WYM 18P

Everything

Also by Lucy Dawson

Everything You Told Me

Lucy Dawson

CORVUS

Published in paperback in Great Britain in 2017 by Corvus, an
imprint of Atlantic Books Ltd.

10 9 8 7 6 5 4 3 2 1

A CIP catalogue record for this book is available from the British Library.

Trade paperback ISBN: 978 1 78239 625 3
Paperback ISBN: 978 1 78239 627 7
E-book ISBN: 978 1 78239 626 0

Printed in Great Britain by Clays Ltd, St Ives plc

Corvus
An imprint of Atlantic Books Ltd
Ormond House
26–27 Boswell Street
London
WC1N 3JZ

www.corvus-books.co.uk

For the Warwick girls, with love.

CHAPTER ONE

'Hey. Wake up, please! You have to wake up now.'

The man's voice sounds curiously distant. I try to do as I'm told, but my eyes feel stuck together – as if I haven't taken off last night's clumpy mascara. Forcing them apart, and squinting, the blurry shape of a head is actually right in front of me, backlit by a small, bright, overhead light. I stare at it groggily and try to focus.

'You have to get out of the car!'

I move, and immediately, a sharp pain grips at the base of my neck from being in one position too long. I'm uncomfortably sprawled across the back seat, with my head jammed against the left passenger door, and my chin on my chest. I attempt to sit up, but my hands only manage to grasp at the air, and I slip a little further, until I finally manage to grab the passenger seat in front with one hand, push down with the other, and haul myself up. My God – I've not had a hangover this bad in nearly twenty years, since I was a student. I moan, and rub my head, before looking down at myself in confusion. I'm wearing pyjamas, the wax jacket my husband refers to as my 'mummy mac', and an old pair of trainers.

'Where am I?' My speech is slurred. I can hear it, I can *feel* it, as if my tongue is a fat, useless slug.

'We are here.'

Yes, but where *is* here? I look around me, completely confused. It's dark outside. I turn back to the blurry head.

'You have to pay me now.'

He has a foreign accent I can't place.

'Pay me now, please. Four hundred pounds.'

Did he just say *four hundred pounds*?

'In your pocket.' He points at me, impatiently.

I stare at him stupidly, my mouth still slightly open. He's young – only in his mid-twenties – thin, a concave chest under a cheap, grubby jumper, with dark, greasy hair and darting eyes, waiting anxiously.

'Come on!' He rubs his thumb and finger together, and points at my coat again.

I reach slowly into one of the pockets, and to my surprise, withdraw a tight roll of notes that has an elastic band around the middle.

'Ah!' he exclaims with satisfaction.

Obediently, I hold it out and he snatches it from me, pulling the band off and quickly shuffling through the notes, counting under his breath.

'Four hundred pounds exactly. Thank you.' He reaches up and clicks the interior light off.

For a moment I'm blind; it's only as my eyes begin to adjust I can see that it's actually starting to turn light outside. The sky is an electric blue, blending down first into yellow and then orange hues almost too perfectly, as if it's been airbrushed. My gaze drops to the dark horizon line slicing through the orange – and a wide expanse of indigo and silvery sea. I gasp as I realize we are on a cliff, overlooking a bay. The tide is in, rolling relentlessly onto a small, exposed stretch of beach on my right. On the opposite side of the hill sits a large hotel; the ground-floor windows all lit up, probably the staff starting to prepare for the day ahead while the guests are still asleep. I know this place, I've been here before, many times. This is *our* place.

'We're in Cornwall,' I say in disbelief. 'But, how...' I spin around urgently and look out of the back window. 'What the hell am I doing in Cornwall?' I say, frightened.

The man shrugs. 'You have to get out now.'

'Get out?' I say. 'What do you mean? I have no idea what I'm doing here!' I reach into my jacket pockets. They are completely empty. No phone, no keys, no purse. I look about me wildly, starting to panic. 'How did I even get into your car? Where did you pick me up from?'

The man looks at me curiously, as if he's not sure whether I'm joking or not.

'I was at my house, in Kent, right?' I question him frantically. 'I was at home. I know I was. Theo and Chloe!' I exclaim suddenly. 'My children! Where are my children?' I lean forward and grab the edge of his sleeve.

Unnerved, he shakes me off. 'I don't know anything. I just drove you here, like I was asked. Get out of the car!'

'But—'

'No!' He refuses, leaning over and flinging open the back door. He gives me a shove. I half fall out, planting my feet down onto soft earth as the shock of the cold air sucks into my gut, and I vomit.

'Not on the seats!' he shouts, angrily.

I hang there for a moment, spit dangling from my lip as I try to catch my breath, but he pushes me again, harder this time, and I stumble to a stand. He quickly yanks the door shut behind me, turns, starts the engine and roars off. It's obvious all he wants to do is get as far away as possible. I watch him helplessly, the wind whipping my hair across my face and making my eyes water as I stand on the exposed hilltop, next to the costal path, completely disorientated.

I don't understand. I went to bed at my house last night, I know I did. How on earth am I now at the other end of the country?

I need help.

I try to walk, but my legs don't seem to belong to me, and, stumbling a couple of steps in the direction of the hotel, I trip on the uneven ground, landing on my knees. The damp from the grass starts to seep through the flimsy fabric of my pyjamas, and as I drag myself up, my whole body feels weirdly disconnected. Standing is making me dizzy. I try another step, but in my confusion, somehow only stagger towards the edge of the cliff.

'Shit!' I gasp, terrified. I should just sit down again, this is too dangerous, I can't—

'Stop!' An urgent voice carries over the air buffeting about my head, and I twist to look over my shoulder. A man is running fast towards me. There is a dog slightly ahead of him, ears flat to its head as it pelts in my direction. It's a collie, and when it reaches me, it begins to leap around, barking madly, its paws scrabbling painfully on my legs. I shriek instinctively and take a step back.

'No!' shouts the man, and in three strides he's there, grabbing my arms and knocking me bodily to the ground. I fall with such force, the back of my head smacks into the turf – and then there is silence.

'Hello! Can you hear me? What's your name?'

My eyes flicker open again. A woman, very close up, is staring down into my face in concern. 'She's conscious. What's your name?' She waits, and I realize she's addressing me.

'Sally.' My mouth is horribly dry, and speaking aloud makes me cough. 'Sally Hilman.'

Some man next to her, who I didn't know was there, appears in my eye line, saying aloud, 'We've got an ID.'

I try to sit up, and several hands reach out to stop me.

4

'Try not to move, Sally,' the woman says kindly. 'We're just checking you over, if that's OK? Making sure you haven't hurt yourself. Stay still just a moment longer for me, I'm nearly done. My name is Marie, and this is Paul. We're paramedics.'

I don't actually have the strength to argue. I turn my head to the side dully, and several pairs of feet about five yards away swim into focus. My gaze travels up the legs, and I see the dog man talking to two police officers. They are standing by a police car that has the blue light flashing, and an ambulance.

'She was kneeling down on the ground, praying—'

No I wasn't, I'd fallen over.

'—then she stood up and started walking towards the edge,' says the man eagerly, holding a rope lead tightly, on the end of which his dog is still leaping around excitedly. Why is he wearing full camouflage combats and top? He looks like a soldier reporting in to his next-in-command.

'—I got closer, and she was crying. Really distressed.'

That's not right either. I wasn't crying. The wind was making my eyes water.

No one says anything, they just carry on checking me. I did just say all of that out loud, didn't I?

'I knew something was wrong and I called to her again to stop,' the dog man says. 'I could see she was going to do it, so I, like, *ran* as fast as I could, and pulled her to the ground. We've been trained to do that in the TA. She did bang her head a bit, but then she just sort of went to sleep. It was weird. Once I knew she wasn't faking it, I let go of her arms and called you. I checked her too, just in case she was carrying one of those EpiPens or wearing an "I'm a diabetic" bracelet, but she didn't have *anything*, just the note.'

My eyes widen. Note? What note? What the hell is he talking about?

5

'I need to get home,' I plead, reaching out to put my hand on Marie's arm, to get her attention. 'My children...'

'Where are they, Sally?' she asks. 'Are they with someone, or on their own?'

'Their father and my mother-in-law are with them.'

'And where do you live, Sally?'

I tell her, and she replies soothingly, 'That's great. We'll sort everything out. It's all going to be OK... She seems physically fine.' She looks away, talking to her male colleague.

'You don't understand,' I whisper in distress, starting to cry. 'My son is only a baby. He'll be needing me.'

'—I knew it wasn't right because of the way she was acting, and people come here to jump all the time.' The dog man is still talking. 'I've got a mate who knows the coroner, and he says body parts wash up loads. Limbs and that,' he adds fervently.

Jump? What's he talking about?

'I wasn't going to jump!' I say to Marie, frightened. 'I nearly fell, but I wasn't doing it deliberately!'

'It's all right, Sally. You don't have to talk now.'

'But I wasn't! Get off me!' I push her hands away, and try to struggle up. Instantly, one of the policemen is alongside us.

'No one is going to hurt you. We're here to help.' He speaks kindly. 'We're making sure your children are all right. Sally, I'm detaining you under section 136 of the Mental Health Act.'

'What?' I say, terrified. 'I haven't done anything!'

'The ambulance is going to bring you down to the police station for now. I'll come with you – it's not far from here – and we'll get everything sorted out, OK? Don't worry. It's all going to be fine.'

'—Anyway, here's the suicide note. I found it in an inside pocket of her coat – tucked well away. I think it's to her husband. See?' The dog man points to something on a small scrap of paper the other policeman is now reading. 'She's definitely married, because she's wearing a ring.' He looks very pleased with himself, and proud. 'Matthew, his name is.'

My mouth falls open. 'My husband's name *is* Matthew,' I say to the other officer, urgently. 'But I didn't write a suicide note, I swear! I went to bed last night at home in Kent, I was waiting for my husband to get home, and then I woke up in the back of a taxi, here.'

'You don't remember anything that happened in between?' Marie asks, casually. 'Literally not a thing?'

'No,' I say, terrified, as I realize it aloud. 'I had a really bad day yesterday, and I argued with someone just before I went to bed, but I *did* get into bed. I'm certain of that, because I wasn't feeling too good. I'd had a couple of drinks, and because I'm not drinking much at the moment it made me feel really queasy... I must have just fallen asleep – so how am I now *here*?' I look around me in disbelief again.

'You don't remember how you got here, but you're certain you didn't come here to jump?'

'Of course I am! At least, I *think* I am...' I trail off, bewildered. 'Did I really have a note in my pocket? Can I see it?'

A small scrap of paper is held out in front of me. The policeman's hand is covering most of it, but I can see the first line.

Dear Matthew,
I don't want to do this any more.

My heart stops – it's my handwriting. I look around me in confusion. I went to bed last night in my house three hundred miles away, and now I'm on a clifftop in Cornwall, holding a suicide note that I've written.

What the hell has happened? How have I lost the last ten hours of my life?

TWO DAYS EARLIER

CHAPTER TWO

'Shhh,' I soothed wearily, jiggling the warm little body pressed to me as we stood underneath the extractor fan whirring at full pelt. My six-month-old's furrowed frown began to relax slightly, and I felt him weigh heavier in my achy, tight arms as he finally slipped into deeper sleep. Well, thank God for that. I glanced at the kitchen clock. 1.37 p.m. I'd been rocking him for an hour and a quarter already. In only another hour, I'd be wrestling him into his car seat so that we could go and get Chloe from pre-school. Most of the day gone already. I looked around the rest of the kitchen and playroom in despair. It looked as if someone had thrown open the door, hurled in the contents of a box of crap, and rushed back out. I closed my own eyes, briefly. Almost instantly, the treacle tide of sleep started to envelop me, and, swaying slightly, I hastily opened them again.

Sadly, the crap was still there. A bottle of Calpol sat on the rug next to the plunger, had leaked a tiny pink pool onto the mat of Theo's baby gym. A pile of wet washing was on the kitchen table waiting to be hung on the rack next to the Aga, the sleeve of one of Matthew's clean shirts draping onto a crumb-covered plate that hadn't made it into the dishwasher from breakfast. Unappetizingly, a pink Tupperware box of orangey spag bol was defrosting on the side for Chloe's tea, alongside two punnets of

11

found-forgotten-in-the-fridge wizened blueberries, one of them organic, the other a replacement no-frills, as the first lot were so tart even I couldn't stomach them.

Matthew came into the kitchen, taking a late lunchbreak, and looked dismayed to find me under the fan settling Theo. 'Can't I make a sandwich?' he whispered. 'I've got another call in ten minutes?'

I sighed inwardly, but nodded, and began to move gingerly over to the playroom sofa. I held my breath and gently began to sit. But the second my bottom touched down, Theo shifted irritably and began to rub his eyes.

I got up quickly again and resumed my rocking while watching my husband gloomily begin to inspect the contents of the fridge. The full bin bag that had been propped up against the kitchen wall since before breakfast wobbled over, so he absently bent and rebalanced it. I'd already asked him twice to take it out; it was making the whole room smell rancidly fishy, but I sensed now was not the time to put in a third request. Matthew had been deeply stressed out over the last few days; a campaign his team had spent months working on was on the brink of being signed off by the client, but kept not happening at the last minute. I didn't need to ask if it had finally all gone through, I could tell from his grim expression that it hadn't.

Instead I looked down at my son and felt so deeply exhausted to my very bones that momentarily, I had to close my eyes again. If only he would just sleep somewhere other than actually *on* me... Or just sleep at all. This too will pass, I began to chant inwardly for the thousandth time. At least second time around, I knew that was actually true. When Chloe was born I'd felt like the world had played a cruel trick on me, everyone had known what it was going to be like, and hadn't told me that I was *never going to sleep again*. But oh dear God, I had no idea what it actually meant to have a baby that literally didn't sleep – until Theo.

I took a deep breath and opened my eyes just in time to see Matthew about to cut up the remainder of the cheese. I hastened over.

'Please can you not eat that?' I breathed. 'I need it for Chloe's tea.'

Matthew put the knife down. I saw a muscle in his jaw flex, he turned to me and said pleasantly, 'Well, what can I have then? There seems to only be some mustard and a courgette.'

'I know. Sorry. The shop is coming tomorrow. There are beans in the cupboard.'

'I had that for lunch yesterday. Forget it.' He turned to walk past me.

'Before you go, *please* could you put the rubbish out?' I whispered quickly, suddenly unable to bear the smell any longer.

He gritted his teeth, but went back over and picked it up. This time, at the rustle of the plastic, Theo stirred in his sleep, flung a fist sideways, and then dragged his surprisingly sharp little nails across my cheek, before jerking and falling still once more. Matthew and I both froze and waited... but our son's eyelids fluttered. He blinked, looked around him in surprise, and both dark eyes alighted on me.

'Oh bugger, fuck, and shit,' I groaned.

'Should we really be swearing like that in front of Theo?' Matthew said immediately. He was right, of course, but pointing it out wasn't exactly helpful. '*I* would have just left moving the rubbish until later,' he added, equally unnecessarily.

'Perhaps if you'd just done it at breakfast, when I asked you...' I bit the bait.

'Right. It's my fault he's woken up. Of course it is. Sorry... What the hell is that?' Matthew peered tiredly down at the floor, then bent over and touched the gaffer tape that was holding the ripped lino together. 'Oh lovely, the bag's leaked everywhere.' He straightened up. 'It's probably not the best idea to put the rubbish *right* on top of that dodgy bit.'

'Have the flooring samples you were going to order arrived yet?' I shot back.

He looked at me meditatively for a moment. 'I think you know the answer to that. I haven't had time. I know you're exhausted, Sal. We're *all* exhausted, but—'

'Well, probably not *quite* as much as me.' I was unable to help myself.

'I've offered to get up at night too.'

'I know, but we agreed that was my responsibility, given you have to actually work during the day.' His pending contract instantly loomed back into my mind. I remembered how worried he was, bit my tongue, and rubbed my eyes tiredly. 'I don't mind, though, honestly I don't.'

'OK, well I've said I'll have him down here for a couple of hours each evening too, so you can get some rest, but you won't do that either.'

'Only because I think it's easier for me to try and keep him settled upstairs. Plus you really can't afford to be tired yourself at the moment, not with your job the way it is. When things calm down, I might take you up on that offer.' I tried to smile, although it felt unnaturally tight. I didn't have the heart to say it, but Matthew was totally useless at getting Theo to sleep, hauling him around awkwardly like a sack of potatoes, which in turn made Theo cry, and meant I would lie upstairs getting more stressed at how unhappy *he* was, which sort of defeated the object. Matthew had been the same with Chloe too, not really coming into his own until she was about two. It wasn't his fault – it was just the way it was.

'We have to face facts.' Instead, Matthew began to bulldozer off down a now well-worn conversational cul-de-sac, and my heart sank. 'We need more help. What about an au pair? A guy at work said it's revolutionized their lives.'

Theo began to grizzle and I jiggled him a little faster. 'I don't think I could cope with also being responsible for some sixteen-year-old French girl living in the spare room and coming home at God knows what hour. And where would your mum or my parents sleep when they come to stay?'

He shrugged. 'I don't know what else to suggest. Things aren't sustainable as they are. It's not easy for me either, you know, working from home when it's like this. And it's not like I don't wake up at night too when he cries. I do. All the time.'

I stared at him as the flint of a row sparked again and my short fuse flared. 'You find it hard to sleep while you're lying in bed in the spare room and I'm pacing the floor for literally hours at a time in Theo's room, rocking him, you mean? Wow. I'm so sorry to hear that. It must be dreadful for you.'

'And once I'm awake, it's really hard to get back to sleep.' If he'd noticed the point I was making, he ignored it.

'You know,' I said, lightly, 'I had – in total – three and a half hours' sleep last night.'

He looked heavenward. 'OK. Never mind.' He glanced back down at his watch. 'Well, that was a fun lunchbreak.' He picked the bin bag up again and walked over to the door.

'I know it's dreadful at the moment, Matthew. Believe me, I know,' I said, with sudden energy. 'I mean, just look at me!' I nodded down at my sick-stained maternity trousers, and the shapeless shirt straining slightly over my doughy tummy. Chloe had only that very morning prodded it and remarked, 'You've still got a bump, haven't you?' before adding darkly, 'There isn't another baby in there, is there?'

Matthew paused, but remained silent.

'I think that's the bit where you say, "Don't be silly, you look great to me".' I tried another smile.

His work mobile buzzed in his pocket. He pulled it out and stared at the screen. 'Oh, just fuck off and leave me alone…' He glanced up. 'Not you, them. You had a baby six months ago and you're getting zero sleep. What do you expect?'

The rather ungallant response stung, but I tried to ignore it. 'I thought we weren't swearing in front of Theo? What I'm trying to say is, yes, it's rubbish, but we just have to hang on another month or so until he's old enough for me to do sleep training with him.'

'Another month?' He looked up bleakly. 'I don't know how we're going to make it to the end of the week, to be honest. Why's the Calpol out, by the way? Is he ill again?'

I hesitated. 'No,' I admitted. 'I thought it was worth a go.'

'We can't just drug him!'

'Well, it didn't work anyway. I thought if—'

But Matthew had already lost interest in what I was saying, and was wrinkling his nose. 'Jesus. This reeks. Right. I've *really* got to go and get on now. Don't forget I've got an eight a.m. call tomorrow too,' he called as he reached the front door. 'So you'll have to do both school runs.'

'I know,' I said in a small voice. 'I'm really looking forward to it.'

'I *have* to, Sal.' He reappeared. 'If I don't get this contract signed off and in by the end of the week, I'm actually going to lose my fucking mind.'

'Seriously! Can you *please* stop swearing! No one is trying to stop you working, Matthew. I promise. I'm trying to give you as much space as I can, believe it or not.'

Theo stepped his protests up a notch, probably picking up on the mounting tension, so I moved over to the kettle to start making up a bottle.

'It's all I do at the moment – work,' Matthew continued. 'I just work, and help you with the kids, and go to the gym. That's it.'

I couldn't be bothered to respond to such a ridiculous statement. I hadn't had more than five minutes to myself for *half a year*. The flame in me died suddenly, and all I wanted to do was find a hole, climb into it, and sleep for a hundred years. Matthew watched in silence as I soothed Theo, and then, without saying anything else, turned and left the room. I heard him pull his shoes on in the hall, then moments later a fiercely cold draught rushed in where he'd left the front door open.

Shivering, I almost called out to ask him to shut it, but too defeated, closed my mouth again. Instead, a couple of fat tears sploshed down onto Theo's downy head, making him look up at me in surprise. I wiped them away gently.

'Sorry, baby boy.' I tried to smile. He regarded me for a moment and then gave me a huge, gummy grin and waved his little fist at me again. I caught and kissed it, more tears blurrily flooding my eyes. 'Don't worry, Theo,' I whispered. 'Mummy's just a bit knackered. That's all.'

He started sucking his fist, and I reached to my left so I could put the radio on. Silence wasn't good. It felt too big. When Chloe had been a similar age, the radio had helped massively with the daytime loneliness of being in the house so much. Although, of course, that was when we'd lived in our tiny, but pristine, flat in London. I looked despairingly at the disgusting frosted pink stripy wallpaper, upon which I'd hopefully daubed three different paint samples when we'd first moved in and I was pregnant, about eight months ago. The blobs were still there, untouched.

The kettle began to bubble as I jiggled Theo. Once his sleep was sorted, I'd put Project House back on the front line. I felt immediately cheered at the thought of new showers that pulsed rather than dribbled, wood flooring throughout, no more patterned carpets, all the Artex gone, a woodburner in the sitting room, a front door that wasn't entirely constructed of swirly glass, and that had a proper handle rather than a catch that skinned the thumbs and forefinger of the person trying to shut it. No more velvet pink curtains or brown kitchen tiles with orange baskets of fruit adorning them, either.

And defiantly, nothing held together with gaffer tape – that went for Matthew and me too. I wanted things back the way they'd been before Theo had arrived. I hated the constant niggling and bickering that came with this stage of having a baby. It wasn't us. I'd also woefully underestimated the increased workload of having two rather than one child, while additionally being under virtual house arrest while I tried desperately to get Theo into a daytime nap schedule. Life was a little like being part of a Milgram experiment. Who would crack first, me or Matthew? Perhaps we'd end up eating each other.

I picked up my phone, the only thing still connecting me to the outside world, and absently googled 'studies into the effects of small children on happy marriage'. The top result to come back was 'Is Divorce Bad for Children?', followed by 'The Implications of Divorce'. Yeah, that'd be about right. I put my phone back down as the kettle clicked off and Roxette's 'It Must Have Been Love' came on.

Oh God, no! I groaned and hastened back over to the radio to find something more cheerful, but it was too late. As if I wasn't depressed enough, the song had already transported me back to being eighteen again, bombing around the country lanes in bright sunshine with my long-term boyfriend from home, Joe. That particular summer had been full of carefree laughter, lots of driving too fast with the windows wide open, fish and chips on the beach as the sun went down... A lifetime ago. I hadn't known I was born.

'This too will pass.' I closed my eyes. 'This too will pass...'

Poor old Chloe looked just as shattered as me when she got home from pre-school, choosing to collapse quietly on the sofa so she could watch *Sarah & Duck* on the iPad, as I made tea.

'Who did you play with today?' I shouted over Theo's dinging as he tiredly sat in his bouncer, and I hurtled around trying to cook pasta.

'Amy,' said Chloe, not looking away from the screen. 'And Harry. Ben hit Harry on the head with a bit of train track.'

'On purpose?' I tried to concentrate on not grating my fingers in addition to the cheese.

'No. He wasn't looking where he was going. Harry cried. And I felt sad because Harry's my best friend. He tried to hug me in assembly.'

'OK.' I gathered the cheese up and put it in a small bowl. 'Well, all you need to say is "Thank you, but I don't want to be hugged at the moment".'

'But I liked it.' She looked up in surprise. 'Can I have the cheese not *on* my spaghetti, please?'

'I'm already doing it,' I promised, smiling as I made a mental note to tell Matthew later about the hugs with Harry.

'Would you like Harry to come and play, do you think?' I asked Chloe during their bath after tea. Theo was squirming around madly in the water as I clutched him tightly under his arm, while trying to rinse crusted sweet potato from between his fingers with my free hand.

Chloe poured some water from a plastic pink teapot and said decisively, 'Only if he doesn't play chase. I don't like it when he and Ben try to catch me and Amy. They pull us by our hoods.'

'Who do?' Matthew appeared in the doorway, leaning in and passing me the towel I'd already carefully laid out ready on the floor, as I lifted a dripping Theo out.

'Could you just pop it back down?' I said, forcing a smile and trying not to sound irritated. Theo, cold and suspended in mid-air, gave an indignant bellow that made Chloe look up briefly.

'I think he needs a feed, Mummy,' she identified, correctly, and returned to her pouring.

Matthew chucked it back, haphazardly. 'Do you mind if I go to the gym tonight?'

I placed Theo down and wrapped him as best I could.

'I'll do Chloe's stories first, of course.'

'I want Mummy to do them,' Chloe said quickly.

'Mummy can't,' Matthew said dismissively. 'She's got to feed Theo. So *who* pulled your hood?'

'Harry. But it was part of a game. I want to get out now too.' She stood up. 'Mummy, I don't want to get married. I want to live here with you, Daddy and Theo.'

I looked up at her, concerned. She'd said the same thing two days ago. The diet of Disney DVDs that she'd been watching almost twenty-four-seven since Theo's birth was obviously coming home to roost.

'You don't have to get married, darling. Not if you don't want to.'

'You might want to get your own place, though,' Matthew suggested.

Chloe and I both stared at him. Chloe's bottom lip began to tremble as I said incredulously, 'She's *four*, Matthew. What Daddy means is,' I reached for her towel, and turned back to Chloe, '*of course* you can live with us. For ever and ever.'

She climbed out, and as I wrapped her, she tried to lean on me. 'Please can you do stories, Mummy?'

'I sure can!' I beamed, as Theo rubbed his eyes furiously before letting out a sharp, cross and hungry wail.

Matthew gestured helplessly. 'I said I'd do them! She'll be fine!'

'No!' Chloe's eyes began to fill with tired tears.

'Just go to the gym,' I said quickly, in an attempt to calm everything down. 'I've got this.'

'Sally, you need to back me up when I say things,' Matthew continued. 'I said I was doing the stories. It doesn't help if you then steam in, take over, and—'

'Shall we discuss this later?' I said with a bright, warning smile. Chloe looked between us uncertainly, and Matthew shook his head.

'I'll be back later then.' He turned and left, without kissing the kids goodnight.

'Right! Pyjamas!' I smiled cheerfully, and tried to move us on quickly. 'OK, Theo. I get the message. Bedtime!'

Once I'd finally read them both stories, sung to Chloe, fed Theo, held him in my arms for long enough so that I could sneak him into the cot without him waking, and crept back out to the safety of the hall, it was eight p.m. I was starving. I wandered down to the kitchen and opened the fridge. I couldn't be bothered to do anything more than cereal. Matthew could have fish fingers, chips and the courgette later when he got in if he wanted. In fact – I considered his ridiculous 'get your own place' comment to Chloe – I could think of several things he could do with the courgette.

Suddenly too tired to even get the milk out, I closed the fridge and sank down onto a kitchen chair for a moment, putting my head on my hands. All I could hear was the white noise machine we'd bought, whirring away in Theo's room through the monitor, but thankfully nothing from Theo himself. His sleep cycles were becoming shorter and shorter, though – I probably only had another thirty minutes before he'd be awake again. It was utterly tortuous. I loved Theo, I really did. But no matter how gorgeous he was, I needed a break. He was attached to me twenty-four hours a day. I was beginning to lose my mind.

I took a deep breath and lifted my head again, just in time to see the most enormous spider saunter casually past me, about an inch away from my foot.

'Shit!' I gasped, and scrabbled to a stand, looking around quickly for something to catch it in. Luckily there was an empty glass Matthew had left on the table. As if aware of my intentions, the spider drew its legs in slightly and crouched still on the lino. I wasn't convinced the glass was big enough, but there wasn't anything else I could do. God – it was *huge*. I gave two short exhalations to psyche myself up and, making a quiet *'eeeeee'* noise under my breath as I approached it, slowly extended my arm out – but as the glass lowered, it scuttled off towards the kids' toys in the playroom. I instantly imagined it popping back out of a box of Lego while Chloe was playing, and shoving the glass down, I legged it around the table, and instead grabbed Chloe's hobby horse, Penelope, lying on the carpet. The spider made another run for it, and with reactions I didn't know I still possessed the energy for, I flipped the head end around, grasped the pole, and whacked it furiously. Penelope unhelpfully neighed loudly, and then made a trotting sound, but I was so determined to finish the job, I just kept whacking. After a few moments more of whacking, neighing, and trotting, I stopped, slightly puffed out, and lifted up the horse to see the poor, now very dead spider mashed into the floor. Using Penelope as a sort of equine broom, I swept the mangled body to the front door and out onto the doorstep, before closing it again and collapsing down onto the carpet.

How the hell had I managed all of that without waking Theo? I exhaled in relief, and then, glancing at the hobby horse, pictured how ridiculous I must have looked. I smiled, and then laughed out loud. What an idiot! But then tears simultaneously rushed to my eyes, and I realized that I was in fact crying. Disconcerted, I made a huge effort to get myself under control and quickly reached into my pocket for a tissue and my phone.

Hey. How are you? I began to text Liv. One friend losing the plot here... I have just annihilated giant spider in house using a toy horse. Would call, but Theo about to wake up. This baby is breaking me. Chat tomorrow? Xx

Right on cue, I heard Theo begin to whimper. Sighing, I hit send, then made my way upstairs.

Matthew was back, and on the sofa in front of the TV eating a fresh batch of pasta when I trudged into the sitting room at ten past nine clutching the baby monitor.

'Oh, thank you for making that.' I nodded gratefully at his bowl as I flopped down on the sofa opposite him. 'Is mine in the kitchen?'

He pulled a face. 'Um, sorry, no. I thought you'd gone to bed. I didn't leave you any.'

'Oh.' I unaccountably felt tears spring to my eyes again. 'OK. No problem.'

He peered at me, puzzled. 'Are you *crying*?'

'I'm just very tired, and hungry,' I whispered.

He breathed out, deeply, and put the bowl down on the carpet beside him. 'I didn't do it on purpose, Sally. I thought you'd gone up for the night. How was I supposed to know you'd not eaten? I'll go and make you some *right* now.' He stood up.

'Don't bother.' I shook my head. 'By the time it's cooked, it'll be half nine, and Theo will be up again.'

He gestured helplessly. 'So what would you like me to do?'

'Nothing. I don't need you to do anything.' I stared glassily at the TV for a moment as I tried to summon the energy to go and get the cereal I'd been going to have in the first place anyway. It wasn't the end of the world. 'Just eat your pasta.'

23

He sat back down. 'I get it, OK? Everything I do is wrong. I'm a constant source of disappointment to you and Chloe.'

My gaze flickered over to him briefly. What was he talking about *now*, a source of disappointment? 'It's only pasta. Just eat your food.'

'No, I don't want it. You can have it.' He pushed the bowl towards me.

'Don't be ridiculous,' I said. 'Have the pasta.'

'You said you were hungry! You obviously want it, which is why you keep saying, *"Just eat the pasta"*. So have it. Take it.'

'Oh my God! I don't *want* it!' I exploded.

'So why make such a fuss about me not saving you any then? Was it just to make the point I'd not thought of you?' He sat back into the sofa and put his hands on his head as he looked up at the ceiling briefly. 'Jesus Christ, I can't take much more of this.'

'You can't take much more of *what*, exactly?' I said dangerously, preparing to do the 'I know you're under a lot of work stress at the moment, but it's not fair to take it out on me and the kids' bit.

'This!' he said, gesturing around him, presumably to encompass *everything*. 'I used to do things. I saw people, we went out with friends. We'd spend time together. I feel like a social recluse, and that my life is just ticking by. Soon, I'll be too old to do cycling, rock climbing, and—'

'When have you *ever* done rock climbing?' I said incredulously.

'The point is these are the best years of my life, allegedly.'

'I wasn't aware me and the kids were holding you back so much. We've got a new baby, Matthew. I mean, honestly, what did you think it was going to be like? Surely you remember this bit from when Chloe was tiny?'

'Don't patronize me,' he said. 'I don't think you understand what it's like for me: the huge pressure all the time to provide

– now we're on one salary – when the house needs doing up, and—'

'OK, *literally* you're going mad,' I said energetically, sitting up a bit straighter. 'The money for the house is just sitting in the bank from the flat sale, waiting for us to get around to sorting everything out. I've got the builder coming over a week on Monday. Sorry I haven't done it sooner, but I've got a feral baby who doesn't sleep *ever*, plus a four-year-old. Yes, we're on one salary, but we knew that was going to happen. That's why we set the funds aside to cover that too, remember?'

He looked down at the floor and said quietly, 'Yes. Of course I remember.'

'Look, I know work is shocking for you at the moment.' I tried to get us back on track. 'But we need to *attempt* to hold onto the good stuff. We've got a house that's going to be amazing when it's finished. Yes it's a 1970s nightmare at the moment, and it's a lot further out of town than we would have liked, but it's still going to be great. You've got two amazing kids. Theo *will* sleep eventually, believe me. We've just got to hang on in there and—'

'You don't have to pep talk me, Sally,' he interrupted rudely. 'I know all of this, I'm trying to—'

'Well then, if that's really true, just stop whingeing and man up.' I lost my patience, simply too tired to prevent myself ripping off the kid gloves any longer, which I might have used to handle Matthew's not-so-good-under-pressure nature carefully, earlier in our marriage.

'Man up?' he repeated slowly. 'Sally, do you even like me any more?'

'Oh, shut up, please...' I collapsed back wearily. 'I. Do. Not. Have. The energy for this.'

'You need to tell me,' he persisted. 'Because we don't have sex, we don't hug, we don't—'

'*Oh my God*!' I put my head in my hands in frustration. 'We've got a bloody six-month-old baby! Of course we don't! But if your life is really *so* shit, Matthew, and you're *that* unhappy, then why don't you just leave? Pack your stuff and go.'

'Maybe I should!' Matthew flashed back. 'Perhaps I *could* be happy with someone else!'

I gasped audibly – and everything stopped. We stared at each other, aware that the line had just been well and truly crossed. Out of nowhere, I thought suddenly about the poor spider, desperately running for cover.

'I shouldn't have said that,' he said quickly. 'Of course I want to be with you and the children.'

I didn't reply. I couldn't. It was one thing to do a cross Rightmove search on houses that I could afford to live in with just the kids after a row – I'd done that plenty of times – and quite often recently, when Matthew had been in a particularly arsey mood, and I'd decided I actually hated him, but I knew that was normal. This was in a different league altogether.

'Perhaps you could be happy with someone else?' I repeated, stunned. 'We're seriously discussing divorce because of a bowl of pasta?'

'No.' He rubbed his temples. 'Of course we're not.'

Through the monitor came the familiar sound of Theo starting to cry, for once a welcome sound.

'I'd better go and see to him.' I got up quickly, and escaped.

By the time I re-emerged to get changed into my nightie and remove what little make-up I was still wearing, all of the lights were off. Matthew had gone to bed in the spare room, as usual. He hated me keeping the baby monitor next to our bed, insisting it kept him awake all night, despite my assurances it was only short-term while Theo and I got used to sleeping in different rooms.

I checked on Chloe, covering her back up with the duvet and gently stroking the hot, damp little curls from her face. She smelt like a hamster.

I crept into our bedroom and eased into bed quietly. I had no idea how things had managed to escalate so badly over nothing – but there was no question Matthew and I had unwittingly strayed into really dangerous territory.

I reached for my phone and texted: I'm sorry for what I said tonight xxx And then I waited.

Me too

That was it? And did he mean he was sorry too, or just that he was sorry for what I'd said as well?

I threw the covers back and sat up. I should just go into the spare room so we could both apologize in person and sort it out properly. I stuck a leg out of bed, and then hesitated. The thing was, he might then want to have sex. He *would* want to have sex – and I was just too shattered. It was all right for him, he'd be able to go to sleep afterwards. I, on the other hand, was going to be up with Theo all night. Feeling mean, I drew my leg back up, shrank under the covers, and quickly turned the light off.

Less than a minute later, I heard the spare-room door creak, the landing floorboards go, and then our door gently push open.

'Sally?' he whispered. 'Are you asleep?'

I squeezed my eyes tightly shut, and pretended I was.

He gave a small, sad sigh of defeat, then whispered, 'OK. I really *do* love you. I promise. Goodnight,' and retreated back off to the spare room.

I hesitated for a moment, feeling like a complete cow for not going after him, but the house had finally, blissfully, fallen silent. I couldn't resist it – and I fell instantly asleep.

CHAPTER THREE

'You should have come and got me,' said Matthew, stirring sugar into his coffee. I was bent over trying to spoon baby rice into Theo, who was bobbing up and down in his bouncer, just to add the frisson of a moving target to my morning challenges.

'There wasn't any point – from about three a.m. he literally wouldn't settle unless I was holding him. I don't actually know how I'm awake,' I confessed, glancing at Chloe, who was singing 'Let It Go' quietly to herself and fiddling with a pair of tiny, plastic fairy wings. 'No toys at the table, sweetheart. Can you eat your porridge, or some of your banana? You'll be really hungry at school otherwise.' I turned back to my own bowl and grabbed a mouthful, before returning to Theo. 'Do you think you'll be able to help me this weekend, Matthew?'

'Yes.' He got up to put his bowl in the dishwasher. 'Keep eating, Chloe. It's time to go in five minutes.'

Chloe looked up. 'Are you taking me, Mummy?'

I glanced down briefly at the purple and flowered jersey button-front nightie Mum had bought me to wear in hospital when I'd gone in to have Theo. I had to stop wearing it, even when it was the only thing clean. I imagined myself arriving at the school gates wearing the fetching ensemble, no make-up, and my unbrushed hair scraped back into a ponytail, and smiled at Clo.

'No, darling, I'm not. Thankfully Daddy's call got cancelled, so he's taking you. Theo and I will come and get you, though.'

'I've finished,' she said. 'Thank you for my breakfast.'

'Go and get your toothbrush then. Good girl.' I watched her clamber down and skip off out of the room.

'She's happy,' Matthew remarked through a mouthful of toast.

There was silence for a moment, punctuated only by Theo beginning to babble as he sucked on his cloth bib. I hesitated, loathe to bring up the row again, and ruin the apparent peace, but I'd done some more thinking overnight while walking Theo around, and knew what I had to say was important.

'Matthew, about last night—' I was about to tell him I was worried we'd become so used to operating at our limits and being pushed to the brink, we were in danger of letting it become our new normal, which wasn't good.

'I don't want to talk about it,' he said brusquely, to my surprise. Picking up his mobile, he glanced at it, stood up and slipped it into his back pocket.

'But—'

'We really need to go. It's twenty past eight already.' He made his way around the kitchen table. 'There's nothing to discuss anyway. It's all OK, honestly it is.' He went out into the hall.

Once I'd closed the front door on them, having helped Chloe find her missing school shoe, zip up her coat, and carefully put her hat on so it didn't mess up her hairclips, I was still feeling a sense of disquiet. While I didn't think for one minute he was seriously considering leaving me for someone else, I couldn't shake the feeling that something almost imperceptible had shifted. Something was wrong. I could feel it.

I reached for my phone.

'Hey,' Liv answered, sounding breathless. 'I'm just dropping Kate at pre-school. What's up?'

'Oh, I'm sorry. Of course you are. I didn't think. I've been up literally most of the night with Theo, and I had a row with Matthew too. I'm a bit all over the place this morning.'

'Oh, bad luck, I'm sorry to hear that. Sorry I didn't text you back last night either. I was out. What was the row about?'

I hesitated. 'You and Jake have discussed divorce, haven't you?'

'Of course!' she said immediately. 'Anyone who's married with children has. If they say otherwise, they're liars.'

'It *is* completely normal, isn't it?' I said uncertainly. 'To say it, but not actually mean it? Even if it feels like you do at the time?'

'Very normal indeed. What happened?'

'Oh, just one of those stupid things that blew up out of nowhere. I'll tell you later when you've finished drop-off. Catch you in a bit.'

'Will do!'

I put the phone back down on the table, momentarily reassured, only to get decisively to my feet again seconds later to fetch a piece of paper and pen from the hall drawer. My point still stood, this wasn't normal for *us*. Liv and Jake actually did argue a lot – they'd had a slight set-to at the very first NCT class we'd met at when we'd been pregnant with the girls, much to the astonishment – and now amusement – of the whole group. It was just their way, but the Jake and Liv model certainly wasn't how *we* operated. This cycle Matthew and I were apparently locked in needed breaking. If he didn't want to talk about it, that was fine. I'd write it instead.

Dear Matthew,
I don't want to do this any more.

I scribbled quickly.

It doesn't matter how it stops, but enough is enough. I really am truthfully sorry. Xxx

There. An unequivocal apology. Carrying Theo upstairs, I carefully placed it on his desk where I knew he would see it, then headed off to get dressed.

He arrived back twenty minutes later, but didn't come into the kitchen to say hello. I made a chicken casserole to sling in the slow oven for the kids' tea, and waited for him to come down to give me a hug, but after almost another hour, he still hadn't appeared.

I tried not to feel piqued – there was no point in my giving with one hand only to take away with the other – but as I got to my feet to take Theo up for his nap, and go to see Matthew at the same time, the food shop arrived. I took the bags in as quickly as possible, stupidly without checking them while the delivery man was still there, and it was only as I began to hurriedly unpack – Theo's dinging from his baby bouncer beginning to morph into full-blown overtired crying – that I discovered one of the bags contained yet another three punnets of blueberries. I was peering in confusion at the inventory, when Matthew wandered in and noticed them instantly on the kitchen table.

'What do we need all of them for?' he said. 'We've already got two lots, haven't we?'

'I don't understand.' I scratched my head. 'I know I didn't order them, but they're here on the list.'

'You must have. You *are* pretty tired at the moment, Sal. Maybe I should take over the weekly shop. We can't really afford to be making unnecessary mistakes like this.'

I looked up in astonishment. 'I'm sorry?'

He held his hands up defensively. 'Don't get angry. I'm trying to help. You're excessively sleep deprived. Of course a couple of things are going to slip.'

'Why is it me that's definitely messed up?' I said. 'No chance you think it could be the shop?

'It's just this kind of thing has a cost implication, Sally. It all adds up.'

A cost implication? Blueberries? Was he actually serious?

'I'm just trying to prevent unnecessary wastage. That's all,' he said. 'It's ridiculous what we spend on food each month. I'm sure with more careful shopping you could reduce things down a little. I know you've got a thing about organic fresh stuff, but there's nothing to stop you buying branded items like baked beans from somewhere cheaper, if you put your mind to it.'

Just like that, all of my good intentions vanished. I stared at him, and despite all of the very reasonable things running through my head, like, 'OK, perhaps you could tell me where I am supposed to find the time to go to two different supermarkets when I barely mange a ten-second shower each morning?' unfortunately, the best my mouth managed in response, was, 'Oh, just fuck off.'

He raised his eyebrows, before saying quietly, 'Right. Well, until you're able to have an adult conversation about it, I'm going to go back upstairs and get on with some work.'

'No, hang on a minute, Matthew,' I said. 'Do you understand how it makes me feel when you act like I'm incapable of even doing a food shop? I did actually used to have a job where I successfully managed a team of people and coordinated numerous major advertising campaigns for several blue chip companies, remember?'

'I'm familiar with your LinkedIn entry, thank you,' Matthew replied. 'You don't have to quote it verbatim to me. *That's* what this is really all about? You miss your job? You want to go back to work early?'

'No!' I said, exasperated. 'I'm trying to say that I think I'm coping pretty well with managing everything here.'

'Who said anything about you *not* coping? I just tried to talk to you about saving some money, and you told me to fuck off. I'll be upstairs attempting to work, if you need me.'

I just about managed not to throw the offending blueberries at his retreating back as he left the room and instead burst into frustrated, exhausted tears. I sank to the floor and sobbed, as Theo, who had fallen quiet, watched me contemplatively. Instantly, guilt flooded over me. He shouldn't be seeing or hearing stuff like this.

'Everything is OK,' I said aloud, and smiled shakily. I wasn't sure who I was trying to reassure, me or him.

I let my head hang for a moment, then got to my feet and tremulously got a drink of water from the tap, which I gulped quickly before reaching over to grab the unwanted plastic punnets and sweep them into the bin. It *hadn't* been me that had ordered too many, it was far more likely to be an online technical glitch.

I was almost sure of it.

After an hour of rocking Theo in his room, I tiptoed downstairs and slumped down gratefully at the kitchen table. It was a small thing, but I'd ordered a fresh almond croissant. The high point of an otherwise pretty crappy morning. I reached for the patisserie bag, slid out the pastry, lifted it to my lips and... through the baby monitor, I heard my son cough, and then start to wail.

'You have *got* to be kidding me,' I said aloud, in amazement. I glanced at the clock. Ten minutes. He'd been asleep for *ten minutes*. I took a deep breath, put the croissant down, and went back upstairs.

Hey, I'm sorry I just missed your call. I texted Liv, glancing at a still out-of-it Theo in the rear-view mirror. I'm sitting in the car on the drive, engine going, having just been for a spin up the A26 with Theo to get him to go to sleep. Things we do eh? If I talk I'll wake him.

You poor thing came back her instant response. Just wanted to check you were OK and see if you wanted to talk re the row?

I considered that briefly, then replied. Am OK.

You sure?

I paused, then confessed. Matthew told me he thinks he could be 'happy with someone else'. TBF that was after I told him to leave if we were making him so unhappy... sigh... In other news, I was getting Chloe dressed this morn and she told me my boobs look 'low'.

You're both very tired at moment. Easy to say things you don't mean, and he probably said that to you because that's HIS biggest fear. That's what his dad did to his mum and him, isn't it, just left? Re boobs:!!! What did you say?

Hmm. I actually hadn't considered that about Matthew. He so rarely talked about his father it was sometimes hard to remember he even existed. To all intents and purposes he might as well not; as he lived in Sydney, Matthew hadn't seen him since our wedding five years ago, and I wasn't sure they'd even spoken since Theo was born.

You might have a point re Matthew. As for Chloe, she's right. Could tuck them in my socks at moment. Once upon a time, I used to go out and do nice things, wearing pretty clothes... I looked down at the unidentifiable stain on the front of the old Gap jumper I was wearing over a pair of black leggings. Jesus. Before kids, I wouldn't have worn such an ensemble around the house, never mind out in public. I sighed. What happened to me?

Anyone around to come and help you today? Your mum? Matthew's mum? Could your brother come over after work?

M's mum at some psychiatry conference in Barcelona. My mum and dad 3.5 hours away now we've moved. Too far for day trip and they're both working anyway. Could ask brother, but he would only bring the bloody girlfriend with him, and can't face bitchy comments all evening. I hate my life.

No you don't. This bit won't last for ever. Sorry I can't come over and give you a hand but got a meeting this afternoon, then Kate needs collecting from after-school club. Would be a bit late by then? Busy wknd too. Got Jake's sister's bday tomorrow, and out for dinner with work girls tonight. Sorry. Hang on in there.

Lucky thing. I let the phone drop down onto my lap. I wanted to be going out on a Friday night and doing fun stuff. But then... I glanced in the mirror at Theo, all snuggled into his car seat, still sleeping peacefully, and softened. Liv would kill to have Theo. She and Jake had been trying for a second baby for ages now, but it just didn't seem to be happening. I looked at Theo again. He was so beautiful. I shifted uncomfortably at the memory of being rushed down to theatre for my emergency C-section. It could have all been so different. I needed to get a serious grip. Liv was right. Things were going to improve.

I glanced up at the front of the house. Yes, it was dated, and needed a lot of work, but we were incredibly fortunate to have made enough money from selling our flat to do it up. It was going to be fun. And perhaps if I got organized, I'd be able to do bath time and bed on my own, so Matthew could go to the gym and de-stress a bit – he obviously needed to. Maybe there were other work problems he wasn't telling me about, perhaps that was behind this sudden need to economize? I looked back at Theo again, and jumped slightly to see that he was no longer asleep, but rather unnervingly looking steadily back at me. I smiled ruefully.

'Come on, then.' I unclipped my seatbelt. 'Let's go and find Daddy, shall we?'

After lunch, having wrestled the contents of a pouch optimistically labelled 'Moroccan chicken' into Theo, I put him on his mat while I made myself a fresh tea to accompany my croissant, but Theo had other ideas, and puked everywhere. Liv rang just as I was scrubbing the carpet.

'Hi.' She sounded breathless and was apparently walking some-where fast. 'Me again. I'm just about to go into my meeting but I wanted to ring and say sorry for sounding all "busy, busy" earlier when I know you're stuck at home. I didn't mean to rub it in. I also didn't actually give you chance to say if you and Matthew have sorted everything out now?'

'I think so. And thanks for calling back again. That's really kind of you. I'm currently wiping some puke off the floor... with my tits, actually,' I deadpanned, 'seeing as they were already down there.'

She snorted. 'Yes, that was sweet of Chloe to make such a per-sonal observation.'

'Oh God.' I grabbed for a muslin. 'I'm going to have to go – Theo's just done it again. Sorry.'

'No worries,' she said. 'Nearly there! It's not long until it all gets much easier again. I promise.'

'Mummy!' Chloe flung herself at me in her classroom and gave me a fierce hug, before releasing me just as quickly. 'How did Theo sleep today?'

I looked at my poor little girl, aghast. Was that really all she heard me go on about? I laughed gaily and hoped that none of the other mums or her teacher had overheard.

'Very well, thanks, darling,' I lied. 'Had a good day?'

'Yes. I wrote a "p" and a "n".'

'Well done you! Can you get your lunchbox? And your hat and coat?'

'Who's at home?' she asked.

'No one. Just Dad.' I smiled. 'Come on, love. Hat and coat, please, quick as you can. I didn't have any change and I don't want to get a parking ticket.'

'You said no one was here!' Chloe said excitedly as we arrived back at the house to discover a taxi on the drive, with the engine running.

'There wasn't,' I said, confused, as I shoved the yellow plastic parking ticket envelope to the bottom of my handbag, where Matthew wouldn't chance upon it. I watched the back, right-hand passenger door open and a slim, elegant leg, clad in a sheer stocking and three-inch patent leather pump, emerged.

'It's Granny!' exclaimed Chloe in delight, and she started scrabbling to undo her seatbelt, as sure enough, my mother-in-law climbed out: the cavalry dressed in Diane von Furstenberg. My heart momentarily lifted at the sight of her, only to be replaced by dismay at the thought of the pig-tip that lay behind the front door. Oh, how embarrassing. Why on earth hadn't Matthew told me she was coming? Wasn't she supposed to be in Spain on some conference?

Chloe clambered out of the car as fast as she could, dashed up the drive, and hurled herself at her grandmother, to Caroline's delighted laughter, as she gathered her up.

'Hello, Chloe! You're so big since I last saw you. What a lot of clever growing you've been doing!'

Chloe adoringly stroked Caroline's ash blonde hair, then wriggled deeper into her arms, as Caroline grabbed at her handbag to stop it slipping off her shoulder. 'How many sleeps are you staying for, Granny?'

'Tonight and maybe tomorrow night? We'll see,' Caroline answered, looking up and beaming at me from over Chloe's head. 'Chloe, sweetheart, hop down for a minute, while I say hello to Mummy. Sally!' She held me at arm's-length for a moment, and inspected me sympathetically. 'What *has* that beastly grandson of mine been doing to you? Come here.' She drew me into a warm hug. 'Now, Matthew called me and said you were on your knees.' She released me. 'And I told him it was just as easy to come here from the airport than go home, so I can lend a hand for a day or two, if that's any help? But I can just as happily stay for a cup of tea, cook you all some supper, and trot off again later this evening if you like. Whatever works best.'

'It's lovely to see you,' I replied truthfully. 'I'm just embarrassed at how disgusting the house is. I'd have had a quick tidy up if I'd known.'

'Oh, for goodness' sake, don't be ridiculous! It couldn't matter less.' She turned to the driver, who had opened the boot, and took a large red holdall from him, the strap of which she also placed over her shoulder, while grasping the handle of her wheelie suit-case in the other hand. She smiled brightly at me. 'Let's all go in, shall we, and decide on a plan?'

I immediately felt better as we all sat down at the kitchen table. Caroline's energy, as ever, was infectious, and her aura of competence hugely reassuring. Utterly content in her own skin, she had no problem being generous to others, which consequently drew people to her. Slightly more than averagely tall, her elegant height also lent her an air of calm resilience. I was convinced that if she'd had the slightest interest in it, she could have been a front-bench political figure. Instead she'd chosen child psychiatry, specializing in eating disorders. Supposedly officially retired, she was still actively involved in several projects and research programmes, and sat on several boards. Her only blind-spot was Matthew. He could literally do no wrong in her eyes, which was sometimes unbearably frustrating, but since Matthew's father had left when Matthew was only four, and she had never remarried, Matthew was pretty much all she had – bar Chloe and Theo, whom she equally worshipped – and her own elderly and infirm mother, who lived in a home near Caroline's house, about twenty-five miles away from us.

I'd once asked Matthew why he thought someone as attractive as his mother had managed to stay single for so long. Certainly I'd never even known her be involved with anyone in all the time we'd been together.

'I suppose it *is* quite sad, really,' Matthew had replied. 'In some ways it was worse that there wasn't anyone else; Dad just didn't want *us*, and him leaving almost destroyed her, I think, because she was so completely in love with him. I only ever heard her talk about him once, to one of her friends – she didn't know I was listening. She said she was never going to allow herself to become that vulnerable, ever again.' He shrugged. 'And she hasn't.'

'Did you bring me a treat, Granny?' Chloe said nonchalantly, as she climbed onto Caroline's lap.

'Chloe!' I admonished immediately, jiggling Theo on my knee. 'It's not polite to ask. You know that.'

'It's all right.' Caroline laughed. 'As a matter of fact, I did. Go and look over there and see what you can find. No, not that bag.' She jumped up as Chloe headed over to the red holdall. 'I'll just pop this one in the cupboard under the stairs, if I may, Sally, until Matthew can carry it upstairs for me. Just a moment, sweetie.' She disappeared, and then returned immediately. 'Let's look in my handbag for a little something, shall we?'

The 'little something' turned out to be two extremely pretty cotton dresses: perfect lightweight cover-ups for hot days. 'I actually enjoy shopping for the children more than myself now,' Caroline confessed. 'Aren't these just so gorgeous?' She'd also bought a very cute sunhat and a surf suit for Theo. 'I thought they might be nice for a summer holiday, later in the year. Oh, you are delicious!' she cooed at Theo, who was staring up at her, equally besotted in his bouncer, while gumming a carrot.

I, however, was picturing the bliss of pre-children holidays: lying on loungers reading books; cocktails and dressing for dinner after a tough day of sunbathing and sleeping. Matthew and I had been good at travelling together. I suddenly also remembered us having drunken and very abandoned sex on a large marble table in a villa in Ibiza. I blushed and glanced down – at the kitchen table I now spent most days scrubbing free of pasta sauce. We should have gone away more, while we'd had the chance. I sighed wistfully.

'We could chat later, about us all going somewhere, I thought?' Caroline suggested. 'A nice, child-friendly resort where you and Matthew can relax. I'll pay, of course, and look after the children. I just think you could do with having something to look forward to. Something like this, perhaps?'

She passed me her phone and I stared hungrily at the image of a tranquil spa treatment room with a sea view.

'Hang on, where's the little video I found? Oh, here!' She reached over and tapped the screen. I watched a bikini-clad woman dive into a pool, then a picture-perfect family run into some waves on a stunning sandy beach, followed by a shot of a man surfing, all set to vibrant acoustic guitar music. Another woman appeared with her small daughter, standing in shallow waves inspecting a shell. Both of them were wearing matching white broderie anglaise dresses, billowing in the sea breeze. The woman looked utterly gorgeous. All tousled sea-salt hair and bare, tanned skin.

'I was thinking maybe next month, or early June, so it's warm, but not too hot for Theo?' Caroline suggested.

Next month? I couldn't help it – my immediate first thought was me on a beach, wobbly, bright white blub stuffed into a bulging black one-piece... But more importantly, Theo wailing through the night as I walked him endlessly around an unfamiliar hotel room. And oh God – the packing...

'Maybe.' I smiled faintly. 'It's a very kind offer, though.'

Caroline gently reached for the phone. 'Well, perhaps it's something to think about. No need to make a decision right now.'

'No need to make a decision about what?' Matthew appeared in the doorway. 'Hi, Mum.' He came over and kissed her.

'A little holiday idea I had.' Caroline waved her hand dismissively. 'Hello, darling!'

'Really?' Matthew looked at her eagerly. 'That would be amazing. Hey, Chloe, we could practise your swimming, couldn't we? How was school, by the way?'

'It was good,' said Chloe, who was drawing a picture at the table. 'Practise my swimming where?'

'On holiday. Granny wants to take us away. That'd be fun, wouldn't it?'

'Matthew...' I tried to get his attention and shook my head slightly, motioning at Chloe, so he didn't get her hopes up. 'It's just a bit hard to plan anything right at the moment,' I explained to Caroline. 'Could we maybe revisit it once I've got Theo's sleep sorted? I know it sounds pathetic, but I can't really think about anything else right now.'

'You don't want to go on a free holiday?' Matthew said disbelievingly.

'Matthew!' I exclaimed, embarrassed. 'Perhaps we can discuss this later?'

'Absolutely. We don't have to decide anything now,' said Caroline. 'There's no rush to plan anything at all. Is there, Matthew?'

'Whatever you want, Sal,' said Matthew flatly. 'Whatever you want.' He came and sat down next to Caroline. 'How was Barcelona, Mum? You're looking very well.'

She reached out and patted his knee. 'Thank you, darling. It was fine. Nice hotel, which always helps, and plenty of time off. I had a lovely wander around one of the squares after supper last night and chanced upon this man doing a fabulous old-school flamenco display.'

Matthew sighed. 'Sounds amazing. I really miss that.'

'What, flamenco?' I teased, clapping Theo's hands, and smiling as he tried to grab them and give them a dribbly suck. 'I never knew you were so into it.'

'I meant I miss travelling. Why do you always belittle my feelings? I am capable of some genuine emotion, contrary to popular belief.'

I looked up in surprise. Chloe carried on colouring, and Caroline took a sip of her tea, her hand still resting on Matthew's leg. Matthew and I locked eyes for a brief moment, before I glanced away first, confused and hurt. I'd only been joking, that was obvious, surely?

'Flamenco is very difficult to master, apparently,' Caroline commented, moving smoothly on, as she reached for her phone again. 'I went to see Joaquín Cortés perform it at the Roundhouse. Here, I'll show you on YouTube. Chloe, come and look at this man dancing!'

Matthew stood up again and sighed. 'I'd better go and get on with some more work. I'll make sure I'm done in time to help with bath time,' he threw to me over his shoulder as he reached the door, presumably for his mum's benefit. He made it sound as if I wasn't able to cope otherwise, and he was firefighting on all fronts, single-handedly keeping everything afloat. 'See you all in a bit.'

'So, what's for tea?' Caroline said brightly, a moment or two after he'd left the room. 'Anything I can help with?'

'Um, no, I don't think so. I'm really sorry, Caroline, about what just happened,' I said. 'I didn't mean to sound ungrateful. Or for either of us to make you feel uncomfortable. Matthew's under a lot of pressure at work at the moment, and things are a little... tricky.'

She didn't miss a beat. 'You don't have to apologize for Matthew to me. I understand perfectly.'

'Thank you. Do you think you could watch the kids for a minute? I'll be right back.' I got up suddenly and made my way out into the hallway, and then hastened upstairs after Matthew. He was already back in front of his computer.

'OK, firstly, I wasn't belittling you, and secondly, can you please not speak to me like that in front of your mum and Chloe?' I said, from the doorway. 'Has something else happened, besides the contract not coming in? You seem to be pretty on edge.'

'*Me?* I'm absolutely fine. Why don't you want to plan a holiday?' He looked up from his screen and fixed me with an intent stare. 'I thought you'd jump at the chance to go away.'

I sighed. 'It's not that easy, Matthew.'

'Yes it is. We just go. I know Theo's tricky, but...' He shrugged. 'We can't stop living *our* lives. I'd love to go away somewhere with you all.' He paused, and added, 'I sometimes feel my needs are very much last on the list. And that's understandable. I get it. I just want "us" back again.'

'I'm not trying to be difficult, Matthew, just practical while Theo's so small. If we can just remember—'

I was about to add that it wouldn't always be this way, but his phone started to ring. He picked it up and said heartily, 'Matthew speaking, how can I help you? Oh, hi Dave. No. Still not in. I know. Right up to the wire again. Lovely.'

He turned away from me to face the window. I looked at his back, the outline of his broad shoulders visible despite the sensible shirt he was wearing, and thought again of us naked in the hotel in Ibiza. Sometimes it was hard to believe we'd ever been those people.

I turned and closed the door quietly behind me on my way out.

CHAPTER FOUR

'You're sure I can't do anything to help with the children's tea?' Caroline asked again, as I appeared back in the kitchen.

'Thank you, but it's just a little chicken casserole I made this morning, so I think we're all sorted.'

'That's impressively organized!' She raised her mug to me in compliment.

I tried to smile, but failed.

She regarded me for a moment, and I wondered if she was going to tackle everything head-on after all, but she seemed to change her mind, and then the subject, by looking out of the window and remarking, 'Oh, honestly – look at that! Raining again! Typical April showers. We need a bit of sun. I must admit, it was beautiful in Barcelona.'

'I'll bet,' I said, relieved. 'I was saying to one of my friends the other day, I'm seriously thinking about relocating us all to California.'

'Oh, not all that again!' Caroline laughed. 'You've only just moved here, for goodness' sake!'

'All what again?' I looked at my mother-in-law, confused.

'You had that job offer to move to America, didn't you?' She took another sip of tea. 'When you and Matthew hadn't been together very long. You must remember, surely?'

'Wow! You've got a good memory. That was years ago! It was

New York, though, not California.' I sat down opposite her. 'Do you know, I'd almost completely forgotten that! It so nearly happened too – they'd sorted out an apartment, flights, everything... We both gave notice on our jobs... I wonder if we'd still be out there now, if it hadn't all fallen through at the last minute? Living the American dream. Imagine!'

'Indeed.'

'Matthew was amazing about it,' I realized suddenly. 'We'd hardly been together any time at all, and yet he was prepared to just up and leave everything here, for me.' I shook my head in disbelief. 'How weird is it to think of Chloe with a little American accent? And Theo might have ended up being called, I don't know, Jayden, or Ethan, or something. Anyway,' I paused and took another sip of tea, 'there you go. Funny how life works out, isn't it? There's no way we'd do something similar now.'

'I'm very glad to hear it.'

'I couldn't uproot Chloe, and my mum and dad would hate being that far away from the children, just as much as you would.'

'How *are* your parents? Still working hard in the shop?'

I nodded regretfully. ''Fraid so. I can't see them retiring any time soon. I worry about Dad in particular, what with him having the two heart by-pass ops now, but...' I shrugged, 'Mum keeps him on the straight and narrow.'

'And what about your brother, Will. How's he?'

'Very well, I think, thank you. I haven't seen him for ages. It's crazy given – like you – he only lives about twenty-five minutes away, but he's been flat out with work.'

'He's still with the same girlfriend, I gather? The famous one?'

'Kelly? Yes. She's just finished her run on *EastEnders*.'

Caroline shrugged, nonplussed. 'I don't watch it, I'm afraid.'

'Me neither,' I said firmly.

'Oh dear. Still not so keen on her, then?' Caroline sympathized.

'Um, that's one way of putting it. I wish it wasn't that way and I – *we* – could get over it, but...' I sighed. 'Have I not ever told you what happened the first day I met her?'

Caroline shook her head. 'I don't think so.'

'Really? Well, Will asked me to come over to his flat for dinner to meet this new woman he'd started seeing. I was about four months pregnant with Theo, and when I arrived, there was a girl standing in the middle of the pavement, pretty much blocking it completely, on her mobile, with her back to me. I didn't want to step into the road, but I was already pretty big – what with it being my second – so I went to squeeze around, but she moved at the last minute, and instead, I kind of bumped into her. I apologized instantly, but she didn't even look at me, instead she said–' turning to make sure Chloe wasn't listening to us, I mouthed – '"you fucking stupid bitch" over her shoulder as I walked past, and then carried on talking.'

Caroline raised an eyebrow.

'I went upstairs, and had only got as far as taking my coat off, when the bell went and his new girlfriend, Kelly, arrived, who was – as I'm sure you've guessed – the girl who had sworn at me downstairs.'

Caroline made a face.

'I know,' I agreed. 'So I wait for her to look embarrassed and apologize, but she gives me this enormous fake smile, and cries, "Oh! You're so beautiful! Look at that neat little bump!" I was completely thrown by such a Jekyll and Hyde turnaround. My first thought was that maybe she wasn't aware I was the woman she'd just sworn at – I'd taken my coat off, and you couldn't ignore my bump – *or* she knew exactly who I was, and just brazened it out in front of Will. In which case it worked, because I was so stunned, I didn't say anything.'

'Hmmm,' said Caroline. 'It sounds like either way, you saw a flash of some true colours there. People often reveal so much about themselves in the most seemingly unimportant moments.'

'Exactly!' I said. 'It was an awful first impression, and a scary demonstration of her ability to turn on the charm when required...' I shook my head. 'I wouldn't go as far to say I took an instant dislike to her because of what I'd seen...' I stopped. 'Actually, you know what? If I'm being honest – I *did* take an instant dislike to her. Anyway, it was obviously mutual, because not long after our first meeting, she made it pretty clear she and I were never going to be the best of friends. We were all in our sitting room – she and Will had been seeing each other for about two months – Will and Matthew went into the kitchen, and to make conversation, I started to ask her how work was going, and she just said, "Look, Sally, it's obvious we don't like each other. Let's just leave it there, shall we? I've nothing more to say to you."'

'Ouch!' Caroline said. 'Yes, there's not much mistaking that, is there?'

'No. There isn't. It's not improved, but the important thing is, we manage to be polite for Will's sake.'

'Do you think he's going to stay with her long-term?'

I fidgeted on my chair. 'I hope not. They're very... different. They're already living together, which I think happened too fast, but they've also only been together for eleven months, and she's still young – well, six years his junior – so,' I shrugged uncomfortably, 'plenty of time for it to burn out yet.'

'The trouble is, there's no telling people, is there? It's difficult, but you have to let them find out the hard way sometimes.'

'True,' I agreed. 'She—' My phone buzzed on the table in front of us, and I stopped to see who the message was from. 'Well, how weird is that?' I said, amazed. 'Talk of the devil – that's Will, asking if he can come over after work today.'

'Please don't say no on my account,' Caroline said immediately. 'I can easily pop out for a bit and leave you to it.'

'No, no. You don't need to do that.' I frowned at my phone. 'How funny. He's practically never around on a Friday night.'

'Perhaps he's got something important to tell you?' suggested Caroline.

I paled, and looked up at her horrified. 'Oh my God, you're right...' I stared at the message on my phone again. 'He's going to propose to her, isn't he?'

We sat in silence for a moment, before Caroline got to her feet, gave my shoulder a sympathetic pat, and put her cup in the sink. 'Sorry, I shouldn't have said anything. If it is that, though, can I give you some advice? Smile and tell him you couldn't be happier... Because regardless of whatever you have to say about Kelly, he will go ahead anyway. I promise you that. My father hated Peter – *loathed* him, in fact – but it didn't stop me from marrying him. There are some things in life you can either make the best of, or let them get the best of you. At least it's Will, and not Chloe or Theo marrying someone you can't stand. It could be a lot worse.'

I shuddered. 'Don't. I couldn't bear that, but I think you're right. Will is going to marry Kelly...' I trailed off as the horrible realization began to sink in. Kelly wasn't just going to disappear off over the horizon, she was about to become part of our family. Even if I didn't have to see her that often, every Christmas, birthday – any celebration at all – she'd be there. I felt sick. It wasn't just that she was so unpleasant, and I wanted so much more for Will than her; she was the kind of person who would take great pleasure in altering the existing happy dynamic of our lives, as she trampled all over them.

Everything was about to change.

*

'But when's Uncle Will getting here?'

'After you're in bed, sweetheart.' I dished up casserole and sweet potato mash onto Chloe's plate, before putting another couple of dollops into the blender jug and blitzing them up for Theo, who was sitting at the table in his highchair sucking yet another carrot.

'Why?' said Chloe.

'Because by the time he's finished work and arrived, you'll be asleep.' I plopped the puree into one of Chloe's old pink plastic bowls, then grabbed a selection of equally pink spoons for Theo to chew and fling around the room.

'Ohhh!' Chloe put her head in her hands and slumped at the table, then as I put her food in front of her, pushed it away and said, 'My tummy doesn't want this.'

'I'm sorry to hear that, darling, but can you tell your tummy I'm afraid it's all there is?' I said, sitting down and starting to spoon the puree into Theo. 'So what was the best bit about school today?'

Chloe sighed. 'Playing with Alice.'

'That sounds fun,' I said, trying to focus and stop thinking about Will and Kelly. Was Caroline right? Should I just say nothing apart from congratulations? But Will and I had always had a very honest relationship. I wasn't really going to stand there and outright lie with something crap like 'I hope you'll be very happy together'. Was I?

'Muuuuummmm!' Chloe tugged on my sleeve. 'I said I want you to feed me.'

'Um, OK,' I said absently, and put Theo's spoon down so I could do a forkful for her.

'Shall *I* help you with your tea, Chloe?' offered Caroline.

'No thank you,' Chloe said. 'I want Mummy.'

'OK.' Caroline smiled, unruffled, and then turned to me, sympathetically. 'Are you all right?'

I gave her a small smile. 'Yes. I'm just a bit—'

'More please, Mum.'

'Sorry,' I said, doing another forkful. 'OK, Theo, yes, you're next... I'm just a bit taken aback, really. Like I said earlier, it's only been eleven months. I suppose in the back of my mind I thought – open wide please, Chloe, sweetheart, I can't do it if you're turning the other way – that they might just have a fling and that would be it. She's a fling sort of girl, if you get my drift. This is pretty much my worst nightmare. Actually, that's not true. My *worst* nightmare is he gets her pregnant... OK, Theo, here it comes... Although, I suppose if they're going to get married, that's going to happen too anyway, and—'

'Sally! STOP!' said Caroline.

'What?' I paused, chastened, spoon in mid-air.

'You're about to give Theo a mouthful from Chloe's plate.'

I looked down at the spoon, aghast, and hurriedly put down the large forkful of solid chicken. 'Oh God! I could have choked him!'

'He's fine,' Caroline said. 'And Will might be coming for some other reason entirely. I feel dreadful. I shouldn't have said anything. This could have nothing to do with – sorry, what's her name?'

'Kelly,' I said grimly. 'And I'm sure it's got absolutely everything to do with her.'

'You know what we should do?' Caroline said half an hour later, as Chloe happily squeezed a flannel over her knees in the bath and Theo chewed a plastic duck. 'Try and sort a weekend away for you and Matthew, together. You need a break. I'd have the children for you.'

'That'd be nice,' I said, considerably more flatly than I intended. I couldn't help it. The longer the day had gone on, the crappier it had become, and at the thought of Will's news lying ahead, I felt almost bleak.

'Oh, Sal!' she said sympathetically. 'I so want to help. I can tell things are –' she picked her words with precision – '*tricky* for you – and Matthew – at the moment, and I hate to see you struggling.'

I assumed she was now talking about what had happened before tea, unless Matthew had told her what was actually up with him, rather than me. 'They're not great, no,' I said quietly. I lifted up a dripping Theo, sat him on the towel on my lap, wrapped him snugly, then shivered. There was a hell of a draught coming from somewhere. 'Can you watch Theo a minute?' I passed him over to her and got to my feet.

Out in the hallway, I realized it was coming from Matthew's office, and went in. He wasn't there, but his window was wide open. As I walked across the room to close it, I noticed my earlier note to him, tossed on the floor. How nice. I picked it up and put it in my pocket, shut the window, then hurried back to the bathroom.

'Come on then, Clo!' I said brightly. 'Time to hop out!'

'I want Granny to do my stories,' said Chloe, and Caroline beamed.

'I think I can manage that! If it's all right with Mummy?'

'Of course it is.'

'Try not to worry about this evening, Sally,' Caroline said gently. 'I know it's hard, but what will be, will be. There's no point trying to fight it.'

'Hi.' Matthew looked up as I came into the sitting room to find him on the far sofa, next to his mother. 'Kids asleep?'

I nodded.

'Thank God. I'm going to get a takeaway so you don't have to cook tonight, and I'm sorry. I shouldn't have spoken to you like that earlier, you're right.'

I glanced at Caroline, who was looking studiously down at her feet. She'd obviously had a word.

'Thank you,' I said. I wasn't really sure what else *to* say.

'I'll order now and go straight away. You'll want to be all done eating before Will and Kelly arrive?'

'Kelly?' I said instantly. '*She's* not coming – it's just Will.'

Matthew looked at his mother immediately. 'Oh right. Sorry, I—'

'He's coming to talk to me *about* Kelly,' I explained. 'I expect that's what you meant, wasn't it, Caroline?'

'My mistake. It doesn't matter,' Matthew said quickly. 'The thing is, the football lot are having a few drinks tonight, and I'd like to go, mostly because my contract finally came in, but if you need me to be here...'

'Congratulations. *I* don't mind if you go, but...' I glanced awkwardly at Caroline. I couldn't blame him for not wanting to stay in, especially when he hadn't left the house all day – but my mum would be gutted if I went out as soon as she arrived for a visit.

'Oh, don't worry about me,' Caroline said. 'I'll just take myself off to bed after we've eaten, if that's all right?'

'Thanks, Mum,' Matthew said absently, frowning down at his phone. 'I'm getting the usual, I take it? Bugger, my battery is about to die, I can't get the menu up. Can I borrow yours, Sal?'

I threw it across. 'The spare bed hasn't got clean sheets yet, I'm really sorry,' I confessed to Caroline. 'I will do it, though.'

'Don't be silly.' She waved a hand. 'I can sort it out. It's no problem. I know where everything is.'

'Sal, what's your code?' Matthew looked up at me. 'It's locked.'

'Two, three, four, five,' I said, and he rolled his eyes.

'I think—' he began, then stopped suddenly, just staring at my screen.

'What?' I said.

He paused and then looked up at me, his face blank. 'Nothing. So, chicken passanda, is it?'

My phone began to ring seconds after they'd both left to collect the food. I almost didn't pick up, I was so desperate for five minutes to myself, but it was Mum, and I knew she'd just keep calling until I answered.

'Hello love!' she said cheerily.

I pictured her sitting in my parents' Dorset cottage, in our little seaside village, fire lit in the sitting room, washing up from tea all neatly put away in the kitchen, draining board dried with a tea towel. She'd have her knitting in her lap, and Dad would be in his chair watching TV, no doubt. Just for a moment, I wished I was there, being looked after by her too.

'How's your day been?' Mum said. 'And how are those little dots?'

'Your grandson has slept a grand total of about three quarters of an hour today.' I leant back on the sofa and closed my eyes. 'And I'm on my knees.'

Mum tutted. 'He's a little tinker. The one thing I could always rely on with you and your brother was that you both slept two hours a day, like clockwork. I don't know what I would have done, without that.'

'Felt like you were going completely mad, probably,' I said.

'You're not going mad, Sally.'

'Really? I don't know how much longer I can cope like this, that's for sure.' I curled up miserably. 'He just *doesn't sleep*, Mum. Last night, he didn't go down till eleven. And then...' I paused. That was right, wasn't it? Was it eleven or twelve? I couldn't quite remember. 'Anyway, the point is, I'm not sure I can hang on for another month until I can do sleep training with him.'

There was a moment's silence and then Mum said, 'Well, I don't see what choice you have, really. I'd come down and help you, but there's no one who can mind the shop. That woman we took on – she's already left because her husband had a stroke. We're interviewing again next week. We've got to get someone trained up before the summer season starts. What about your brother and Kelly? Can't you ring them? They're only half an hour away. Will would *love* to come and help you. In fact, hasn't he rung you himself yet?'

'Well, hold that thought for a second, but Caroline actually turned up out of the blue earlier. I think Matthew must have called her as she only arrived back from Spain today.'

'Really? Oh, I am glad. That was very sensible of him. At least you're not totally on your own now.'

'True,' I admitted. 'Although, obviously, I wish it was you and Dad here instead.'

'We do too. The house felt so quiet after you all left last weekend. It was *such* a lovely Easter.' She sighed. 'That beautiful little girl collecting her eggs for her basket, when we did that hunt in the garden. So why did you say hold that thought about Will?'

I took a deep breath. 'Well, I think you know why. He's asked if he can come over tonight, completely out of the blue. What's he coming to tell me then, Mum?'

'Nothing, as far as I know.'

I frowned sceptically. 'Really? He's not coming to tell me he's getting married to Kelly?'

'I haven't spoken to him, love. I've no idea.'

I hesitated. Will would have definitely told my parents if he'd proposed, and Mum would be beside herself if he actually *was* getting married.

'Oh, well, that's good,' I said, feeling suddenly much more cheery. 'I must have got the wrong end of the stick. Mum, do you mind if I go now? I don't mean to be rude, but I could really use a moment to myself before Matthew and Caroline get back with the food, or the kids wake up again, or Will arrives. Is that OK?'

'Of course it is,' she said generously.

'You and Dad are all right, though?' I said quickly.

'We're absolutely fine.'

'Good. And this *is* all going to get better with Theo, isn't it?' I added, a little desperately.

'Yes!' she said. 'It was exactly like this with Chloe too, don't you remember?'

'Not really,' I admitted. 'I think I must have blocked it out.'

'Well, I can tell you it was. And you *will* survive. I do hope you have a better night with the little man tonight. Give them both a hug and kiss from me, won't you? Dad sends his love too.'

Once she'd gone, I happily remembered my croissant. I got to my feet and headed off to the kitchen. It might have taken me all day to finally find five seconds to eat it, but I'd got there eventually. Thank God.

I found the empty scrunched-up patisserie bag on the side, next to the hob, among a scatter of flaky pastry crumbs. Matthew hadn't even bothered to throw the bag in the bin.

I stared at the debris. Logically, I knew it was hardly crime of the century, but it just about summed my life up. My mood having turned on a sixpence again, I had a sudden overwhelming desire to scream with frustration, at the top of my voice. The walls of the house began to shrink in on me in a rush, and I realized I was actually shaking with supressed rage. Hands fumbling, I undid the back door quickly and escaped out into the side passage and the cold, crisp night.

'Fucking, fucking hell!' I gasped aloud, as the freezing air hit my skin. I stared up at the twinkling stars miles and miles above me, and just as quickly, my anger began to dissipate, leaving me standing under the enormous night sky, feeling utterly broken, tiny and alone. 'I can't do this any more,' I whispered in disbelief. There was no room for me. I was being swallowed alive by the constant demands of my family. I didn't *want* to do this any more! And I hadn't even got to eat my croissant. I let my head hang, and then from inside the house I heard the determined shout of my baby... I looked up at the sky once more in desperation, then I turned and went back in.

I came down from Theo's room to discover Matthew and his mum had come back with the food. Matthew was nowhere to be seen, however, and Caroline had already finished; her empty plate was at her feet on the carpet as I went into the sitting room to find her watching TV. She got up instantly.

'I'll get yours now, Sally. I've been keeping it warm for you.' She hurried out to the kitchen and came back in with my meal on a tray, accompanied by a glass of water.

'Thank you.' I curled my legs up under me and took it gratefully.

'You'd be able to do something like that in here,' she remarked, pointing to *Grand Designs*. 'On a smaller scale, of course, or you could have bi-fold doors out onto the garden. That'd be lovely. It's so exciting to think about everything you can do to this place!'

I ate peacefully for five minutes before being interrupted by a sudden, loud rumbling on the drive. 'What on earth is that?' I said, confused. I set my tray on the floor, jumped up and pulled back the curtain, only to find Matthew helpfully dragging the newly emptied wheelie bin noisily up the drive with him. I opened the window, leant out, and pleaded in a desperate whisper, 'Matthew! *Please* stop! I've literally just put Theo down!'

He stared back at me. 'Well, he's not going to hear me from upstairs, is he? I'm only putting the bin away, that's all.'

'Please, *please*, can you not?' I begged. 'I literally can't bear it if he wakes up again, and it's so bloody loud!'

Matthew gritted his teeth. 'Sure. I'll just leave it here then, shall

I?' He pointedly set the bin down right in the middle of the drive. 'I think I'm just going to go out now, if that's OK?'

'I think that's probably best, yes,' I said in relief, and closed the window. Caroline turned the volume up and diplomatically said nothing.

'I know I probably seem obsessed with noise right now,' I said a moment later, having started to eat again. 'I'm just...' I struggled and failed to articulate everything. 'Things will just be a lot easier when Theo starts sleeping, that's all.'

'Of course they will. It's enormously hard, this stage,' Caroline said generously. 'So hard, I could only do it once! Matthew was such a nightmare sleeper when he was little. I couldn't have gone through it again even if I'd had the choice.' She leant back on the sofa. 'It was also very different when we were all having babies. I mean, I was only twenty-two when I had Matthew. I hadn't got an interesting career I had to leave, and my parents were around all the time because they had retired. They looked after Matthew a lot. But your parents work, I still work – to all intents and purposes – although I *am* winding down this year. The point is, you certainly don't have the same support that we all enjoyed.' She sighed. 'And it must be very hard to have to leave a career midway through. It's such a great deal to give up. You've had to cope with an awful lot of demands on you, Sally, and you're under such strain in so many different ways right now, never mind the effects of severe sleep deprivation. I think you're doing amazingly well.'

At her kind words, my eyes flooded with tears. 'Thank you. I can't help but feel I *should* be coping better than this, though; it's the second time around, after all.'

'Oh, Sal, don't cry.' She went to get up, but Matthew came back in, and I hurriedly wiped my face.

'Everything all right?' he said, looking between the two of us.

'Absolutely fine,' Caroline said smoothly. 'Listen, I think if you don't mind, I'm going to turn in. Barcelona was a bit full-on, and I wouldn't say no to catching up on some rest. I'd offer to settle Theo back tonight if he wakes, but you won't want me to, will you?' She turned to look at me.

'No,' I confessed. 'Thank you for the thought, but I'll do it.'

'Well, I'll rest up tonight so I can go on duty tomorrow during the day, then.'

'It won't be long before I come up myself. Hopefully my brother will be—'

But before I could finish saying 'arriving anytime now', the doorbell rang. Caroline and Matthew exchanged a worried look, which was odd, and Caroline got up instantly.

'I'll just go and get my phone from the kitchen, then I'll come back and say goodnight.'

'And I'm going to answer that door, before Will rings again and wakes Theo.' Matthew hurried out into the hall.

I heard my little brother say a jolly 'Hello!' and then loudly whisper, 'Shit, sorry!' presumably in response to Matthew urging him to be quiet.

I put my plate down and got to my feet in anticipation. Sure enough, Will appeared around the corner, still wearing his overcoat and outdoor shoes, having apparently not been allowed to stop in the hallway.

I opened my mouth to tell him how nice he looked, but then I realized why my husband and mother-in-law were so ill-at-ease, because from out behind him – tiny and slim as ever – stepped Kelly.

CHAPTER FIVE

She regarded me coolly through dark eyes, and removed a stray lock of her long glossy brown hair from her face. No ring, however, I noted with instant relief, as she flashed me one of her wide, impossibly white smiles.

'Hi, Sal.'

She was the one person I hated calling me that. She somehow made me sound like a yokel farmhand, but I managed not to say anything other than, 'Hello, Kelly. You look very well.'

I took in her bare, brown legs beneath the tight, berry-red pencil skirt she'd teamed with nude, four-inch heels. Given she must be aware it was only just April, I suspected her choice was designed to show off what I assumed must be a fake tan, but this time I was wrong.

She raised an immaculately drawn-on eyebrow and said smoothly, 'Thanks. I've just got back from Tenerife, shooting the campaign for my new swimwear range.'

'How nice.'

'Well, it was work.' She shrugged. 'I did some filming for a new six-part series while I was out there too.'

'Great,' I said, deliberately not asking her anything more about it, as she obviously wanted me to. 'Come in and sit down – but would you mind removing your shoes first?'

She scowled slightly, and looked at Will, who was already undoing his.

'It's just because of the kids,' I explained. 'Theo rolls around on this rug, you see, so...'

'OK,' she said tightly, and putting her bag down, kicked them off, looking considerably less elegant.

'Thanks so much.' I smiled.

'Would you like me to put the kettle on before I go? Cup of tea, anyone?' Matthew looked between us warily, and added quickly, 'No? OK, well, I'm sorry I can't stop, but I'll be back later, Sal. And before you ask, it'll be probably just after eleven.' He smiled, but I saw Kelly note the edge to his tone, as well as the fact he didn't kiss me goodbye. 'Nice to see you, Will, Kelly.' He gave us all a brief wave as he hurried out, closing the door behind him.

'So how are you, sis?' Will stepped forward and gave me a hug. 'You're looking pretty fabulous yourself.'

I gave him a grateful smile. It was a kind lie; I looked like a rolled ham. While my maternity trousers might be holding my tummy in, they were also creating several unflattering bulges as the fat tried to escape over the top of the waistband. I shot another incredulous look at Kelly's outfit, and then her Sophia Loren hair, as I tried to remind myself she was ten years younger than me and didn't have kids – but even so, what styling secret did celebrities have access to that the rest of us didn't? I touched my own scraped-back ponytail self-consciously. I hadn't had it cut or coloured since Theo was born. The only famous person I was channelling was Francis Rossi.

'Right,' I said, dragging myself back to the room. '*I'll* make us a drink. What can I get you? Tea? Coffee?'

'Before you do that,' Will gently put an arm out to stop me, 'we've got a bit of news, actually.'

'Oh right?' I stopped short, completely caught off guard. 'What's that then?'

My brother let go of me, took a step over to Kelly, cleared his throat nervously, and took her hand in his.

I froze. Oh *no*...

'Kelly and I are getting—'

The door opened behind them and Caroline appeared. 'Sally, I'm terribly sorry to interrupt, but I can't find my phone charger. I wonder, have you seen it?' She smiled apologetically. 'Please do excuse me.'

'Not at all,' I said, still staring at my brother in dismay. 'Will, you remember my mother-in-law Caroline. And Caroline, this is Will's girlfriend, Kelly.'

Will released Kelly, who turned to face Caroline full-on. I saw a puzzled look fleetingly pass across my mother-in-law's face as she recognized Kelly after all. Kelly *loved* this bit... the moment when it dawned on people meeting her that they were in the presence of a FAMOUS PERSON. She was only a soap actress, for God's sake.

I watched Caroline hurriedly rearrange her features as she placed her, and she politely extended a hand. 'Delighted to meet you. I'm Caroline Hilman.'

I couldn't see Kelly's face, but she put out a perfectly mani-cured hand. 'Kelly Harrington.' I waited for her to add some-thing demurely like, 'Yes, I'm on TV. No, no – please don't be embarrassed... it happens all the time...' Blah, blah, blah... But before she could say anything, Caroline began to back away.

'I really am sorry for intruding. Would you excuse me? Very nice to see you again, Will, and to meet you, Kelly. Goodnight all.' She glanced sympathetically at me as she withdrew, and it dawned on me that she and Matthew already knew about Will and Kelly getting married.

They *all* knew, except me.

Will turned back to me. 'OK, let's try that again. Tell you what, let's also get a little glass of something celebratory!' He ducked out into the hall and reappeared with a plastic bag, out of which was sticking the neck of a bottle of champagne. He lifted it free and passed it over, with a hopeful 'please be happy' look. 'So, as I'm sure you've guessed by now – a bit of fun – Kelly and I are getting married!'

Kelly stared at him.

'Sorry,' he said quickly, 'when I say "bit of fun", I obviously mean we're completely thrilled.'

I took the champagne slowly and looked up at my brother. Just for a moment I saw the little boy that I'd tied a lead onto when I'd made him into my dog, aged three and seven. He gazed back at me worriedly, and I realized I was very much being handled with kid gloves. This announcement was being downplayed and broken to me as if they were expecting some catastrophic fallout as a result.

I turned to Kelly, his future wife: a ruthlessly ambitious, and totally insincere, future wife. She would inevitably meet someone else in her line of work one day, who was more glamorous, richer, or with greater influence than my brother – I heard Caroline's advice echo in my head.

'Congratulations,' I said, despite suddenly very much wanting to let the bottle slip from my fingers. Not her. Anyone but her, Will. She doesn't deserve someone as good and as lovely as you. You're a very intelligent man, but you're not diamond-hard like her. She will walk all over you and leave you completely destroyed without so much as a backwards glance.

A small, satisfied smile played about Kelly's beautiful mouth. 'Thank you, Sally.'

'No, really,' I said, 'I'm delighted for you both.' And I offered her my hand.

Her eyebrows flickered with surprise, but she reached out too. As Will looked on, I flinched slightly as we touched, her long nails briefly resting on the fleshy part of my palm. I suspected she would have liked to dig them right in, but we let each other go, and I turned to Will, who enveloped me in an enormous hug.

'Thank you,' he whispered.

'Let's get this open then, shall we?' I said, trying hard to keep my smile in place. 'So, when did this happen?'

'Two days ago,' Will said, now grinning happily. 'I flew out to surprise Kelly. There was this amazing sunset and—'

'He'd planned it all,' Kelly interrupted. 'We had a private table on the roof terrace of this penthouse suite. It was incredible!'

'No ring, though?'

Will laughed. 'You're kidding me. There was no way I was even going to attempt getting that right.'

'We're going shopping tomorrow,' said Kelly, smugly.

I tore the wrapper from the neck of the bottle and untwisted the wire before easing out the cork noiselessly.

'Well done,' said Will, impressed.

'I'll just get some glasses.' I picked up the baby monitor, walked out into the hall, and once I was in the kitchen, quietly opened the cupboard, reached for three flutes – and then closed my eyes briefly.

He was actually going to do this. She was going to become a permanent fixture.

Shit.

'Sally?' I jumped and turned to see Will standing behind me. 'Are you OK?'

'Of course! Just getting these.' I held them aloft.

'I meant OK with what I've just told you,' Will said. 'I'm very aware that you and Kelly aren't the best of friends, and I wanted to pick my moment, so we could all really talk about this, if need be.'

I considered that, and said carefully, 'That's very sweet of you, but it's not about me and what I think. As long as you're happy, that's all that matters.' I paused and then was unable to prevent myself adding, 'You are happy, aren't you? You're one hundred per cent sure this is what you want? I ask because you've only been together eleven months, and I promise you, Will, whatever faults exist in your relationship will go under a magnifying glass a million times over once you have children, and if you're not strong enough, it won't survive.'

Will looked concerned. 'Are you and Matthew all right?'

'We're fine,' I said quickly. 'It's just, Kelly is—'

'—right behind you,' said a voice, and I swung around guiltily. Kelly was holding her shoes in one hand, her bag in the other, and regarding me icily. 'I just came out to put these by the front door.' She lifted the bag and shoes up. 'And to ask if I could use the loo. So what was the end of that sentence? Just out of curiosity. Kelly is...' She waited.

'I was going to say, "very career-driven".' I lied. 'And I don't think it's fair to expect you to just give that up, but equally I know Will wouldn't want to put any children you have into nursery. Would you, Will?'

They both looked totally bewildered, as well they might.

'Riiiight,' Kelly said, and shot a 'what's she on about?' look at Will.

'Well, thanks for that, Sal,' Will said. 'It's certainly the kind of thing we will, if and when we need to, discuss.'

'Great!' I said. 'Anyway, let's go back into the sitting room. Theo will wake up properly if we chat in here. We're right under him. The loo is just out there, Kelly.'

'Thank you,' she said, shooting me another quick glance of disbelief as she tiptoed past.

Back in the sitting room, Will picked up his now full glass. 'You're sure you're all right?'

'You mean because of what I just said about your kids going into nursery?' I rubbed my eyes. 'Yes, it was a bit random. Sorry.

I'm shattered, that's all. I just didn't phrase it very well.'

'OK,' he said uncertainly. 'Well, just for the record, and in answer to your question, I am very happy. Happier than I think I've ever been.'

There was a moment's silence. 'Well then, there's nothing more to say, is there?'

'Give her a chance, Sal. You'll like her if you do, you really will. Could you try – for me? Maybe start again?'

We both looked up as Kelly appeared back in the room. 'Well, now, I'd just like to say I'm sorry,' I said, as I picked up my glass, 'because you were obviously nervous about telling me what is a *huge* deal for you, and I don't want it to be that way. This is happy news, not something you should have to subdue. I'd like to raise a toast to you both – the happy couple.'

They both lifted theirs, but I suddenly thought I heard Theo, and simultaneously remembered I'd left the monitor in the kitchen. 'Sorry, excuse me a minute,' I said, jumping up and putting my glass down. I stood at the bottom of the stairs for a moment, listening, when the door opened and Will appeared again.

'Sally, seriously – are you all right?'

'Absolutely!' I whispered, putting my fingers to my lips. 'I thought I heard Theo, that's all. Just let me grab the monitor and I'll be right back.'

When I returned, Kelly passed me my glass. 'To the happy couple,' I repeated, and we finally chinked glasses, before drinking.

Kelly cleared her throat. 'I actually have something to say too. Sally, you are very important to Will, and therefore important to me. I love Will very much, and I want to make him happy. If you'll let me, I'd like to do my best to become a part of your life, as well as a part of your family. I know it won't happen overnight, and it will take time and effort, on both our parts. But I'm willing to invest that time, and I hope you will be too.' She exhaled, and Will reached for her hand, kissing it briefly. She smiled at him, then she turned to me and looked me straight in the eye.

If I hadn't known that she was an actress, or witnessed first-hand the kind of unpleasant, immature behaviour she was capable of, I would have believed every word she said, but as it was, we both stared at each other for a moment, before I said, 'Of course I will.' There was a pause, and I added, 'So obviously Mum and Dad know about this, and I think Matthew does too?'

Will nodded. 'You're the last to know, yes – but by no means the least. Like I said, I didn't want you to have to hear this along-side everyone else, it needed a better moment than that.'

'We've already told *my* family as well, but obviously we wanted to tell you in person before releasing the details to the press,' Kelly said seriously, and I supressed a smile. 'What?' she snapped, irri-tated. 'There will be a great deal of interest, actually.'

'Kelly...' murmured Will.

'Sorry, I'm sorry,' she said immediately. Perhaps I'd misjudged them. Will didn't seem to be letting her get away with much at all, if anything.

We drank the champagne. I asked them if they had set a date. They had – December the tenth.

'I've wanted a Christmas wedding for as long as I can remem-ber!' said Kelly with child-like excitement. 'A fur-trimmed cloak, candles and Christmas trees!'

They asked if Chloe would be their bridesmaid, and I said of course she could – she'd be thrilled. Will told me he was going to have two best men, both university friends of his, and then they asked me if I would consider doing a reading at the service. I politely said if it was what they wanted, I'd be happy to. They told me about venues they had already considered – including, to my horror, the hotel in Cornwall that had long been mine and Matthew's secret bolthole.

'Will told me how much you two love it there, and we looked at it, only it was a bit too small,' Kelly said crushingly, but to my relief. I didn't want it to be taken over by their memories. Instead she showed me pictures on Will's phone of some vast stately home they had already booked. It was no joke, this really was going to happen. I poured myself a second glass.

'Please don't tell anyone where it's going to be, though, will you?' Kelly said. 'Reporters will call you and try to find out, but the best thing to say, all the time, is "no comment". We've got an exclusive deal with one of the magazines –' oh, how naff. I looked at Will in dismay – 'and they won't want anything leaked.'

'We *might* be doing a deal,' Will said firmly. 'I'm still up for sneaking off and doing it on a beach somewhere, just the two of us.'

Just for a second, Kelly looked fed up, but then sighed and said, 'OK. We might be doing a deal. Anyway, just don't say anything, Sal… If that's all right,' she added quickly.

'Of course. A bit more?' I offered the bottle to them. They exchanged a quick glance. 'Sorry, yes, I have finished mine rather fast,' I said instantly. 'But hey, we're celebrating.'

Kelly shook her head primly. 'I'm driving, thank you.'

'I'll join you,' offered Will, but as I lifted the bottle to his glass, Theo woke up.

By the time I got him back down, another half an hour had passed, and I came back downstairs to find Will and Kelly waiting in the sitting room, ready to make a move. 'I'll just go and get my shoes,' said Kelly, and disappeared.

'We'd happily stay longer, but I can see you've got your hands full,' Will said.

'Yeah, sorry about that,' I said tiredly. 'Everything's a bit mental at the moment.'

'Hang on in there. I think you're doing an amazing job.'

'Thanks,' I said, and to my huge annoyance, and out of nowhere, my eyes filled with tears. 'Oh for goodness' sake!' I wiped them away with my sleeve. 'Ignore me, I'm just exceptionally sleep deprived. This is not me being sad about your wedding, I promise.'

'I've got a problem… I'm going to have to borrow some of your shoes, Sally, because mine seem to have—' Kelly reappeared and then frowned at me. 'Why are you crying?'

'I'm fine.' I waved a hand defensively. 'Sorry, why do you need a pair of my shoes?'

'Well, the heel has just snapped off mine, which is completely bizarre. I don't think I've ever known that happen. Ever.' She held them aloft.

Was she suggesting I'd nobbled them? Why on earth would I do that? 'There are some of my boots in the cupboard under the stairs.'

'You mean *wellies*?' Her eyes narrowed.

'Yup. They're probably a bit big, but you can hang onto them as long as you like.'

She left the room to go and find them and I felt pathetically pleased at the thought of her having to clump off home in them under her pencil skirt. Sure enough, she looked completely ridiculous as we all stood by the front door. Her earlier goodwill seemed to have vanished alongside her style.

'So I won't tell Chloe about her being bridesmaid yet?' I said politely.

'What, in case something goes wrong and we call it off, you mean?' Kelly snapped.

'I meant because you'll want to tell her yourself, won't you?'

'Oh,' she said, clutching her broken shoe to her body like a child. 'I see. Sorry.'

'You tell her, Sal, it's fine,' Will said quickly. 'Listen, it's been lovely to see you, and I hope Theo stays down now. We'll sort out a lunch soon or something.'

The second they'd gone, I rushed into the kitchen, grabbed my phone and called Mum. 'I asked you outright if they were getting married and you said you had no idea,' I said, not even bothering with hello. 'How could you not tell me?'

She sighed. 'Oh love, he asked me to keep it to myself, and it wasn't my news to tell in any case. I take it they've just left?'

'Yes, *they* have. So you also knew Kelly was coming too, just like Matthew and Caroline did? Why is everyone being so weird and tiptoeing around me like this? OK, they're getting married, and yes, I don't like Kelly *at all* – and no, I wouldn't choose in a million years for Will to marry her – but what can I do about it? I just have to get on with it, don't I? So why are you all acting like I'm about to go off on one?'

'No one's being weird, Sally. Your brother just wanted to be gentle with you about this, that's all. You're right, it's no secret that you two girls don't see eye to eye. Mostly, though, we all know you've been finding things very difficult recently, so—'

'Mum, I haven't been "finding things difficult",' I interrupted. 'They *are* difficult. My son doesn't sleep, my husband has been stressed out to hell and back, and – *oh, for fuck's sake, Theo! Give me a fucking break!* Mum, I have to go. Theo's up *again*. I'll call you back later, OK?'

Once Theo was finally back in his cot, I returned downstairs and collected up the glasses and the remainder of the bottle. I took them into the kitchen and reached for my phone, on which I was keeping a record of Theo's sleeping, in a pointless attempt to spot some sort of pattern. All the list of times was actually proving was that I was up a lot, and that there was no pattern. Nonetheless,

I dutifully entered 'up 8.30, asleep 9.15'.

We all know you've been finding things difficult...

Recalling Mum's earlier comment – as I sat down heavily at the table – really hurt. I'd like to see any of them get up seven times a night and still function rationally the next day. I took a sip of my half full champagne and bleakly thought about Kelly's smug little grin.

The floor creaked and I looked up to see Caroline.

'Hi,' I said flatly. 'You were right.' I raised my glass to her. 'They're getting hitched, but then, of course, you already knew that... Although,' I thought back to her advice about how to react to Kelly and my brother, 'I do appreciate you trying to give me the heads-up. That was kind.' I picked up the bottle. 'Would you like some?' I stood up to get her a glass before she could answer, and when I turned back, she was sitting at the table, head in hands.

I stared at her, puzzled. That was a slightly melodramatic reaction on my behalf. She breathed out audibly and let her hands fall away to the table. She had her eyes closed, screwing them up, as if she were in pain. She seemed to be on the brink of some momentous decision. Just as suddenly, she sat up straight and looked me right in the eye, making me jump.

'Sally, if someone had close proximity to Chloe and Theo, and I was concerned that person was potentially dangerously unstable, and might be going to behave in a toxic manner that would do severe damage to both Chloe and Theo, you'd expect me to intervene and prevent it, wouldn't you?'

'Of course,' I said instantly.

She reached out and clasped my hand urgently. 'You can't even allude to the conversation we are about to have. I could lose *everything*. You understand that, don't you?'

'Caroline, what are you talking about, *who* has proximity to the children and is toxic...? Oh my God. You mean Kelly, my brother's girlfriend – fiancée?' I corrected myself, looking at Caroline in disbelief. 'You know her?'

'I can't answer that.'

My eyes widened. 'You've *treated* her?'

Caroline said nothing, but looked at me steadily for a moment, and then repeated, 'I can't answer that.'

'Jesus – you have, haven't you?' I whispered. 'And she's *dangerous*?' I picked up my drink in shock and took a large mouthful. 'I knew she was extremely unpleasant, but... I can't believe this!'

Caroline cleared her throat and adopted a light, conversational tone. 'You know, part of my job sometimes means I bump into clients, or former clients, when I least expect it. My protocol, and it may well be different for other practitioners, is to take my cue from the other person. If they are comfortable to acknowledge me socially, then I respond in like, appropriately. If they pretend they don't know me, then in turn, I won't divulge our relationship. Instead, I act as if it is the first time I've met them – as quite possibly they might be with a friend, or partner, who is unaware that they've had treatment, and that must be respected as part of patient confidentiality. It's an interesting conundrum.' Her voice wobbled slightly. 'I think I will have a little of that champagne, if I may.'

I hurriedly poured her some and she took a grateful sip as I drank some more of mine too. I got what she was trying to say, without saying it. She *did* know Kelly.

'But you're a child psychiatrist,' I said after a further moment of uncomfortable silence. My mind was racing.

'That's right,' she agreed. 'And adolescents.'

'You deal with eating disorders.'

'Among other things, yes I do. It's my area of specialism, though, you are correct.'

I tried to concentrate; my head was beginning to swim. Kelly

71

was exceptionally slim. But an eating disorder? I'd had no idea.

'In what way is she dangerous?'

'It's important to remember, of course, that people can do things as children that they would never do as adults, and with rehabilitation, they can turn their lives around,' continued Caroline, as if she hadn't heard me. 'But sometimes, you do seem to come across patients who, despite your best efforts, appear to be beyond help.'

'Jesus…' I said. 'What the hell did Kelly do?'

'I didn't say she did anything,' Caroline said instantly.

'OK. So you can't tell me. Fine.' I tried to think. 'Hang on, she's famous. I mean, not mega famous, but surely if she'd done something *really* horrific, some journalist would have found out by now, wouldn't they?'

Caroline said nothing.

'I have to tell Will this.'

'You mustn't,' said Caroline immediately. 'I will lose *everything*, Sally. While I can't stay silent in the knowledge that someone might have, shall we say, an agenda, and could potentially be placed in sole care of Theo and Chloe, Will is different. Adults can make decisions for themselves. Children can't.'

'You're really freaking me out now. What do you mean, an "agenda", and how does it involve my children?'

Caroline exhaled. 'I'm not saying I know anything specific at all, or that she has disclosed any direct threats towards any of you to me. She hasn't. If that were the case, I'd be going straight to the police. This is so difficult… How can I put this?' She paused. 'Did you know that there are links between eating disorders and infertility?' She looked at me, and waited.

'Infertility? Kelly can't have children?' My mind was reeling.

'I didn't say that, no.'

'Right,' I said slowly, 'but – hypothetically, of course – someone who couldn't have their own children might be in danger of developing an unhealthy attachment to someone else's, perhaps?' Incongruously, I yawned.

'I'm sorry,' Caroline said. 'I'm really not saying I have proof of anything that might be a reality *now*. Look, I've kept you up later than you should be and we don't need to do anything tonight. We'll talk more about it all in the morning, OK? Try not to panic.'

'But I couldn't possibly go to bed now!' I said, astonished. 'I need to know exactly what—'

Before I could continue, my phone lit up suddenly on the table in front of us, with a message. I picked it up and peered at the screen. 'It's Will. He's at home, but Kelly's on her way back over! She's left her phone here, apparently. Oh God. Do you think she's actually coming back to see you?'

Caroline looked anxious. 'Hell.' She put her head in her hands for a moment, then lifted it just as suddenly. She stood up quickly. 'I'll go back up to bed now. *If* she asks for me, which I'm sure she won't, tell her there was a change of plan and I've gone home.' She hastened out into the hall, and then came straight back in, holding an iPhone. 'This must be hers. It was on the side, next to your keys.'

'Here, give it to me.' I reached out – just in time to hear a car pulling onto the drive. 'That's her now. You'd better go!'

I looked down at the screen, which was showing the start of a text message that Kelly had received from someone called 'The BFF'. God, what were they, twelve? It read: **How did it go telling the mental bitch sister then? Did she...** But the rest remained frustratingly hidden, and the phone was locked. Mental bitch sister? How charming.

I made my way out to the hall and waited, arms crossed apprehensively, only to jump when eventually a figure quietly appeared on the doorstep. Through the glass, a hand lifted and a soft knock followed. I took a deep breath, reached out, and opened the door.

'Hello.' Now that my brother wasn't with her, she wasn't smiling anywhere near so fulsomely as she held out the wellies. 'I thought I might as well bring these back, too. Nice touch, by the way. So you want to tell me exactly what this is all about, then?'

'I don't know what you mean,' I said, warily appraising her through new eyes.

'Oh, come on, Sally. Four-hundred-pound shoes don't just snap themselves, and I don't believe you just wanted a kick out of me looking a dick in those boots either. Let's talk about why you took my phone out of my bag. What were you looking for on it?'

'I didn't take anything!' I exclaim. 'You're sure *you* didn't leave it here deliberately so you had a reason to come back? I didn't notice your mobile on the side, because I was saying goodbye to my mother-in-law, who has had to go home unexpectedly.'

'What are you on about now?' Kelly briefly looked up in irritation. 'Of course I was going to come back and get my phone! You seriously think I'd leave it here with you?' She returned to the screen and her eyes widened as she saw the message, obviously realizing I'd read it. 'That's awkward,' she murmured, then laughed and shrugged briefly. 'Oh well, that'll teach you. People who go snooping rarely find out anything nice about themselves.'

I swallowed, refusing to rise. 'Is that everything then?' Then I yawned again. I actually couldn't help it – I wasn't trying to be provocative.

She snorted slightly. 'Sorry. Am I keeping you up? Well, just before I go, Sally – seeing as now we *are* on our own – there *is* something I want you to know.'

So she *had* left it here on purpose, giving her an excuse to return, alone. I tensed immediately.

'You need to— *ATISHOO!*' she sneezed suddenly, and theatrically, making the hallway practically shake. There was a moment's

74

pause and then Theo wailed from upstairs.

'Oh no...' she said. 'I *am* sorry.'

I didn't take my eyes off her. 'You stay right there.' Reluctantly turning my back on her, I hurried up the stairs to shut Theo's door before he woke Chloe too. Hurrying back down again, I found her leaning on the doorframe, letting all of the cold air in, still waiting. 'Whatever it is you have to say to me, you have five seconds.'

She stared at me. 'Do you have any idea how rude and condescending you are sometimes?'

'I mean because Theo is now crying. As you can hear,' I said.

She rolled her eyes. 'They just wake up, Sally, it's what babies do, despite you permanently making everyone tiptoe around on eggshells.'

'Says the woman with all of the experience of having no children of her own.' The words were out of my mouth before I'd even appreciated the significance of what I'd just said.

She stared at me again. 'Well, lovely a conversation as this is, what I really want to say is: I don't know exactly what it is that you're planning, but go crying to your brother all you want, stamp your little foot, whisper poison in his ear from dawn till dusk if it makes you feel better. It won't change anything. You're not going to break us up – I *am* going to marry Will, and there's nothing you can do to stop it. When I want something, I get it: jobs, men, whatever...' She smiled at me. 'You would be very ill-advised to try and take me on.'

I probably would have dismissed such a ludicrous statement previously, I might even have laughed, but in the light of Caroline's revelations, instead I felt the shiver of adrenaline rush through my body, and I stepped forward. 'Are you threatening me?'

Her smile vanished and she straightened up. 'Sorry?'

'I don't care who you think you are,' I continued, my voice

starting to shake. 'Or how many crap storylines you've acted out, which have somehow given you the impression you can behave like that in real life. But I will tell you this – I'll stop at nothing to protect my family. Do you understand me? Absolutely nothing.'

She didn't say a word, just moved even closer, so she was now inches away from my face. 'Have it your way then,' she whispered softly as I tried not to flinch. 'You want a fight? You just got yourself one.'

She spun on her heels so suddenly, I jumped. Heart thudding as I watched her walk to her car, I shut the door quickly – wishing I could slam it – then dashed upstairs to Theo. Mercifully, it only took me ten minutes to get him back down. Hopefully he might now do his one three-hour stretch of the night before he woke again.

Next, I crept into Chloe's room and checked on her. She was sprawled out across her bed, the covers pushed off onto the floor. I tucked her back in and tiptoed into the hall. Caroline's door was shut and I could see from the crack underneath it that the light was off. Everything was as it should be, but by the time I made it into my own bedroom, having silently removed my make-up, brushed my teeth, and taken a paracetamol, I was exhausted and wracked with anxiety.

You want a fight? You just got yourself one.

Trying to force Kelly from my mind, I took off my top and my grubby jeans. I automatically searched the pockets before putting them in the dirty clothes basket, only to find my note to Matthew again. I tossed it on the bedside table, then climbed into bed, thudding my head heavily down onto the pillow. I was starting to feel dizzy and sick too. I already hugely regretted drinking the champagne. I'd only had a glass and a bit, but I had no tolerance for booze any more.

I reached for my phone and, yawning, began to try to make a short list of things I needed to buy in the morning, but try as I might, Kelly kept looming back into my head. She'd deliberately engineered an excuse to come back and confront me.

Dangerously unstable.

Potentially toxic.

This, the woman my brother was going to marry, who also had an agenda that may or may not present a danger to my children. I was going to have to stay awake and talk to Matthew about this, when he got in; I couldn't not. I would just doze, with the light on, until he got back. I closed my eyes and my mobile began to weigh heavily in my hands. He'd be back soon. He'd said he wouldn't be late.

You want a fight? You just got yourself one.

Kelly's whispered promise was my last conscious thought, before my eyes closed, and I was gone.

CHAPTER SIX

'That's absolutely everything, exactly as it happened, right up until I fell asleep,' I say to the doctor opposite me in the small interview room at the police station. 'So yes, I would agree that I have been under a lot of stress recently, and yes, I remember feeling unnerved when I went to bed last night – because of the argument I had with my brother's fiancée – but I honestly don't recall feeling suicidal, or thinking that I wanted to do anything to hurt myself.' I swallow nervously.

The doctor says nothing, just scribbles something on her pad of paper. I wait for a moment, and when she remains silent, I start to panic and continue desperately, 'As for the note I had in my coat pocket – the one the man found after he bundled me to the ground when I was attempting to walk down to the hotel *to get help* – now I've read all of it, I'm absolutely certain it was the one I wrote to my husband after our argument on Thursday. I can see that put in this context it looks bad – it looks *very* bad – but I meant I didn't want to argue with him any more; that's what I'd had enough of. Not life in general. I was actually saying sorry to him, not sorry for ending it all. I can see how it might seem to an outsider, though. If you didn't know what had *actually* happened...' I'm babbling. I make a huge effort to stop, reaching forward for my plastic cup and taking a mouthful of water.

'You're not sure how the letter came to be in your coat pocket, however?'

I shake my head. 'No, I don't have an explanation for that. The last time I remember seeing it, I think I was putting it on my bedside table.' I want to add, 'And it's terrifying me that I have no memory of the last ten hours, and no idea what's happened to me over that time. It's not even a question of my not being able to remember anything, it's more as if someone has hit a pause button I didn't know I had, and everything else has carried on around me.' But then I get the impression this doctor is only concerned with making sure I'm not so mentally ill I ought to be hospitalized. So I don't.

'OK, Sally, thank you,' she says eventually. 'As I explained to you at the beginning of our interview, it's my job to assess you, because you were detained under section 136 of the Mental Health Act. I've concluded that I don't believe it's in your best interests to detain you any further. I will be in contact with your local Crisis team, so they can provide you with some ongoing support.'

'Thank you.' I want to cry with relief, but manage not to, mindful of my needing to appear rational and stable. 'I just want to get back to my children.'

The kind police officer clears his throat. 'We've been in touch with Kent Police, who have already attended your home because you were reported missing by your husband, at around half past eleven last night. As I said to you earlier, they have informed us that your son and daughter are safe and well. Normally what would happen next is that we would ask your nearest relative to collect you, but we are going to take you back to Kent.'

I try not to betray any emotion at all, but oh, thank God! I assumed Matthew would have to come, and by the time he's driven here and we've driven back, I wouldn't be home until late tonight – and I'm beyond desperate to see Chloe and Theo. Perhaps that's why they are driving me, because they know I have a baby.

'Wait,' I say slowly, a horrible thought occurring to me. 'You're *sure* there's nothing wrong with Theo or Chloe? That's not why you're taking me all the way back, so I get there as fast as possible, because there's an emergency? No one has hurt them, or taken them from the house? They're not missing? You're absolutely sure they are safe?'

The police officer looks concerned and says, 'Yes, I'm sure. Do you have a reason to believe they are in danger?'

I hesitate. Not specifically, no. Kelly threatened *me*, not them, and I haven't had a chance to talk to Caroline properly yet about the concerns she raised last night. 'Sorry, I'm overreacting. I'm just very thrown by everything that's happened; my being here and not knowing why. Nothing is making much sense right now. I just want to get home and see for myself that everything is OK there, even if it isn't normal here. That's what I meant.'

He nods, seemingly satisfied, and I fall silent, but it's too late, the seed of doubt has been sown in my mind. Stepping out into a beautiful spring morning as we head to the car is not a relief. If someone had told me this time yesterday I'd be having several hours child-free, I might have wept with gratitude, but as I climb in, I'm unable to think of anything but Chloe and Theo. I feel sick with supressed panic. Please God, they are OK. If she has hurt them, or done anything to them at all, I will kill her. I huddle on the back seat, staring at picture perfect scenery flashing past, in silence. How can I not remember being driven by a stranger in the opposite direction, mere hours ago? There's not even a spark of recognition. It's terrifying. And what the hell was that note doing in my coat? How did it get there? My fingers curl around it, now in my pocket, as I think about the waves pounding relentlessly onto the beach and my staggering around on the clifftop above them. I nearly fell. Limbs wash up all the time, that man said.

I shudder and draw my coat a little tighter around my shoulders, as out of nowhere, the image of me plunging through the air, arms outstretched, appears in my head. I imagine the freezing water closing in over my head, and have to shut my eyes to force the picture away. I couldn't possibly have gone there deliberately to throw myself off. It's beyond belief.

I hate my life.

I don't know how much longer I can cope like this.

But they're just things you say. Aren't they?

You've been finding things very difficult.

I'd remember planning something like this, though. Surely? Who forgets deciding to kill themselves? And remembers nothing about actually putting that plan into action?

I snap my eyes open again.

'Are you all right, Sally?' the kind officer asks, and I jolt suddenly, because the open countryside dotted with cows has somehow become four-lane traffic and noise barriers.

I blink and look around me, eyes wide with confusion. 'Where are we?'

'The M25,' he says, turning to look at me. 'You've slept most of the way.'

What? That's impossible! We only left Cornwall moments ago! I try to sit up, but slump again, the movement making me wince. My head feels as if someone has stamped on it, it's pulsing with pain, and my eyes are sandpaper raw on the inside with fatigue. Instead I glance weakly at the car clock, but he's right, it's now 2.45 p.m. My mind might have been racing with questions, unable to switch off, but my body had other ideas, the opportunity of a quiet car, and the rumble of the road, proving too much.

'We should be there in just under an hour.'

I attempt to focus. I might be back in time to do Chloe's tea. It'll have to be fish fingers, there won't be enough time to do the chicken I had planned to roast. I wonder if Matthew took her to ballet and swimming like normal? I really hope so; she'll have needed the diversion from my not being there. What will he have even told Chloe? Thank God Caroline was at ours. She will have helped him handle it properly, and more importantly than anything else, she will have made Chloe feel safe. Because she will be safe. She has to be. I dig my nails into the palm of my hand at the thought of my little girl, bewildered and frightened, asking where I am. Nearly there. Nearly home.

We arrive back at quarter to four. My parents' car is on the drive – parked at an uncharacteristically odd angle that betrays an emergency arrival – but our car is nowhere to be seen. I bite my lip anxiously, and only just restrain myself from pushing past one of the policemen as he walks alongside me, so that I can run ahead.

He knocks on my own front door and we wait in the quiet of the sleepy close for someone to answer, the only noise being the nearby chugging of my neighbour Ron's lawnmower making the first cut of the year. Ordinarily, I would probably be inside cursing Ron and the diligence of his domestic-maintenance activities, while trying to get Theo to nap.

A figure silently approaches behind the glass door, which opens to reveal Caroline. She looks strained, and tired, but gives me a kind smile as she steps to one side and says, 'Hello, Sally,' in a totally normal voice, as if I've just popped back from the shops.

She extends her hand to the police officer once we're in the hall. 'Hello. I'm Dr Caroline Hilman.' She smiles again and pauses to let the doctor bit resonate. 'I'm one of the board members of Abbey Oaks, a private provider of psychiatric support and therapy, not far from here. I'm also Sally's mother-in-law, so I'm rather wearing two hats today. Now, I'll just be a moment, then I'll come back to sign any paperwork you might have.' She speaks politely but firmly, and without waiting for an answer, leads me away.

She takes me into the sitting room, where I discover Mum and Dad sitting edgily on opposite sofas. Mum exclaims, 'Oh!' at the sight of me, before covering her mouth with her hand. Her face is all puffy from crying, and her eyes start to fill with tears again as she jumps to her feet and rushes across the room to pull me into her arms, stroking my hair and kissing me. 'You're safe now. We'll look after you, I promise, and everything is going to be OK.'

I pull back urgently. 'Where are Chloe and Theo?'

Mum shoots a glance at Caroline, which makes my heart momentarily fall away from my body, and I spin around to face my mother-in-law. 'Caroline?'

'They're absolutely fine,' Caroline says. 'They're out with Matthew, and will be back anytime now.'

'Matthew's got them on his own?' I say anxiously. He's never taken them out together before. It's still cold enough for them both to have needed coats, and maybe even a hat for Theo.

'It seemed sensible for Chloe not to be here when the police car arrived, and for everything to have a chance to settle down a bit,' Caroline says reasonably, then adds gently, 'He'll cope.'

'But you promise me they're OK?'

'You know I would never lie to you about something like that,' she says.

'Has Chloe asked where I am?'

'We said you'd gone to work today. She was fine. If it's all right, I'll go and deal with the police, shall I?'

I nod, and she leaves the room.

I turn back to Mum, and we all just look at each other, no one knowing what to say.

'I'm so sorry,' Mum blurts, after a moment more. 'Last night you told me you couldn't cope, and I didn't listen properly. I'm so very sorry, Sally. It's just Theo is your second baby, and you seemed to be doing really well. Yes, you've been very tired, but it never occurred to me that it might be the post-natal depression you had with Chloe back again. I googled it all this morning on the way down, and the symptoms could have been written for you: crying a lot, no energy or confidence, overwhelmed, and,' she shifts awkwardly, 'irritable. I can't believe I've been so stupid. I'm listening now, though, and we will help you. We're *all* going to help you.'

I rub my eyes wearily. God, I feel horrendous. 'All of those symptoms apply to every single woman who has a baby, though, don't they?'

'Yes, but not every woman has an emergency caesarean and nearly loses their son, like you just did with Theo. And with Chloe, you didn't realize you were depressed, did you? It was your midwife who spotted it.'

'*She* thought I had post-natal depression. I never believed I did.'

'But then, like you said last night, you can't really remember how you felt after Chloe was born, because you blocked it out.' She looks at me anxiously.

'I meant I blocked it out as in I don't want to remember a pretty challenging part of my life. I didn't mean I literally can't remember it. Mum, can I just sit down a minute?'

'Sorry, love,' she apologizes again. 'Of course you can. I didn't mean to overwhelm you.'

I sink down onto the sofa. 'It's OK. You're not the only one with questions. I don't understand how I can't remember anything beyond getting into bed last night. I have no idea what happened to me for about ten hours, I don't know how I got to Cornwall, or why I was there.'

'Will said you were in tears last night at one point, and that at times you weren't making much sense.'

I falter. 'Yes, that's true, but...'

'You also told me you felt like you were going completely mad and weren't sure how much longer you could cope.' Mum's own eyes well up again. 'You *can* trust us, Sally. It's OK. It's OK to tell us what you went there to do.'

'But that's the thing. I *can't* tell you because I don't know.'

'They said you had a letter on you,' Mum whispers, 'to Matthew, saying goodbye.'

I shake my head. 'No, that really is wrong. And when Matthew gets home, I'll prove it to you. It was this.' I reach into my pocket and pull out the now well-worn scrap of paper. Mum shrinks back from it as if it's cursed. 'It's just a note I left on his desk after a row last week. He'll tell you. I've no idea how it wound up in my coat. It doesn't make any sense.'

Caroline comes back into the room. 'The police have gone.' She sits down on the sofa. 'You're going to get a call from the Crisis team later today. They may visit in person. It depends how efficient the out-of-hours services are here.'

There's a pause, and then I say, 'Caroline, I was just saying to my mum and dad: this morning, I woke up in the back of a cab, and I have no idea how I got there, and yet I had the exact money to pay for it – which is both surreal and completely terrifying.' I take a deep breath. 'After Kelly left, I know I settled Theo, I checked on Chloe, and I saw your light was off, which is when I went to bed. Did you see or hear anything suspicious, or unusual after that?'

She shakes her head. 'Once I was certain Kelly had gone, I waited in my room in case you wanted to come and talk to me about anything.' She looks pleadingly at me, and I know she's referring to our conversation about Kelly's past, and their relationship. 'But everything went quiet, so I put my earplugs in. We'd already agreed that I wouldn't get up with Theo in the night, and I wanted to be rested to help you in the morning. I was expecting him to be awake a lot, of course, and I was tired after the conference, so...' She shrugs helplessly. 'It didn't even occur to me doing that might be a problem; wearing them seemed a *sensible* thing to do, if anything. I was out like a light and didn't hear a squeak.'

'So it was Matthew who discovered I was missing?'

'Yes. When he came back from the pub, you weren't in bed, so he thought you were sleeping in with Theo. Theo woke up at about half eleven and started crying. When he didn't stop, Matthew went in to see what was wrong, and discovered you were gone.'

I have to grip the arm of the sofa at the thought of my baby becoming steadily more desperate for me, and thinking he'd been abandoned in the night.

'Did Chloe wake up too?'

'Thankfully, no, although I honestly don't know how. Matthew came and found me, we called the police, and then everything went from there.'

Oh God, poor, poor Matthew. 'That must have been horrendous for both of you. I'm so sorry.'

'It's OK, Sally,' she says gently. 'Theo was all right. He did settle back.'

I nod, overwhelmed with guilt that I was not there. Where was I, when my baby was calling for me? What was happening to me?

A movement out of the window catches my eye, however, and distracts me. Our car is pulling up onto the drive. They're back! I jump up as Matthew climbs out. He doesn't see me, but instead opens the passenger door for Chloe. I catch my breath at the sight of her blonde head bobbing around the edge of the Renault, and then she appears in front of the glass. She peers in excitedly, and as she sees me, her face lights up, and I just about hear her shout, 'Mummy!' Her sheer delight both makes me laugh and simultaneously sob, as we both turn and bolt for the front door. I get there first and throw it open in time to hear Matthew – carefully lifting Theo out of his car seat – calling after her to slow down, in case she trips.

She breathlessly flings herself at me, almost knocking me off my feet. 'Mummy! Mummy!' she repeats, hugging my legs fiercely. The relief of reunion seems almost more than she can cope with, because she suddenly gives a random little leap and miaow.

'Oh what a sweet little cat,' I manage to say, recognizing a well-played game she particularly likes, as I pick her up and clutch her to me, closing my eyes and just holding her tightly. 'What's your name?'

'Ella,' she squeaks.

I savour the familiar sweet smell of her hair as I picture myself staggering around on the cliff edge. It makes me feel physically sick. 'I missed you,' I say, trying not to let the emotion in my voice betray me, because Caroline's right, Chloe needs everything to get back to normal as soon as possible.

Matthew appears on the doorstep, the change bag slung over his shoulder and Theo snugly wrapped in his car seat. Theo is wearing both a coat and a hat. Matthew pauses, stares at me, eyes wide, and stumbles in over the step slightly.

I instinctively step forward, still holding Chloe, one hand out to brace Theo – but instead, lifting Theo's seat to the side so he doesn't get bashed, Matthew envelops us with his free arm, wrapping it tightly around me and Chloe, before resting his forehead down on my head, and sighing shakily.

'Bear hug!' Chloe says, a little uncertainly, and wriggles free, forcing Matthew to release us. He sets Theo down gently on the carpet, and, as Chloe starts to kick her shoes off, I reach to unclip Theo's straps.

'Hello,' I whisper, as Theo regards me solemnly. 'Hello baby boy.' I smile at him, swallowing down the lump in my throat, and after a moment's pause, his face splits into a huge grin. I lift him out and into my arms, and turn to see Matthew watching me. I can tell he is bursting to say something, and I look at him worriedly, hoping he'll wait until Chloe skips off into the sitting room, but he's clearly unable to contain it any longer.

'I'm so sorry,' he says. 'It's all my fault.'

'No it's not,' I say, bewildered, hugging Theo's sturdy little body to me.

'Yes, it is,' he insists. 'I should never have gone out. It was Will's news, wasn't it? That was the trigger. Or did something else happen?'

I dart a look at Chloe, and then put a finger to my lips, before transferring Theo onto my hip, to take his hat off and unzip him. 'Did you have fun with Daddy and Theo, Clo?' I ask. 'Where have you all been?'

'For a babychino,' Chloe begins. 'Daddy said I could have a—'

'Sally!' Matthew steps forward in desperation, interrupting her. 'Please! Talk to me! You need to—'

'Hello, Chloe!' Thankfully Caroline appears in the sitting-room doorway, before he can continue. 'Did I just hear you say you've been for a babychino? What fun! Come and tell me what you had with it; a cake, I bet, or was it a cookie? Shall I take Theo for a moment too?' She glances between us, concerned, and holds out her arms.

I don't want to let go of Theo for a second, but she's right – the kids shouldn't see any of this. Reluctantly, I let her take him. 'Thank you, Caroline.'

I wait until they have all disappeared into the sitting room, and closed the door. Matthew and I stand opposite each other in the hallway.

'I really am so sorry,' he says again, and to my horror, his eyes begin to fill with tears. I have never seen Matthew cry before. 'I've let you down so badly, Sally. I've behaved like a child. Yesterday, when you were gone, I've never been so frightened... I thought I was going to lose everything... I knew you'd been thinking about leaving me – after what I saw on your phone. So when I discovered you were missing, I—'

'Sorry, what did you see on my phone?' I'm completely bewildered.

He reaches for a tissue from his pocket to blow his nose. 'When you gave me your mobile to look for the takeaway menu, the last page you'd been on came up – the one with all of the stuff about divorce on it. "Is divorce bad for children"; "The true cost to children of marriage break-ups".'

My mouth falls open. 'No, no! You've got it all wrong! I was messing about online. I googled the effect of small children on marriage. I wasn't researching divorce options behind your back. Oh, Matthew! You must have been devastated. Why didn't you just ask me about it?'

He wipes his eyes with the back of his hand. 'I've been trying to talk to you for a while. The last time I did, you told me if I wasn't happy, I should leave. I was too frightened to bring it up again after what I saw on your phone, in case you just said that was it, it was over. I know you. Once you've made up your mind about something, there's no going back.'

'I wasn't going to leave you!'

'Well, that's what I thought had happened when I discovered you'd gone – especially when we realized the money had vanished too. But then I found your phone and I knew something was very wrong, so we called the police. When they said where you were, and what you'd gone there to do...' His voice breaks.

'Sorry, I don't understand. What money is this?'

He looks up at me again. 'It's OK, Sal. It's not important. Trust me, I don't care what you've done with it as long as you're safe. I'm just so ashamed that I haven't given you enough support, that I didn't appreciate how stressed you've become, and—'

'Matthew, I have no idea what money you're talking about!'

He gives me a strange look. 'Mum's holdall, under the stairs? You didn't take it?'

'No. It had cash in it? How much?'

He pauses, swallows nervously, and says, 'All of it. Everything we have. Sixty-five thousand pounds.'

CHAPTER SEVEN

'You're not serious?' I say slowly.

He's not laughing. 'You really don't know what's happened to it?'

I gasp. 'What on earth was all of our money doing in a *bag under the stairs*?'

'You can tell me, Sally,' he insists. 'It's OK.'

'I didn't take the money!' I raise my voice, frightened.

He looks concerned and gets to his feet. 'Sweetheart, calm down,' he says. 'I don't want to make you upset. Please, I want to help you, I—'

The sitting-room door opens, and Caroline and my mother appear. 'Is everything OK?' Mum says anxiously.

'I've just told Sally about the bag going missing.' Matthew looks at his mother.

'Ah,' she says, as if she's been expecting this. She straightens up a little, as if preparing herself for the firing line. 'It's entirely my fault, Sally, Matthew isn't to blame. About two weeks ago, I approached Matthew and asked him if I could temporarily borrow the money that you made from your flat sale. I was aware you had a large sum in the bank, ready for your building work to begin. I wanted to use it to bail out a small, but vitally important, women's refuge that was being forced out of their building by a developer attempting to buy the property from under them. We had a very tight window in which to come up with a counter bid. I had some assets that I wanted to gift the refuge, which would have covered it, but the property owner refused. He wanted cash. So, I put a large stake up myself, and asked Matthew if I could have the sixty-five thousand of your money to make up the rest. I promised him I'd pay you back as soon as I could.'

'You said yes without discussing it with me?' I turn to Matthew incredulously.

'I asked him not to involve you,' Caroline says. 'I was worried that you might, understandably, persuade him not to lend me the money, and I couldn't take that risk. It was *so* important I got it, Sally. There were women with children, they had literally nowhere to go... But they are all safe now, and that's thanks to you and Matthew. I had the money with me, in full, when I arrived last night, to return to Matthew.'

'Obviously I meant to take the bag out from under the stairs and put it in Mum's room, like she asked me,' Matthew continues, 'but by the time I got around to it, Theo was down, and I was worried about clunking around and waking him up, you'd already got stressed about me dragging the bin up the drive – that's not me having a go, by the way,' he adds quickly. 'Anyway, I was going to take it to the bank today, but...' he trails off.

'It had to be cash that I gave you back, otherwise there'd have been a tax implication, you see, on the assets I'd liquidated,' Caroline explains.

'So, do you have it?' Matthew asks me. 'It's OK if you took it, Sally. Like I said, the most important thing is that you're safe.'

My mouth gaping slightly, it's my turn to sink to the floor, overwhelmed, as I just look up at them both.

'Did someone steal it from you?' Matthew crouches down desperately and takes my hand. 'Did that make you panic, and is that why you decided to—'

'Matthew,' interjects Caroline, 'perhaps now isn't the right time for this. Sally has literally just got back, and in view of what she's been through, I think we should save this conversation for later.'

I try to compose myself. 'I had four hundred pounds on me to pay the taxi with. If you're saying there was a load of money under the stairs, I suppose it must have come from there, but I don't know that for sure. I certainly don't remember taking it.' I put my head in my hands. 'That can't be right, though. If I only took four hundred pounds, where's the rest of it gone? There's something else strange too.' I reach into my pocket and pull out the so-called suicide letter, and pass it over to Matthew. 'See? It's the note I put on your desk after we had the row about the pasta. How did that get into my coat?'

He scans it, and then looks up at me uneasily. 'Sal, I've never seen this before.'

I feel like I'm falling down the rabbit hole. There is a long, uncomfortable pause. 'Yes you have,' I try again. 'I wrote it while you were taking Chloe to school.'

'But, I would have said something to you if I'd read it. I wouldn't have just ignored it.'

I hesitate. I did think it was a bit off that he'd said literally nothing. 'You really didn't see this?' I squint up at him, confused.

'I don't understand, why you were writing me a note in the first place?' he asks gently. 'Why didn't you just wait until I'd got back and discuss it then? You don't usually *not* say something, if it's on your mind.'

'You said you didn't want to talk about it, that's why.' I stare at the letter and my own handwriting in confusion. I feel as if I'm going mad. I *did* write it for him – and I found it on his floor, I'm sure of it.

'Let's get you upstairs and into bed.' Mum comes over and puts her arms under mine, and helps lift me to my feet. 'You're very clearly exhausted, and are obviously in no fit state to be talking. As Caroline's pointed out, the money just doesn't matter right now, and no one thinks you had anything to do with it disappearing.' She glares warningly at Matthew.

'I'm not going crazy, Matthew, I promise you,' I say urgently. 'This is just… bizarre, and really scary, actually.'

'I'll replace the money again anyway,' Caroline says suddenly. 'If I hadn't have asked to borrow it, we wouldn't even be having this discussion now. The fact that it has gone missing is therefore really my responsibility. The money was – after all – lent to me in good faith. I was also very wrong to ask Matthew not to discuss it with you, Sally. You're his wife, and of course he should have talked to you. I was blinded by what I considered to be the importance of what I was going to do with the cash, but that doesn't make it acceptable. I'm very sorry indeed. This time, there won't be any confusion at all. Once I've organized the funds, I'll transfer the money directly into your account. Any tax liability is my problem. Please don't give any of it a second thought. Your mother is right, it's far more important that we focus on *you* right now. Why *don't* you have a little rest for a bit? You look exhausted.'

'I'm OK, thank you, though. I just want to go and be with the children.'

'But isn't that part of the problem?' Matthew says. 'You're with them *all* the time. You haven't had a break in God knows how long. Everyone's here, we can look after Chloe and Theo. Go and rest.'

'That's kind of you,' I say, 'but I *really* want to be with them.'

'Don't get agitated, please, sweetheart,' Mum pleads. 'No one's saying you *can't* go and sit with them. We're worried about you, that's all. Come on then, let's go through.'

I don't say anything, not trusting myself to speak, and we all head into the sitting room.

If truth be told, I'm worried about me too.

I sit with the kids while they have tea, just as I would normally, although I've let Mum do the cooking. Caroline respectfully defers to Mum – which I am grateful for – and takes herself off into the sitting room to watch some rugby on TV with Matthew and Dad. I feed Theo, and Mum busies about in a deft flurry of oven gloves and baking trays. Chloe is clearly delighted to have everyone here, chatting away happily about what she did in ballet, and the massive dive she did off the side at swimming. If it wasn't for the fact that this morning I woke up in the back of a car at the other end of the country in my pyjamas, to a stranger demanding £400, it would be a very nice Saturday afternoon.

I smile at Theo as I spoon the mashed potato, pureed carrot and broccoli that Mum has effortlessly produced into his hungry baby bird mouth, while trying to hide my shaking hands. I'm making a huge effort to appear calm, but I feel ill with anxiety and confusion; there's an actual tight ball of tension in my stomach. Are they right? Did I really do all of this myself?

'You're doing very well, best little boy!' I turn to Chloe, who is sitting next to me. 'And you're doing very well too, best little girl.'

'Best *big* girl,' she corrects me, while still looking pleased.

'Sorry.' I plant a kiss on her head, before turning back to Theo and supressing a yawn determinedly. I'm physically exhausted, but they must see me coping, being normal. I've noticed that they haven't left me alone with Chloe or Theo for a single minute since I've been back. Are they still worried that I'm a danger to myself?

'Who else knows about last night?' I ask, trying to keep my voice casual.

Mum stiffens – she's bent over the washing-up bowl, scrubbing the big saucepan within an inch of its life.

'Well, your brother and Kelly, of course. Will is very upset. It was all I could do to stop him from coming over here to wait for you to get back. He's worried that he's responsible for what's happened, because of what he told you last night.'

That really *is* crazy. 'Mum! I'm far from his fiancée's biggest fan, but I'd hardly respond in such a dramatic way.' I try to stay oblique in front of Chloe.

'He means was it the straw that broke the camel's back, I think.'

'Oh, I see.' I fall silent for a moment. 'Did Kelly tell you all that she and I had a heated exchange of words just before she left here?'

Mum stops scrubbing and turns around. 'No. What happened?'

'Who are you talking about?' Chloe looks up curiously, realizing that something interesting is going on.

'Uncle Will, sweetheart,' Mum says. 'He's getting married and he wants you to be a bridesmaid! Isn't that fun?'

'I need a poo,' says Chloe.

'OK, off you go.' I pull back her chair, so she can get down. 'But come straight back because you're halfway through tea. It was when Kelly was here on her own,' I continue, as Chloe scampers off. 'The last thing she said to me was if I wanted a fight with her, I'd got one. She'd come back to get her phone, which, actually, I remember thinking at the time was weird. She's usually surgically attached to it. Theo woke up and I left her downstairs on her own. Oh my God!' Something suddenly occurs to me. 'She'd been in the cupboard under the stairs earlier, because her heel snapped and I lent her some boots!'

Mum looks blank.

'She made a big deal out of it, suggesting I'd broken her shoe on purpose, but that's where Caroline's holdall was – which she would have seen – the one that's now missing... Along with sixty-five thousand pounds of our money.'

'Sarah Jayne Tanner!' Mum exclaims, like I'm fourteen again, and she's just found a packet of fags in my underwear drawer. 'Kelly is a challenging girl in many ways, but to make an allegation like that, based on absolutely nothing at all other than the fact that you don't like her, is unforgivable. If you don't know what happened to the money, that's fine. No one is blaming you. But don't just make something up.' Mum is appalled.

'I'm not making this up.' What was it Caroline said about Kelly? Some children do things that they wouldn't do as adults, but others are born evil, and beyond redemption? That was surely alluding to some sort of criminal propensity. What if seeing Caroline so unexpectedly yesterday triggered something in *Kelly*?

'Caroline's already said she will repay you in full,' Mum interrupts.

'Yes, but then she'll be sixty-five thousand down.'

Mum glances at the door and lowers her voice. 'Oh well, there you go. I'm sure she can afford it.'

'Mum!' Now I'm appalled. 'It's an enormous amount of money, and OK, she's not destitute, but she's not got a huge disposable income either.'

'She told Matthew not to involve you, remember?' Mum whispers pointedly.

'She also said she was sorry. She can't just be expected to walk away from losing—'

'Sally, I know what you're doing,' Mum interrupts, throwing down the cloth to come and sit opposite me as she takes my hand. 'It's very convenient to have this missing money to try and focus everyone's attention elsewhere, but I don't care if you flushed it down the loo, note by note. You don't need to do this. Or the "I can't remember anything, I just woke up in a taxi" bit either. If you don't want to talk about what happened last night, that's OK. I just want to help you get better. All I know for sure is that my little girl – who I love more than anything – was found confused and distressed last night, a long way from home in a very dangerous situation. Regardless of how that happened, or why – it *did* happen, and now that you're a mother too, try to understand why I want to be here to look after you, make sure you are safe, and help you. Please, will you let me do that, as you would if it were Chloe we were talking about?'

I don't answer, because next to me, my phone begins to ring – an ID withheld call. I almost don't answer, then remember Caroline telling me the Crisis team would be getting in touch.

'Mum, I should probably take this. Can you take over with Theo?'

She nods and takes the spoon from me.

'Hello? Yes, this is Sally Hilman. Yes, I can.' I stand up. 'Just hold on a moment, please.'

I go straight up to my bedroom for a bit of privacy, where I spend the next five minutes listening to a woman called Maureen, who has the most droning voice I think I've ever heard.

'Well, as I explained to you, *Sally*,' she says – she's used my name about five hundred times throughout the conversation and is speaking very deliberately – 'we are here to provide short-term acute care and *support*. You don't feel you need a home visit and that's *fine*. I'm happy with everything you've told me and I appreciate you have the support of your mother-in-law in a professional and *personal* capacity. Which is, of course, *great*.'

'Can you come and wipe my bottom?' yells Chloe – which just about sums up my feelings on this phone call too.

'Excuse me just a minute,' I say, then cover the phone and shout back. 'We talked about this, darling. You can do it yourself now.'

'But I don't want to,' calls Chloe.

'I'll sort it,' says Matthew suddenly, appearing from nowhere, and striding quickly across to the bathroom.

'Sorry about that,' I say to Maureen slowly, realizing he's been listening outside the door all along.

'It's *fine*, Sally. Now I'm going to pass some discharge information across to your GP so they can be in contact with you. I expect it will be early next week. But if anything changes and you need support in the meantime, please contact us again. Have you got a pen and I'll give you a number. You have? Oh, that's *great*.'

'Well?' Matthew reappears as I hang up.

'I'd have definitely killed myself if I'd had to listen to her for very much longer.' I rub my neck tiredly and try to smile.

Matthew's jaw drops in horror. 'Sally!'

'Sorry,' I say immediately, chastened. 'I was just trying to lighten the mood.'

He looks down at the floor. 'I don't think we can really trivialize this. It's not fair on any of us, least of all you.'

'I really am sorry.'

'So did she say anything helpful? Offer you any support?'

'Daddy!' shouts Chloe. 'I can't turn the tap off and the floor's all wet.'

'Shit… Coming!' he calls.

'I'll go.' I automatically get to my feet. 'I can sort her out.'

'No, no.' He holds out a hand. 'I've got this. It's fine. Everything is under control.'

He hurries out of the room before I have a chance to say anything else, leaving me to sink back down onto the bed redundantly. I glance at my phone. Have I really just spent five minutes talking to a Crisis team about support for a suicide attempt I don't even remember making?

Everything is under control… Except me. I don't feel under control at all.

I think about Kelly again, and Mum's reaction to my accusation. If she's right, and *I* took that sixty-five grand, what on earth have I done with it? I literally have no idea. No idea at all.

After the kids have had their bath, Mum insists on giving Theo his bottle and settling him for me. I actually don't feel well – I'm badly nauseous – so I let her, but warn her that when he kicks off, to come and get me, not to try and struggle on through. I'm therefore amazed to see her slip out of his room after only fifteen minutes, giving me a silent thumbs-up as I'm sitting in Chloe's room, reading her stories. Thank God Matthew can vouch for what Theo has been like, otherwise surely no one would believe I wasn't making it all up. It's a freak occurrence, surely? He'll be awake again in a minute.

Chloe is thrilled to have me to herself for a change, snuggling into my shoulder as she sits in bed, and I park alongside her on the floor. She twists my hair absently as she listens attentively to *Mrs Pepperpot*, followed by *Ella Bella*, then last but not least, a *Brambly Hedge*. It's the one about Primrose getting lost in the woods and her mummy and daddy finding her.

'You weren't here when I woke up today,' Chloe says as we get to the last page, where Primrose is safe in bed and her mummy is tucking her in.

I pause. 'No, I wasn't,' I say. 'I went to work. Do you remember Dad and Granny told you?'

She nods. 'Granny did my porridge, but she put the banana *in* it, not in the bowl on the side. I didn't like it.'

'Well.' I put the book down, and as she lies back on her pillow, looking up at me with her bright blue eyes, I lean over and gently stroke her head. 'Granny just doesn't know how we do it, that's all. I'll put it in the bowl on the side tomorrow for you, OK?'

'You don't have to go to work again?'

'No.' I shake my head. 'Not for a long, long time.'

'Good,' she says decisively.

'I love you so much, Clo,' I say, my voice breaking slightly.

'I love you too.' She turns over, away from me. 'You can turn off the light for songs now, Mummy.'

I do as I'm told, and start to sing as she happily burrows down into her duvet, clutching Dog, who has accompanied her to bed since she was ten months old, and is now shiny where once he was furry. I look around me in the soft rosy glow of her nightlight at her cosy, pretty room. It's real life Brambly Hedge. I want her always to feel this safe, to have me to love her, and take care of her. As her blonde hair slips through my fingers and her small face begins to relax and soften at the sound of my voice, I imagine her life if something were to happen to me, something that would mean I wasn't there for her any more. It's been my biggest fear since the moment she was born, and I am suddenly hit so hard with complete clarity, I almost gasp aloud – winded – as I realize there is absolutely no way on God's green earth that I got in that taxi last night intending to kill myself.

I am tired, suffering from exhaustion even, severely sleep deprived, and yes, at times depressed – but I am not even close to being as desperate as some poor, poor person would have to be, knowing that a child or children they loved more than anything would be left behind, and yet still feel they had no choice but to end it all. Chloe and Theo make me want to live for ever. I never, ever want to be parted from them.

So what *did* happen last night?

Continuing to stroke her head, I pick up my phone and click onto the notes icon, and my log of Theo's sleeping. The last entry reads: *up 8.30, asleep 9.15 p.m.* Next, I tap the clock icon and go onto my stopwatch. It's still scrolling and is currently on 22 hours 23 minutes. I was trying not to let Theo go longer than four hours between feeds up until the ten o'clock evening one. Why would I have started a countdown I had no intention of completing? Or diligently made an entry to my pathetic sleep log? As I return back to the notes, I also spy a shopping list. The date next to it reads that it was composed yesterday, at 9.30 p.m. So just before I left the house to take my own life, I made a list for the following day consisting of tuna, sweet potatoes and Babybel? I don't think so.

Heart starting to beat a little faster with the excitement of proof, I open my call list. If everyone else is right, I should find an outgoing call to a cab company, at around 9 p.m.

The whole thing has been cleared. There is no list of any recent calls at all.

I immediately stop stroking Chloe, who has already fallen asleep, and sit up straighter. I never clear the history on my phone. I have no reason – or the time – to.

So if I didn't do that, who did? And what were they trying to hide? The identity of the cab company *they* called?

I get to my feet uncomfortably, my legs having stiffened up, and as quietly as I can, creep out of Chloe's bedroom. I'm pulling the door gently to, when there's a whisper of 'everything all right?' behind me, which makes me jump and spin around on the spot.

It's Matthew. 'I was just folding some clean towels.' He motions to our room behind him. 'She went down OK then?'

Considering this is the man who can't even put his socks in the dirty clothes basket when he's standing right next to it – to say nothing of my mother already having the entire house standing to attention despite being in it less than a day – I am immediately suspicious of the towel-folding alibi. It must be his turn to be on watch.

'She's fine,' I say in hushed tones. 'I think I might go and have a rest. Would you mind telling the others I'll be down in a bit?' I walk around him to our room.

'I'll come with you,' he whispers.

Yup, definitely on watch. 'I'm not going to do anything, Matthew. I really am just going to lie down.'

'Oh absolutely! I know. I'm just tired too, and I thought it would be nice to be able to give you a hug.' He shrugs awkwardly, and I sigh.

'OK. Come on then.'

We climb, self-consciously, onto the bed and lie still alongside one another for a moment, before he reaches out and pulls me to him, so that my head is resting on his chest and he has his arm around me. Neither of us speak, we just lie there.

'We haven't done this in a while,' he says eventually.

'I should almost jump off a cliff more often.'

I feel him tense instantly. 'Sally, please, you've got to stop this. You have no idea how it felt last night, to be looking for you everywhere, Theo screaming the place down.'

'Matthew, I wasn't going to kill myself.' I twist slightly and look up at him. 'I'm sure of that now. So how *did* I get into that cab? And the note in my pocket – who put it there, intending it to be mistaken for a suicide letter? You're certain you didn't notice it on your desk yesterday? When I picked it up from the floor last night, it looked as if it had been dropped. Although the window *was* open; I'd gone in to shut it,' I remember. 'Perhaps it had blown onto the floor earlier and you hadn't seen it?'

'I definitely didn't see it. You really don't need to do this, Sal. Mum explained how low you were last night about Will and Kelly getting engaged, and I know there's been other stuff too. You weren't even vaguely excited about Mum's holiday idea. A totally free holiday! You absolutely refused to commit to it at all—'

'Because I'm about two stone heavier than usual right now, not for any other reason. Matthew, the call list on my phone has been erased. You said you found my mobile and that's what

103

made you panic that something had happened to me. You must have looked at it to see who I'd rung, or to see if anyone had contacted me?'

He says quietly, 'Yes, I did. There was nothing on it at all. As you say, the whole thing had been deliberately cleared. All of your messages had gone too – like you'd shut the whole thing down and just signed off.'

There's a moment of silence. 'You think *I* did that?' I say, amazed.

'Oh Sal,' he says, his voice breaking slightly. 'Please stop. I can't bear watching you act out this whole charade, trying to justify the letter you had on you, or insisting that it was odd you had four hundred pounds in cash when there was a bag stuffed full of money in the house that's now vanished, or why was it Cornwall you wound up in, when we've spent some of our happiest times there. People struggle, they find things difficult, impossible even. You've been looking after the children practically single-handedly for six months now: anyone would be at breaking point. The trouble is, yes, you've been depressed at points, but overall, you've seemed to be coping so well, I didn't appreciate how bad it had got. No!' He stops abruptly, chastising himself. 'That's crap. I didn't take the notice I should have done, because I was so absorbed with my work. In fact, you ought to be furious with me for not supporting you enough! Everyone ought to be shoving this in my face and shouting: "Look what you made your wife do!" Not trying to pretend it didn't happen! I don't know what made you change your mind, or if it really was that bloke who told the police he saved your life, but either way, *thank God* you're still here.' He sits up, suddenly livid, and says energetically, 'Say it! Tell me I'm a worthless bastard. There is no shame in what you did, it's heartbreaking, and I'm a lucky, lucky man that this didn't end tragically. I could so easily be having to spend the rest of my life explaining to my two beautiful children why they don't have a mother, and it would be all my own fault.' A tear slips down his cheek, and he wipes it away angrily. 'Mum said that people often do it because they think their families will be better off without them. Please, *please* don't ever think that! We – the kids, me, your mum and dad, *everyone* – need you so, so much, Sally. It would devastate all of us if anything happened to you. You must promise me you won't ever, ever do this again. We'll get you help, all the help you need, someone to talk to about how you feel, and some practical support too. Hey, you could go back to work!' He looks at me eagerly. 'No one says you *have* to be a stay-at-home mum. I know we talked about it being the way we wanted to bring our kids up when they were really small, but plenty of women would rather work, and that's fine. I'm *fine* with that. Whatever you want, we'll make it happen. I just love you so much.'

I stare in amazement at such an impassioned speech. 'Matthew,' I take his hand, 'I didn't clear my phone. I have no idea why or how I was in Cornwall. I cannot account for the ten hours I've been away from home. I'm not even saying I can't remember; it's like they never happened. There's nothing there – just a blank space. I'm telling you the truth!'

He lets his head hang for a moment, then rubs his eyes wearily. 'OK,' he says, 'so, what are you saying – that you might have chosen to block it all out?'

'No!' I say, frustrated. 'Did my mum tell you I'd said that about the period after Chloe was born? I didn't mean it literally.'

'You could ask *my* mum about it, I suppose,' he suggests, ignoring me. 'I don't know if it's even possible to supress memories, but she will.'

I'm about to ask him why he won't just take my word for it, and trust me that I'm telling the truth, when the baby monitor crackles and the familiar sound of Theo waking shatters the stand-off between us. I knew he wouldn't be down for long.

I get up, but Matthew reaches for my arm. 'Just leave him for a minute, see if he sends himself back to sleep.'

'He won't. He'll just wake up even more and be harder to settle. We're way past that stage, Matthew. It's like I've told you before, we've just got to wait until I can do proper sleep training with him.'

'But—'

'It's only going to be another month at most. We've coped this far.'

His eyebrows shoot up in disbelief.

'Oh, Matthew, I *have*!' I whisper. 'I *am* coping! I looked at Chloe while I was settling her and I knew, I just *knew*, there's no way I was trying to kill myself last night. I nearly fell, but I wasn't going to jump.'

'*That's* what this new-found certainty about last night is based on?' He looks incredulously at me.

There is a creak on the floorboards outside our room. Someone is walking past to Theo's bedroom.

'Great. Now Mum's gone in and he'll get properly upset.' I throw an arm up in exasperation. 'He doesn't know her well enough for her to be doing this. He'll freak out.'

'What are you talking about? He saw her all last weekend for Easter, and she's been here all today. They arrived at seven a.m., Sal. She put him down for his nap this morning, and after lunch.'

I sink back down onto the bed and put my head in my hands in frustration, as I try to stay calm. 'Look, could you all *please* just let me do what I've been managing on my own for the last *half a year*? If you really want to help, that's what you can do.'

Through the monitor, we hear Mum whisper firmly to Theo, 'Night, night, Theo, time to settle down and go to sleep. Night, night, darling,' followed by the sound of his door gently closing. There is a brief pause, and then Theo goes absolutely ballistic.

'See?' I say, almost relieved, and stand up – but then, just as suddenly, there is silence. Theo simply stops. I actually hear him *sigh*. And then there is quiet, apart from another creak on the floorboards as Mum makes her way back downstairs. I gape in disbelief, partly at the ease with which that just happened – and partly at the total, brutal unfairness of it when I have been trying so, so hard, for so long to get him to do exactly what he's just done in under a minute.

'Just let us help you, Sally,' Matthew pleads quietly. 'Come on, let's go downstairs and ask Mum about this "blocking things out" theory.'

Caroline and I sit in the playroom while the others tactfully retreat into the sitting room. I'm huddled on the sofa, clutching a mug of tea that Mum insists on making me, and Caroline sits on the floor, leaning her elbow on the sofa, as it's slightly too small for both of us to sit on at the same time – we'd practically be on each other's laps.

'You don't have to do this, Sally.' She looks up at me. 'I just want you to know that, but by all means talk to me if you want to. It goes without saying that I won't discuss anything with anyone else – unless, of course, I think you're a danger to yourself, or someone else. But I honestly think you'd be better talking to someone who is removed from your situation, and has no connection to you at all. Your GP can arrange that, or I can recommend some colleagues – none of whom would discuss whatever you said with me, I hasten to add.'

'I want to ask you more about Kelly.' I lower my voice discreetly, and her smile fades. 'Has she tried to make any further contact with you?'

Caroline looks over her shoulder at the closed door, and then turns back to me. 'No, she hasn't.'

'You didn't see her doing anything suspicious while she was here, did you? While I was upstairs with Theo?'

'No, I didn't.' She pauses. 'I heard her car pull off the drive, but I stayed in the bedroom like we agreed, so she wouldn't see me.'

'I haven't had a chance to tell you yet, but Theo woke up just after she arrived – or rather, she woke him up – and I left her downstairs. She would have had time to pick up your bag and put it straight in her car, and she knew it was there, she'd seen it earlier. I know you can't tell me if she's ever done anything like this in the past, but let me put it to you this way: do you think she's capable of stealing that money?'

Caroline hesitates. 'Yes, she is, but… do you have proof that's what she's done?'

'It wasn't me, Caroline.' I look her right in the eye. 'I promise you it wasn't. I'm appalled at you losing sixty-five thousand pounds. It's a huge sum of money! Surely you want to report this to the police?'

She shakes her head. 'No, I don't. I'm not having you put under that level of stress and scrutiny. It's not fair, and it's not worth it. It's one thing to have the police think that this is an attempted suicide – which, very sadly, I have to tell you they are used to dealing with all the time – and quite another to bring a significant theft into the equation.'

'You're going to let her get away with it?'

'I take it you *don't* actually have proof that Kelly took the money, then?' she says gently. 'In which case, what option do we have? Accusing her would create a firestorm that I can't even begin to explain to you. There is a Chinese proverb that reads: "If you are patient in one moment of anger, you will escape a hundred days of sorrow", and *another* that says: "If you corner a dog in a dead end, it will turn and bite". Both are very sound recommendations in this case. Whether it was Kelly who took the money – or something else happened to it – I'm going to consider its loss a worthwhile investment in peacekeeping, and you should do the same. Let's just leave it there.'

I look at her in shock. 'But—'

'Now, Matthew said you have some questions about repressing memories,' she says firmly.

'I don't – he and my mother seem to think it's a possible explanation for what's happened.'

'OK.' She rubs her eyes tiredly, and just for a moment looks exactly like Matthew, and Chloe. 'Well, I think you're talking about psychogenic amnesia or dissociative amnesia.'

'Amnesia? You mean like Jason Bourne, when he blanks everything out because he can't cope with having assassinated that married couple with the little girl?'

'Sort of, in that it goes well beyond normal forgetfulness, but the kind of personal identity loss you see in the movies is very rare in real life. You're talking – or Matthew and your mum are talking – I think, about situation-specific amnesia, which might result from an overwhelming event: a post-traumatic stress, if you will. The hypothesis is that whatever happens is so psychologically painful, or horrific, that the brain simply "shuts out" the event, and the repressed memory, or memories, only resurface over time, perhaps with therapy or because they are triggered by another memory or event. Cases *have* been documented where some sufferers were unable to remember trying to kill themselves several hours previously.' She pauses. 'But equally, a person with this kind of amnesia will usually repeatedly have periods where they can't remember information about themselves, and that's not applicable in this case. People can also have what are known as "fugues", which is where they might travel to a new location during a temporary loss of memory or identity. But *that* usually happens over a period of days. Neither of these conditions fit your scenario, Sally, although I should stress I'm not making a formal diagnosis here,' she warns. 'That would be totally inappropriate on numerous levels.'

'But you don't think I blocked anything out deliberately?'

She doesn't say anything for a moment, but looks at me, contemplatively. 'I don't think you can repress something that never happened in the first place, no. But like I said, this is not a formal diagnosis.' She gets to her feet. 'You should know that Matthew and your parents have all asked me to stay tonight, in a professional capacity. I've said that I don't think it's necessary, because I don't.'

'Thank you.' That's a vote of confidence at least.

'I'll come back in the morning, though, first thing. Hopefully that will placate them.'

'Fine. Whatever they want.'

'OK.' She nods. 'I'll go and let them know. Now, before I do: I'm happy to give you a sleeping tablet tonight. It seems your mum has broken Theo, in the nicest possible way, so you could let her take over.'

'No, thank you.' I *will* prove to them all that it's business as normal.

'Well, I'll leave it in the bathroom so you can have it if you want, and not if you don't. I must say, I think it was rather unfair of Theo to acquiesce quite so quickly, but I now seem to remember it being a common thing in years gone by – the idea that you'd break a baby's bad sleep cycle by someone else taking over other than the mother. I wish I'd thought of it sooner to help you. Anyway, at least you might get some rest now, I suppose.'

'Caroline, I'm sorry, but I'm not finished yet. I still need to talk to you about Kelly's intentions towards Chloe and Theo, as we discussed yesterday. Exactly why are you afraid for the children?'

She sighs, and then sits back down. 'Yes, I've been worried about what I said to you, and wondering if I let my own feelings as a concerned grandmother overwhelm my professional objectivity. Put more crudely, did I overreact in the heat of the moment on seeing Kelly, and should I have exercised more caution over what I said? Almost certainly. It was completely irresponsible of me to have frightened you badly without being able to be specific, and I'm so very sorry. I do want to reassure you, though, that if I had anything concrete to go on that represented a threat to Theo and Chloe *now*, I would be the first person alerting the authorities. What we talked about last night—'

'Kelly being dangerously toxic, and because of not being able to have her own children, possibly having designs on mine, you mean?' I remind her pointedly. 'That's *pretty* specific, isn't it?'

'Hang on. I understand why you're reacting like this, Sally, but I'd like to explain – and say what I should have last night. I genuinely don't believe there is anything to be gained from unnecessarily kicking a hornets' nest. Everyone, including Kelly, has a right to a past, and it's something none of us can escape. Does that, however, mean it must always affect how we are viewed going forward? In an ideal world, no. *But*,' she holds up a hand as I begin to protest, 'I *do* think it's appropriate that we exercise a degree of caution. I told you I was intervening because I was concerned about Chloe and Theo potentially being placed in the sole care of a particular person. Now I've brought it to your attention, I don't believe it will be an issue any more, and I'm certainly confident that there are enough of us physically here at the moment and around the children that it's not something we need to worry about right now. I would much rather be focusing on you, and getting you the help you need.'

'Yes, well that's the other thing,' I say. 'I don't think I need any help. I found a shopping list on my phone for items I intended to buy today, and I'd started a timer off last night so I knew when I next needed to feed Theo. Those aren't the actions of someone who was planning to kill herself, are they?'

Caroline looks at me sympathetically, but says nothing, and I must admit, spoken aloud they don't sound hugely compelling arguments.

'More importantly, though,' I clear my throat, 'I'm now certain I could never do something like that to Chloe or Theo. I know it seems pretty damning, my having that note in my pocket, but I didn't put it there, and I genuinely can't remember anything from after I went to bed. So where does that leave us? Someone must know what happened to me.'

Caroline looks startled. 'You think *Kelly* had something to do with your disappearance? That's what you're suggesting?'

I hesitate. 'Well, she certainly hates me – she genuinely believes I'm trying to break up her and Will. In fairness,' I confess, looking Caroline straight in the eye, 'she's right. If I could, I would.' I think about Kelly standing inches away from my face, whispering her threats. 'I very nearly fell when I was on that clifftop, Caroline – and I can't help but think that would have suited Kelly very nicely indeed. She'd have protected her relationship with my brother, and she'd have stood to be far more directly involved in Chloe and Theo's lives. She was also the last person I saw before I woke up three hundred miles away, having told me that if I wanted a fight, I'd got one.'

'You'd argued?' Caroline says, looking deeply troubled. 'What about?'

'Will! She accused me of trying to come between them, and told me she was going to marry him – come what may.'

Caroline exhales, heavily.

I fall silent for a moment. 'So would your advice still be to stand by and let my brother marry her, when he's completely unaware what she is capable of?'

'Oh Sally, people are capable of lots of things,' she says gently. 'It's whether they actually do something that matters. This isn't a battle you should be focusing on right now.'

'You don't believe she was involved then?'

'I can see now that perhaps I shouldn't have discussed my fears with you at all. I'm so very sorry. It's coloured your whole attitude towards Kelly, and that's dreadfully unfortunate. Lord, I've made such a mess of all of this.' She closes her eyes for a moment. 'Look, as far as Kelly goes, I wouldn't give her any more cause to believe she's right and that you *are* trying to break her and Will up. Don't go looking for trouble, and it won't come looking for you. Forget the money too, it's done – it's gone. Please *don't* worry about the children, because they are safe, I promise you. And if you say you don't need any help going forward, then OK. I trust you. So, in answer to your question,' she gets to her feet once more, 'that's where we're left: armed and forewarned, but heading into a fresh start nonetheless. Now, it's time we all went to bed.'

CHAPTER EIGHT

O ur bedroom door is, as usual, wide open so we can hear Chloe if she gets up, but with the exception of the familiar whir of Theo's wind machine humming through the monitor, the house is silent. It's only ten p.m., but Matthew, my parents and the children are all asleep.

Ordinarily I would be luxuriating in this, savouring the warmth of the bed, the softness of the pillow, and the peace, but instead, I am turned on one side, facing away from Matthew. I can't switch off. Caroline still believes I tried to kill myself. She looked at me like she might a child, badly fibbing to cover something they've done wrong, when I tried to discuss Kelly's possible involvement in my winding up on that clifftop.

Is it really so completely ludicrous an accusation, though?

Or, actually, bang on the missing money?

Why the hell can't I remember what actually happened?

I twist to face Matthew, but still unable to settle comfortably, turn back just as quickly. I simply do not understand how ten hours of my life can be a complete blank. How is that even possible?

I snatch up my phone in frustration and google memory loss.

If you're reading this because you're worried you have dementia, rest assured you probably haven't. A person with dementia won't have an awareness of their memory loss.

> More common causes of memory loss are depression,
> stress or anxiety.

Matthew sighs restlessly in his sleep, disturbed by my moving about, and turns over. I momentarily freeze, then quickly place my phone face down on the mattress, in case the lit screen wakes him properly. I'm so used to Matthew choosing to sleep in the spare room that having him lying next to me again feels really weird. I wait for a moment for him to re-settle, then start again, clicking on depression first.

> Depression is about more than simply feeling unhappy or
> fed up for a few days. Depression affects people in different
> ways and can cause a wide variety of symptoms. At its
> mildest, you may just feel persistently low in spirit, while at
> its most severe, depression can make you feel suicidal and
> that life is not worth living.

This is no good – it's just a definition of depression itself, nothing to do with memory loss at all. I sigh, exasperated, and am about to put my mobile down, when I remember Matthew in tears earlier, having found that information about divorce on my phone. I quickly clear the search completely and set the phone carefully back on the bedside table, before turning over – at which point I jump horribly, because Matthew is lying there, eyes wide open, quietly watching me.

'Jesus Christ!' I gasp. 'What are you *doing*?'

'Catching you clearing stuff off your phone about depression causing suicidal thoughts.'

I flush. 'I was looking up causes of memory loss. One of which is apparently depression.'

He doesn't say anything, just looks at me.

'Matthew, you didn't "catch" me doing anything. I swear!'

'Last night, when you were missing,' he ignores me, 'I phoned Liv from your phone, in case she knew where you were, but she didn't. Like all of us, she was beside herself. Once you'd been found safe this morning, I called her back, to let her know, and when I told her the circumstances, she was horrified. Then she confessed you'd sent her text messages over the last couple of days that she hadn't taken seriously, saying things like "this baby is breaking me" and "I hate my life".' He pauses for a moment, and I agree, it does sound truly awful, spoken so baldly like that, completely out of context.

'You must know I didn't mean it literally, though, surely?' I say slowly. 'Everyone does that sort of thing, all the time!'

'I don't,' he says. 'I don't tell my mates I hate my life.'

'Oh, come on, Matthew. I don't actually hate it – it's just a whingey thing you say when you're knackered. That's all.'

'She knew all about our row, and told me you'd asked for some advice about divorce.'

'Hey, back up a bit.' I move away from him, urgently. 'I asked her if it was normal for a couple to *discuss* divorce, and yet not mean it. Anyway, Matthew, it doesn't matter what Liv said. *I'm* telling you that wasn't how it was. She—'

'And then she told me this isn't the first time you've tried to kill yourself.'

I freeze for two, maybe three seconds, before the shock of his words implodes in my head and I'm dragged backwards into a vacuum, where everything starts rushing past me; like falling through the inside of a kaleidoscope – brightly coloured shards of my life flashing by – until with a jolt, I arrive at my small room at university. I can see myself sitting, sobbing on my single bed. My knees are hugged up to my chest, as I rock backwards and forwards, because my heart is freshly ripped into pieces, and I can't sit still with the pain. Joe – at another university some two hundred miles away – has just called on the halls of residence phone to tell me that he doesn't want a long-distance relationship after all. With impeccable timing, given Dad has had his second heart attack some twelve days earlier, he says he thinks we ought to take a break for a while. 'I'll come up,' I plead. 'I'll get on the first train I can and we can sort this out.' 'No, don't do that,' he insists. He's sorry, but he's made up his mind, and it's important to be honest with me.

It's the first time I've experienced the perfect storm of rejection, heartbreak, grief and fear all at once – and that night, I do something *really* stupid. My two best friends on my corridor get me some vodka from the on-campus Londis, to drown my sorrows. One of them – in her first year of a drama degree and obsessed with *Pulp Fiction* – casts herself as a female Tarantino, and enjoying the way it sounds and how she imagines she looks saying it, strides into my room clutching the bottle and a packet of fags, waves them around and shouts, 'Fuck him! Drink some of this, smoke these, and in the morning, start the rest of your fucking life better off without him!' We down a *lot* of vodka, and then they stagger off to their rooms. I climb under my duvet, but much more than half-cut, and through tears that I can't seem to stop, my pissed teenage mind is still desperately looking for a way to hold onto this first boy I've ever loved. I blurrily decide that if something awful were to happen to me, Joe would realize what I mean to him and come running back. So I get back out of bed, and, picturing him sobbing by my bedside while I'm hooked up to a life support like the one I saw Dad on less than two weeks earlier, I open a bottle of paracetamol – this being back in the day when it was still possible to buy more than ten at a time over the counter – swallow the contents, and lurch back to bed.

I wake up the next day feeling like I've slept amazingly well – but sober, am scared witless by my actions of the night before. Particularly when I realize there were about twenty pills in the bottle.

I have a *lot* of time to think about it over the next forty-eight hours that I spend vomiting. I could have killed myself. How did it *not* kill me? This is also in the days of no Internet, so there's no immediate answer, and therefore, of course, no one that I ask. In fact, I tell not a single soul about this sordid, deeply private moment of my life until some sixteen years later, when, while becoming closer friends, Liv and I – heavily pregnant and watching a movie while eating cake balanced on our bumps – have one of those intense disclosure/bonding sessions about the boys and men we have loved and lost.

'I honestly don't know how you're not dead,' Liv said in amazement. 'Some people can tolerate drugs better than others, I guess. You were so lucky!'

'It never occurred to me that I might actually die, I only got as far as imagining him doing some mad dash to the hospital to rescue me.'

'The classic teenage cry for help.' Liv shook her head in disbelief.

'No. It really wasn't,' I corrected her. 'I think I was partly still reeling because of what had happened to my dad, and was just very pissed and very stupid.'

I reach out and grab Matthew's arm. 'Did you hear me? I said I was very pissed, and an idiot. I was also only nineteen. I don't know what impression Liv has given you, but—'

'You swallowed twenty paracetamol?' Matthew is looking frightened and bewildered, almost as if he barely knows me. 'Six years we've been married, and you never thought to mention this?'

'It was private,' I say. 'And it has no bearing on my life now, whatsoever—'

'Really?' he interrupts. 'You don't think this might have been relevant when you were struggling after Chloe was born, too? That I had a right to know?'

'No. I don't. To both questions. Look, you and I both know it wasn't easy after Chloe, but Christ, Matthew – tell me a single person that doesn't find it hard having their first baby! I don't think I was any more depressed than any other new mum. And I'm not depressed now. In fact, I'm coping better than I did first time around, because I *know* that it's going to get better. What happened at university was really dumb, and a very long time ago. Liv had absolutely no business telling you about it.'

'She didn't feel she had a choice. She was worried not saying anything might put you at more risk, if we didn't have the full picture.'

'Oh my God!' I look up at the ceiling and try very hard to stay calm. 'This is why none of you believe me about last night, isn't it, because of what Liv has told you all? Look, this is not something I have a problem with. I was not going to kill myself!'

'What would you think, Sal, if you were me?' he asks, his voice quiet. 'My wife who "hates her life" and has been looking into divorcing me, disappears in the middle of the night with sixty-five grand in cash. Naturally, I think she's left me and our children. The next morning I find out she was actually prevented from jumping off a cliff in Cornwall by a passer-by, and she had a suicide note on her. Her best friend tells me I ought to know that a long time ago she attempted to kill herself at university. Then my wife comes home. She can't explain where the money is, she tries to tell me the note was in fact one that I've already seen – only I haven't – and says, yes, I am correct: she took a paracetamol overdose twenty-one years ago that she never told me about, but don't worry, it's not related to *this* situation at all, and can I please

119

not just trust her when she says that actually, she has *no idea* what happened last night? That's it. That is her explanation. Would you believe you, Sal?'

'Yes. I would. Because it's true.'

'Oh, Sally, don't treat me like this. Please. It's insulting.'

'I'm not saying it doesn't look bad, but—'

He laughs incredulously. 'Oh, OK. That's good. At least we agree on that.'

'Matthew, stop!' I say, on the brink of tears. 'Please. I'm your wife. I'm telling you that I have no idea how I wound up on those cliffs – and I'm *frightened*, Matthew. I went to bed and woke up three hundred miles away! Forget what Liv told you. Trust *me – help* me!' I let go of his arm and take his hand imploringly. 'I love Chloe and Theo so much. I would never, ever do that to them. There has to be another explanation for what happened last night.'

His eyes well up again too, and he hesitates. 'Go on then,' he whispers. 'What *is* the reason? What really happened? Tell me.'

There is a long pause. I want to tell him my suspicions about Kelly, as well as everything Caroline has disclosed to me about her. But not wanting to reveal how his mother has already betrayed Kelly's patient confidentiality, I stay silent.

'I can't,' I confess eventually, and Matthew sighs heavily.

Theo begins to cry down the monitor, and I start to get up.

'No,' Matthew says. 'You need to rest.' He throws back the duvet and climbs out of bed. I listen to him walk down the hall and wait for Theo to begin crying when Matthew picks him up, but instead my husband gently and successfully starts to soothe our baby back to sleep in a way I didn't even know either of them were capable of.

What the hell has happened to my world overnight?

My phone buzzes in my hand. I glance down at the screen – it's a message from Liv.

How are you?

I don't even think about it. My fingers flash over the tiny keyboard angrily.

You told him? WTF?

The three dots scroll as she starts to type back.

I had to. You have two kids Sally. You don't have the right to make selfish choices now.

I gasp in amazement. Well, I guess it's a good job I *haven't* just tried to top myself. That's some pep talk, Liv.

You're ANGRY with me? I message.

Three dots…

Yes. I am. Very.

Wow. All I can do is sit and stare at the screen for a second, in shock, but then the three dots start furiously scrolling again.

So many people love you. You have so much in your life!

Oh, OK. I think I get it now. I hesitate, then type.

Is this more about your stuff than my stuff? I promise I know how lucky I am to have two kids. Would never, ever hurt them. I don't remember what happened to me last night.

A pause, and then the dots begin to ripple. I wait, but then they stop rolling – and vanish.

Let's discuss tomorrow? I request. It delivers instantly, but I'm still holding the phone having had no response – she usually acknowledges texts with an 'x' – when Matthew comes back into the room.

'Sal, you need to get some rest,' he says, climbing into bed next to me. 'Put your phone down.'

I do as he asks, and he rolls away to the other side of the bed. But I can't sleep. Of course I can't.

Once I'm certain Matthew has definitely drifted off, I reach for my phone again, this time doing a search on Kelly Harrington. The latest news item flashes up. It's a link to the MailOnline.

The picture that I see when I click on it makes me exclaim so loudly, I don't know how I don't wake the whole house up. My future sister-in-law is beaming like the Cheshire cat on steroids as she holds her left hand up in what appears to be an Instagram selfie. *'It's true! I'm so happy!' Proud Kelly Harrington confirms engagement and shares first pictures of a very bling ring!* gushes the headline.

Kelly Harrington shares her happiness after her boyfriend proposes during a romantic holiday in Tenerife!

I thought she said she was out there working? Another shot of Kelly in a swimsuit cut up to her armpits, draped over some sun-drenched rock like a lads' mag Andromeda, sits alongside the text.

The beautiful twenty-seven-year old actress – I thought she was thirty? – *tweeted 'It's true! I'm so lucky and so happy!' after a source* – Kelly herself, then – *told MailOnline that her partner of just under a year, TV exec Will Tanner, had gone down on one knee at sunset. It seems he went all out with his ring choice too, opting for a stunning solitaire for his celebrity beauty, which reportedly cost a whopping £70,000!*

Seventy thousand pounds? My mouth falls open.

Will doesn't have that kind of cash! Even if he did, he wouldn't spend it on a ring – that's obscene! I scroll down and peer closely at the square-cut rock squatting on her slim finger – and then it's as if her fist smashes right through the screen and punches me full in the face with the realization.

OK, Caroline, *now* I know exactly what happened to your money.

CHAPTER NINE

'You're wrong, Sally, and you've got to stop this.' Mum bangs around my kitchen in her dressing gown, getting knives and forks out of the drawers for the cooked breakfast sizzling on the Aga. 'Of *course* that's not how much the ring cost. I spoke to Will last night, after they went shopping yesterday afternoon, and he warned me that the figure Kelly's representative was going to feed the press was very exaggerated. She's in the public eye, it's almost expected that she have the perfect clothes, nails, hair – and jewellery. People want their stars to be glamorous and removed from reality, don't they? You want to see them getting off yachts in Cannes, not pushing shopping trolleys around Aldi.'

I stare at my mother. 'She's not Elizabeth Taylor, Mum. And Will's not Richard Burton either. Even if it's worth half what the papers say, we both know he couldn't afford to pay that either. So how *was* it financed?'

Mum whips around and points a fish slice at me. 'I mean it. Stop it. We discussed this last night. She didn't take Caroline's money.'

'It's the perfect out. Got some cash you need to lose fast? Buy a rock that no one knows the exact cost of and stick it on your finger.'

'Oh, Sally! Can you even hear yourself? I've never heard any-thing so improbable.' Mum flips the bacon in the pan and pushes it down aggressively.

'Well, I woke up in Cornwall yesterday with no idea how I got there. *That* happened. I don't see how this is any more impossible to believe. Does Will actually know that our money is missing?'

'Please don't say anything,' Mum begs suddenly. 'He's already so worried about you. Even though I've told him you're home safe with us, all he wanted to do was come and be here for you yesterday. They both did.'

'She didn't want to be here for me at all, Mum. Kelly and I argued. Remember?'

'That was then. Everything's changed now, because of what's happened. She wants to support you, just like the rest of your family.'

'No, she doesn't!' I exclaim. I'm desperate to tell Mum what I've learnt about her future daughter-in-law. 'If you had any idea what—'

'You didn't take Caroline's money, did you?' Mum asks suddenly, lowering her voice.

Her unexpected question completely draws me up short. 'What? No! Of course not!'

'I think I might have been tempted to, if I were you – even if it was just to hide it for a bit and teach Caroline a lesson. The bloody cheek of it, going behind your back and asking Matthew to lend her your savings.'

'I haven't taken it *or* hidden it. I didn't even know all that cash was here on Friday night.'

'Really? If someone left a big bag downstairs in my house, I'd have a nosy around in it. Perhaps that's just me.'

'Mum, please listen. I'm trying to tell you I'm genuinely worried about how Kelly is—'

'Good morning,' says a voice behind us, and we both jump guiltily as I turn to see Caroline standing in the archway of the playroom. Mum self-consciously tightens her dressing-gown cord at the sight of Caroline's hot pink Issa jumpsuit, an outfit most women half her age couldn't pull off as well. I don't ask *her* to take off her pointed black pumps with their three-inch heels. I wouldn't dream of it. Caroline would consider it the height of bad manners to be asked to remove her shoes.

'How are we all this morning?' She smiles at us.

'Very well, thank you, Caroline,' says Mum graciously. 'Would you like a bacon sandwich?'

'No, thank you,' Caroline says kindly. 'It smells wonderful, though. Would you like me to marshal the troops?'

'Thank you. Chloe's upstairs in her room getting dressed, and Matthew's changing Theo's nappy,' I say, not quite able to meet her eye.

'Well, how very civilized,' Caroline says. 'Did you manage to get some sleep last night?'

'A bit,' I lie. 'Listen, would you both excuse me a minute? I think I've just missed a call.' I reach into my dressing-gown pocket and pull out my mobile. 'It might be the Crisis team again.' I pretend to scan the screen. 'I'd better just check my voicemail.'

I pass my father in the hall on his way into the kitchen, clutching the Sunday papers. 'Hello, love,' he says. 'You're looking much brighter this morning. I've just been to the petrol station to get these, and I chose you a magazine while I was there. I thought you could have a quiet sit down with a cup of tea later. Your mum and I will watch the kiddies.'

I take the glossy interiors magazine he's proffering, touched by the small but very thoughtful gesture. 'Thanks, Dad.'

He smiles kindly, reaches out and ruffles my hair, before walking into the kitchen. There's a lump in my throat and I have to force myself to get a grip, before hastening off to the downstairs loo. I've probably only got about another three minutes before either one, or both, of the children will want me.

I close the door quietly and sit down on the loo seat. I very plainly don't have anyone's backing or support, but I think I've got to phone Will and talk to him about Kelly. If the situation were reversed, and Will had serious concerns about Matthew, I'd want to know. I'd consider it a betrayal if he *didn't* tell me, and I actually don't feel I have any choice but to talk to him anyway, given this is about keeping our family safe – my children in particular. I meant what I said to Kelly: I'll do anything to protect them. But what exactly can I tell Will? Without being able to divulge Caroline's information, I run the risk of him reacting exactly the same way the others have to my accusations, or actually an awful lot worse – he loves her, after all. I want Kelly out of our lives, but at the cost of potentially losing my brother? I exhale slowly. No, I have to do it. I have to tell him my fears. It's the right thing to do.

The phone rings to the point that I'm expecting his answerphone, but at the last moment, he picks up with a sleepy, 'Hey, Sal, are you all right?'

'Oh, I'm so sorry,' I say immediately. 'I've woken you up.' I forget no one except people with small children in the house are ever up before nine on a Sunday.

'It's fine. I've been by my phone in case you wanted to talk.'

I hesitate, but just manage to say, 'Thanks. That's kind of you. Listen, Will, can I discuss something privately with you for a moment? Would you mind going somewhere where we can't be overheard?'

'Of course.' He sounds worried, and there's a pause, before he returns back to me. 'I'm in the spare room now. Go for it.'

I take a deep breath. 'So, tell me about your shopping trip yesterday!'

He pauses again, before saying slowly, 'Er, OK. To buy the ring, you mean?'

'No, to Sainsbury's,' I try to joke. 'Yes, of course the ring!'

'Um, we went to this place Kelly knows. Well, she knows the daughter of the owner. We both liked the same one pretty much straight away, and we bought it. There's not much else to tell, really.' There's another silence before he says, 'It didn't cost anywhere near what the papers are saying, if that's what you're worried about.'

OK. Here we go.

'I am a bit concerned, yes,' I say. 'I just don't want you over-stretching yourself to keep up with a lifestyle you're not necessarily needing to be a part of. But then, for all I know, Kelly contributed to the cost?' I wince at such a completely crass way of trying to find out if she pulled out a huge wodge of cash at the till.

'Sally,' he interrupts gently, 'Kelly's honestly not like that, she had no expectations at all. I'll tell you in confidence, it cost me seven thousand – which is still a lot of money, but her friend's dad gave us a *really* good deal.'

There's absolutely no way the ring in that picture was only seven grand. I immediately lose all attempts at subtlety. 'You paid, then? Not her?'

'Of course I paid!' He laughs. 'Jeez, you're not telling me that Matthew made you cough up for *your* ring? How have I never known this?'

'We actually didn't buy one at all, if you remember,' I say absently. 'Mine is a family heirloom from his grandmother.'

'Oh right – nice. The best kind.'

'I suppose so, although I think—'

'Kelly was so excited,' he cuts across me. 'It was really nice. In fact, she was so busy gazing at her finger, we got back to the car and she realized she'd left her handbag in the jewellers. Daft moo. I had to drop her off and go around the block so she could race back in and get it.'

I stop instantly. 'She forgot her handbag?' Given all of the bags I've ever seen her with are designer and extremely expensive, I find that very hard to believe.

'Yeah. Luckily her mate's dad had put it out the back, but her pal had also arrived in the interim. Eight times I did that bloody loop while they were in there, probably just shrieking at each other.' He laughs.

'You know us girls,' I say slowly. 'Tell me, what's the ring like? Is it platinum or white gold? What cut is the stone?'

'Oh God, Sal, I don't know!' he exclaims. 'It's sort of square. And platinum, I think.'

'Platinum, you think...' I repeat in disbelief.

'That's the most expensive one, isn't it? Yes, it's definitely that. We got a lot of bang for our buck, as it were.'

I'll bet she did. It's completely obvious to me what's happened. Kelly came out with the more modest ring that Will paid for, then she faked a reason to go back – and secretly upgraded while he was in the car. As long as she'd come back with a ring roughly the same shape, he'd have been none the wiser if it was larger, worth three times as much, or thirty-three times. The fact that she also knows the jeweller makes me even more certain that's what she's done. She probably had the ring she really wanted pre-selected and on standby – and if they know her personally, they're not going to question cash, are they? Caroline's were completely genuine notes, after all.

'Well, don't forget to add it onto your insurance policy, will you?' I tell him. 'Rings have to go on individually.'

'She's already got it covered. Her agent sorted it, I think.'

There! I *am* right, because that's just weird. Why on earth would her agent be arranging something like that? *This* is how I can make him see exactly what kind of person Kelly is. I don't even need to bring up everything else. She's hung herself.

'Will, you need to ask her if you can add it to *your* policy, and tell her you need the diamond certificate.'

There's a long pause. 'Sally, I think it might be easier if you just tell me what the problem is.'

'I'm pretty sure the ring she's wearing now isn't the one you chose together,' I say carefully, making sure I say nothing about the missing money. 'I think she might have swapped it for something a little more... extravagant while you were in the car.'

Such a long silence follows, I actually think I've lost him for a minute. 'Hello? Will?'

'I'm still here.'

'Just ask her, that's all I'm saying.'

'Kelly wouldn't do something like that. She'd know how much that would hurt my feelings. The whole point was we chose it together and it was as much as I could afford. She couldn't buy a ring for seventy thousand either. Soap stars don't make anywhere near as much money as everyone thinks they do.'

There's a sudden knock on the door, which makes me jump. 'Mummy?' says a small voice. 'The door's stuck. I can't come in and I need you to do me a plait, please.'

'I'm coming, Clo. Will, I'm sorry, I've got to go. I'll call you back in a bit, if that's OK?'

'It's fine,' he says distantly. 'I'll be here.'

I hang up and open the door. Chloe is standing outside holding my hairbrush and a hairband. 'I've got everything.'

'Did you get them all yourself? Well done!'

She nods proudly, passes them to me, and turns around. 'Can it start low down?'

'Of course, darling.' I draw her closer to me and start to brush, taking care to hold the hair tightly as I tease the knots from the ends so it doesn't pull. She stands beautifully still as she waits patiently for me to be done, and I glance at her delicate arms and the perfect sweep of her tiny neck. I begin to plait, and clench my jaw suddenly at the thought of Caroline saying last night that there are enough of us around the children at the moment for any threat to them not to be a problem. What the hell kind of reassurance is that supposed to give me anyway? Someone is either dangerous, or they're not. It was the right thing to call Will. There's no doubt in my mind.

'Have you finished, Mummy? I'm hungry.'

'Yup – all done!' I twist the band into place. Dangerous and devious... I don't want that woman near any of us. 'Come on – let's get you some food.'

We go back into the kitchen to find everyone – bar Caroline, who is sitting on the sofa clutching a cup of tea – eating breakfast.

'Here's yours, love.' Mum gets up hurriedly and passes me a plate heaped with eggs, bacon, mushrooms and tomato. 'And yours, Chloe.'

'Thank you, Granny Sue,' she says politely, and sits up. 'Can you push me in, Mummy?'

I get up and do as she's asked, then sit back down opposite Matthew. 'Do you want me to do that?' I nod at the bowl of baby porridge, which he's very slowly and carefully spooning into our son.

'No, thank you. I need to get better at this, and I'm enjoying it.' He smiles at Theo. 'Yes I am! Aren't I? Daddy's enjoying it. Everything all right with the Crisis team?' he asks ultra-casually.

I glance at Chloe, who is tucking into her food, good little girl. 'Yes, thank you. Would you come to the park with me later, Chloe?'

Her little face lights up, and she nods happily. 'I'm going to show you how I can go down the slide *backwards*.'

'No! I don't believe it. You can't do that?' I pretend to be amazed. She grins and says, 'I *can*!'

'You don't think you ought to stay in and rest today?' Matthew says. 'I can take Chloe to the park. Sue, you wouldn't mind putting Theo down this morning, would you, so Sal can go back to bed?'

'Of course I wouldn't,' Mum says. 'Matthew's right, you should take advantage of us being here.'

'But I—' I start to protest, only for Caroline to interrupt with a gentle, 'I think the park is a great idea, Sally.' I look at her gratefully, and she adds firmly, 'You and Chloe should go, just the two of you.'

'We used to call that a kitten adventure,' Chloe says suddenly. 'If it was just me and Mummy. Just me and Daddy was a mousey adventure, and if it was me, Mummy, and Daddy, it was a puppy adventure.'

'That's right, clever girl,' I say, remembering that we used to say that all the time, but then I'm distracted by my mobile buzzing in my pocket with the arrival of a text message. I reach in and pull out my phone, expecting Liv, but to my surprise, it's Will.

Just had it out with Kelly. You were right. She swapped ring.

'No!' I exclaim aloud, without thinking.

'What?' Matthew says, as everyone else looks up too.

Had massive row – she was hysterical. Apparently she 'didn't want to hurt me' but my offering not quite up to scratch, so she thought she'd 'top it up' herself… Don't tell anyone else please. Not sure how I want to play this yet. Might pop over and see you all later, depending on everything here. Thanks for heads-up. X

'It's nothing,' I say immediately. Will's not sure how he wants to play this? What does that mean? He's considering calling it all off?

They are questions that remain frustratingly unanswered for the rest of the day. I try to text him again later, while we are at the park, and then later still to see if he wants to join all of us for a roast that Mum is making, but he doesn't respond.

131

It's only once Caroline has just left to go home at 7 p.m. that there's a loud knock at the front door.

My parents look up from *Country File*, and Matthew jumps to his feet. 'Mum must have forgotten something. She's going to wake Theo!' He rushes out of the room, only to return apprehensively a few moments later. 'Sally? Door for you.'

Confused, I get up, and pulling my bobbly but comfy and favourite cardigan tightly around me, I make my way out into the hall. I'm expecting Liv – who I haven't heard from all day – or maybe even Will, but the person I actually discover standing on the doorstep, incongruously holding a huge bunch of flowers, some chocolates and a magazine, while looking absolutely furious – is Kelly.

In contrast to the glossy girl from the Instagram picture I saw last night, her eyes are slightly red from crying, she's got no make-up on, and her hair is tied back in a ponytail. She's wearing a simple long-sleeve black top over dark skinny jeans, and some battered old Converse, but she actually looks amazing. Almost a completely different person. As she glares at me, I can see we are about to have a conversation stripped back of any pretence too.

'It was you, wasn't it?' she says. '*You* call, and out of the blue, Will is suddenly asking me for diamond certificates and insurance documents. You really hate me this much? You're *that* jealous? Will would have been none the wiser if you hadn't stuck your nose in. All you've done is hurt him – again.'

'Me?' I say in disbelief. 'I wasn't the one who deliberately left my bag at the jewellers so I could go back and swap the ring before anyone got a picture of me wearing the "sub-standard" offering my poor brother worked so hard to provide you with.'

She flushes hotly. 'Don't you dare make out you know anything about me!'

'I know a lot more than you think,' I retort, unwisely.

132

Her eyes narrow and, after a moment's pause, she says dangerously, 'And what exactly is that supposed to mean, Sally?'

I realize instantly I've said far too much, and am teetering on the verge of betraying Caroline. Desperate to deflect Kelly's attention, I blurt, 'Why did you do it? You found some spare cash lying around the house you thought you'd invest?'

She turns completely white and whispers, 'No! Of course I didn't.'

'You're lying. I can tell. I know you stole the money!'

Her expression changes again. '*Stole* it? From who?'

'My mother-in-law,' I say quietly, and watch carefully for her reaction.

She laughs incredulously. 'Oh my God! You really are completely mad, aren't you? I've always known you've got issues – but this is on another level.'

'I *know* you took the sixty-five grand.'

'*Sixty-five thousand pounds?*' She shakes her head in disbelief. 'OK, Sally – despite what we said to each other on Friday night, after you wound up in Cornwall, I actually was going to just back off and leave you alone. You're ill, and I get that, but you just can't drop it, can you? You keep coming back for more, and I've told you, *I'm not letting you do this to me.* You know, all of my friends keep saying you'd be like this with whoever Will was with, but I don't agree. This is personal to me, I know it is. What did I ever do to you? I'm just a nice, ordinary girl.'

'No, you're not.'

She considers that for a moment, and then throws her head back as if she's in a spotlight. 'Yeah, actually you're right. There's nothing ordinary about me. But, you know, I'm actually not just a pretty face; I'm also way smarter than you give me credit for, and if it's any consolation, Sally, *I* believe you. I don't think you tried to kill yourself.'

'Oh? And why's that?' I say slowly.

'I know exactly what you've done – you don't fool me for a second. People who really want to kill themselves, do it. They really *commit* to suicide. You think you're so clever with your little games, don't you? Taking yourself off to Cornwall in a taxi and your PJs: "Woohoo, everyone, look, I'm going to jump off a cliff..."' She stares at me in disgust. 'Nothing makes a husband buck his ideas up like a wife literally on the edge, eh, Sal? Being a bit more attentive now, is he? Plus, of course, now everyone is on your side. No one can be angry with poor little Sally when she interferes where she's not wanted, because she's so vulnerable at the moment, we couldn't possibly upset her. Except, here's the thing, Sal –' she takes another step closer to me, letting the flowers hang loosely in her hand. Caroline's warning not to kick the hornets' nest begins to reverberate in my head, while I try to stand my ground and wonder if she's about to hit me – 'normal people don't pull attention-seeking stunts like this. You are *deranged* to have done it.'

'I didn't do anything!' I exclaim. 'And you know that. You were the last person who—'

'Oh, just shut up! I've not stolen a penny from you. And for the record, the ring cost nowhere near that amount. You need to learn not everything you read in the papers is true. But most importantly, from one actress to another, here's some profes- sional advice: you don't want to overplay this. Otherwise every- one might think you're *really* unstable, and that's a different game altogether, trust me.'

'Have you got the door open out here, Sally? There's a wicked draught coming through... Kelly!' Mum appears alongside me, beaming, but then looks concerned. 'Are you all right, love? Where's Will?'

'At home. Everything's fine, I just wanted to pop over with

these for Sal,' Kelly says earnestly, absolutely all trace of anger having flicked off like a switch, as she holds out the flowers, chocolates and magazines. 'I know they're not much – but I wanted Sal to know I was thinking about her.'

'Isn't that nice!' Mum says. 'You came all that way!' She looks at me pointedly.

'Thank you, Kelly,' I say dutifully.

'You're very welcome. You've been through so much, Sally, but please don't forget where we are. Just call again, and I'll be there. I'm not going anywhere, I promise you.'

CHAPTER TEN

By a quarter to seven, the house is warming up nicely for Monday-morning chaos. Theo has been babbling in his cot for half an hour, having already been fed when he woke up at six, and put back in his cot. I haven't got him yet, not just because I'm clinging to my one sacrosanct rule that the kids don't get properly up before seven o'clock, but because I'm lying in bed thinking about Kelly, turning up on the doorstep last night out of the blue. She is completely determined to stay in Will's life. She left me in no doubt about that.

Matthew begins to crash around in the shower, and Theo instantly changes tack as he realizes someone else is awake, and starts clamouring noisily to be rescued. I reluctantly drag myself up and go through first to check on Chloe, who is sitting in bed flicking through some books.

'Morning, darling, how are you? Sleep well?' I give her a business-as-usual smile. 'What do you fancy for breakfast?'

'Boiled egg, please. Is it a school day today?' she asks.

'Yup. Granny Sue and Grandpa have asked if they can take you. That's fun, isn't it? I'm just going to change Theo's nappy, then we'll get you dressed, shall we?'

'Can I come and get Theo up too?' She scrambles out of bed and dashes past me.

Pausing to grab her uniform and the hairbrush, I also stop

en route outside the bathroom and knock on the door. 'Matthew? Don't forget, Mum and Dad have to get through the shower too, will you? I'll go and start Chloe's packed lunch, but can you come down to sit with Theo as soon as you're dressed?'

'Will do,' he shouts back, unusually equably. Normally he hates being chivvied. 'I'm nearly done.'

I go through to find Chloe has climbed on the side of Theo's cot and is squeaking, 'Good morning' repeatedly to him, at an ear-piercingly high pitch. Theo has pushed himself up onto his tummy in his Grobag and is craning to look at her. I arrive in time to see him pulling his knees up to his chest in very credible preparation for crawling.

'Let's stop that, shall we?' I pick him up hastily and wrestle him onto the change mat while Chloe continues to jump around and screech. 'Sweetheart, can you not make that noise? Please?' I ask her, smiling, despite it being a really horrible sound.

'Everything all right in here?' Matthew suddenly appears around the edge of the door, clad in a towel, hair damp, and looking – I'm surprised to find myself thinking – very attractive. 'Do you need me to change him?'

'Um, no, thank you.' I self-consciously pull my gross nightie down so it covers my legs and bottom a little better.

'You sure?' he says, concerned. 'I don't mind, if you feel like you need a moment? You sound stressed.'

'I'm really fine,' I assure him, and he nods, then disappears.

I sounded stressed? I didn't think I did.

Everyone might think you're really unstable, and that's a different game altogether, trust me.

Disquieted, I push Kelly's voice from my mind as I bend to gather Theo up and get to my feet. I need to try not to let her into my head, that's exactly what she wants. I should never have said I knew more about her than she realized, though, that was insane.

She's going to put two and two together and deduce Caroline's the source, surely? I basically did *exactly* what Caroline warned me not to. Should I give Caroline a heads-up? I probably ought to. There was no need for me to accuse Kelly of stealing the missing cash either. Will is going to pursue where Kelly got that kind of money from in any case, it would have come out anyway, without my needing to take a wrecking ball to it.

I just need to go and see him, and have this out with him properly. I wonder when he's working from home next? That would be the best solution. We need to sit down and discuss things calmly, without anyone else interrupting.

'MUM!' Chloe tugs on my sleeve, bringing me back to the room. 'I *said* I want bunches today!'

'OK, OK,' I say quickly. 'Sorry, Clo. Bunches it is. Let's go downstairs and do them, so I can put Theo on his mat with some toys.'

As we pass the spare room, Mum calls out, 'Sally! Is that you?'

Opening the door, I put my head around to see Mum sitting up in bed brightly, holding a mug of tea in one hand and a Maeve Binchy in the other. Dad is sitting on the armchair in the corner, already dressed in trousers, a shirt and tie, and a neatly pressed jumper. His coat and shoes are also laid out next to him. He's obviously been ready for some time.

'Morning, love,' he says, not looking up from *A Guide to Britain's Beaches.*

'Now, Dad's showered and I've already done Chloe's packed lunch,' Mum says briskly. 'And breakfast is all laid too. Once Matthew is out of the bathroom –' she continues apace as my brain struggles to keep up with this extra information – 'I'll just zip through quickly and wash, shall I? What time do we have to go?'

'Um, eight fifteen.'

'Granny Sue, Mummy's going to do me a boiled egg!' interrupts Chloe.

'Lovely!' Mum smiles. 'So that's settled then?'

'What is?'

'Oh Sally, do concentrate!' She rolls her eyes patiently. 'I'll go through next, then you. I'll be five seconds.'

'Bathroom's free!' yells Matthew.

'There!' Mum sets her cup down, throws back the covers and, voluminous nightie billowing, leaps up and grabs her towel and washbag. 'I'll be quick as quick!' She whisks around the door like the White Rabbit.

I wish I had her energy. Maybe I would have if I'd slept better; Theo seems to be creeping back to his old ways. Still, I've no time to dwell on that now.

'Come on, Clo, let's go and get you dressed. Ow!' I wince as Theo grabs a fistful of my unbrushed hair and yanks it. 'Let's not do that, darling. Dad, do you want an egg for breakfast?'

He looks up amiably from his book. 'I'd better wait and see what your mother says. I think she had toast and cereal planned.'

'It's just an egg,' I say gently. 'Have one if you want one. It won't make you late.'

'Well, that would be very nice then, thank you,' he says. 'Matthew's already put Chloe's car seat in for me, and I've programmed the satnav. So we're all set. I'll come down in a minute then, shall I?'

'Mum, you have to say, "I bet you can't get to the kitchen before I do",' Chloe says eagerly, sneaking past me as we leave the room.

'I bet you can't get into the kitchen before I do,' I repeat obediently.

I really worry sometimes about what will happen to Dad if, by some hideous irony, Mum dies first and he's left to think for himself. I'm not sure he knows how to any more. I don't even really remember the time *before* he was ill when Mum didn't do everything.

'Clo – don't rush on the stairs! I don't want you to trip!'

'I won't!' she calls back. 'See? I won!' She beams as I appear in the kitchen seconds after her. 'Can I watch something on the iPad?'

'Yes, darling, you can,' I say, as I spot her lunch, which Mum has left out on the side. I put down the uniform and hairbrush, and pick up the four clingfilmed-within-an-inch-of-their-life bread rolls, which are sitting alongside an apple and – completely inexplicably – a hard-boiled egg. What time was Mum up – 1950? All Chloe needs now is a bottle of ginger beer. I peer at the contents of the rolls, which, I can just make out, appear to be cheese. 'Wonderful,' I sigh, and hasten over to put Theo in his bouncer.

'What's wrong?' says Chloe suspiciously. 'Why did you say "wonderful" like that?'

'Because Granny Sue's done you cheese rolls,' I say, quickly grabbing the bread and reaching into the fridge to pull out mayonnaise and cucumber.

'But I don't like cheese in sandwiches,' Chloe says worriedly. 'I have a Babybel in the pink box *next* to my sandwiches. Which I want to be tuna.'

'I'm sorting it out now.' I snatch a tin from the cupboard. 'Can you start getting dressed? It's OK, Theo, Mummy's here. I'll just do this and then I'll get you out.'

Chloe frowns. 'What's that noise, Mummy? I can hear knocking.'

'Sally!' bellows Matthew simultaneously, from upstairs. 'Did you hear me? I said there's someone at the front door! I'm still not dressed – can you get it?'

I look down at my purple flowery nightie. Oh sod it, I give up. Who cares any more?

'I'm on it!' I shout back, as I put the tin down and dash out into the hall. Sure enough, someone is waiting on the doorstep. I unlatch the chain and throw it open, to find *Kelly* standing there again. In the twelve hours that have passed since we were last opposite each other like this, she has reverted to full glamour mode. She's heavily made-up, with sunglasses perching perkily on top of bouncy, freshly washed hair. The figure-hugging bright red dress she's teamed with impossibly high shoes looks utterly out of place, given she's also holding a walking stick in one hand, and what looks like a covered casserole dish balanced on her hip with the other.

I fold my arms over my chest self-consciously. Of all the people I'd hate to see me looking like this, she pretty much tops the list. Before I can say anything, however, Chloe appears at my side, clutching her school dress and looking up at Kelly curiously.

'Well, hello!' Kelly widens her eyes dramatically and gives Clo a massively OTT 'I'm talking to a child' smile, before bending down so she can invade her personal space properly. 'I *love* your uniform! Are you getting ready to go? Do you like school?'

Chloe doesn't say anything, just looks at her warily and shrinks back behind my legs.

'Go back into the kitchen, sweetheart, and keep an eye on Theo for me, will you?' I say quietly. 'I'll be right there.'

'Bye Clo-Clo!' Kelly waves cheerily, then, once my daughter has gone, she turns to me.

'What are you doing here again?' I stare at her. 'You need to stop this, Kelly. It's becoming weird.'

She takes a deep breath and forces a smile. 'Oh, have a word with yourself, will you? You know exactly why I came over last night – I was beside myself. But I'm here *now* because I shouldn't have said some of what I did. You're obviously going through a very tough time, and I ought to have been more sympathetic. I know I could have just phoned, but I wanted to come over and apologize in person.'

'You know it's barely half seven in the morning, right?' I say slowly.

'Of course I do,' she snaps defensively, but then seems to catch herself, and smiles again. 'I mean, yes I do, thank you, Sally. I'm filming all day today and I wouldn't have been able to come over at all otherwise, but I really wanted you to see how serious I was about this. Here – I've made you something.' She tries to hold out the casserole dish, but struggles slightly. 'Sorry, can you just take this stick for a second? I get labyrinthitis from time to time – it's an ear and balance thing – and I'm a bit wobbly today.'

I resist the temptation to say perhaps she'd be better off in considerably more sensible shoes, in that case, and reach out to take the stick as she takes the dish in both hands, then holds it out to me too. I stare down at it, then take it, not sure what to say. This is completely bizarre. What is she trying to pull now?

'It's chicken,' she offers, taking back the stick.

'Thanks.'

There's an uncomfortable pause for a moment, and then she says, 'Fine. Well, I'd better go then. Before I do, though, I wanted to say, I didn't steal any money from you. I would never do that. I *did* swap the ring, but I genuinely didn't think I was doing anyone any harm. That certainly wasn't my intention. I just wanted you to know.' She turns and starts to walk back down the drive towards a black car, out of which climbs a be-suited man to open the passenger door for her.

Mum appears alongside me, an apron on and sleeves rolled up. 'Sally, why are you re-making Chloe's lunch? Wait – is that Kelly again?' She looks confused as the car begins to pull away.

'Yes. She's made me a casserole.'

'Well!' Mum says, amazed. 'First coming all that way last night with those lovely gifts to cheer you up, and now this? You see? She *is* trying. I told you.'

'Mum, I just want to get back inside, I'm in my nightie,' I say, noticing Ron staring at me from across the way, while busily vacuuming the inside of his car as if that's a normal thing to be doing at half seven in the morning. 'Hi Ron!' I call tersely, and he half waves back, forced into acknowledging he's looking right at us.

'Well, here then – I'll take that stew.'

'No. You're not touching it. None of you are.' I turn around and head back into the kitchen, yanking the lid off and then stamping my foot down on the pedal of the bin, before turning the whole pot upside down. The contents plop into the bottom of the bin bag like someone being violently sick.

'What on earth are you doing?' Mum says, her mouth falling open.

'I don't want any of you eating that, especially not the kids.'

'Right,' Mum says slowly. 'Is that why you're re-making Chloe's lunch too? Have I done something to upset you as well? I'm so sorry if I have.'

'No, no.' I shake my head, exasperated. 'It's nothing like that. Look, I don't want to go into why I don't trust Kelly. I just want to be careful, that's all.'

'Careful of what, love?'

'Like I said, I'm not going into it now.' I nod down at Chloe, who appears to be playing, but I can see she is listening to every word. 'Mum, I'm not going mad – please don't look at me like that. None of this is a big deal, I promise. Chloe doesn't like cheese, so I'm making her tuna for lunch, and I don't want her eating Kelly's food. That's it. OK?'

'OK,' Mum says, and gives me a big smile. 'That's absolutely fine.'

'Great,' I say flatly. Thanks so much Kelly. Mum now obviously thinks I'm having another 'moment'. 'Come on, Chloe, let's sit up. It's nearly time to go.'

*

At precisely 8.15 a.m., Theo and I, both now dressed, are watching my parents strap Chloe into her car seat when, to my surprise, Caroline's Mercedes pulls around the corner and up onto the drive.

'Morning all.' She smiles, looking immaculate as she climbs out, wearing a sharply tailored blazer over a pair of wide-leg cropped trousers with heeled pumps. She must be stopping off on her way to something work related. 'I'll take Chloe to school if you like, Sue? Save you a trip?'

'No, no, it's fine, thank you, Caroline.' Mum smiles. 'Bob's programmed the satnav now, so it's no bother. We'll stick to the plan, shall we? You go in and have a cup of tea with Sally and Theo.' She motions pointedly at me and widens her eyes in an exaggerated fashion. I wonder if MI5 realize what an asset they missed in my mother? She beams at us again and climbs into the car, firmly shutting the door, before giving a little wave.

'Please tell me they haven't dragged you over here just to sit with me while they take Chloe to school?' I ask, as Caroline arrives alongside Theo and I, and we watch them reverse carefully down the drive, my father's parking sensors dutifully bleeping. 'Even if Matthew wasn't working at home today, I'd be perfectly safe.'

'Oh, look at that dear little girl. She's so gorgeous.' Caroline sighs as they disappear out of sight, then turns to us. 'And good morning to you too, handsome.' She takes Theo's hand in hers and gives it a gentle shake, before bending slightly to kiss it. 'I'm here because they all want me to persuade you to ring the GP so you can get an appointment today. Matthew in particular is very worried about what your friend Liv told him, and he thinks you need some support as soon as possible.'

I stiffen slightly. 'So he did share my moment of teenage madness with all of you then? I thought he had.'

She gestures helplessly with her arms. 'I don't think he should have done either, Sal. It was private to you, and I said that to him.'

It's my turn to sigh. 'Let's go and make that tea. Does this happen to you every time someone you know on a personal level has a crisis, or a breakdown of some kind? People just expect you to sort everything out because of what you do for a living?'

'Pretty much,' she agrees, as we go back into the house. 'I don't mind, really; it goes with the territory, and I'm careful not to take responsibility for more than I feel comfortable with. It's different with you, anyway. You're my daughter-in-law. Of course I want to help.'

'Not that I've had either a breakdown or a crisis,' I say quickly, putting Theo down on his mat and handing him his singing octopus. 'Although,' I hesitate anxiously, really not wanting to have to confess that I've messed up, 'something slightly unfortunate did happen last night.'

'Oh?' she says, getting two cups out of the cupboard. 'Tea or coffee?'

'Tea, please.' I sit down next to Theo, avoiding having to look her in the eye. 'Kelly came over and I said something stupid to her.'

Caroline has her back to me as she's filling the kettle, and at first I don't think she's heard me. She sets it back down on its base, flicks it on, and slips her jacket off to reveal a crisp navy tunic top, before placing the blazer over the back of one of the kitchen chairs. She looks down at me expectantly.

'So what happened?'

'I saw a picture of Kelly wearing her new engagement ring on the MailOnline, with a report saying it cost seventy thousand pounds. I can't go into details, but my brother confirmed she did something devious on Saturday and, suffice to say, that's where your money has gone.'

Caroline's eyebrows shoot up in surprise. 'You know this for certain?'

'She denied it, of course, but pretty much, yes—'

'You actually confronted her?' Caroline cuts across me.

'I accused her of stealing the money, yes.' I take a deep breath. 'I also told her I knew more about her than she realized.'

There's a pause. 'Ah,' Caroline says, 'I see.'

'I know, I know,' I say miserably. 'I'm so sorry. I don't know what I was thinking. I backtracked very quickly, and neither of us made any direct reference to you at all, but she reacted badly regardless. That was last night, but she was back here at half seven this morning too.'

Caroline says nothing, just waits for me to continue.

'This time she was very apologetic, and brought me a casserole she'd made. It was utterly surreal. Was she like that when you treated her? Completely Jekyll and Hyde? I've not told anyone else about my accusing her of stealing the money, by the way,' I add.

'I think I'd probably keep it that way,' Caroline considers carefully. 'Listen, Sally, while I can see this is all really bothering you – and I promise we'll come back to Kelly – I don't think we should completely lose sight of what else happened this weekend. In fact, what time is it?' She turns and glances at the kitchen clock. 'Coming up to half past eight. That's when your doctor's phone lines open for same-day appointments, I think? As I said, Matthew and your parents are very keen for you to get some support from your GP.'

I don't say anything for a moment, just pull the string on the octopus for Theo again, who grabs it as soon as the music starts to sound. 'And do you agree?'

'I'm not sure that they really understand what is going to happen at that first appointment, let's put it that way,' she says. 'I thought it might be helpful instead if you and I ran through it briefly. Your GP is going to have a ten-minute slot for you and, quite simply, there won't be time to cover any psychological challenges you may or may not be experiencing, once he or she has established you're not actively suicidal – which you're evidentially not. What they *will* do, however, is take your history, examine you, and discuss any physical symptoms you might have had, or have. Now, the thing is,' she takes a deep breath, 'yours is such an *odd* story, it's not going to cleanly fit a diagnosis. At first they're going to wonder if it's amnesia of some kind – but as we've already discussed, amnesia doesn't present like this. So at that point, your GP is going to start wondering if you're telling the truth, or if perhaps there is something else psychological going on.'

I look up at her immediately. This time the pause is much longer, broken only by Theo starting to clatter some stacking cups that he's found. 'We've already been here. I *am* telling the truth, Caroline.'

'OK,' she says slowly, 'then that's going to leave them with no option but to start having to consider some of the much rarer possibilities.'

'I don't understand.' I'm confused. 'Rarer possibilities like what?'

The kettle boils, but she ignores it. 'Mental blackouts or memory loss can have physical causes: like head injuries, underactive thyroids, alcoholism... and brain lesions or tumours.'

'Brain tumours?' I repeat stupidly. Theo, happily waving around the white cup, looks up at me and smiles.

'Yes. They are going to have to consider testing you for all of those things. Are you absolutely sure you want – or need – to put Matthew and your parents through the very real worry of all that?'

'Caroline, I swear to you, I'm telling the truth!' I say urgently. 'I can see you think it's an "odd story", but I promise you, I've not made it up.' I swallow. 'When you say these causes are rare, just how rare are we talking?'

'Very unlikely indeed.' She closes her eyes briefly, and rubs her hand tiredly across her face, as if she's trying to think of another way to approach this. 'It's just that this is going to scare everyone so badly, particularly as most GPs are lamentably inept at handling this sort of thing, and blunder in there with no thought, just announcing they're sending you for CT scans without so much as a by-your-leave. Then there will be the agonizing wait for the results, only for them to come back negative, and—'

'But what if they don't come back negative?' I whisper. I can feel my pulse starting to flutter faster with fear.

Caroline stops short suddenly. 'You haven't *already* been diagnosed with something and you just haven't said anything to anyone, have you?'

'No!' I say, now completely bewildered. 'Of course not!'

'Well, then, they will come back negative, Sal, *because they are all really rare.* That's entirely my point.' Then she adds gently, 'Are you quite, quite sure that you don't remember a single thing between going to bed on Friday night and waking up on Saturday morning in Cornwall? Literally nothing?'

'Yes, I'm sure, Caroline.'

My tone must be terse, because she adds quickly, 'I'm not saying you know what happened, or you're trying to be dishonest about it, Sally. I'm really not. I'm simply asking you if you remember anything. I am making no judgement whatsoever, so please don't be alarmed. You're quite safe and everything is OK.'

I look down at the floor, starting to feel sick. Why is she talking to me like that? As if I'm a patient? 'Well, then, in answer to your question, no, I don't remember anything at all,' I repeat for the hundredth time, as calmly as I can, before reaching for Theo and getting to my feet shakily. 'Could you hold him for a minute? I just need a moment.' I take a couple of steps over to the table and hold him out to her.

'Of course,' she says, concerned, taking him. 'Where are you going?'

'Only to the downstairs loo,' I say. 'That's all.'

'You're sure you're OK?'

'I'm fine,' I lie. 'I'll literally be five minutes.'

Closing the door behind me, I sit down on the loo lid and, pulling out my phone, I type *brain lesions and tumours*.

> **Brain lesions (lesions** on the **brain)** refers to any type of abnormal tissue in or on the **brain**

reads the first article, running alongside a deeply incongruous sidebar advert for 'the perfect floral skirt'.

> Major types of **brain lesions** are: traumatic, infectious, malignant, benign, vascular, genetic, immune, plaques, **brain** cell death or malfunction, and ionizing radiation.

Well, that all sounds really shit.

I swallow anxiously, and read on.

> **Q:** What are the symptoms of a **brain lesion?**
> **A:** Headaches, vomiting, vision changes, changes in mood, behaviour and concentration, memory loss or confusion.

Jesus Christ. So, pretty much exactly how I felt when I woke up in that taxi. I try to stay calm. What did Caroline say the other physical causes of memory loss were? I pull up the main NHS site.

> Memory loss can be a sign of something serious and should be checked by a GP, but if you're reading this because you're

> worried you have dementia, rest assured you probably
> haven't. A person with dementia won't have an awareness of
> their memory loss.

Didn't I already read this last night? I frown. I'm sure I did… *I can't remember.* Matthew would think that was me trying to be funny, but I'm not laughing.

> Common causes are head injuries or a stroke. Less common
> are an underactive thyroid gland, alcohol misuse, bleeding in
> the brain, transient global amnesia (problems with blood
> flow to the brain, which causes episodic memory loss) or
> brain tumours.

Tumours again. Theo begins to cry in the kitchen, but I stare at the words on the screen, finding myself unable to move. I can't have a tumour. I just can't. Theo's crying becomes louder. I get to my feet automatically and unlock the door.

My baby is rubbing his eyes crossly when I reappear in the room, and as he sees me, he begins to whimper again and holds out his arms to be taken.

'Tired already, I'm afraid,' Caroline says. 'I'll put him down for you, if you like?'

'It's OK, I'll do it.' I reach out for him, desperate suddenly to hold his reassuringly solid and wriggly little body. 'But I just need to make that appointment first.' I feel awkwardly in my jeans pocket for my phone, balancing Theo on my hip, and start to search for the number of the surgery in my contacts list.

Caroline says nothing, just gets up and begins to pour water from the kettle into the two mugs.

I have to hit call-back several times, but I get through eventually and arrange an emergency same-day appointment for 2 o'clock.

I'm just hanging up when Matthew walks into the kitchen holding an empty mug.

'Oh, hi Mum.' He feigns surprise at the sight of Caroline. 'I didn't know we were seeing you today.'

'Sally's just made the doctor's appointment,' Caroline says quietly, making no effort to play along with the pretence. 'It's at 2 p.m., right, Sal?'

I nod, and Matthew blushes guiltily. 'OK, well – that's good. I can drive you, if you like? I'll get back to work now, then, if I'm going to take some time off this afternoon. See you both later.' He vanishes, clearly embarrassed. Or at least he seems to be. I barely notice.

I'm remembering how it felt to be age twelve, not *that* much older than Chloe, scared and sitting in the hospital corridor with Mum, watching Will playing with one of his *Star Wars* figures, when a doctor emerged from a room to our right and said solemnly to Mum – who had gripped my hand – 'Mrs Tanner, I'm afraid your husband has had a heart attack.'

I hold Theo tightly to me, that image now being plastered over with the words *brain tumour, brain tumour, brain tumour, brain tumour...* I try to blank my mind and push the thought away – only for it to begin to play on an increasingly loud loop instead, deep inside my head.

CHAPTER ELEVEN

In the car on the way to the doctor, both Matthew and I are quiet as he drives. Thank God he isn't able to read my mind. He'd crash immediately.

I cannot believe Caroline asked me if I've *already* been diagnosed with something. She obviously believes it could be an explanation for what happened on Friday.

So she thinks I went to kill myself to spare everyone the pain of losing me slowly to a serious illness or life-threatening condition?

Well, first off, if I'd been told I had something like that, I'd have definitely told Matthew. I'd also cling to any chance at all to stay with Chloe and Theo, for as long as I possibly could. What parent wouldn't? I'd want to help prepare them for losing me, particularly Chloe, so that she felt safe about it, and understood what was happening. I'd want to explain that I was going to heaven, but that it was a very long way away and I wouldn't be coming back. That no one really knows what heaven is like, and we only go there once we die, because sometimes – not often – people get ill and the doctors can't make them better. I'd want her to have a chance to say goodbye.

My eyes fill with tears, and I have to turn to look out of the window so Matthew can't see. Until this morning, it hadn't occurred to me that there might be something physically wrong with me. I try to swallow down my distress and stay calm. I know Caroline says it's all very rare, but rare isn't impossible, and suppose— Jesus! Another horrific thought slips into my mind, unbidden – suppose I *have* already been diagnosed with something like a brain tumour, *only I can't remember it*? No, that really is lunacy – and surely that's not even possible? Who could forget something as hideous as that? And it's not as if I've experienced any other memory loss – it's just those ten missing hours on Friday night. I take a deep breath. I have to try to relax. The GP will know. I'd have gone to him or her in the first place with any worrying symptoms... And as Caroline pointed out, they'd have referred me onto a specialist. There would have been tests and scans, which in turn would have been documented. I can ask to see my medical records when we get there, and make sure for myself.

I close my eyes for a moment, and lean back on the seat, suddenly completely overwhelmed. Everything is jostling for space in my mind: memory disorders, tumours, Kelly, missing money, Matthew crying, Liv, bottles of paracetamol, suicide notes, taxis, Chloe looking up at me with those big blue eyes, saying, 'You weren't there when I woke up, Mummy'. It's all a tangled, frighteningly confused knot, which feels like it's getting bigger and bigger.

'You realize this is the first time we've been out on our own since before Theo was born?' Matthew's voice cuts through the confusion, then he adds carefully, 'When everything has calmed down a bit, I'd really like to take you somewhere. At least we know Theo *can* go to sleep for other people now. We could go for dinner or something.'

'That would be nice.'

He glances across at me. 'How are you feeling about this?'

'What, the doctor's appointment?' I look out of the window. 'Um, pretty scared.'

He frowns, hesitates, then reaches out and takes my hand in his. 'I'll be there, and I'm not going to let anything happen to you. This is about you being supported, not caught out. She can't just make an arbitrary decision about your future, Sal – you do know that, don't you?'

He thinks I'm scared of being sectioned again. I can see Caroline's right – Matthew very clearly has no idea of what's actually to come. I don't correct him, but think instead about the first time he took my hand like this – eight years ago now – and how desperate I was for him to touch me.

I'd attended several work meetings with Matt Le Bonk (slightly unoriginal moniker, given we were an ad firm), after all of which I told myself – and several trusted colleagues – that it was totally inappropriate to have personal relationships with clients... But oh my *God*, he looked good in a suit. In spite of everything, I smile briefly at the memory of me trying to concentrate on discussing tedious campaign details in various dull boardrooms, Matthew nodding with careful consideration and taking copious notes. Both of us, as it turned out, trying not to imagine ourselves in bed with the other.

'What's funny?' Matthew asks, putting the indicator on and turning left onto the street where the surgery is.

'Hmmm?' I look across and almost tell him, but oddly, I feel shy and awkward. We're so out of practice at this. 'Oh, nothing.'

I turn back to the window again, picturing the client launch event on a preposterously glamorous hotel rooftop overlooking London, where everything changed. The evening was a huge success. We had a little too much to drink, which led to... walking through Hyde Park, him taking my hand, then us kissing. Dinner out. A cinema date. Dinner at mine. Dinner at his. Sex. Sex. Sex – several weekends spent almost completely in bed. Introducing him to my friends. Introducing him as my boyfriend. A first weekend away, learning to surf in Cornwall – me trying to prove I could be sporty and outdoorsy. A luxury weekend in Paris – me giving up on the pretence and admitting I preferred galleries and cocktails. Meeting families. Disastrous weekend in Scotland. First huge row. Beach holidays. Skiing holidays. Moving in together. Promotions. Buying the flat. Buying furniture. Proposal in Cornwall at the hotel where we had the first weekend away. Wedding venues. Wedding dress. Wedding food. Wedding, everything all about the bloody wedding. Sick of wedding. Never want to see another invitation or band playlist ever again. Hen weekend. Lovely, incredibly fast wedding; immediately want to repeat it. Honeymoon spent mostly asleep and dimly aware of probably never looking that good in a bikini again. Pregnancy test. Panic-buying whole of John Lewis baby department. Exhaustedly and bewilderingly watching Matthew hold Chloe for the first time. Lots of daytime property shows. Routinely arriving for the last ten minutes of numerous expensive baby classes. Holiday in Cornwall, returning after two days with ill baby. Mind-numbing toddler groups. Return to work. Crying a lot: miss Chloe horribly, tired, guilty, doing five days' work in three. Start to go out a bit more in evenings. Attempt to get back into gym routine. First hot holiday. Fall pregnant. Look enormous very quickly. Realize will never wear bikini ever again, full stop. Sell flat. Buy house. Pack. Unpack. Get crib out of new loft. Smugly wash saved baby clothes, as convinced new baby is a girl. Shock as midwife holding my hand the right side of the screen tells me I have a boy. Watching Matthew finally introduce a shy Chloe to a tiny Theo lying in a plastic cot, while thinking I have never felt so lucky and happy.

OK, maybe a lifetime already spent together, but it's not enough.

Matthew takes his hand away to change gear, and I place mine back in my lap. We haven't even had a chance to get over Theo's birth yet. I know who we were, and how we got here, but I don't recognize what we've become. We need time to find ourselves again and learn how it all fits into life's new shape... or what I thought was life's new shape. I close my eyes briefly. I can't be seriously ill. I just can't. Theo and Chloe can't afford for me to let them down. There's no other option. This has to be OK.

'Here we are.' Matthew jolts me back as we pull into the surgery car park and, miraculously, straight into a space. I try to steady myself as he switches off the engine and turns to me. 'I'd like to come in with you, if that's all right? Unless there's stuff you want to tell the doctor that you'd rather not say in front of me? You know, your night at university, that sort of thing?'

I hesitate. Should I tell him he has to wait outside and protect him from everything until I know for sure what diagnosis I'm dealing with? But he already looks so worried, it's not fair to keep him completely in the dark, even if I'm trying to do it to be kind.

'It's OK to come in,' I say. If the shoe were on the other foot, I'd want to be told immediately, even if there was a chance he might be seriously ill. This is something we ought to face together. 'But can we just talk about what they might be going to tell us quickly?'

He looks at his watch. 'I don't want us to be late.'

'Matthew, no doctor ever runs on time.'

'Well, it'll be sod's law they do today if we're sitting out here. Come on, you can talk to me once we're in there.' He climbs out and closes the door firmly.

We're in the waiting room, listening to several old people with hacking coughs, and watching a three-year-old happily empty several holders of leaflets about giving up smoking and signs of strokes, when he turns to me and says, 'So what did you want to say about this?'

I shake my head. 'It's OK. Don't worry.' I can hardly talk to him about it now, and in any case, I'm actually starting to feel very nervous indeed.

Matthew takes my hand again and squeezes it. 'This is going to be OK, Sal,' he whispers, then leans over and drops a kiss on my forehead. 'Try and relax. You're allowed to feel anxious, but everything is going to be all right, I promise you.'

Oh, Matthew – please God you're right. I try to take my mind elsewhere. 'I hope Mum's going to be OK with getting Theo down for his afternoon nap.'

'She'll be fine. He actually slept better over the weekend, didn't he?'

'Yes,' I admit. 'Which I have to say I think is grossly unfair of him.'

Matthew snorts gently. 'Yeah, it was. But *I* know how bloody hard you've worked all this time, Sal. I'm so annoyed with myself that I didn't step in and try to break the cycle of him needing you to get back to sleep sooner, though. I should have done. I'm sorry.'

'Well, you say that, but we were only a month away from properly sleep-training him. We would have got there if... events hadn't overtaken us.'

'You think?' he says, after a pause.

'Of course! Things weren't *that* bad. In any case, he was up to his old tricks again last night. I had to get up with him at—' But my words die on my lips as a buzzer goes, and over the head of the receptionist, a sign flashes up: Appt Sally Hilman. Dr A Sawyer, room E.

I inhale sharply. 'That's us.'

Matthew gives me a look of concern. 'Sally, this is going to be fine. I'm not going to let anything happen to you.'

As we walk into the small room together, having knocked politely, a woman about the same age as me turns and gives us a friendly smile. 'Hello. I'm Dr Sawyer.'

'I'm Sally Hilman and this is my husband Matthew. I'd like him to stay, if that's all right?'

'Of course!' She stands up and pulls over another chair. 'Please, do sit down, both of you... So, Sally,' she turns to me. 'I've actually received your discharge information from the Crisis team since your call this morning. You've had a rough couple of days?' She looks at me sympathetically.

'Not my best, no.' I try to smile.

'How are you feeling now?'

'Er, pretty frightened, to be honest.'

Matthew takes my hand.

'What's particularly bothering you?' Dr Sawyer asks calmly.

I try to clear my throat. 'I don't know how much the Crisis team have told you, but I went to bed on Friday night as normal and woke up in the back of a taxi on Saturday morning three hundred miles away on a clifftop. The hours in between seem to have just vanished. I've had a complete mental blackout. Nothing like this has ever happened to me before. At first, for a number of reasons, everyone was concerned that I was attempting to commit suicide, but I'm convinced that's not the case. I am obviously very concerned about why I can't remember what happened to me, however. I was sick on the Saturday morning when I woke up in the taxi, and my vision was blurred. I also had a very bad headache. I've been excessively tired recently, and I also think it's fair to say I've been quite irritable and short-tempered.' I pause, take a deep breath, and squeeze Matthew's hand tightly to brace him. 'I'm aware all of that could be symptomatic of a physical condition like a brain tumour.'

Matthew, who up until now has been listening carefully while focusing on a spot on the floor, immediately jerks his head up and looks at me in shock. Oh God, I *should* have made him wait and discuss this in the car with me first. I can see exactly why Caroline was worried now.

'In fact, there's something else I just need to clarify, if I may?' I ask quickly. 'There isn't anything in my medical records at the moment to indicate I've *already* been diagnosed with something, is there?'

Dr Sawyer blinks in surprise, then turns to her screen and scans it. 'No, there's nothing here at all. You can read for yourself, if you like. The last record I have for you is for a post-natal check-up back in January?'

I glance at Matthew, to make sure that's sunk in. 'I only ask because on Saturday, I had what appeared to be a suicide note in my pocket – it wasn't, I hasten to add – and my mother-in-law told me she was worried I might have already been diagnosed with a terminal illness; presumably because that's about the only circumstance under which she can imagine I might have considered suicide. An attempt on my part to spare everyone a lot of suffering, I suppose.'

'*What?*' Matthew exclaims, completely horrified. His hand has gone limp in mine.

'Sorry, sweetheart, just a second.' I turn to him beseechingly, then back to Dr Sawyer. 'I really want all of us to be very clear that's not the case. You have no record of my being tested for anything so far?'

'None at all. But you *do* have symptoms now?' Dr Sawyer prompts. 'Have you still got this headache?'

'No.'

'You haven't been waking each day with a headache or pain?'

'No.'

'And when you did have it, was it worse when you coughed or sneezed?'

'Not so I noticed.'

'You were also sick on Saturday morning too, and had visual problems?'

'Yes,' I confess. 'My sight was blurry when I first woke up, shortly before I vomited. The pain in my head was pretty excruciating, like the worst hangover I've ever had.'

'OK, Sally.' She looks at me reflectively for a moment. 'Well, we'll take a look at you now, and I think we'll also run some blood tests. I'll see if we can get one of the nurses to do that while you're here so you don't have to come back again later. I'm also happy to refer you for a CT scan too. Then what I'd like to do is book you in for another appointment for the end of this week, so we can run through everything in more detail then.'

'Sorry, what are the blood tests and CT scan for?' Matthew interrupts.

'We'll do a full blood count, renal function, liver function, bone profile, and thyroid function, to make sure that there isn't a reason like high calcium, an infection, or an underactive thyroid behind Sally's symptoms. The CT is to make sure there isn't any kind of condition affecting the brain,' Dr Sawyer says. 'These unusual things can present sometimes, and it's important that we rule them out, but I would stress that they are rare.'

'You don't think this sounds like amnesia of any kind, though, do you?' I say.

'No, I don't. Transient global amnesia doesn't present like the episode you've described. Are you on any other medication at the moment, Sally?'

I shake my head. 'I had a glass or two of champagne on the Friday night, and I've not been drinking alcohol at all recently, but that wouldn't account for blacking out like that, surely? My mother-in-law did offer me a sleeping pill, but – no, wait.' I stop suddenly. 'That was last night, anyway. Sorry. I'm getting confused – like I said, I'm very tired—'

'Whoa, sorry. Can we just stop here for a minute?' Matthew cuts in, looking very frightened indeed. 'Sally, you don't have a brain tumour. That's not possible.'

This is dreadful, but I had no choice but to be honest with the GP about everything. It's too important. I squeeze his hand again. 'Even if I do have something, we'll deal with it, OK?'

'No, no, no.' He shakes his head vehemently. 'This isn't... right. What I mean is,' he turns to Dr Sawyer, 'we've been under massive stress recently. Sally's been amazing, but life has been extremely challenging for her. She had a very traumatic birth with our son six months ago. She had to have an emergency section, and our son needed to be resuscitated immediately after delivery. They put an airway into him –' to my horror, Matthew's voice wobbles suddenly and his eyes fill with tears – 'and took him straight down to the special care unit. He was there for a couple of days and it made things like feeding him very challenging for Sally. Sorry.' He swallows and tries to gather himself.

I had no idea he had been so affected by what happened – or is he actually upset about what he thinks I was trying to do on Friday night? Because I'm not sure, and don't want to say the wrong thing, I end up saying nothing at all.

'I mean, he's fine now, and Sally is too, although she picked up an infection. It was just a very, very scary time. We've found it quite hard to get back to normal since then. Particularly as our son doesn't really sleep. Sally's been dealing with the nights completely on her own so I can hold down my job, but over the last few days she's been – very understandably – vocalizing to our family and friends that she can't cope any more, telling them that she hates her life – that kind of thing. But on top of all of that, after what happened on Friday, her friend told me that Sally has in fact tried to commit suicide before. I'm now really desperate that Sally gets some support with this, if it's some sort of post-natal depression, because I don't want whatever happened on Friday to have been the start of something; some sort of trigger. I'm saying all of this really badly, but this isn't a brain tumour.' He looks at me pleadingly. 'It just isn't,' he whispers.

I turn back to the doctor. 'Is it possible that if I did have a brain tumour I might have behaved in an extreme way that I now can't remember? Like taking myself off to the other end of the country in the night?'

'Yes, it's possible.'

I hesitate. 'Can tumours also alter your behaviour? Make you irrational, or paranoid?'

'People with tumours may experience negative changes to their personality, yes.'

'Would I be aware that I was behaving like this?'

'Well,' she says carefully, 'someone might not realize that their behaviour has changed, or become problematic, no. Let's wait and see what the results of the tests are before we jump to any conclusions, though, shall we?'

Back in the car, we've been driving to collect Chloe from school in silence for about five minutes, when I finally clear my throat.

'Matthew?' I say tentatively.

He jumps slightly, and turns his head worriedly to me. 'Yes?'

'I'm so sorry you had to see all of that happen to Theo when he was born.'

He doesn't say anything, but I watch his fingers grip the steering wheel a little more tightly.

'It must have been horrific for you.'

'I thought I was going to lose you both,' he says simply. 'You were on the table and they were stitching you up while they were trying to get Theo to breathe—'

'You saw that too? Them working on me?' I'm appalled.

'I saw some of it, yeah,' he says flatly. 'It was a much smaller screen than when Chloe was born, which I wasn't expecting.' He exhales. 'And then when it all started to go wrong...'

I wait for him to continue.

'I felt so helpless. Two of them were sewing you up, the other lot were putting the mask over Theo, and then when that didn't work and they put the tube down him...' He shakes his head. 'He was so fucking tiny, Sal.'

'I'm so, so sorry, Matthew. You should have told me.'

'Of course I shouldn't!' he exclaims. 'I wasn't the one it actually happened to, was I? You had enough to deal with.'

'Do you think about it still now?'

He doesn't look at me. 'Yes. I tend to get flashes of it when I'm not expecting it.' He clears his throat. 'I've dealt with it all quite badly, I think.'

I simply had no idea at all about this. And I've just taken him to an appointment where he's been hijacked with the news that there might be something else new and seriously wrong with me, on top of also thinking I tried to commit suicide two days ago. My poor, poor husband.

'But listen, this isn't about me. I'll sort myself out, and I don't want you to worry, because I can handle it. It was quite a shock to hear *you* come out with all that at the doctors, though.' He stares at the road ahead. 'You mentioned Mum had some concerns? Did she discuss them with you?'

'Yes, she did, but I'm glad. She was worried that my not telling the truth, and insisting I can't remember what happened, was going to lead Dr Sawyer down a path that would unnecessarily frighten everyone. The thing is, I *am* telling the truth, and while it obviously *has* scared you, and I'm very sorry for that, I honestly have no memory of Friday night at all – and until your mum brought it up, I didn't even know my not remembering what happened might be caused by something being physically wrong with me. So I'm actually very grateful to her. I didn't want to have to tell the doctor everything, but what choice did I have? It would be completely irresponsible of me to have some symptoms and *not* get checked out as soon as possible, wouldn't it? For Chloe and Theo's sake.'

His jaw tenses and he doesn't say anything for a moment, but then suddenly bursts, 'Actually, I'm just amazed all that doctor gave you was that patient health questionnaire to take back next time.' He nods tersely at the piece of paper I'm holding in my lap. 'Tell me what question nine says again? In the last two weeks have you—'

'—had thoughts that you would be better off dead, or of hurting yourself in some way,' I read.

'Jesus Christ!' He shakes his head crossly. 'I mean, forget everything else fundamentally – that doctor had, seated in front of her, a woman with a baby who's had a tough time recently, has told everyone she can't cope, and it turns out in the past she took a paracetamol overdose! What the hell point is there in that fucking questionnaire?'

I look at him carefully, but stay quiet. He's really frightened. That's what this outburst is about.

'I'm sorry,' he says a moment later. 'It's just... the one thing I'm clear about is that I love you more than anything. I just want to keep you and the kids safe, and all of us together.'

'I know,' I manage eventually. 'I love you too.' We pull up outside Chloe's school, and Matthew starts to look for a space along the already crowded roadside.

What on earth will we do if there is something wrong with me? I can sort everything else, but not that. Somehow my own body already feels slightly alien... Although that is completely

164

absurd. I don't know for certain that anything is the matter. I need to hold onto that.

Having found a very tight space, Matthew eventually manages to squeeze into it, and turns the engine off. 'Are you all right? Do you want me to go in and get Clo?'

I nod, not quite trusting myself to speak.

'You don't want to come too? She'd like that – it's not often we get to pick her up together.'

He's right. Chloe will be so delighted to see us both that she'll come running towards us, arms outstretched, shouting, 'Mummy! Daddy!' and I don't know that I'll be able to keep it together. She doesn't need that.

I shake my head, my eyes bright with tears. 'I think I'll just stay here, if that's OK?'

Matthew looks at me and says shortly, 'There's nothing physically wrong with you, Sally. Those tests are going to come back just fine.' He opens the car door. 'I'll leave you the keys, just in case.' He climbs out, and I watch him stride towards the gates and bang in through them.

He gets so angry under pressure. I know that's just how he copes, but I wish he wouldn't. It doesn't make it any the easier; in fact, it just adds to the stress.

It occurs to me suddenly that even if Caroline is wrong and I'm not OK, I'm still won't be able to explain why I put the note in my pocket. Or why I cleared my phone down. But then, I suppose that's the whole point about irrational behaviour – you can't explain it, only what causes it. Far more importantly, suppose I do it again and this time I actually *do* fall. I try to swallow my rising panic. I just can't be ill... I *can't*!

There's a sudden knock at the window and I jolt, to see one of the mums standing alongside the car, holding her daughter's hand, a lunchbox and several bits of paper with drawings on them in the other. I open the door and am immediately assaulted by a heady waft of perfume.

'Hi, Sally.' She smiles with the passive-aggressive steel of someone pissed off at being held up for point five of a second longer than they have to be because of the sheer stupidity of *everybody* else around them. 'Do you think I could ask you to pull back so I can get my car out?' She nods at her massive Lexus. 'It's a bit tight.'

'Sorry, Lydia. Matthew was on a mission,' I apologize, and for reasons best known to myself, opt to slide inelegantly across to the driver's seat rather than getting out and walking around.

I have to arch my bottom up to get over the gear stick, which makes me lose my balance a bit, and, yelping in alarm, I stick my right arm out, which in turn makes the buttons on my already straining shirt ping open over my boobs, revealing my bra. I look up to see the mum and her daughter watching me incredulously, as I perform my bizarre in-car yoga.

Face flaming, I carefully ease our Renault back as they climb into their Lexus, and the mother waves tightly – it's actually closer to a fist-shake than a gesture of thanks. I'm instantly reminded of Kelly as the Lexus roars off, only to have to stop impatiently at the red traffic lights at the top. Everyone is just getting in her way.

I watch them pull away again determinedly and think about Mum telling me I'm wrong about Kelly, she's played no part in this; Caroline telling me this morning to stop concentrating on Kelly; Kelly herself insisting I'm crazy, she's totally innocent... I close my eyes. After this morning at the surgery, surely I should concede I might have been unduly paranoid and obsessive about her?

Except I know Caroline warned me about Kelly – that definitely happened. And Kelly swapped the ring too. It's hardly as if my fears are totally baseless... But then I have to accept it is also possible I had no control over what my body was doing and my mind was thinking on Friday. Maybe the very fact that I'm thinking about it all now is irrational?

I realize suddenly it's not a question of not knowing who to trust around me. What's truly terrifying is now I don't know if I can trust myself.

CHAPTER TWELVE

Chloe chatters away as we drive back, but for once I'm quieter, letting Matthew field. I open the window as we head down one of the more open stretches of road and feel the cool air chill my skin, closing my eyes and letting the sound of Chloe and Matthew's voices wash over me. My head is spinning with questions and fears that I have no answers for. I can't make sense of anything. I feel as if I'm trying to grasp at the finest of silvery threads, but they disappear like smoke as my fingers curl around them. All I am able to hold onto for certain is that I would not ever knowingly hurt myself. But it feels nowhere near enough to anchor myself to.

'Sal?' Matthew taps me. 'Chloe's cold.'

'Oh, sweetheart, I'm so sorry.' I lean forward instantly and do the window up again. 'Is that better, are you OK?' I spin around to look at her fretfully.

'Hey, it's OK. She's fine, aren't you, Clo?'

Our daughter nods, busily watching videos on my phone of herself when she was about two. Matthew reaches out and takes my hand in his, holding it gently, until he has to change gear and is forced to let me go again.

We eventually pull up on the drive, and I reluctantly undo my seatbelt as Matthew switches the engine off. Mum is going to have twenty questions for me, and she's going to be scared out of her mind when I tell her I've got to go for a CT scan… But as we approach the front door, there are more immediate problems to hand. I can hear Theo crying before we've even managed to make it into the house.

'What on earth?' Matthew says in alarm, and fumbles with the key in the lock in his haste, before the door swings open to reveal my poor mother, desperately rocking and shushing an absolutely scarlet and completely wet-faced Theo, alongside an equally harassed-looking Caroline, who is helplessly watching on. Both women's relief to see us is palpable. Theo has clearly been crying for some time.

'Hey!' I exclaim, and hurry over, gathering my little boy into my arms. His sobs immediately begin to subside and I feel him start to relax. 'What's wrong?'

'I have absolutely no idea,' Mum says. 'He was fine, we were having a lovely time. I read him some stories and put him down for a nap, and that's when it all started. He was crying and couldn't settle, so I went in, picked him up – and then he just wouldn't stop.'

'There, there.' I rub Theo's back. 'There weren't any sudden noises? No one else has been here? It's just been the three of you in the house?'

'Oh, for God's sake, Sally!' Mum explodes suddenly. 'Please don't start all that again! My nerves won't take it. *Of course* no one else has been in the house!'

I stare at her in surprise. 'I just meant he didn't hear a strange voice, or someone delivering something that might have freaked him out? He's not normally like this.' I inspect Theo with concern. 'Hey, hey! It's all right, I'm here.'

Chloe looks on in interest, kicking off her school shoes, before coming over to Theo and stroking his foot, crooning helpfully, 'Oh, poor baby boy!' as she's heard me say before. 'He just wanted Mummy,' she says simply, and then wanders off into the sitting room.

'I think that's about the size of it, to be honest,' Caroline admits. 'He honestly wasn't at it for more than twenty minutes, though, just to reassure you. Although it felt a hell of a lot longer than that, didn't it, Sue?'

'Yes,' says Mum, 'it did.'

'Your mother has done sterling work. I think I'll go and put the kettle on, shall I?'

She escapes off to the kitchen, and Mum turns to me. 'I'm sorry. I didn't mean to get all snippy. Do you mind if I just go and have a sit down in the other room for a moment?'

'Of course not. I might see if I can get Theo to nap now, even if it's just for ten minutes. Maybe he's just overtired. I assume he's not actually slept at all?'

'You assume correctly.' Mum looks at Theo in amazement. 'My goodness, young man. You've aged me at least ten years today...' She pats me feebly. 'You have the patience of a saint, Sally.'

'Hey, Clo, let's go and put a film on for Granny Sue and you can all have a little rest,' Matthew says. 'Do you want a tea too?' He looks at me.

I shake my head. 'Thanks, but I'm not sure how long I'll be upstairs for.'

I check Theo's room thoroughly once I get up there, but I can't see anything out of the ordinary, and he's so completely worn out by his exertions, that after less than five minutes, I'm creeping back down. I stick my head around the sitting-room door to see Chloe happily snuggled up in the crook of my dad's arm, both of them intently watching the *Tinker Bell* movie, and Mum with her eyes closed, leaning back in the armchair. I watch them all for a moment, snapshotting the scene in my mind, before withdrawing quietly and tiptoeing off to the kitchen to say I will have a cup of tea after all, only to find the door slightly ajar. I'm about to push it open when I realize Matthew and Caroline are in there having a row. They are conducting the whole thing in whispers, but it's a row nonetheless – about me.

'I don't care! You shouldn't have said anything to her at all!' Matthew is hissing. 'She was terrified, talking about brain tumours and asking to look at her medical notes. The GP actually said that she was "happy" to send her for a CT scan, like she was placating her or something.'

'But darling, I went out of my way to explain to Sally that it *won't* be anything like that, and if—'

'My point is,' Matthew interrupts, 'it completely detracted from the very real mental support she needs right now. I know you've been helping her, and she trusts you, but there ought to be someone outside the family she can talk to.'

'Oh Matthew, come on!' Caroline says. 'Don't be so absurd. She was nineteen, for God's sake! She doesn't need help.'

I feel a rush of gratitude as Caroline takes my corner.

'Yes, she does,' insists Matthew doggedly.

'You know that's not true, Matthew.'

There's a long pause, and I wait, hardly daring to breathe.

'She also said you asked her if she'd already been diagnosed with something – and if *that's* why she went to Cornwall,' Matthew persists. 'Was that really necessary?'

'What's far more pertinent is her continued insistence that she can't remember a thing about Friday, from when she went to bed, until she woke up again in the taxi. Don't you think?' There is a long pause. 'She and I talked about it again this morning.'

Matthew sighs. 'She said the same thing in the car on the way home too – and that she felt she had no choice but to tell the doctor the truth.' There is another long silence. 'I'm still terrified that at any moment she could—'

But I don't get to hear the end of that sentence, because a small but piercing voice suddenly says, 'Mummy?' right behind me, making me leap into the air. I spin around to see Chloe standing there, clutching one of her plastic beakers. 'Is this old water or new?' she asks, holding it aloft.

'Old. I'll get you some more.' I take the cup from her and walk into the kitchen.

'So the funds should be cleared in an hour or so—' Caroline looks up easily. 'Oh, hi Sal, I was just saying to Matthew, I've paid the sixty-five thousand into your account.'

Well, you weren't saying that at all, were you? I don't challenge either of them, though. Instead I look her in the eye and say sincerely, 'Thank you.'

She looks surprised. 'You don't have to thank me. I borrowed it – it's only right I pay it back.'

I wasn't talking about the money, although I'm still incredulous that she can just walk away from such a vast sum. Kelly *must* have some sort of hold over her – something I'm unaware of. It's got to be why Caroline isn't calling the police. I know that she said she doesn't want to involve them because it will mean me being dragged into everything, which is very kind of her – but who really does that if sixty-five grand is at stake, and it's not as if I've done anything wrong, so why should I worry about the police investigating what's happened? And given Caroline doesn't think I'm ill, she can't be worried about that being a factor either.

Although now, I don't really feel as if I have the capacity to care about the cash any more. In comparison to what might actually be at the root of everything that's happened, the missing sixty-five grand oddly doesn't seem so important after all. I'd exchange millions for a guarantee that I'm not, in fact, ill.

'So everything's sorted,' Caroline says firmly. 'It's as if none of it ever happened.'

Once the children have been fed, bathed and wrestled into bed, I come down from sorting Theo, prepared to face a barrage of questions from Mum about the visit to the doctor – only to find there is already a serious four-way conversation happening in the sitting room, about the 'practical arrangements' going forward.

'I'm very worried about how Sally's going to cope on her own, especially as she needs to be conserving all of her physical energy,' Mum is saying as I appear in the doorway. I'm not sure she's realized I'm actually back in the room. 'The trouble is, we've been away from the shop for three days now, and it can't stay closed indefinitely. I feel dreadful about this, but we need to go home no later than tomorrow, really. The best thing, I think, is if Sally and the children come home with us until the test results come back.'

'Mum, I'm right here,' I say. 'I can hear you.'

'Bob – do you think you could manage the shop on your own until the end of the week if I do opening and cashing up with you?' She ignores me and looks at Dad anxiously. 'That way, I can properly look after her.'

'Hang on a minute!' I interject again. 'Chloe's got school, Mum. We can't just up-sticks and—'

'She's got *pre*-school.' Mum turns to me. 'A few days off won't hurt her. It will do her good, another little break by the sea. You know she loves it up there, staying in Will's old room. You can have your bedroom back too, and we'll put Theo in the spare room, so everyone's got their own space. I think it could be a real tonic for you, to come home and rest. You could see some of your old school friends!'

'Mum, I haven't seen most of them for about twenty years.'

'I agree that Sally needs some extra support at the moment...' Matthew begins carefully.

173

I look across at him tiredly. Yes, I know you do. I heard what you were about to say to Caroline earlier – you're terrified I'm going to have another flip-out and disappear off again to do God knows what at any moment.

'Good,' Mum cuts across Matthew. 'Well, then could you drive them all up after work tomorrow? I know it's a big ask, but—'

'I was going to say I think it might be better if she and the kids stay here,' Matthew continues. 'If they—'

'What do *you* want to do, Sally?' Caroline turns to me suddenly. 'We'll do whatever you feel most comfortable with.'

'I think I'd like to be here for when the blood test results come back from the GP at the end of the week,' I say gratefully. 'And I've got the CT scan on Monday afternoon in any case.' I imagine myself having to deliver bad news to Matthew down the phone, some two hundred miles away from him in Dorset.

'You know you're going to be just fine, though, don't you?' He looks me squarely in the eye, as if he's reading my mind.

'We could have you back in time for the appointment on Monday,' Mum says. 'Of course I don't want you to miss *that*.'

'I'd be happy to move in here for a few days, if that helps?' Caroline offers.

'It *would* be good to keep the kids' routines going as normal, if we could,' Matthew says quickly. 'You're sure you don't mind, Mum?'

My mother frowns, and opens her mouth to disagree, but thank God, I'm saved from having to wade in between them by my mobile vibrating in my back pocket. Pulling it out, I see it's a text from Liv.

'I'm just going to look at this.' I step over to the window and turn my back on all of them.

Couldn't not make sure you're all right. You must be devastated. Didn't she know there was someone watching? Stupid cow.

I frown and text back straight away.

Did who know what? Don't know what you mean?

OMG. You haven't seen it?

Underneath is a link, which I click on.

It takes me straight through to the MailOnline, and a thumb-nail picture of Kelly, immaculate in her red dress and heels, ear-nestly holding out the casserole dish to *me*, dressed in my revolting purple maternity nightie, also apparently leaning on a walking stick, hair all over the place and not wearing a scrap of make-up. I look beyond mental.

Caring Kelly offers some hands-on support, days after romantic engagement... reads the strapline beside it.

I gasp aloud, and blood starts to crash in my ears. I scroll down and there's another, larger image. My buttons are half undone, exposing my bra... Oh dear God, you can also see the line of my granny knickers under the nightie, the huge ones that I bought so I wouldn't rub my C-section scar straight after Theo was born, but that I've carried on wearing out of habit and because they're actually really comfortable.

'What's wrong?' Matthew says immediately, looking up. He gets to his feet as I hold out my phone, my hands shaking.

He looks at the picture and his mouth falls open. 'Shit!' he says, appalled, and then passes the phone straight to his mother before turning to me and putting steadying hands on my arms. 'Look at me,' he says. 'It's just a picture, not a good one, but just a picture. It doesn't mean anything.'

'Oh, Sally!' I hear Caroline exclaim behind me. 'This is outra-geous!'

'Everyone I know is going to see this.' I swallow, as my husband looks back at me. 'All of our friends, people I was at school with, everyone from work, my clients, the mums from Chloe's school... Everyone, Matthew!' My voice begins to waver as hot tears of humiliation flood my eyes. I feel as if I'm in the dream where you're on the loo in a crowded place and everyone's pointing and laughing at you – only this is actually happening. 'I can't believe this. Can I see it again, please?'

My mum is now holding the phone, and she looks across worriedly at my father.

'Mum, *please*!' I beg. 'Can you just give it back to me?'

She gets stiffly to her feet and hands me the phone. I quickly start to scan the text underneath the image.

Former *EastEnders* star Kelly Harrington took a break from her more glamorous day job to give a little something back when she visited a local charity, based near the London home she shares with her new fiancé, TV executive Will Tanner. Down-to-earth Kelly proved she's a hit in the kitchen as well as on screen, taking with her some home cooking for the residents to enjoy.

'It's very important to me that the mental health services in this country, who are facing cuts to their services like never before, are given the support they need to continue the vital work they are doing,' said Harrington. 'Mental health issues are nothing to be ashamed of, and sufferers need our help and understanding.'

Mental health issues?

RESIDENTS?

In perplexity, I scan through the other four pictures of Kelly and me that run under the piece. In all of them I'm holding the walking stick – like I'm completely infirm – and appear confused; as, frankly, I was, given it was barely 7 a.m. I put one hand on my head in shock, and just hold it there, staring at the pictures that are now *everywhere*, and which I can do nothing about.

'Give the phone here.' Matthew takes it from me, reads the article, then drops the mobile dismissively on the sofa. 'No one you know is going to think any of that is about you. It's plainly a mismatch of text and images. The story is meaningless, and the photos aren't great, but it's not *that* bad.'

'Not that bad?' I look at him incredulously. 'We've both pushed images for a living for years. A picture paints a thousand words, remember? The camera never lies… She was "visiting a mental health charity"?' I whisper aloud, in shock. 'Oh my God…'

My phone begins to ring.

'It's Will, love. Should I answer it?' Mum asks, picking the phone up off the sofa and looking at me anxiously.

I don't say anything. Mum hesitates, and then answers anyway. 'Hi, sweetheart. Yes, it's me. Yes, she has. Just now. They've only just gone on then?'

I knew Kelly was up to something when she just appeared this morning and performed that complete about-face. And all that shit about having labyrinthitis, it was just so she could pass me the walking stick and I'd get snapped with it. She must have phoned a photographer and tipped him off the second she got back from threatening me last night. Something like this requires premeditated thought and planning.

'Why is she doing all of this to me?' I turn to Matthew, wide-eyed with fear.

'Why is who doing what?'

'Kelly,' I whisper. 'I'm not being paranoid. I know I'm not. She did this on purpose. She's done *all* of it deliberately. But *why*?'

'I don't think now is the best time to talk to her, love.' Mum is looking at me anxiously. 'She's very shaken up. Yes, I can. I will. OK. Bye then.' She looks up at me. 'He says Kelly is absolutely devastated.'

I exclaim aloud, in disbelief, '*She's* devastated?'

'Everything's been completely confused, apparently. She visited a charity this afternoon in Hackney. She's agreed to be their patron and they'd set up a publicity event where lots of photos were taken. Her people then did a press release and sent it out, only Will says some journalist mixed up the pictures with some shots a paparazzo took of you and Kelly earlier this morning.'

'Rubbish,' I say immediately. Is that what she meant when she said I needed to learn not to believe everything I read in the papers? She was going to teach me the lesson? 'She has deliberately made me look completely unstable.'

'I really don't think she would go there, Sal, not given what she knows you did on Friday night—' Matthew begins.

'I wasn't going to fucking kill myself!' I shout, before he can finish.

There is an ugly and uncomfortable silence as they all stare at me.

'Will said Kelly is putting a retraction up on her website now and tweeting it,' Mum ventures, after a moment more. 'She's going to do whatever she can to make sure people realize the mistake.'

'A retraction?' I swing around to look at Mum. 'No! Tell her to stop! She mustn't! Give me the phone – quick!' I scrabble to her website, but it's too late. There is already an uploaded selfie of Kelly, with photogenic tears sparkling on her cheeks, looking stricken.

Beyond heartbroken! she's written beneath it. *This morning I went to visit someone who's been having a tough time. This private moment was captured by a photographer.* The one that you'd told to be there, you mean? *When you work in my industry, you accept you're fair game, but my family and friends are not, and I cannot condone this gross intrusion into my personal life. To make matters worse, the pictures were incorrectly used to illustrate a story about my visiting a mental health charity today, which I fitted in during a break in filming for my new six-part series for ITV,* Beyond Suspicion, *which will air this autumn.*

I simply don't believe this. She's actually plugging her new TV show while supposedly apologizing for publically humiliating me?

Not only has the charity concerned lost a much-needed opportunity to publicize their work, as the photos showing their new logo were NOT used, the person in the photograph – my future sister-in-law, Sally Hilman – is understandably mortified, not, I'm sure, because she believes anyone's mental health issues are something that need to be hidden away, but because she was just going about her business trying to lead a normal life. Not cool, newspaper people, not cool... On their behalf, I'd like to say a massive SORRY, SALLY! And chin up, babe. Kelly xxxx

I actually shriek, and fling the phone away from me.

'Sal, what's wrong now?' Mum asks, coming over to me. 'Kelly's only trying to make good what—'

'She's named me!' I put my hands on the side of my head. 'Don't you understand how this all works? She's actually printed my name, so now every time someone does a Google search on me, *this* is the picture that will come up! And you think Kelly doesn't know that?'

'Sal, calm down. Please!' Matthew pleads. 'You're going to wake the kids.'

'Calm down?' I turn to face them all, looking at me apprehensively. 'This woman is wrecking my life. She needs to be stopped! Why can't any of you see what she's doing to me?'

I look at Caroline, silently imploring her to back me up, but she lowers her gaze and says nothing at all.

CHAPTER THIRTEEN

M um's phone bleeps as she's finishing tucking me into bed. 'Sorry!' she says immediately. 'It's just a text message. I'll put it back on silent.' She pulls it out of her pocket and inspects the screen. Her mouth falls open, and completely uncharacteristically, she whispers, 'Bitch!' before hurriedly shoving it away again.

'Who was that?'

'Penny Blakewell. *You* know...'

I stare at her blankly.

'She always does the cricket teas, won't let anyone else get involved, keeps the urn locked in her shed. She's asking if the pictures are you, if you're all right, and if there's anything she can do to help.' Mum flushes. 'I never liked that woman.'

'This is just the start. I told you people would see it.'

'Yes, well, Penny Blakewell certainly doesn't let much get by her...' Mum hesitates. 'Why *were* you holding a walking stick, though?'

'Because Kelly asked me to!'

'All right!' Mum says. 'It won't do you any good to get het up again and have all of that adrenaline flooding your system. You don't want to put your body under any unnecessary strain at the moment. I expect the doctor reminded you of that today, didn't she? Matthew was telling us she gave you a very comprehensive range of tests. That's good, isn't it? Wonderful that she's taking you so seriously.' Mum tries to give me an encouraging smile, but I can see the strain in her eyes – and it makes me hate Kelly all the more, for putting her through this. 'Shall I bring you a cup of tea in a minute?'

'I don't want you to give these tests a second thought, Mum, especially the CT one.' I reach out for her hand. 'I'm sure they're going to come back completely negative.'

'You don't have to try and protect me, Sally,' she says. 'We'll deal with everything if we have to. Now, are you sure I can't get you anything before you go to sleep?'

'Knock, knock!' My door opens gently and Caroline appears. 'Can I come in?' She tiptoes over and sinks down onto the edge of the bed. My phone buzzes as she does, and I reach out and turn it off.

'People you haven't seen in years messaging to tell you they saw you in the paper today?' Caroline nods at it.

'Some of them, yes,' I say flatly. 'Others are just concerned friends, that sort of thing.'

'I'd keep it turned off if I were you. Very wise.'

I glance over at Mum. 'I think I would like that tea, actually, if that's OK?'

She nods, visibly relieved to have something practical to do. 'I'll be right back.'

I wait until I'm sure she's gone downstairs, before turning to face Caroline.

'You know when you and I talked this morning, before the doctors? Do you really believe I'm not ill?'

'I don't think there is anything physically wrong with you, no.'

'That means if you're right, I still have no answer for why I can't remember anything about Friday night, and what was responsible for making me black out. As soon as I start thinking about *that*, I can't let go of why that note was in my pocket, and why my phone had been deliberately cleared, as if someone had wanted it to look like I was intending to kill myself. I've already told you I think that person is Kelly, and now she's set up those humiliating pictures of me on purpose. I also *know* she swapped her engagement ring for something substantially more expensive after your money went missing, and you'd already warned me to be on my guard around her. Kelly herself told me if I wanted a fight, I'd got one. Every part of me is screaming that something is really, badly wrong, and I need to do something to stop her, but...' I pause for breath, exhausted. 'The fact that you could help me, by telling everyone about her – but you won't – is making me worry that I might actually have some sort of warped obsession with Kelly; that I could be suffering from some sort of paranoia. It doesn't *feel* like I am, but then I suppose it wouldn't, would it? Essentially, I don't know if I can trust myself any more, and it's terrifying me.'

'Are you asking me to make that call for you?'

I hesitate. '*Does* it sound completely insane to suggest Kelly could have done something to me that might have made me lose my memory?'

'You mean like give you a drug of some sort?'

'Yes.' I look at Caroline, frightened.

To my enormous relief she doesn't shrink back from me, or look at me as if I've just said something impossibly far-fetched. Rather, she says quietly, 'There *are* several sedative drugs that can cause memory loss, yes.'

My eyes widen, but I say nothing, just wait for her to continue.

'It's incredible, really – they're available on prescription for the treatment of insomnia or anxiety, and yet their effects are so potent they're being widely abused in far more sinister ways; mainly in the form of drink spiking, leading to date rapes – or thefts.'

'So if they're available on prescription, presumably someone could have them with them at all times, quite legally?'

'Yes.' She nods. 'As long as they've been obtained through a prescription. The reason perpetrators usually get away with using them for criminal purposes is that some sedatives can leave the body after as little as twelve hours, so it's virtually impossible to prove the drug was ever administered in the first place.'

'Kelly was alone with my champagne,' I say. 'When we were about to toast their engagement, I left the room to listen for Theo, and Will came after me. She definitely had long enough on her own to put something in my drink. But wouldn't I have tasted something was wrong with it?'

Caroline shakes her head. 'One of the other controversial things about these sedatives is they don't always have an unusual taste or smell. Do you remember that sleeping pill I left in the bathroom for you? The Zopiclone? It leaves a metallic taste in your mouth, so it's unmistakable if you've taken it. Flunitrazepam was reformulated too, so that when it's dissolved in liquid, the drink turns blue, but the old pills are still widely available. You'd be more familiar with it as Rohypnol – it's the date rape drug. That's usually only prescribed by psychiatrists, though, because it's not on something called a formulary, which is a list of stipulations like cost, or a need for specialist guidance, which govern what GPs can prescribe.'

'So if Kelly was still seeing a psychiatrist, she might be on it? What's it used for?'

'It's used medically as a sleeping pill. It's about seven times stronger than Valium, and in fact it's usually prescribed in situations where Valium has ceased to have an effect on the patient because they've developed a tolerance to it – perhaps as a result of addiction.'

'If you accessed her medical records, would you be able to see if she was taking it?'

Caroline says carefully, 'I know that is, of course, a hypothetical question and not a request. *If* I had access to her records, yes, that sort of detail would be documented. However, there's no national database of records. The government has just wasted billions of pounds trying to implement one, and it doesn't work. So I'd have to be employed at the practice treating her to have access to that information. Even if I was, it would be highly unethical to do something like that. I'm not saying it doesn't ever happen, but it's something most health care professionals wouldn't dream of doing.' She pauses, and then says urgently, 'I can't even tell you how much I regret our conversation on Friday night, Sally. I should have kept my fears to myself. But please, *please* try to remember that I would never let anything happen to Chloe and Theo. Equally, all patients have a right to rehabilitation, and we have no proof that Kelly did anything to you on Friday night.'

'Well, couldn't you at least just tell the others what you told me about her, so they have the opportunity to make their minds up for themselves? And then they also won't just think this is about me going mad?'

'But, my darling girl, we've been over this already too. I only discussed anything with you at all in the context of protecting the children, because they can't protect themselves. Adults can, and there is no need for anyone to be told anything. Breaching patient confidentiality in that manner would mean the end of my career, but you know, I'd actually do it in a heartbeat if I thought there was any real risk to the children, *only I don't*! So in fact, sacrificing myself wouldn't achieve anything anyway. If a patient tells me himself, during a session, something like he intends to stab someone, then yes, of course I can tell the police – I'm *supposed* to tell them – but that's not what has happened here. I actually only have your word for all of this, with no evidence of Kelly's alleged wrongdoing whatsoever. You asked me to make this call for you, and here is what I think: stop pursuing Kelly now, because you have nothing to gain from going down this road, and everything to lose.'

I draw back from her slightly. 'What do you mean? What will I lose?'

'The police told your husband and the rest of your family that you were rescued by a passer-by in the early hours of Saturday morning, distressed and walking towards a cliff edge. Your best friend then told Matthew this was not your first suicide attempt. There is no reason for everyone not to believe these separate, credible sources. Sometimes, what *appears* to have happened can be just as powerful as something *actually* happening. Your predicament is a perfect example of the whole being greater than the sum of its parts. It's all about perception. Your parents and Matthew are already terrified you are unstable, and even believe you might be physically ill. How is it going to appear to them if you announce baldly that Kelly – who they are all aware you dislike immensely – drugged you and stole a significant sum of money from your house? Do you think they, or your brother, will believe you? Or will they think these are the protestations of an increasingly paranoid and mentally ill young woman, who perhaps ought not to be left in charge of her children any more, as she doesn't appear to be safe around them... Not when she doesn't have a shred of evidence to support her wild claims. Because you don't, Sally,' she reminds me gently. 'You really don't, and that's the insurmountable problem here. Can you *really* not see where your behaviour is leading, if you keep this up?'

'So *back me up*!' I exclaim, scared. 'They'll believe me if you tell them everything you know about Kelly.'

'Sal, we're just going around in circles here.' Caroline closes her eyes, as if she's trying to muster strength. 'For the last time, you're asking me to make a gross breach of my duty of reasonable care. I'd be reported to the General Medical Council and probably struck off – and that's just the professional rather than personal recriminations. I've already compromised myself enough by making such a huge mistake on Friday. You just told me you're not sure if you can trust your own judgement, and I think you're right to be worried.'

'You don't believe Kelly is responsible for what happened on Friday night, then?'

Caroline looks at me steadily. 'The person's behaviour I'm really concerned about at the moment is yours. Try, please, to let this go – for Theo and Chloe's sake. They need you. Don't give your parents or Matthew more ammunition than they already have.'

'Has Kelly already contacted you, and you just haven't told me?' I realize aloud. 'What did she say? Did she threaten you too? Is that why you won't help me?'

'OK, I think we have to stop talking about this now, Sally.'

'What if we go to the hospital immediately? Perhaps some of whatever she gave me is still in my system. They can do tests. I know you said that date-rape drug can't be found after twelve hours, but it might have been something else, and not that.'

'Sally, almost all drugs leave the body after seventy-two hours. If you ingested something on Friday night and it's Monday evening now, there's not a single hospital test that's going to be able to find anything. We *have* to stop this now.'

'Well, what side effects would I have had, if she'd given me a sedative of some kind?' I persist doggedly.

She sighs heavily. 'There are numerous side effects: nausea, paranoia, a loss of balance, hallucinations, visual problems, but—'

'That's almost exactly how I felt when I woke up in the taxi.'

'I'm not saying it wasn't, but...' She shrugs helplessly. 'The taxi driver didn't give you a receipt, or a card that would mean he could be traced?'

'No. He couldn't get me out of the car fast enough – all he wanted was his money. I was completely disorientated, it never occurred to me to get the number plate. It wasn't a marked car either, just a minicab, and he sounded foreign.'

'And the man who rescued you? He didn't see the taxi?'

I shake my head. 'He arrived after the cab had gone.'

'So you have no proof. At all. You cannot force your family to accept Kelly did this to you. You have to move on from this, Sally, for your own sake.'

'Even if I believe I was abducted from my own home? I'm supposed to just watch the person responsible marry my brother, knowing that *he* could then be at risk – never mind letting him think it's OK to have children with her? And do I then also have to distance myself completely from him to be sure I'm still protecting Theo and Chloe? Or do I keep Will and Kelly as part of our lives, but permanently walk on eggshells in case I enrage her again?'

'Only you can decide how best to go forward from this,' Caroline says quietly. 'I'm so sorry for you, Sally. As I said to you on Friday night before all of this unfolded, there is no greater threat to the happiness of a family unit than when an outsider is brought into the mix. Over the course of my career, I have seen families – who would have never believed for a second that they would find themselves not talking to each other – collapse completely, all because someone's new partner has altered the dynamic. It's not always the fault of the interloper, either.' She shifts position. 'A colleague of mine – a woman who should have known far better – made the life of her future son-in-law absolute hell. He was a lovely boy, but it wouldn't have mattered if he'd been the archangel Gabriel, she'd have found something wrong with him. No one was good enough for her daughter, that's what she said.' Caroline shakes her head. 'But here, of course, that's not the case. I understand how this news about Will marrying Kelly has made you feel, but Kelly isn't going anywhere, and in actuality, I do think it would perhaps be beneficial if you distanced yourself from Will a little. At least temporarily.'

I fall back onto the pillows miserably. 'I wish some stranger in a car would just take *Kelly* away. Somewhere where she'd never be able to bother any of us again.'

Caroline hesitates. 'I know you don't mean that, Sally.'

'Yes, I do.' I lift my exhausted eyes and look at her. 'I'd do anything to have her out of our lives.'

'I'm going to say it again – I don't believe you mean that,' she says deliberately. 'You wouldn't, for example, want to cause Kelly actual harm, would you? I'd like to be certain that you understand the difference between a verbal threat and actually presenting a clear danger to Kelly. You don't feel you want to get her back for what she's done to you tonight, for example? Earlier on you said she needed to be stopped. What exactly did you mean by that?'

'I was asking for your help. I wanted *you* to stop her by telling everyone what you told me, but I understand now why that can't happen. Don't worry, Caroline – I'm not going to hurt Kelly. I think I'd like to try and get some sleep now,' I whisper. 'Would you tell my mum I don't want that tea after all?'

'Of course.' She looks relieved, and gets up. 'I hope you manage to get some rest, and that the path you're going to choose to go down seems clearer in the morning.'

She reaches out, squeezes my hand, and makes her way out, quietly closing the door after her.

I reach for my phone, switch it back on, and call up the pictures again. There I am with my nightie gaping over my saggy boobs and bulging tummy… holding the stick… I shut my eyes. They are out there now, being seen by everyone that matters to me and some that shouldn't, but do — to say nothing of being idle fodder for the prying eyes of complete strangers. I look mad. I gather the duvet around me miserably. Of course Kelly did this deliberately. I don't understand how I am the only person that can see it.

But if no one else is going to help me, I have no choice but to address this myself. Will *must* understand what kind of woman his future wife is, before it's too late and she's in our lives — my *children's* lives — for ever.

I simply can't stand back and let it happen. I know I'm right about Kelly, and tomorrow, I'm going to put a stop to all of this, once and for all.

CHAPTER FOURTEEN

'Chloe went off to school very happily this morning,' Mum remarks, cuddling Theo to her, as I take a mouthful of coffee while we sit at the kitchen table.

'You've done so well to keep things completely normal for her, Sally,' Dad says, wiping down the draining board before hanging the tea towel carefully over the oven door. 'You should be very proud of yourself.'

'Thanks, Dad.'

'So,' Mum continues brightly, 'have you decided what you're doing yet? Are you coming back with us, or is Caroline going to stay here?'

'I'm coming back with you, if that's OK?' I drain my mug and set it down.

'Oh, I *am* pleased!' Mum exclaims.

'But I haven't told Matthew yet, so can you keep it under your hat? You weren't going to leave until after lunch anyway, were you?'

'We can do whatever is easiest,' Mum says instantly, starting to bounce Theo on her knee and then clap his hands, much to his delight.

'OK, well I was thinking that if you leave about two-ish, you could maybe set up the kids' bedrooms, so then if Matthew drives us up after tea, when we get there, I can just put them straight to bed.'

'Of course. In fact, their rooms are already set up,' Mum admits. 'I did them quickly before we left on Saturday, in case…' She trails off and I don't think any of us really want to pursue whatever the end of that sentence was.

'Well, that's perfect then,' I say quickly. 'Matthew can work at yours tomorrow and drive back here after supper. Then come back and get us on Sunday or something.'

'We'll work it all out.' Mum waves a hand. 'Do you want me to help you pack?'

I shake my head. 'No thanks, but I do need to ask you a pretty big favour.' I clear my throat. 'Would you look after Theo for me this morning? I want to pop out.'

'Oh yes?' Mum says easily, not missing a beat. 'Pop out to where, love?'

'I want to go and see Liv. We've had a bit of a falling out since Friday.'

'Why's that then?'

'She's really angry with me, because of what she thought I was trying to do. She's desperate for another baby, and she can't wrap her head around how I could have been planning to leave Chloe and Theo. I want to sort everything out with her properly before I come up to yours. It's not good to let these things fester. She only lives about half an hour away. I'll be back by two at the latest.'

Mum opens her mouth to protest again. 'But you've got a three-hour journey ahead of you, and we need to sort—'

'Just let her go, Sue,' Dad says suddenly. 'She wants to see a friend, that's all.'

Mum closes her mouth, pursing her lips, and seizing my chance, I quickly get to my feet, gather up my phone, purse and car keys, and then hasten over to kiss Theo, suddenly anxious.

'The only thing is… you're still happy to put him down again after what happened yesterday?'

'Well, Matthew's here, isn't he?' Mum says stoically. 'If the worst comes to the worst, I'm sure we can tick Theo over until you get back.'

'Get back from where?' says Matthew, appearing suddenly in the kitchen doorway holding his empty mug.

'I'm popping over to see Liv,' I explain.

'Why?' Matthew says immediately.

'Because I'd like to!'

'You're taking the car?' Matthew says doubtfully.

'Of course! How else would I get there?'

'Well... OK then,' he says slowly, and I just about manage to refrain from saying I wasn't actually asking his permission. 'Can you take Theo's car seat out, though?' He adds. 'He might kick off and it would be helpful to go for a drive with him if he does. And Chloe's too – just in case you get stuck in traffic or something and we need to pick her up. Liv's expecting you, I take it?'

'Yes, of course she is. But can we please just do the seats now, so I can get going?' I force what I hope is an easy, relaxed smile.

Matthew eyes me steadily. 'Sure. I'll do it now.'

'Thanks. I'll get my shoes on.' I go out into the hall and slide open the crammed-full drawer in the sideboard. 'I might take some sunglasses too,' I say out loud. 'It's brightened up quite a lot, hasn't it? You should at least have a nicer drive to yours now, Mum.' I rummage around in among the used batteries, screw-drivers, loose change, unopened post, and pull out some old glasses – then I spy the glint of what I'm really looking for: the spare keys to Will's flat, which he gave me when he first moved in ages ago, in case of emergencies. I remove them silently and slip them into my pocket, before turning around and holding the glasses aloft. 'Got them!' I smile. 'Right then, I'll see you all later.'

*

My phone beeps yet again on the passenger seat as I turn into Will's road. I pick it up, in case it's Mum or Matthew with a problem about Theo, but glancing at the screen quickly, I see this time it's an ex-work colleague, who I haven't heard from since Chloe was born. I fling the phone back down and pull sharply into an unexpectedly free space a stone's throw from Will's flat. I know what the text will say, the same thing as all of the others: Hey Sally, saw you in the Mail. Are you OK? Xxx

Yeah, I'm great, thanks. Beyond humiliated that everyone thinks I've gone mad and live in a secure facility where we're only allowed to dress in fat pants and nightwear. Thanks for your consideration/ nosiness (delete as appropriate). What have *you* been up to for the last five years?

I turn the engine off and pick up my phone again. Maybe this is the reality of what it takes to get some actual human contact from people these days. If you want to prise people's attention from their screens, it's going to take a pretty big bang – like being handed a food parcel by a minor celebrity in little more than your underwear. I sigh, and text back.

Long time no speak! How have you been?

Her response is immediate.

I'm good thanks! Life is completely manic! Feet never touch the ground! You know how it is. So weird to see you in paper! Didn't know you knew Kelly Harrington?

No, *this* is weird… And yes, I can see you're flat-out busy…

I don't bother responding this time. Instead, I call Will.

'Sal!' He picks up straight away. 'You all right?'

'I'm fine. Are you at work at the moment? Can you talk?'

'I am at work, yes, but it's fine. I've got a meeting in about ten minutes, so now's a good time. I was going to call *you* this morning, actually, but you beat me to it!'

'Yeah, well, I just wanted to say sorry I wouldn't speak to you last night. I was…' I pause. 'A little emotional.'

'Of course you were. I understand completely. I hope Mum managed to explain just how upset Kelly was about it all too?'

I grit my teeth. 'Yes, she did. I don't want Kelly to think I'm still angry with her, though, because I'm not. Perhaps I should call in and see her or something?'

'Well, that would be nice, I'm sure she'd love that,' Will says carefully, 'but she's not at home. She's filming today.'

'Oh, I didn't mean now,' I say quickly. 'I'm just on my way to a friend's house, and then me and the kids are off to Mum's for a few days. I meant when we're back maybe?'

'That'd be great. We'll work something out.'

'Sounds good. So you two sorted everything else then, after the ring incident?'

Will hesitates. 'Yes, we did. But like I said on Saturday, thanks for having my back. I appreciate it.'

'No problem. Well, I'd better go, I've arrived at my friend's now.'

'OK. Have fun, and safe trip to Mum's later.'

'Thanks. Lots of love.'

I hang up. Good. As suspected, they're both out. Clutching my phone, keys and purse, I climb out of the car. Bleeping it shut, I look both ways and quickly cross the busy road, before arriving at the front door. Just for a moment, I waver, but then I remember exactly why I'm here – and how important it is. I press the buzzer for Will's flat, just to double check, but it's exactly as he's already told me: no one is home. There is no response through the intercom, and after a moment, I lift the first of the two keys and open the communal front door. Letting myself into the large entrance hall, I make my way over to the shallow stairs and begin to pad up them, ready to smile easily in case I pass one of their neighbours, but everything is silent; the doors to the other flats stay closed. My phone starts to ring, making me jump guiltily, and even though it's Liv, I don't pick up. I need to concentrate. I'll call her back later.

When I reach Will's front door, my heart gives an extra thud, despite my knowing there is no one there. I just have to be quick, that's all. In and out. I take a deep breath, slide the key into the lock, and swing the door open...

I actually haven't been around to the flat since Kelly moved in, and things have certainly changed. The first thing that hits me is the sickly, heady smell of Star Gazer lilies, coming from a vast vase in the fireplace. Looking around me, the only piece of furniture I still recognize is Will's battered old leather chair, over in the corner; other than that, everything is different. The walls are now a soft dove colour, Will's sofa – our old one – has gone, and been replaced by a very expensive-looking corner unit arrangement, in grey velvet. There's a large, deep-pile rug where his much smaller one used to be, which now covers practically all of the exposed wooden floorboards, making it feel much cosier and almost cocoon-like. There are strategic lamps everywhere, a pile of glossy magazines in a neat fan arrangement on a bleached wooden coffee table, and some large black-and-white shots of New York hanging on the walls. It's within a whisker of being WAG-tastic – but in spite of myself, I absolutely love it. It's a sumptuous, touchy-feely room for grown-ups. I want to climb onto the velvet sofa, curl up like a cat, and go to sleep.

I walk over to the sideboard and put down my purse and the keys, before briefly picking up a picture of Kelly and Will. It looks like it was taken in a restaurant; he has his arm around her, and she's laughing. I have to admit they look extremely happy. But then she's also an actress, so who knows what her real motivation was?

I look at Will again. Whenever I think of my brother, he is smiling. In fact, he's pretty much permanently fixed in my mind as a chubby, red-cheeked three-year-old, lying on his back, shrieking with hysterical laughter as I tickle him. I know he's a grown man now, but I will always associate him with that sound of innocent joy. No matter how old he gets, and whatever happens. I don't want to have to distance myself from my little brother. I love him too much. So I have no choice but to do what I've come here for. I put the photo down, take a deep breath, and head off in the direction of the bathroom. I might as well start there. If I had a prescription of heavy-duty sleeping pills, is that where would I keep them?

In the small, neat room, I pause in front of the gleaming, mirrored bathroom cabinet. Am I really going to do this? Go through Kelly's personal belongings in the hope of finding, at the very least, whatever she spiked my drink with?

Actually, yes I am. She drugged me and put me in a taxi that took me miles away from home, and the safety of my family. I just need the proof.

With no further hesitation, I open the cupboard. It's full of the usual bathroom stuff: nail clippers, spare toothbrush heads, a new tube of toothpaste, Nivea, plasters, some razors, mouthwash – but my eyes alight on a prescription packet. I pick it up and examine it. *Ms K Harrington* is typed neatly on the label of what is a popular brand of contraceptive pill. I grimace and put it back. I quickly start to rifle through the other boxes and packets, but it's all paracetamol and ibuprofen.

Bending down, I pull open the cupboard under the sink. Spare loo rolls, refill pads for the loo brush, Tampax, bleach – nothing else.

Maybe her make-up bag? I walk smartly down the corridor into their bedroom. It's a nice room, very calm. She's painted it pale blue, and it's got lots of white photo frames on the walls. This time the pictures are all of the two of them in various exotic locations. They've certainly packed a lot into their eleven months. I glance quickly at their bed. Her side is obviously on the right; surprisingly, there are a couple of historical fiction books on the bedside table that I've read and enjoyed, and on the shelf below – her make-up bag and another toiletries bag.

The first is chock full of expensive brands. I've never seen so many powders, bronzers, lipsticks and eye pencils away from a beauty counter. I zip it back up quickly – there's nothing I'm after. The toiletries bag seems, at first, much more promising, but it's just more paracetamol packets – mostly empty this time – various nail varnishes and remover, a pumice stone, some eye drops, a Barbara Cartland-esque mask, and some sort of anti-aging serum. No sleeping pills. Exasperated, I zip it back up. They've *got* to be here somewhere.

My eyes alight on a chest of drawers. Underwear drawer. That's where everyone puts secret things. I hurry over to it and yank it open. It too is absolutely full – of distressingly tiny bits of lace and chiffon. Christ, people actually still wear thongs? Feeling very uncomfortable, I rifle through, unearthing a jewellery box, which is empty apart from one small blue box. Within that is a nondescript wedding band, a dull gold pair of rather cheap-looking heart earrings, and a long, plain link necklace. I close it all back up and push past a saved Valentine's day card. Still nothing... I slam the drawer shut and try the next one down, this time full of nightwear. There's nothing in there either, except two unopened packs of Kleenex and a framed picture of a small blonde girl, a little younger than Chloe – three, perhaps – crouching in a field of buttercups, smiling impishly, outstretched hand full of golden yellow blooms, next to a happily smiling woman dressed in a 70s maxi dress, but *then*, behind that – *yes*! A small bottle. My fingers close around it and I pull it out triumphantly.

The brown glass pill bottle reads *Miss K Harrington*, followed by *Ignatia 30c*, whatever that is. Below that, there appears to be a company name and contact number. Inside the bottle there are about twenty small pills. Could this be what I'm looking for? If it's not, why is it hidden away? Still holding my phone, I hold it aloft and take a picture of the bottle, making sure her name is in clear view, before emailing it to myself, then pull the drawer wider so I can hide the pills away again. That's when I see another photo frame, the back facing up. Out of curiosity, I pick it up, but my heart stops as I flip it over.

It's a picture of my children. Chloe smiling at the camera, hugging a three-month-old Theo. I know exactly when it was taken: at Mum's birthday. Why the hell has Kelly got this hidden away in her drawer? I swallow queasily as I stare at the picture, my pulse beginning to quicken, and I start to feel both very frightened and angry.

'How bloody dare you!' I whisper aloud, in disbelief.

'My sentiments exactly,' a voice says behind me, making me gasp and spin around in shock, only to find Kelly standing in the doorway, filming me going through her belongings on her mobile phone.

CHAPTER FIFTEEN

'I won't hesitate to call the police if I have to,' she says, 'regardless of the implications for you this time. You should also know I've already texted Will, who's on his way. Just so we're both clear, OK?'

'Why have you got this picture of my children?' I demand, holding it up, my hand shaking slightly.

She's still filming me. 'It's a photo your mum gave Will that he particularly likes. It's his birthday next month, so I've had it framed for him. I haven't wrapped it yet, so I've kept it out of sight in my drawer. More to the point, what are you doing in our flat, Sally, going through my things?'

'I didn't break in,' I say immediately. 'I've done nothing illegal.'

'Yes, you appear to have a key, which was news to me.'

'Will gave it to me when he moved in, for emergencies.'

'And you think Will would be OK with you using it like this, do you?'

'I didn't think anyone was here.'

She stops filming and then appraises me with contempt. 'Evidently. I kind of worked that one out for myself. I was in the kitchen making a cup of tea when I looked out of the window and saw you getting out of your car. I thought you'd come to see me, and I'll be honest, I didn't much feel like chatting, so when the intercom rang, I didn't answer it. When I looked out again your car was still there, though, so I assumed someone must have let you in downstairs after all. Annoying, but it happens. I stayed in the kitchen and waited for you to knock on the front door, and then go away when there was no answer. Imagine my surprise, Sally, when instead, I hear a key in the door, and then you let yourself in like you own the place, *which of course you fucking don't.*'

Now there are no witnesses, she makes no effort to hide her anger, and spits the words out. 'You can't seriously be looking for the sixty-five grand, because we both know I didn't steal that from you, so why *are* you here?'

'You're correct, I'm not looking for the money, because it's sitting on your hand right now.' I nod at the ridiculous diamond brick catching the light on her third finger.

She briefly looks heavenward. 'Oh my God, give it up! It didn't work, OK? Your sad little plot failed, and you know it. Stop trying to flog this very dead horse. I'm going to ask you again: why are you here?'

'You already know why, Kelly. You've hated me from the moment you met me, when you called me a fucking bitch in the street. You can't stand sharing Will with his family, and I know *I* make you particularly angry. The thing is, I've been warned about you. I know what kind of person you are, what you're capable of – and it doesn't matter what you try to do to make it appear to everyone as if I've lost my mind, I'm not going to let you damage me or my family any more. That's why I'm here.'

She continues to stare at me. 'I have never sworn at you in the street. Ever.'

'It was right outside this flat,' I interrupt. 'I was pregnant, and I accidentally bumped into you while you were on the phone, which was when you called me a bitch.'

'It didn't occur to you I might be saying it to the person I was actually talking to? Not you? Or maybe I thought it was just what happens to me all the time; people deliberately shove into me because I'm famous – particularly girls – because they weirdly get off on it. I've had people try to trip me up, drinks spilt over me on purpose. I probably thought *that* was what you were doing. I'm used to women not liking me because of the way I look, and the job I do, but at the very least aren't *you* supposed to be older and wiser than this?'

'Oh, come on,' I say. 'You're seriously asking me to believe you're totally innocent, when just last night you set up those pictures of me?'

'OK, yeah, I did those.' She shrugs unrepentantly and crosses her arms. 'I told you not to believe everything you see in the papers. Hopefully you know that now.'

'But that's not all you've done, is it?' I persist, and I take a deep breath. 'The pills you drugged me with on Friday night – are they the ones I've now got a picture of on my phone?'

Her expression stays impassive, but she doesn't take her eyes from me. 'What did you just say?'

'I've got a picture of your pills, which I've emailed myself,' I repeat.

'No, the bit about me drugging you. You're not actually serious?'

'Yes, I am. Are the pills you used the ones in your drawer?'

She starts to laugh in disbelief, and pushes past me, yanking the drawer open. 'You mean these?' She pulls out the small bottle. 'These are a homeopathic remedy. I keep them in my drawer because they're light sensitive and meant to be stored in a cool place. How stupid are you?' she begins, but then trails off. 'Actually, that can't be right, because I *know* you're not that stupid. Anyone who's devious enough to see her husband slipping away from her, and so engineers an entirely fictitious scenario designed to scare the shit out of him and make him realize how much he really loves and needs her, isn't stupid *at all*. You used to be in advertising too, I think? So you're even used to making up crap professionally. That's what I *thought* this was all about.' She stops again for a moment, and regards me warily. 'I had you down as just another head-fucked middle-aged housewife married to someone you shouldn't be married to any more, playing selfish games with no thought to those caught up in the crossfire.'

'Oh, Kelly, please!' I say. 'Must you always say everything like you're imagining yourself on screen? It's not only melodramatic and insincere, it's exceptionally annoying.'

'OK then,' she says simply. 'I feel like I *want* to tell you how your nasty little stunt had your younger brother in tears at the weekend, and that you have no idea what this is going to cost you in the future. One day, Chloe and Theo will find out what you did on Friday night, and about the "overdose" –' she makes air quotes with her fingers – 'you took when you were nineteen, and because of what you've done, they will never, ever be the same again. *You'll* never be the same to them.' Her voice begins to shake with energy. 'You will never be a mum they can rely on completely.'

I think suddenly about the ring, chain and small heart earrings tucked away at the back of her drawer, and the picture of the smiling little girl with the woman in the maxi dress.

'Kelly, you seem to have some very strong – and intensely personal – feelings about all of this,' I interrupt, 'and I wonder if there's some stuff going on with you that you might be transferring onto me?'

'Just shut up,' she says, much more quietly this time. 'You don't mean that concern for a second, and even if you did, you're really arrogant enough to assume you have any of the answers when you don't even know what the questions are? I worked out my "intensely personal" stuff a long time ago, with people far more skilled than you could ever hope to be, thanks very much.'

She means Caroline? Is she finally about to bring up her

relationship with my mother-in-law? I hold my breath, but she falls unnervingly quiet once more and just stares at me. I'm on the verge of filling the unbearable silence when she says suddenly, 'You're lying again, aren't you? You don't really think I've drugged you, any more than I believe you're suicidal. You're not even close to being in that place. You never have been. There's more to this, something that – oh my God!' Her mouth falls open suddenly. 'You absolute bitch. Where have you hidden it?'

'Where have I hidden what?' I stare at her in confusion.

'*That's* why you're here. You said you just needed proof, and you emailed a picture to yourself. What have you planted in my flat, to look like they're mine?' She turns and starts to pull the clothes from the drawer, rifling through it. 'I'll find it – and he won't believe you, whatever you've done, and whatever you've faked. You won't make him leave me. God, you nasty, nasty piece of work.'

Then, just as suddenly, she swings around wildly. 'You think you're so clever, but it's your word against mine, Sally. And you're right, everyone already thinks you've lost your mind.'

Confused, I watch her hit a button on her phone and hold it up to her ear. I hear a female voice answer, 'Hello?' and at the sound, Kelly resets her features into a face of panic, and, putting on a terrified voice, she says tremulously, 'Hello, Sue?'

My mouth falls open. She just called my *mother*?

'It's Kelly.' She gulps, making it sound as if she's in tears. 'Sally's here and Will's on his way, but she's angry and distressed, and I'm not sure what I should do. She's very confused. Yes, I know. No, she isn't. No, I haven't. I didn't want to, but I will if you think I should?'

My heart stops as I realize what she's doing. Oh no, no, no... 'Kelly, stop!' I say, frightened, and I step towards her. 'Give me the phone!'

'Don't!' she shrieks suddenly. 'Don't come near me, Sally!'

'I haven't touched you!' I exclaim as she dodges past me, runs into the bathroom, and slams the door shut. I hear the bolt slide across, and I suddenly remember turning to Matthew when we were watching her thick chav character on TV mouthing off, before slapping her fictitious sister around the face, and remarking bitchily, 'You know they all get cast as themselves, don't you?' Jesus Christ, I couldn't have been more wrong.

'I've locked myself in the bathroom,' I hear her shout, as I rush down the hall after her and rattle the handle.

'Kelly, please don't do this to Mum, she'll be really frightened!'

'She's trying to get in! What should I do? I don't know what to do! I think I need to call the police!'

'Kelly! I just want you to stop this!' Panicked, I bang on the door again, which is how Will finds me as he bursts into the hallway, panting with the exertion of having run up the stairs.

He quickly looks at the closed bathroom door, me standing right next to it, and gently reaches out a hand. 'Sally? It's OK. Everything is OK.'

'You don't need to talk like that,' I say as calmly as I can. 'I know how this looks, but it's absolutely not what you think. Yes, Kelly's in there.' I point behind me. 'But she's perfectly safe.'

'Will, is that you?' Kelly calls from behind the door, sounding as if she's weeping with fear.

'Oh, come on, Kelly!' I shout in frustration. 'You *know* it's him!'

'Sally, can you try not to raise your voice? Could you go and stand by the front door, please?'

I shake my head incredulously, but do as I'm told. If I fight this, he's never going to believe me. Caroline warned me, she *told* me not to kick the hornets' nest. Oh shit – she also asked me if I intended to hurt Kelly... I have to try to stay calm, because – I realize suddenly – this really does not look good. It was desperately stupid of me to come here. What was I *thinking*?

I turn to see Will knock gently on the door. 'Kel? It's me. You can come out. Everything's OK.'

The bolt slides back, and she appears, her face red, with eyes puffy from crying. I watch her in amazement. How does she do that so convincingly? Then I notice she's clutching a pair of nail scissors, like a tiny knife. Presumably to defend herself with? She's unbelievable!

She lets them clatter to the floor and falls into Will's arms. 'I was so scared,' she sobs. 'Just get her out of here. I can't handle this, not today of all days. Please, Will!'

'It's OK, we're going now. I'll drive her home in her car and I'll be back as soon as I can. Are you going to be all right?' Will looks at her in concern.

She nods, and then gulps. 'She was going through our things. She's insane!'

'Shhh, shhh, it's OK,' he soothes. 'Everything is going to be OK. I'll be right back.' He lets go of her gently and turns to me. 'Come on, Sal.' He tries to smile at me, but I see instantly it's an effort, because he's my brother, and I know him almost as well as I know myself. He believes her. He believes her one hundred per cent.

I don't say a thing, just glance back at her bleakly as he ushers me out of the door, but she refuses to meet my eye, simply turns – and without saying another word to me, walks into their bedroom and closes the door.

CHAPTER SIXTEEN

'You didn't need to do this, I could have just driven myself home.'

'It's fine,' Will says. 'I'd rather know for sure you get back safely.'

'Kelly was in no danger whatsoever.' I look at him staring at the road ahead. 'I didn't go there to hurt her – I called to check neither of you were at home, remember? You told me you were both out.'

'That's because I knew Kelly wouldn't want to see you today. I said she was filming because it was easier than having to explain why you couldn't go around. It's the anniversary of her mother's death – although that's actually irrelevant. You shouldn't have been in the flat full stop, Sal, and while I get that you *did* call me, you also told me you were going to a friend's house, which was a complete lie.'

'I'm sorry to hear about Kelly, and yes, you're right,' I say quietly. 'I shouldn't have done what I did. I know what you're thinking. You're worried that I'm ill. Mentally, if not physically. But I need you to trust me when I say that I'm neither, and like I just said, confronting Kelly wasn't the reason I was in your flat.'

He doesn't say anything for a moment, then, still without looking at me, asks, 'I assume you were there looking for your missing sixty-five grand?'

I raise my eyebrows in surprise. Had it not been for Kelly just phoning Mum and making out that I was attacking her, I would tell him the truth about what I was actually looking for – but there's no way I can do that now. They'd have me sectioned again by the end of the day. 'You know about the stolen money?'

Will nods. 'Kelly told me you accused her of taking it. She didn't steal it, though, Sal. I see why you might have come to that conclusion, given that you know she swapped the ring for one a lot more valuable the day after the money disappeared, but that's honestly just a horrible coincidence.'

Hang on. He's talking as if he almost *understands* why I was in their flat? And he's certainly nowhere near as angry as I thought he'd be. Neither is he speaking to me as if he thinks I'm treading a very thin line between madness and sanity. My heart thuds. I might actually get away with this if I'm very, very careful.

'You haven't told anyone about Kelly exchanging the ring, have you?' Will asks anxiously.

'No, I promised you I wouldn't, and I haven't.'

He looks relieved. 'Thank you. The trouble is, she *did* pay for the ring upgrade in cash – which looks dodgy as hell, obviously, and although *I* know where the money came from, I know what your reaction – and most people's reaction – would be, if I told you.'

'Why don't you try me?' I say slowly.

He takes a deep breath. 'When Kelly's dad died, she discovered he had all of this money they didn't know about. They'd lived in this really modest three-bedroom place, which they kept after their dad died – Kelly's brother had been living there with his girlfriend – but they all decided to sell it last year. When they were clearing out the loft they found half a million pounds in cash. It was stuffed in Sainsbury's bags in a box.' He looks across at me nervously.

I pause. 'You're joking, obviously.'

'No, I'm not. It's true. They didn't tell anyone, because of the tax implications. Kelly and her brother and sister just went on a really amazing holiday together and bought new cars, stuff for their houses, that kind of thing. Kelly's still got quite a bit of her share left. Or at least she did until she bought the ring, and the rest is going on the wedding itself. In a way, it's nice that she can do this with it, I suppose. It's like her dad is still involved somehow.'

'And when exactly did Kelly tell you about her dad's money?'

'On Sunday night.'

'Right. You don't think that it's at all odd that my mother-in-law puts sixty-five thousand pounds in our cupboard under the stairs – which she's also withdrawn for tax reasons – on Friday night, that then goes missing?' I say. 'And the very next day, your fiancée buys a very expensive item of jewellery with a pot of cash her dad had "hidden" in carrier bags, also for tax reasons?'

'I think it would help if everyone started using banks, like normal people, yes.' He tries to laugh. 'But like I said, I also think it's a coincidence.'

But what he's describing isn't like unexpectedly bumping into someone you know on holiday... This is the kind of coincidence that is *so* extreme, and *so* surreal, that it can mean only one thing: someone has overplayed their hand and real events are colliding with their fictitious ones to reveal them for exactly what they are...

Nothing but a pack of lies.

'Did Kelly tell you she deliberately set up those photos of me?' I ask, after a moment's silence. 'She admitted it outright at the flat.'

He frowns in dismay. 'Really? She honestly said that?'

'She said it was to teach me a lesson not to believe everything you read in the papers. She also had a go at me for my "pretending" to be suicidal, and said she didn't believe for one second I was in "that place".'

Will exhales heavily. 'I'm very sorry about that. Please don't think I'm trying to detract from the difficulties you're having right now, but Kelly is finding things pretty tough herself at the moment. Like I said, it's the anniversary of her mother's death, which she's still very much struggling with.'

'I genuinely had no idea both of her parents were dead. Didn't you say on Friday when you got engaged that you'd told Mum and Dad, and her parents too?'

'No, I said we'd told her *family*. I meant her brother and sister, and she's got a stepmother who she's close to.'

'When did her mother die?'

'Kelly was fourteen.'

'Oh!' I say without hesitation. 'That's really sad. I'm sorry.'

Will glances sideways at me. 'They told Kelly she'd had a brain haemorrhage. Then her father died three years later from cancer.'

'That's dreadful,' I say instinctively.

'If I tell you something else, do you promise I can trust you? I'd like to put some context behind the hurtful things Kelly said to you at the flat.'

'Of course you can trust me.'

'Just before her father died he told Kelly and her brother and sister that her mother had actually killed herself.'

'What?' I'm appalled.

'He'd lied about it to protect them until they were older, but the thing is, death certificates are public records and he was worried that once *he* died, they might see their mother's and realize that the coroner had recorded a verdict of suicide. He obviously hadn't reckoned on becoming so ill, so soon, himself. I think it's fair to say he was probably stressed to oblivion, hence the bags full of cash. He wasn't a man left with much faith in trusting anything or anyone.'

'Kelly finding that out must have been like having her mother die all over again.'

Will shoots another sideways glance at me. 'Yes, I think it probably was. Anyway, everything has become even more complicated since Kelly got her big break at work. While her mother's suicide is not something she'll probably be able to keep private for ever, no one has stumbled on it so far. If anyone pushes in interviews, she just gives them the original version of the story that she was told. I mean it, Sal, you really can't tell anyone this, but I promise Kelly didn't steal that money from you.'

All that loss in Kelly's life *would* perhaps explain why she is so obsessively terrified of something coming between her and Will. Presuming it's all true. But then who would lie about something like that? It could also explain why she went off the rails when she was younger and ended up in counselling.

I reach for my phone and google Ignatia.

Homeopathy: The remedy for loss, heartache and pain.
Most homeopathic kits will have Ignatia in them, listing it as a treatment for bereavement, shock or grief.

I start to chew my lip worriedly, and put the phone back in my lap before looking out of the window. She can't possibly be telling the truth about everything. Can she?

'Getting engaged has really stirred a lot of things up for Kel,' Will continues. 'She's thinking a lot about how neither of her parents will be there for the wedding.' He falls silent for a moment. 'She's had a great deal on her mind and is pretty upset. I take it you didn't find anything when you searched the flat, obviously?'

'No,' I admit. 'I didn't find a thing.'

*

'Hi sweetheart!' Matthew opens the front door and gives me a beaming smile – except it's so heavily laced with worry, I know instantly that Mum has told my husband what just happened at Will's. Matthew, however, is determinedly pretending everything is absolutely fine. 'Thanks for driving, Will.' He proffers his hand to his brother-in-law, who, with just as much forced jollity, takes it and they both pull into a brief back-slap hug. 'Are you coming in? Want a coffee?'

Will shakes his head. 'No, I'd better get back. Kelly's not feeling so great. But thanks.'

'I really am grateful. Sally's heading up to your mum's in a bit –' I look at my husband, surprised. Mum's told him then? – 'so it's really helpful to have her back in plenty of time to go.'

'Will!' There's an exclamation behind Matthew, and Mum appears, arms outstretched. 'Thank you so much for doing this.' She pulls him into an embrace too and adds soberly, 'You're such a good boy.'

It's honestly as if someone actually *has* died.

'You're coming in?' Mum stands to one side to let him past.

'Thanks, but I really ought not to. I'll give you all a call at home tomorrow. At yours, Mum, I mean.'

'We'll look forward to it, love.'

'Let me at least drive you to the station.' Matthew reaches into his back pocket for his keys.

'Honestly, I'm fine.' Will dismisses him with a wave. 'You guys have got a long enough journey in a bit, anyway. I can walk. It's only five minutes.'

'Uncle Will!' cries a small voice, and Chloe dashes into the hall, shyly peeping out from behind Mum.

'Ah, hello there, Shorty,' Will says with a smile. 'How are you?'

'We're going to Granny Sue's for – how many sleeps?' She looks up at Mum uncertainly.

'Maybe as many as four!' Mum smiles.

'For four sleeps! And I'm going to be in your old bedroom,' Chloe tells him excitedly.

'Well, is that so?' He reaches out and ruffles her hair. 'You mind out for the crocodiles I keep under the bed then, won't you?'

Chloe's smile slips slightly, and she looks at me anxiously.

'He hasn't really got crocodiles under there, Clo, don't worry. He's just joking,' I assure her.

'I'm so sorry.' Will turns to me aghast. 'I have no idea why I just said that.'

'Because you're a K.N.O.B.,' I spell out. 'You can sleep in Mummy's old bedroom, Clo, and I'll sleep in Uncle Will's, if you like,' I offer.

'Or I can sleep in there *with* you,' she suggests.

I shoot Will a deadpan look.

'And on that happy note...' Will says. He kisses me and bends to kiss Chloe quickly too. 'Safe journey, you lot. Bye!'

We wave as he ambles off down the drive and until he reaches the end of the close, where he turns to wave back brightly, before rounding the corner and disappearing. Thank God. That almost felt *normal* when he left just then.

'That was nice to see Uncle Will,' Chloe says. 'But I do *not* like crocodiles.'

'I absolutely promise there aren't any, Chloe, he was just being silly. Now, why don't you go and choose some things to pack in your backpack to take to Granny Sue's?'

'I already have,' she says. 'I did it with Daddy.'

'We're all packed,' Matthew says, 'and the car's loaded. We're completely ready to go.'

'What?' I say in surprise. 'But aren't you meant to be working?'

'No, no. It's fine.' He waves a hand. 'I've sorted it.'

'But when you say you've packed...' I begin anxiously.

'Me and your mum did it.' He nods at my mother. 'I'm pretty sure we got everything, but you can go and check, if you want? I've got the monitor, Theo's room thermometer, the blackout blind, the Grobags, nappies, her toothbrush, stories—'

'Dog?' I check, nodding at Chloe.

'I put him in, Mummy,' Chloe says confidently.

'We've got the lot, Sally,' Mum says.

'So, let's go!' Matthew reaches into his other pocket and checks for his mobile. 'I'll get Theo.'

'Guys, please, hang on a minute,' I implore. 'We actually can't leave now, otherwise we'll be on the road when Chloe and Theo need tea. What's the big rush for, anyway?'

'I've packed her some sandwiches,' Mum says. 'You're going to have a car picnic, aren't you, Chloe?'

Chloe nods gleefully.

'It won't hurt, just this once, if she doesn't have a proper evening meal,' Mum adds firmly. 'I'll make sure we feed her up again tomorrow. Theo's got one of his pouches, and I've made up his bottle. Do you want to pop to the loo then, darling? It's a long journey.'

Thankfully, she actually does address Chloe with the last question, although I wouldn't be surprised if she meant me. They are clearly all determined to get me away from here as soon as possible.

'*I* need to pack, though,' I point out.

Mum shakes her head. 'I've done you too. And yes, I put in your make-up bag, and all of your lotions and potions. You're only coming for three days anyway, Sally.'

'But what about things like my phone charger? And where *is* Theo?' I ask, starting to feel really stressed.

'He's in the sitting room with your dad, and my mum,' Matthew says.

'Your mum's here?' I say instantly. 'Oh good! I need to ask her something.'

'Well, can you make it quick?' Matthew looks at his watch. 'It really would be helpful if we could go sooner rather than later. It's just, that way, I won't be back again too late.'

'You're coming straight back here tonight?' I say, astonished. 'But that's a six-hour round trip!'

'I've got to work tomorrow, so I don't have any choice. I'll be fine, though, don't worry.'

'Hello, Sally.' Caroline appears in the hallway too, holding Theo. 'I'm going to stay here until you get back at the weekend, if that's all right? So you can relax without worrying it's all going to hell in a handcart and that you're coming back to chaos.' She nods at Matthew.

'Thanks, Mum.' Matthew rolls his eyes, albeit good-naturedly.

Then the three of them smile at me, and I realize that they are now all completely united, and that *is* what's happening. Whatever they believe happened this afternoon has just sealed the deal.

'Fine,' I say wearily. 'I'll just go to the loo as well then, and we'll get in the car. Has Theo got a clean nappy?'

'Of course he has,' Mum says smoothly. 'I just changed him myself. Didn't I?' she croons, and holds out her hands to Theo. 'Come on then, young man.'

'I'll just pass him to Matthew, shall I?' Caroline plants a kiss on Theo's head. 'Then he can pop him straight in the car. You be a good boy for Granny Sue, won't you?' She hands Theo across to Matthew.

'You did pack coats for us all, didn't you?' I ask Matthew.

'Yes!' he says, exasperated. 'I'm going to get in the car now. See you later, Mum. I'll be back about eleven-ish, but don't wait up.' He waves with his free hand, and heads resolutely out of the door.

'Bob?' Mum calls. 'We're off now. Are you ready?'

Dad instantly appears in the sitting-room doorway, wearing his lightweight anorak and holding a thermos.

'Maybe I'll quickly *try*,' says Chloe, slipping off her backpack and dashing to the loo.

'You get going, Mum, I'll wait for Chloe,' I say, determined at the very least to talk with Caroline before we go.

'All right, love. Now, we're not following you, we're just going to make our own way back – Matthew thought that would be easier, in case you need to stop somewhere. *If* you get back before us, you know the spare key is under the brick on the patio?'

'Yes, Mum.'

'Good. Bye then, Caroline. Thanks so much for everything.' Mum leans over and air kisses Caroline, then adds meaningfully, 'We'll stay in touch.'

I manage to refrain from making any comment about that.

Dad kisses Caroline politely too, and I stumble slightly as I step back to let him pass, leaving just the two of us in the hallway.

'You poor thing.' Caroline makes a sympathetic face. 'You're exhausted, aren't you? Will you try and get some sleep on the journey?'

'I didn't know Kelly was going to be there, Caroline,' I say earnestly. 'I promise I didn't go to confront her. Everything's taken a really bizarre turn, though. She did set up those pictures, so we were right about that, and she had a photo of Theo and Chloe hidden away in her drawer, which really freaked me out. She said that it was for—'

Caroline shakes her head firmly. 'No, Sally. It's not proving helpful for us to keep having these kinds of discussions.' She motions to the door. 'Why don't you get in the car? I'll wait for Chloe.'

'Wait, please! I need to ask you something. When you counselled Kelly about her mother's death, which obviously you would have done, I imagine she expressed a lot of confusion and anger about her father keeping her mother's suicide from her until just before he died?'

Caroline's face is absolutely impassive. She registers no surprise or confusion whatsoever. So it *is* true.

'Will told me everything this afternoon,' I continue. 'I assume it's what triggered Kelly's issues and made her become the person you felt you needed to warn me about, but then Will also told me this very implausible tale Kelly had spun about her father leaving her some cash. I feel so confused, I don't—'

Caroline holds up a hand. 'I'm not going to discuss Kelly with you any more, Sally. While I don't think that you meant for everything to escalate as badly as I understand it did this afternoon, your parents and Matthew were badly frightened by Kelly's earlier call to your mother, and you can see – I'm sure – that this situation, at the very least, isn't constructive? I think a day or two away – just a change of scene – might be very helpful in rebalancing some perspectives.'

'Sorry, what do you mean "rebalancing"?' I say slowly. 'I—'

'You went through Kelly's personal belongings and accused her of drugging you with a harmless homeopathic remedy.'

All the blood rushes to my face. 'How do you know that?'

'Your mother called Kelly again while you and Will were on your way back here. I arrived just in time to find them doing a FaceTime with Matthew. Kelly was very distressed.'

'Did she see you?'

'No. I waited in the kitchen until they'd finished.'

'Do Matthew and my mum believe her?'

'They are very concerned indeed, as you might expect. I haven't told them that you *do* believe she drugged you, and that you were, I suspect, looking for evidence. Currently, it's your word against hers. Are you still absolutely certain you didn't intend her any harm?'

'Of course not!' I look at her, frightened. 'I told Will I was looking for the missing money.'

'Right. Just on a very base level, Sally, strip everything else away; your theories, what everyone does or doesn't know – and repeat back to yourself that you *went through her belongings*, and tell me you think that's a perfectly rational way to behave. You wouldn't be concerned about that alone, if you were us?'

I open my mouth, but falter, and before I can say anything more, Chloe appears at the top of the stairs. 'I did one!' she tells us happily. 'And I washed my hands.'

'*What* a clever girl!' Caroline beams. 'Now, come on, darling – let's get your backpack, because Daddy and Theo are already waiting, and poor old Mummy wants the bathroom too, I think. I'll take her out, Sal –' Caroline turns briefly back to me – 'but don't slam the door behind you, will you – otherwise I shan't be able to get back in. That would be no good, would it, Chloe?' I hear her carry on chattering to Chloe as they trot out together, leaving me standing in the now silent hallway, completely alone.

'Are you still getting loads of messages about the photos in the paper?' Matthew nods at my mobile, as I peer at it while he drives.

'Not so much now, no.'

'Why don't you put your phone down for a minute, Sal?' he suggests gently. 'It always makes you car sick, reading on the move.'

'Mummy, when were there dinosaurs?' Chloe asks from the back. 'A hundred and twenty-two?'

'A hundred and twenty two years?' I ask. 'No, darling. Longer ago than that.'

'Hmmm.' She ponders that. 'Was it eighty-eight-to-ninety-one FM?'

In spite of everything, I smile and turn to Matthew. 'I think we might be listening to Radio Two a little too much, don't you?'

He smiles briefly, but says nothing.

'Longer than that, Clo,' I answer. 'Dinosaurs were alive millions and millions of years ago.'

'Can you ask *me* questions now, Mummy?'

'I think Mummy's just going to have a peaceful few minutes,' Matthew interjects, flicking the indicator on and moving into the fast lane. 'OK, Clo?'

Chloe sighs heavily.

'Tell you what, just give me two more seconds and I'll ask you some in a moment, OK?' I promise, hitting Go on my Google search for 'Kelly Harrington mother'.

Kelly Harrington – Wikipedia, the free encyclopedia.
Harrington's mother, **Denise Harrington**, was a dance
teacher, who Harrington has said inspired her to...

'Mummy, I don't want cheese sandwiches. I don't like them.'

I put my phone down. I'll have to look at this properly later. 'What don't you like about them?'

'The cheese.'

I smile again. 'Well, don't worry, baby girl. We'll stop and get you something else.'

'Thank you, Mummy.'

'You're welcome, darling.'

Matthew puts his foot down a little more. 'I'd rather not stop, actually. Can't we just keep going?'

'But Theo's going to need us to stop too.'

Matthew looks at his sleeping baby boy in the rear mirror. 'Really? He looks flat out to me.'

'He won't be for much longer. He's definitely going to need us to stop so he can have something to eat.'

'So am I,' says Chloe. 'Something that isn't cheese.'

'OK, OK, guys.' Matthew holds up a hand. 'It's fine. We'll find somewhere when he wakes up, then.'

'Mummy, I need the loo.'

I see a muscle flex in Matthew's jaw and wait for him to roll his eyes heavenward, or do a 'for God's sake' rant, but he doesn't. 'It's not a problem, Clo,' he says soothingly. 'We'll pull in, have tea, and go to the loo at the next place we see, OK? And maybe we won't drink a whole box of apple juice in one go next time, though, like I said, hey?'

'Granny Sue said it was a treat for my lunch box.'

'I know,' he says. 'Good old Granny Sue. The trouble is, sometimes people think they know what the best thing to do is, but actually they don't. Never mind, though.'

I look at him again quickly. Was that directed at me?

Matthew keeps his eyes on the road and says nothing more.

Feeding both children at a Costa is predictably hard work. Chloe only eats two bites of a tuna toastie but scoffs the huge cookie Matthew unwisely buys her, resulting in an enormous and immediate sugar rush that has her bouncing on her seat and spilling her drink everywhere. Theo completely flips out when I try and change him on the fold-down baby changer in the disabled loo, as they are his most hated thing; followed by Chloe bellowing with her hands over her ears when she sets off the hand dryer – her most hated thing. Theo is also very reluctant to get back into his car seat again. He cries in the back for what feels like an age, frazzling all of our nerves, before finally falling asleep from sheer exhaustion, followed five minutes later by a relieved Chloe.

We drive in blissful silence for a moment or two, before Matthew whispers quietly, 'I'm sorry. That was my fault. We probably should have left later. I'm just really tired, that's all.'

'You couldn't have just stayed and worked from Mum's tomorrow?'

He shakes his head. 'I've got so much on at the moment, Sal. I need to be at home where I can get into the office easily, if need be.'

'We didn't have to come up just because Mum wanted it to happen. We could have just stayed put. Your mum would have helped me.'

Matthew shifts in his seat. 'I think a change of scene would do you good.'

I open my mouth to respond to that, but before I can, he says quickly, 'So has there been any more fallout from the photos in the paper, then? Are people still trying to contact you?'

'Um, a few today. Some old work people, a couple of the NCT lot, two of the school mums texted. I didn't actually speak to any of them, though; it was all a bit overwhelming, to be honest.'

'You didn't actually go to Liv's today or speak to her in the end, then? That was just a cover for going to Will's, I assume?'

'Yes,' I confess. 'Liv's actually still pretty angry with me because of what she thinks I was going to do in Cornwall.'

Matthew hesitates. 'I think perhaps it's a hard subject for people to understand, because they try to put themselves in that position and can't imagine how someone might make a choice like that – when the desperately sad reality is, it's a situation the person concerned has no control over.'

I glance at him, questioningly.

'I've been chatting with Mum about it a bit this week,' he explains. 'Not in relation to you,' he adds quickly. 'Just about the subject in general.'

'I see.' I fall silent as I try to imagine Caroline also counselling a devastated and grieving Kelly, and saying exactly the same thing to her that Matthew has just said to me, but somehow I can't picture Kelly as a teenager – I can only see her the way she is now.

'I gather you all had a FaceTime call with Kelly today, where she told you I accused her of drugging me on Friday night,' I say quietly.

He tenses. 'Yes, we did. She was... pretty upset. Is it true? That's what you said to her?'

I hesitate for a moment before admitting, 'Yes.'

Matthew inhales sharply.

'I thought I'd find proof,' I say. 'I could lie and tell you I was looking for the missing money, but I think it's important I'm honest with you, of all people...' I trail off. 'I was convinced she was to blame for everything that's happened.'

'Only you're not now?' He concentrates on the road ahead.

I hesitate. 'I don't know,' I say truthfully. 'I've found out some things I wasn't aware of, about her mother's death, which actually makes sense of some of her actions – and she *did* deliberately have those horrendous pictures of me put in the paper, it wasn't a mistake – but then she's also flat out denied having anything to do with the money going missing, or my winding up in that taxi. She seemed... almost believable...' I rest my head back on the seat. 'Except Will also told me this ridiculous story on the way home about Kelly's dad having half a million pounds in cash in his house when he died, and that Kelly, her brother and sister kept it, and Kelly used her share to pay for her engagement ring – not, as I thought, our money.'

'You thought she bought her engagement ring with our missing money?' I can tell Matthew is keeping his tone deliberately casual.

'Yes. Will's asked me not to tell anyone this, so please don't say anything, but Kelly secretly upgraded the ring Will bought her for something a *lot* more valuable – in cash – the day after our money went missing. I know that for a fact. And I just can't help but think the stuff about her dad's money is just too ridiculous a story, and too much of a coincidence, to be true.'

Matthew raises his eyebrows, but says nothing. Encouraged, I continue. 'I don't know if you still think I'm trying to cover up what I was actually planning to do on Friday night, but I truthfully have no memory of it. I mean, obviously *something* extraordinary happened – people don't just wake up at the other end of the country in the back of a taxi. On the one hand, knowing Kelly published those photos of me makes me think anyone capable of doing something that devious would also be capable of stealing our money – and drugging me to create a diversion.' I pause to catch my breath. 'But then I hear myself saying it out loud like that and it sounds so ludicrous! I also *don't* have any proof that she's done anything – except she's got form, and she hates me.'

Matthew puts a steadying hand on my leg. 'Sally, just stop. You need to calm down. We don't need to go through all of this now. I don't want you getting upset again. The kids are asleep, and in case they're not later, shouldn't you try and rest yourself? It's not that—'

'The more I think about it, though, the more implausible the story about her dad's money becomes,' I continue. 'How come she's never told Will about it before? I'd tell you if I found out Mum and Dad had that much cash shoved in the loft...' I pause. 'But then, I guess, we've been married for six years; they've hardly been together for the blink of an eye. Oh my God – I'm going around in circles, Matthew.' I lean my head back exhaustedly.

'So just stop thinking about it all, please!'

I ignore him. 'My head is absolutely buzzing with everything that's happened. *Surely* she'd have told Will if she genuinely had that much money in cash? You couldn't find a more trustworthy person than my brother, and they were engaged by that point.' That reminds me of her scathing assessment of *our* marriage. 'By the way, she also told me she thinks we shouldn't be married any more.'

'Excuse me?' Matthew looks outraged, and immediately forgets he's trying to pour oil on troubled waters. 'She said what? It's none of her business!'

'She said I was a sad, middle-aged woman, who had pulled a selfish stunt to get you to notice me again.'

'How dare she!' He's furious. 'I might not say it enough, mostly because we seem to spend twenty-four hours a day firefighting these two,' he nods in the mirror at our two sleeping children, 'but of *course* I notice you. I notice you all the time, working your arse off for us, and she couldn't be more wrong: being with the three of you is the most important thing in the world to me. When I've had a shit day at work – and believe me, there have been plenty of them recently – I come into the kitchen and you're doing tea, Chloe is colouring at her little table, and Theo is in his bouncer, and I know I *have* achieved something.' He pauses. 'I would be lost without you. It's as simple as that – and things are only going to get better. I don't know how, yet, but we *will* move past all of this, and it *will* all be OK. Kelly can go to hell!'

I look at my poor, exhausted husband in concern. I certainly wouldn't have chosen for it to happen like this, or *because* of this, but neither am I going to pretend Matthew hasn't been support-ive, and isn't trying his hardest, because I can see that he's giving it his all.

'Bizarrely, though, she's got a point in that we've talked prop-erly more in the last couple of days than we have in months.' He takes a deep breath. 'She isn't right, is she? This wasn't a much more elaborate version of what you did at university to get your boyfriend back?'

'Of course not!' I exclaim in disbelief.

'Maybe not on a conscious level, but...' He trails off.

I'm horrified. 'Not on an unconscious *or* conscious level. I was completely disorientated and terrified when I was on top of that cliff, alone and with no idea how I got there. You think I did that for attention?'

'You're right, I'm sorry,' he says quickly. 'I'm really sorry, I shouldn't have even asked. I really do want you to try not to even think about Kelly over the next couple of days, and give your brain a complete break. Regardless of your motivation, or otherwise, you can't go around letting yourself into other people's homes. It's just not... normal.'

'I was desperate to find proof of what happened to me. You don't understand that at all? You wouldn't have done the same in my shoes?'

'No, I wouldn't.'

'Even to protect Chloe and Theo?'

'What?' Now he looks really scared. 'What are you talking about?'

'Your mum used to treat Kelly – as a patient. I'm not supposed to tell anyone, she shouldn't have told me – she could get struck off for it, apparently – but she warned me Kelly is potentially dangerous. That's really someone you want around our children for the next God knows how many years?'

'I can't believe Mum would have said that to you,' he says carefully. 'I think, at the very least, you must have misunderstood what she meant.'

'No! I didn't,' I say with energy. 'Ask her – ask her yourself!'

'OK, easy, Sal. I'll talk to her, OK?'

'You promise?'

'I promise.'

Once we've arrived, he's helped me settle the kids, unpacked the car, and had a coffee, it's time for him to go, and we stand opposite each other on my parents' doorstep in the dark, breathing in the cold, clean air. I'm shivering slightly, and have my arms wrapped around myself.

'Could you please send me a text when you get back, so I don't worry?'

'But it'll be really late, I don't want to wake you, or Theo.'

'Please?' I squint up at him worriedly.

'OK. Now please go in and go to bed, you look shattered.'

'You're probably right, you know. I'm sure I will benefit from some... distance.'

'That's all this is,' he assures me. 'Some breathing space for you – a chance to clear your head a little bit. Try not to overthink things. Will you do something else for me? Don't contact Kelly, OK?'

'I have no intention of going anywhere near her.'

'Good.' He sounds relieved. 'I'll come and get you at the weekend. Sooner, if you need me. Just call.'

I nod again, gratefully. 'Thank you. But you will talk to your mum, about what I said, won't you? She's going to be upset that I've told you, but I can't do anything about that. You had to know.'

'You're sure you're going to be OK?'

'Yes.'

'I love you, Sally.'

'I love you too.'

He leans in and kisses me softly. It isn't the hurried brush of lips we usually barely manage. I can't actually remember the last time we kissed like this, and my tummy flips over.

'I'll see you on Saturday.'

'OK.' I try to smile, suddenly feeling unaccountably teary.

'Hey, don't cry,' he says. 'Everything is going to be all right – I promise.'

He hugs me, then kisses me again, this time more briefly, and turns to walk to the car. It's like being seventeen again and saying goodnight to my boyfriend, standing on my parents' step and wishing he didn't have to go home.

I watch him climb in, and the headlights flash on. He doesn't pause to wave, just pulls away. I listen until I can't hear the car any more, then, shivering again, I turn and head back into the house.

CHAPTER SEVENTEEN

'Oh Theo, don't, sweetie, please!' I beg, as Theo bats away his spoon, knocking it out of my hand and sending yet another glob of his breakfast splatting onto the pram. I jump up hastily, grabbing the damp cloth again, and try to sponge it off.

'I must say, it *is* a nuisance that we forgot the high chair,' Mum says, watching me. 'I'm sure I told Matthew to put it in.'

'It's OK.' I scrub at the stain. 'I should have told you all to just wait so I could check everything. I don't know what I was thinking.' I rub my eyes tiredly and pick up Theo's spoon to rinse under the tap. 'Apart from anything else, this is just too big to have inside the house. Whole travel systems like this were very popular when we had Chloe; they're much lighter and more user-friendly now.'

'Oh, it's a super pram,' Mum says, surprised. 'It's very clever the way it converts from lying down flat to sitting up now Theo's that bit older. Don't get rid of it, will you?'

What, in case Will and Kelly want it? Let's not even go there, Mum.

'So!' Mum says brightly, changing the subject. Clearly she doesn't intend to either. 'What would we all like to do today?'

I glance out of the kitchen window at the fat raindrops sliding down the windowpane. 'Well, I think the beach is out.'

'Oh,' says Chloe, slumping disappointedly over her bowl of Cheerios. 'I wanted to do some digging.'

'We'll do that tomorrow instead, shall we?' Mum suggests. 'The weather's going to be much brighter later in the week. I had an idea, though, for this morning. I wondered, Chloe, would you like to come to the shop and have a go on the till?'

Chloe nods, and looks excitedly at me, barely able to believe her luck at being asked to play shop – one of her favourite games – for real.

'Then on our way back, I thought we could go to the bakery and choose a cupcake to bring back here for lunch, and then this afternoon, if it's still raining, we can do some colouring and then make some scones for tea. What do you think?' Mum smiles at her.

'Yes please!' Chloe jiggles in her seat, unable to contain her delight. I can't help but smile too. At the very least, being here is absolutely brilliant for her.

'Good!' says Mum, pleased. 'Well then, if you've finished your breakfast, go get your toothbrush from the little pink mug, bring it down, and we'll do your teeth.'

Chloe is already scampering off. 'What do you say, Clo?' I call after her as she disappears upstairs.

'Thank you for my breakfast!' she shouts back.

'Don't run while you're carrying the brush,' I add fretfully, then turn back to Theo. 'I think you're done with this too, aren't you?' I get to my feet again to wash his porridge bowl, but Mum beats me to it, jumping up and whisking it out from under my nose.

'I'll do that. Would you like another cup of tea?'

'No, thank you.'

'You're sure? The kettle's just boiled.'

'Honestly, I'm fine.'

'It's not a problem, I'm making one anyway. You might as well.'

'OK then,' I sigh, giving in, and Mum nods approvingly.

'Good girl.'

'Actually,' I consider, 'if you're off in a minute, I'd better go and get dressed. I'll bring the kids over after Theo's nap, shall I? That'll give her a good half an hour in the shop.'

'Oh, I meant I'll take Chloe over so you can rest,' Mum says, surprised. 'And there's really no reason why I can't take Theo too, is there? Couldn't he have his nap in the pram? Although,' she says suddenly, 'thinking about it, perhaps it would be better if I dropped Chloe off with Dad, and then I popped back here, then I can just go back again to get her for lunch. Yes, we'll do that.'

'But that's a lot of faffing about for you, Mum. I can just bring them myself once...' I trail off. 'Hang on, you're not suggesting all that so I won't be on my own with the kids, are you?'

Mum colours hotly. 'Of course not!'

'Or left on my own completely? I'm not going to do anything, Mum,' I say slowly. 'You know that, don't you?'

She busies herself with getting fresh teabags out.

'Mum?'

'Well, look then, why don't I take Chloe, you stay here with Theo and put him down, and we'll come back for lunch all together,' she suggests. 'There. Everyone's happy. But I do want you to rest while we're out. And I mean actually rest. Sleep if you can, or at the very least read a book or watch some TV – Dad's lit the woodburner in the sitting room – but no going on your phone. Chloe's got her little umbrella and wellies, so we're all set – and the fresh air will do her good. We'll *definitely* be back at lunchtime, though – and no, not because I'm worried about you being on your own,' she adds firmly, which means that's exactly what she's worried about. 'Now, if you're going to go and get dressed, why don't you have a nice bath and hair wash too, while I look after Theo and clean the breakfast things up?'

'Are you sure? I'll be quick.'

'You can be as long as you like,' she says. 'Take your time and enjoy it. Here, you can take your tea with you.'

'Thank you. And I promise you've got nothing to worry about this morning, Mum. We'll be perfectly safe.'

'Of course you will,' she says, with her back to me as she wipes up a spilt splash of milk. 'Now, go on – up you go.'

It *is* pretty wonderful to have a proper shower that actually has some pressure, and – unlike our rubbish one at home that's hardly better than standing in a mist of light rain – actually gets all of the shampoo out of my hair. The room is lovely and clean, the towel is fresh and fluffy, but best of all I don't have a small person eyeing me beadily from his bouncer like a tiny time-trial judge, as I leap around hurriedly lathering and rinsing before my two minutes are up.

I don't feel quite so cheery as I go through the bag of things Mum has packed for me, however, discovering that she has somehow managed to select the frumpiest clothes I own. Some of them I've not even seen for a couple of years. I have no idea where she found them. There's a Fat Face shirt and cardigan that Matthew very sweetly bought me for my birthday, and that I absolutely loathe – the shirt is checked gingham and the cardigan dove grey with a waterfall front. I actually thought I'd smuggled them to Oxfam. The jumper I discover next is too small – because I shrunk it while testing the dry-clean-only theory. There's a White Company black jersey top with bell sleeves and a very low-cut front. It's OK, but looks horribly 80s given all she's selected trouser-wise are some blue jeans – unless I go for the M&S burgundy cords, pointedly included because she bought them for me, or some black leggings. I scratch my head as I look at them all. It's like having individual pieces from lots of different jigsaws. Nothing goes together. Well, I guess I won't be leaving the house for the next three days.

I've not got my hairdryer either, which is far more of a disaster.

'Just use mine,' Mum says in surprise when I appear in the kitchen to ask politely which bag she put it in, to discover Chloe happily making a macaroni necklace, and Theo starting to whinge slightly, on the countdown to needing his nap.

I have a go with her dryer, but it's so tiny it does absolutely nothing, so I give up and decide to let my hair dry naturally for once, as Theo begins to kick off downstairs.

He does at least go down surprisingly well, and by ten o'clock I'm back in the quiet kitchen, clutching the monitor; the only other sounds being the familiar *tick tock* of the cuckoo clock on the wall and the light pattering of rain on the windowpane. Mum and Chloe have already left.

I sink down onto one of the kitchen chairs and reach for my phone, only hesitating at the last moment, as I remember my promise to Mum. That reminds me that the woodburner has been lit. I make a cup of tea and make my way through into the sitting room.

The neat room is warm and cosy, the curtains tied back to reveal my parents' pretty cottage garden. The beds are full of glistening clouds of forget-me-nots and damp lily of the valley. I sink down into Dad's chair next to the fire. Mum put a couple of logs on before she left, and they're fizzing and hissing as they start to catch.

I sigh, lean my head back, and stare at the flames flickering behind the spotless glass door, thinking uncomfortably back to Caroline yesterday, telling me gently but firmly that going through Kelly's things is, at best, irrational. How the hell has everything changed so quickly in just five days? I barely recognize my own life.

Setting my tea down determinedly on the bookshelf to my left, I decide I don't want to think about it any more. I'm so very tired.

I snuggle down a little deeper. For once there is no tidying up to do, no washing to fold or put on. Theo is out for the count.

Perhaps I will just have ten minutes. I close my eyes... and my phone immediately bleeps with a message. I try to ignore it, but needily, it bleeps a second time because I haven't read it, and curiosity gets the better of me.

It's Will.

Hi. Didn't call last night as knew you were driving to Mum's, but need to speak to you. Obv Kelly told me what you said about her drugging you. You didn't think to mention this yesterday in car on way to yours? Very concerned. When can we talk?

Oh God. I just can't do this now. I put the phone on silent, just for a moment, pop it on the side, and desperately close my eyes. I'll have two minutes, then call him.

About another thirty seconds pass before the doorbell goes. It's a shrill, old-fashioned ring, like a bell in the servants' quarter, and I snap alert, jumping immediately to my feet. If they press it again, Theo will *definitely* wake, and he's been down just long enough to pep himself up enough so that he won't go back to sleep. I hurtle through the hallway and fling the door open, to discover the only school friend I still really keep in touch with, Mel, standing on the doorstep.

'Ed *said* he saw your car outside last night!' she exclaims, delighted. I smile weakly and hold the door wider as she hurries in out of the rain. 'It's so lovely to see you!' She hugs me. 'What a treat to have you back home again so quickly.'

'I was going to call you this morning,' I lie guiltily. 'We only got here late. Do you want a cup of tea?'

'I won't, thanks. I'm not stopping, I've got to get to the chemist to pick something up for Nan. Where is everyone?' She looks around, surprised.

'Matthew's gone home as he's working, Mum's taken Chloe to the shop, and Theo's asleep.'

'House to yourself – nice!' She nods approvingly, then looks at her watch and kicks off her shoes. 'Tell you what, I'll just come in for five minutes.'

My shoulders sag slightly as I follow her through into the sitting room. Bang goes my nap.

'Your hair looks different,' she remarks. 'Have you done something?'

'Washed it. I'm letting it dry on its own.'

'I do that all the time. Easier, isn't it?' She flops down onto the sofa. 'So, you've had a shit couple of days then?'

'You saw the photos.'

'Yeah,' she commiserates. 'Didn't you get my message on Facebook?'

I shake my head. 'I shut down my account to stop people posting about them on my wall.'

'Ah – that explains it,' she says. 'I told Ed it would be something like that. I texted you too, but I didn't realize the bloody thing hadn't sent till after Ed had got back with the Chinese and told me he'd seen your car, so I thought, I'll just go around in the morning.' She folds her legs up under her. 'So what was all that guff they said about you having mental problems? I know we don't speak *all* the time, but I said to Hayley yesterday, "I think she would have told me if there was something like that going on. She was all right at Easter!"'

'Hayley from school, Hayley?' I ask weakly.

'Yeah. It's shocking, isn't it, the way they just print lies like that? Kelly must be fuming! I can't believe she and Will are actually getting married, by the way. How do you feel about it? Do you still hate her? Are they going to do *Hello!*? I so would if I were them.'

'I don't know, really, Mel. We haven't discussed it yet.'

'No, I don't suppose you have, given what's happened. On the plus side, love, at least all your bits and pieces were covered. I'd have been hanging out all over the shop. So, is Chloe going to be a bridesmaid? That'll be so cute!'

'Yes, she is.'

'Ahh. Grand!' She looks delighted. '*I* know what I was going to ask you. It obviously all happened first thing in the morning, because you hadn't got your face on, and I said to Ed, she doesn't leave the house without at least her mascara, but why were you holding a stick in the pictures?'

'I was holding it for Kelly. She was having some balance issues.'

'Oh really?' She looks interested. 'What, like an ear infection or labyrinthitis? I get that sometimes.'

'Mel, is everyone talking about the photos?'

'What, from here, you mean? Everyone from home?'

'Yes.' I wait hopefully. Maybe it's already old news.

'Yeah, they are' she says regretfully. 'I can't lie. You know what it's like here, Sal, there's bugger all else going on. Mostly people have been asking if you're all right, like,' she taps the side of her head, 'up here and that. But don't worry,' she adds hastily, catching sight of my expression. 'It's because they're just gutted for you and worried, that's all. It's not about everyone being nosy and gossiping.'

'So everyone thinks I've gone mad?'

She wrinkles her nose. 'Not mad, no… just… a bit fucked-up. Everyone knows you've got a new baby and how hard that is. They care, that's all. People want to help. I did hear one funny thing, though. Hannah Davies said Christine Newly told her you did a bunk to Cornwall and the police picked you up in your underwear on a clifftop and had to take you home.' She giggles.

'It was my pyjamas – and I hadn't done a bunk.'

Mel's jaw drops. 'It's *true*?'

'Who told Christine? Do you know?'

'Um…' She's staring at me, momentarily lost for words.

'It'll be my mother somehow, won't it?' I shake my head. 'Telling someone she thinks she can trust.'

'What were you doing on a cliff in Cornwall in your pyjamas?' Mel asks, confused.

I take a deep breath, as I prepare to explain for the umpteenth time. 'I woke up in the back of a taxi on the clifftop. I don't know how or why I got there.'

She frowns. 'Were you pissed?'

'No.'

'Did someone spike your drink? That happened to Ed's sister's friend in a club in Newcastle. She was chatting to this bloke, and next minute she woke up back at her house. She literally had no idea how she got home.'

'You believe me?' I exclaim in surprise.

'Of course.' She looks thrown. 'Why wouldn't I?'

'Because nobody else does. Not even Matthew. Everyone thinks I was going to commit suicide.'

'*What?*' She laughs, then her face falls as she realizes I'm serious. 'That's crazy! You'd never do a thing like that! Ever since I've known you you've wanted the husband, kids, good job, nice house. You've got it all. Why would you throw it away? I mean, I know some people get depressed anyway, and that sort of stuff stops mattering to them, but I only saw you two weeks ago! You were fine. Knackered, but fine. You were just the same as always.'

It's so reassuring to hear someone talk about me – and to me – so normally, that I discover I'm near to tears. 'Thanks, Mel.'

'Hey,' she says, noticing instantly. 'Don't cry, pet!' She slips off the sofa, comes and kneels on the carpet next to me, and takes my hand. 'I don't understand,' she continues, genuinely puzzled. 'Why doesn't anyone believe you? Hasn't Matthew ever seen the news? Women get their drinks spiked all the time. You can't leave them unattended anywhere, not even for a second.'

'The thing is, I wasn't out when this happened, Mel. I was wearing pyjamas, remember? I went to bed at home, just like I always do – then I woke up in Cornwall the next morning.'

There's a long pause.

'OK, yeah, that is a bit weird,' she admits. 'In fact, that's *really* weird.'

I falter. I'm desperate to trust her; to tell her everything. She's known me for ever – and perhaps some advice from someone outside the situation is just what I need. Mel likes a bit of gossip as much as the next person – in fact, most of my local news comes via her rather than Mum – but once she understands how serious this is...

'I know you only have a few minutes,' I say desperately, 'but can I ask your opinion on something?'

'Of course,' she says immediately, and sits down properly. 'I'm all ears. Go for it.'

'So do you believe Kelly had nothing to do with what happened to me, or do you think she's lying?' I conclude, some five minutes later.

'Bloody hell!' Mel exhales slowly, gets up from the carpet, and sits back on the sofa, stunned. 'Well, I can see why you're stressed now.' She pauses. 'On the one hand, that's tragic about Kelly's mum, and I can see why her thinking you were pulling some sort of attention-seeking stunt would have big time pushed buttons for her – and she was pissed about the whole ring thing too – but does that also make her guilty of everything else? I just don't know. On the other hand, she's a professional actress, and she seems to be going out of her way to deliberately warp your own family's perception of you while behaving really deviously. Setting up those photos of you was just plain unnecessary. Plus, of course, Caroline had already warned you not to get on her bad side.' She considers everything, then continues, 'And, like you, I can't help but think it's pushing it a bit to believe that she and her brother and sister wouldn't have found all of that money from their dad straight away after he died... Although it's possible, I suppose. It *is* weird that she didn't tell Will about it until now, though. Or just unlucky. Ah shit – I honestly don't know, Sal.'

'It's not just me, is it?' I ask. 'It all seems to point to her, but she outright flat denied it when I confronted her.'

'Well, she would, really, wouldn't she?'

'I suppose so.' I rub my eyes wearily. 'I said to my mother-in-law last night, I wish she'd just... disappear.'

'I completely understand that,' Mel says.

'No, you don't,' I say miserably. 'I want more than anything to get her out of our lives. Caroline told me she was dangerous. How do I trust her around my kids? And I can already see that she's turning Will against me. Even my mum is completely taken in. She's going to wreck our family, I know it.' Tears well up in my eyes again as Mel sits there helplessly. 'Sorry,' I whisper, wiping them away.

'You don't have to apologize. I just wish there was something I could do.'

'Me too!' I try to smile. 'I'll be all right in a second. I'm just very tired. You know how it is, it always makes things seem worse, I think.'

She nods. 'Definitely. Look, Sal, I'm really sorry to have to do this, but Nan's going to do her nut. I'm going to have to go. How long are you back for?'

'Going home on Saturday, I think.'

'OK. Could I come and see you tomorrow? I'm working later today.'

'Of course. Thanks for listening.' We get to our feet. 'Mel, I know I don't need to say this, but...'

She smiles briefly. 'No, you don't. I won't say a thing. Don't worry.'

Nonetheless, as I close the front door behind her, my temporary sense of relief at being able to confide in someone drains away and I experience such an ominous sinking feeling, I have to lean on the door briefly with my eyes shut.

'Fuck it!' I say aloud, furious with myself, only to jump as the bell goes again. Mel must have forgotten something in her haste to get going. As I start to throw the latch back, I hear Theo give a sudden shout upstairs, and frustrated tears fill my eyes again.

An absolutely enormous bunch of flowers greets me. 'Sally?' says the delivery man holding them.

'Yes.' I stare at the mixture of tulips, gerbera and lilies as I wipe my eyes. 'Sorry.' I reach out for them. 'I don't mean to be crying. You just need me to sign something, I expect?'

'No. Er, Sally, it's me?' he says, embarrassed.

I look up quickly at the stranger standing in front of me, and yet, as I stare at him, I realize there is a familiarity to his features – the eyes especially – and then I see it immediately, and gasp at the twenty-year-old boy staring out of the middle-aged man's face.

'Joe?'

He smiles hesitantly. 'Hi.'

'What on earth are you doing here?' I stammer incredulously. It's one thing to have had Liv drag Joe so pointedly back into my life last Saturday, when she told everyone what I did when he dumped me; it's quite another to have him actually standing here in the flesh.

A movement over Joe's shoulder catches my eye and I look across to see Mel standing by her car, frantically waving at me, then pretending to actually pick her jaw off the floor, before mouthing 'OMG!' and making a furious phone shape with her hand, before leaping into her car and roaring off.

Joe turns around to watch her careering off around the corner. 'Was that Melanie Jackson?' he asks. 'I don't think I've seen her since school.'

'Yes, it was.'

He turns back to face me and we just stare at each other in silence, before it's punctuated by the indignant yell of Theo upstairs.

'And...' he begins slowly, 'is that *your* baby I can hear?'

'Yes, it is.' I don't appear capable of more than three words at a time.

There's another pause. 'So... are you going to invite me in, and *get* your baby?' He laughs suddenly, at what must be the expression on my face – a sound I haven't heard in nearly twenty years.

Completely dazed, I stand automatically to one side, he walks in, and I close the door behind him.

CHAPTER EIGHTEEN

J oe is sitting on the sofa nearest the window when I come back
in with Theo, who eyes him suspiciously as we sit down on
Dad's chair.

'Ah!' Joe says. 'She's cute. What's her name?'

'Theo.'

'Oh, sorry.' He pulls a face.

'It's OK, it's my fault for dressing him in his big sister's flowery
babygrows. He doesn't wear them out, obviously, just to sleep in,'
I explain unnecessarily.

'Sure.' He nods understandingly. 'It makes sense, after all;
they're out of them so quickly, aren't they?'

'You've got two boys, I think?' I say politely.

He looks slightly surprised. 'Yes, I have.'

'Mum keeps me up to date with all the local news,' I explain
quickly. 'So you must be here visiting *your* mum and dad. Last I
heard you were in Plymouth?'

'Portsmouth.'

'Oh, right. Sorry.'

We lapse into a brief and uncomfortable silence, which thankfully Theo breaks by starting to wave his arms around cheerfully, as
Joe glances down at the flowers he's rested on the carpet, suddenly
appearing to wonder what on earth he's doing here. I'm struggling
to reconcile this grown man with the skinny twenty-year-old who

has been fixed in my memory for so long. He's dressed in middle-aged-dad dark blue jeans with smart black shoes, topped off with a tucked-in navy shirt: the off-duty uniform of the type of chap who works and plays hard, and still likes to try and stay fit, but doesn't really have the time or energy any more. Then again, with my damp hair, low-cut black top that is embarrassingly gaping over my cleavage, and black leggings tucked into socks, I am hardly in a position to throw stones. In fact, I think of the two of us, the passage of time has probably been less kind to me. On the odd occasion I've idly wondered what it would be like to bump into Joe again, neither of us looked like this in my imagined scenario, that's for sure.

Joe clears his throat. 'I've been at Mum and Dad's for a couple of days, actually, and, well...' He pauses. 'I heard what happened in Cornwall and... saw the pictures.'

I go very still and don't say anything.

'That is to say,' he falters, and tries again, 'I gather you've been having a tough time. A really tough time. And I wanted to come and see if you were all right, and to let you know I was thinking of you. That's all. Mum told me you were back.' He looks up at me earnestly. 'But now I'm actually here, I can see I'm intruding. You've got things you need to be doing,' he gestures helplessly at Theo, 'and I'm probably the last person you want to talk to.' He frowns suddenly. 'Sorry, Sal, I should have thought this through. Look, I'll go. This was horribly insensitive of me, I'm really very sorry.'

Before I can say anything, I hear the front door bang, and Mum suddenly bursts into the sitting room, panting. 'I've been ringing and ringing. Why aren't you answering your— Oh!' She draws up short and just stares at Joe. 'Joe Ellis,' she says, glancing first at me, then down at the flowers, then back up at Joe coolly. 'Well, this is a surprise.'

'Hello, Mrs Tanner,' Joe says politely, getting to his feet. 'It's been a while.'

'Yes, it has, hasn't it? How are you, dear?' She puts her head to one side sympathetically. 'I gather your wife has just left you?'

'Mum!' I say, shocked.

Joe flushes. 'Um, yes, she has. Or asked me to leave, to be more precise.'

'So you're back living with your parents?'

'For the time being.'

'Ah, well that'll be nice for your mother, I'm sure. It hasn't affected your job then, being all the way across here?'

'No,' Joe says. 'I can work remotely, so luckily that's all fine.'

'Oh, I *am* glad.' Mum looks disappointed. 'Now I'm going to have to be very bossy, I'm afraid, and remind Sally that we have to leave in about twenty minutes. We're all going out to lunch, you see, Joe. We've got a bit of a drive to get there.'

'Oh, of course. I'll leave you to it.' Joe reaches into his back pocket and fumbles for his car keys. 'It was very nice to see you again, Mrs Tanner. Please do pass my best on to Mr Tanner. I hear he's in rude health, which is great.'

'Thank you.' Mum smiles obliquely.

'I'll see you out.' I get up and pass Theo to Mum. 'Perhaps you can watch Theo while I go and get changed.' I shoot her a look, which she innocently ignores.

On the doorstep, Joe turns back. 'It's been nice to see you again.'

'I'm sorry about that.' I gesture over my shoulder, back towards where Mum is cheerfully chatting to Theo in the sitting room.

'Not at all, it's my fault turning up unannounced – just bad timing. I hope you have a good meal.'

'No, I meant Mum being chippy with you.'

He smiles sadly. 'Oh, that. It's OK. I deserved it. Mothers never forget.'

'No,' I admit. 'They don't. I'm sorry to hear about you and your wife, Joe.'

'Yeah, me too.' He squints down at the ground, and for a horrible moment, I think he's going to cry, but then I realize he's actually just lost for the words that might cover the enormity of it all, and his evident grief. 'It was… complicated.'

'You don't have to tell me,' I say quickly. 'Not if you don't want to.'

'Sally!' calls Mum from inside. 'Theo needs you!'

For God's sake, Mum! 'I'll be there in a minute!' I shout furiously back over my shoulder.

'It's all right, you go,' Joe says. 'I actually shouldn't have come, Sal. I could see immediately what your mum thought, and it isn't *that*, really it isn't. When I heard what people were saying about you, it made me very angry, partly because there will always be a corner of my heart that has your name written on it.' He smiles briefly. 'But also because no one has the right to second-guess what's going on in anyone else's life. I've got two little boys, I know how challenging everything can be for a couple at the best of times.' He shrugs. 'It happened to my wife and me – we didn't make it.'

I feel really sad for him. 'I wish there was something I could say.'

'There is, actually.' He looks up again. 'I know it's incredibly selfish, but I also wanted to tell you I was sorry. I never apologized properly for the way I treated you when we split up. I was an obnoxious little prick, and I let you down at the worst possible time, when your dad was so ill. I hope you can forgive me.'

'Oh, come on! It was twenty-odd years ago!' I begin awkwardly. 'You don't need to—'

'Sally!' There's another firm shout from within the house.

'Mum, I swear to God…' I spin around and yell warningly, pausing for a second to make sure she's got the message, before turning back to Joe.

'No, I really do need to apologize,' he says. 'I'm not arrogant enough to assume that my appallingly cavalier behaviour had any lasting effect, I just very much regret hurting you at all – particularly in light of my own recent experiences – and I hope that if you are having some difficulties at the moment, they are short-lived, and the path becomes smoother again very soon.'

I can't help but smile. 'You haven't lost your charm, I see.'

'Or my capacity for bullshit, depending on who you're talking to,' he says wryly, then looks appalled. 'Not that I mean for one second what I just said was all a load of...'

'Joe, please. It's really fine,' I say firmly, and it actually is. I reach a hand out to him. 'Apology accepted.'

He hesitates, and then takes my hand in his. We'd look ridiculous to anyone passing, two grown adults about a foot apart, hands clasped, but we just stand there for a second or two, locked in a brief moment where the past collides with the here and now, and may well be all we ever have again.

We drop hands.

'I'll let you go back in,' he says. 'Your mum's probably about to spontaneously combust.' He smiles mischievously. 'Tell her I asked you to come and look me up at Mum and Dad's in case you fancied a drink or something while you're here – which of course you can, if you'd like some company.'

'I'll bear that in mind. Thanks.' I grin.

He inclines his head gently, turns, and walks down the drive towards what I assume is his dad's car. I can't imagine a Jag is really his style – yet.

'Take care, Sal,' he calls out, blowing me a kiss as he gets in.

I watch him go, waving as he rounds the corner and then disappears, before leaning on the door frame soberly for a minute. Separated with two small boys. Wow. There but for the grace of

God... I suddenly want to call Matthew and tell him how much I love him. How lucky we are.

I walk back into the sitting room to find Theo happily sitting on the carpet gumming his toy firefly, not in need of me at all, of course. I look at Mum and raise my eyebrow pointedly.

'What?' she says defensively.

'Going out to lunch? Theo needs me?'

'Well, I'm sorry, Sally, but if he thinks he can arrive at the party after the band's packed up and demand an encore, he's got another think coming.'

'He just split up from his wife!'

'Exactly.'

'And thanks, by the way, for the heads-up on that piece of information. You didn't think to mention it to me?'

Mum stays mutinously quiet. 'You'll understand one day, when Chloe meets her Joe Ellis.'

I don't say anything to that, partly because the thought makes me feel ill. Instead, I say quietly, 'He knew about me being picked up in Cornwall.'

Mum drops my gaze. 'I thought he might. I'm very sorry about that, Sally. I trusted someone I shouldn't have on Saturday, when I felt a little overwhelmed by everything. Unfortunately she didn't keep it to herself. Make no mistake that I'll be taking it up with her, though. Now, I ought to get back to the shop, really, to get Chloe. I only came back to see why you weren't answering your phone. Why haven't you answered any of my messages? I was worried, and I didn't want to ring the landline in case it woke Theo.'

'I put my mobile on silent so I could close my eyes for a minute. I'll put it back on now. There, all done. Why were you calling anyway? Is Chloe OK?'

'She's fine.'

'Then why... Oh Mum, you weren't checking up on me, were you? I've told you, there's no need for you to worry!'

'Well, you say that, and I come home to Joe Ellis sitting here, cool as you like. Lucky I did come back,' she adds darkly.

'He was hardly here for more than a minute before you came charging in.'

'Hmmm,' she says. 'Well, just you remember, you have a husband who loves you very much. And the grass is never greener.'

'Oh, honestly!' It's my turn to scold. 'Don't be ludicrous. Joe came around to say hello, that's all. Seeing as you *are* here, though, I'm just going to pop to the loo before you go, if that's OK?'

'Yes, it's fine. Be quick, though, or Chloe will be wondering where I am.'

Upstairs, I actually go into my bedroom. I can't help but check my appearance critically in the full-length mirror – only to wince. Mum's out of her mind if she thinks Joe might have had any dishonourable intentions towards me. I should think the poor bloke had the shock of his life when I opened the front door. And how embarrassing that I didn't even recognize him. I cringe afresh and sink down onto the bed for a moment. And now I'm going to have to tell Matthew that he was here, too. I lie back and stare up at the ceiling. Great. That's going to be fun. Thanks to Liv, I think Joe has featured more in my life this week than he has in the last two decades.

I hesitate and reach for my iPad, sitting next to the bed, and tap 'Fields of Gold' into YouTube. It's ridiculously indulgent and foolish, but as the music starts – the other of the two songs I most associate with Joe – I close my eyes for a second, and immediately I'm back in the teenage bedroom at his parents' house, lying on his single bed, the duvet and pillow smelling faintly of Fahrenheit aftershave. The window is open. It's warm outside, and I can hear the seagulls lazily calling to each other in the otherwise sleepily still, late afternoon. God, I loved him. I can remember so clearly what it felt like to be that girl: just starting out in life, long summer days, eating supper outside in the garden with his parents, which we never did at home, driving my little car down the country lanes on my own back to Mum and Dad's, feeling utterly happy and free... A lump wells up in my throat and I realize to my huge surprise that all this time I've assumed it was Joe walking away that broke my heart, when actually I think it was the loss of myself that did it. I stopped being that girl after what happened, and the sheer stupidity of what I did to try and win him back.

I reach out and stop the music abruptly, before getting up and heading off downstairs.

Mum looks up from where she is sitting on the carpet with Theo and smiles tiredly as I come back in. I walk over and drop a kiss on the top of her head.

'I'm sorry for all the sleepless nights I've given you,' I say sincerely, and then I sit down next to her, taking Theo gently from her. 'What Liv told Matthew, about my taking all of those pills, was very private information and not something I ever intended for you, or anyone, to know. I was drunk out of my mind when I did it.'

Mum's eyes start to shine, and she just nods, for once unable to speak.

'But I absolutely swear to you, I wasn't attempting to kill myself on Friday night.'

She reaches out and half squeezes my arm, while half using it to help her get to her feet. 'I really do have to go and get that little girl. She'll be starving. She's been having a lovely time with Dad. You know, the one thing all this has made me think is that we live too far away from each other.' She wipes her eyes quickly. 'Three hours is too much. I want to be in Theo and Chloe's lives all the time. I don't suppose you might think about moving home? The schools are very good, and you've got lots of people who know you here, and as *Joe* said,' she still struggles to say his name, 'so many people work remotely these days. Perhaps Matthew could too?'

'Perhaps,' I say. 'We have only just moved, though, Mum.'

'Oh, you won't stay in that house,' she says, brushing her skirt off and walking to the door. 'You'll do it up and sell it on. It's not your forever home. I feel it in my bones. Right, I'm just going to put a cauliflower cheese in the oven. If I'm not back in twenty-five minutes, could you take it out again?'

After she's gone, I reach for my phone, Theo sitting on my lap. Matthew picks up immediately.

'Hey,' he says worriedly. 'You all right?'

'I'm fine. I just wanted to say that I love you and I miss you,' I say. 'And I'm looking forward to seeing you, and coming home at the weekend. Hang on, Theo.' I hold the phone out of his reach as he tries to grab for it. 'Matthew, I need to tell you something. Joe – my ex – was just here.'

'At your parents'?' he says sharply.

'Yes. He brought me some flowers because he'd seen the pictures of me in the paper and heard I'd been picked up in a distressed state in Cornwall. Mel said exactly the same thing. The whole village is talking about it – which is nice. Theo, darling, please wait a second! I put them both right, but the reason I'm telling you about Joe is because I don't want it to seem like it was a secret meeting, which it wasn't.'

'He just brought you flowers. He didn't want anything else?' Matthew demands sceptically.

'No, nothing. I just didn't want you to think I was trying to hide anything from you, that's all. I meant to ask you too – have you talked to your mum yet, about what I told you last night? The information she gave me about Kelly, I mean? Ooof!' Theo makes another swipe for the phone, misses, and scratches me instead, then, frustrated by his efforts, bursts into tears.

'Yes, I have. It sounds like you've got your hands full. Can your mum take him for a sec?'

'She's not here. They're all up at the shop.'

'Oh right... You and Theo are alone at home then?'

'Yup. Shall we chat later?' I say reluctantly as Theo starts to wail properly. 'I probably am going to have to go, I think, but I really do love you. Just so you know.'

'I love you too. Just quickly, when you say you put Mel and Joe right about what really happened in Cornwall, what did you tell them?'

'Oh, I explained I haven't gone mad, and I don't have any mental issues. I didn't offer them an alternative explanation; I couldn't – I don't have one, do I?'

He pauses. 'I'm really sorry everyone is talking about you, Sal. That must be very hard.'

'It's OK. Mum's packed me such dire wardrobe choices I'm not actually going to be able to leave the house in any case, so it's not like anyone is going to have the opportunity to point fingers and inspect me for themselves. OK, darling! Mummy's nearly finished. I'm going to have to go, Matthew.'

'Sure. I would like to talk to you about what happened in Cornwall, though. I don't want you to think that we're just going to quietly sweep everything under the carpet, but I just think we should wait until your results from the tests come back clear first.'

'Um, OK,' I say warily. 'Has something changed? You were adamant before that I wasn't ill.'

'No, no, it's nothing like that. Listen, we'll talk later. You go, Theo sounds like he's losing the plot completely. Will your mum be home soon? They're up at the shop, you say?'

'Yes, they're coming back for lunch. Let's speak in a bit then. Bye, love.' I hang up.

Despite my earlier misgivings about confiding in Mel, it is actually a huge relief to have someone believe me, and Matthew actually does seem marginally calmer about everything today, which can only be a good thing.

'Come on, Theo, let's go in the other room, shall we, and see what we can find?' I smile at my son, who eyes me balefully, unconvinced, before starting to cry. My phone also starts to ring again, and glancing at it, I see its Will. I can't answer now – not with Theo like this.

Wincing guiltily, I let it go to voicemail.

Anyway, I still haven't worked out what the hell I'm going to say to him.

CHAPTER NINETEEN

My mobile starts buzzing at about 7 a.m. At first, I think it's my alarm and fumble around for it on the bedside table, only for it to stop of its own accord. Gratefully, I assume it's gone into snooze mode, until it dawns on me that, of course, I've not had to use an alarm for some months now.

I prop myself up on my elbows. I can hear the kids playing downstairs. Mum must have taken them to give me a lie-in. That's so kind of her. I yawn and reach for the phone. It must have been someone trying to ring me. I peer at the screen. A missed call from Will. This early? I know I didn't call him back yesterday, but still…

It starts to ring in my hand. It's him again. This is weird. Something's wrong. I brace myself and pick up.

'Hey,' I say, rubbing my eyes. 'You OK? I'm really sorry I haven't called. I know what it is you want to discuss.'

'Was it you?' His voice is shaking with anger, and I immediately come to properly.

'Was what me?'

'Don't try that,' he says warningly. 'You have done nothing but lie to me since you broke into my flat. Just tell me the truth now. Was it you who told the press about Kelly's mother? It's a straight answer: yes or no?'

I freeze instantly. Oh my God, Mel… What have you done?

'Of course not.'

'It's everywhere! Kelly got a Google alert. She's absolutely devastated. And guess what – they know about her upgrading the ring too. So my next question is, given you're the *only* person I told about that, do you want to change your mind about the answer you just gave me?'

'It wasn't me!'

'OK, then who *did* you tell?'

I swallow. 'Mel.'

'*Mel?*' he says in disbelief. 'As in Mel from home? You're not serious? You *know* what it's like around there! They all tell each other everything about everyone!'

'I asked her not to! She's my oldest friend. I needed someone to talk to, Will. She promised she wouldn't, and I really didn't think she'd—'

'But what about the promise you made to me first?' he cuts in. 'The one where I specifically asked you to keep it all to yourself? Remember?'

'Yes, of course I do.'

'So then help me out here, Sal.' He's becoming angrier, and really shouting now. I don't think I've ever heard him yell like this. It's horrible. 'What part of the system broke down? I mean, what the fuck were you *thinking*? Oh Jesus,' he gasps, then falls silent for a moment. 'You meant to tell Mel, didn't you? Because you *knew* she wouldn't be able to keep it to herself, and something like this would happen.'

'No!' I'm horrified. 'Of course not!'

'I know you've never liked Kelly, but until yesterday I had no idea how deep it ran. To accuse her of drugging you is insane enough, but to do something like this... You know this will destroy her brother and sister too, don't you?'

'I did not do this deliberately, Will, I swear to you. No, I don't like Kelly, but I would never, ever do something so underhand – or betray you. You must know that, surely?'

'I can't talk to you right now, Sal. I'm sorry. I'm going to have to go.'

'Will – wait!' I plead.

'No, Sally, I have to, or I'm going to say something I regret.' And then he hangs up.

I stare at my phone aghast. He's never hung up on me, ever. I call him back immediately, but it goes straight to answerphone.

'Please pick up; let me explain,' I beg in my message. 'I'll hopefully talk to you in a bit.' I click off, wait a few seconds, and then call again – but still no answer. Instead I type Kelly's name into Google. The three most recent stories pop up, and I feel sick as I read:

Heartbroken Kelly buys OWN ring!

TV's Kelly Harrington was spotted paying for her own engagement ring, only days before details surrounding her mother's suspicious death emerge. We say, swap the man, not the ring, Kel!!!

Devastated Kelly Harrington discovers mother's suicide after father's death

Soap star Kelly Harrington was forced to confront her painful past, when her dying father revealed that...

It's off!

Has Kelly Harrington changed her mind already? The TV beauty was seen returning her engagement ring at the weekend. The star – who tragically discovered that her mother, a dancer, took her own life when...

Oh God. This is horrific. I text Mel instantly.

Will is absolutely devastated at everything in the papers today. What have you done?

As I wait for a response, I look at the message I've just sent and shift position uncomfortably. It's like reading a message addressed to myself. Will's right, I shouldn't have told Mel. Of course I shouldn't... I close my eyes. She didn't do this because of what I said about wishing there was something I could do to get rid of Kelly? Surely? I wait a moment more, but nothing comes back from her – a guilty silence?

'Sally!' calls Mum sharply from downstairs. 'Will you come here, please?'

Will's just told her then. I take a deep breath and go downstairs to face the music.

'Right, that's Will's car now.' Mum drops the curtain edge. 'Come on, Chloe, darling, we need to go if we're going to get that ice cream.'

'Can't I stay and say hello to Uncle Will?' Chloe says reasonably.

'We'll see him when we come back,' Mum says firmly. 'He's staying tonight so there'll be plenty of time then.' She turns to me. 'Try and make him see that you didn't mean it to happen. That's the bit that's hurting him the most, I think. It's half eleven now. We'll be back in half an hour for lunch. Theo will be up by then, won't he?'

I nod.

Mum pats my arm briefly, then reaches for Chloe's hand. I wait in the sitting room and watch through the curtain as they both appear on the drive, talking briefly to Will, who nods stonily at something Mum says, overnight bag slung over his shoulder, but smiles down at Chloe as she tugs on his trouser leg, and then rests his hand on her head for a moment. Somehow it makes me feel even worse that he's making an effort to be kind and smiley with her, when it must be the last thing he feels like. Mum kisses him, then she and Chloe take their leave, and Will walks towards the house. I take a deep breath... and moments later, he's there, right in front of me, standing in the sitting-room doorway.

'Theo asleep?' he says unsmilingly, letting the bag fall to the floor.

I nod. 'Mum told me what Kelly said to you. I'm so sorry that she's taken this so badly, Will, and asked you to leave.'

'Are you? I thought you'd be delighted.' He flops down on the sofa and looks up at me. 'Isn't this part of what you've been working towards, us splitting up?'

'No.' I look at him, confused. 'And certainly not the way you make it sound, like I'm on some sort of crazed vendetta.'

He doesn't break his gaze. 'I'm giving Kelly the space she asked for. She's not thrown me out, she knows it's technically my flat, but yes, she wants to think everything through. At the moment she can't see that we have a future.' He waits for that to sink in. 'She's furious that I told you about her mother, devastated on behalf of her brother and sister that it's all come out like this, and just in pieces, really. I specifically asked you not to tell anyone, Sally. This has all happened because of you.'

I look down guiltily.

'I know you two have never really got on, and that's fine. I mean, obviously I'd have liked you to, it makes me sad that you don't, but it's one of those things. I had hoped that you'd at least be able to be polite to each other for my sake, but I really didn't expect anything more than that. I had pretty low expectations.'

'Will, if it had just been about—'

'Can you let me finish, please?' He holds up a hand. 'I didn't know where to put myself after what happened to you last Friday. I felt I'd completely let you down. I was devastated you'd not been able to talk to me about how you must have been feeling, and I wanted to do whatever I could to support you. I still stand by that, but you know, Sal, part of me actually now hopes you might be ill, and that there might be a justification for you behaving like this, because even before all this shit in the papers happened, going through Kelly's belongings was completely unacceptable behaviour. You then went on to attack her, and accused her of drugging you, as well as stealing sixty-five thousand pounds from your house.'

'I did *not* attack her,' I say hotly. 'That's an outright lie. She was deliberately trying to scare Mum by making out that I'd gone mad or something!'

Will focuses on me intently. 'She was frightened of you, Sal. Actually frightened. She said you were behaving erratically, and it's pretty hard to refute that in the face of your allegations. Why didn't you just raise these concerns with me, rather than go through our flat?'

'I knew you wouldn't believe me. You all think I'm suffering from some sort of delusional paranoia, and that I'm increasingly mentally unstable, which is just what Kelly wants you to think.'

'No, she doesn't. She thinks you've made all of this up. The whole thing, right from winding up in Cornwall through to "being ill" – because she's convinced this is about you and Matthew having problems, and you trying to do something about that. Like I say, *I'd* almost rather believe you're ill – although either way, it's very clear to me you need help.'

'*Or* you're completely wrong, someone has tried to hurt me, and none of you are helping me protect myself, or my children.'

'Let me ask you this outright, then: do you honestly think Kelly drugged you and stole that money from your house?'

I hesitate. 'Yes, I do.'

A strange look passes over his face. A mixture of disbelief, anger, pity – and fear.

'And so here I am, back at square one,' I say. 'You all think I've lost the plot.'

'*Or,*' he mimics me, 'you know *exactly* what you're doing. Surely you can see, though, that implicating other people, people that you don't like, to make it appear that in fact *they* are—'

'Will, don't tell me you actually believe her crap story about her dad hiding half a million quid in shopping bags in the loft?' I interrupt. 'Kelly knew sixty-five grand was in the holdall under the stairs at mine, she saw it when she went looking for the spare pair of shoes after hers broke, remember? I don't understand why you – and Mum, for that matter – have such a problem believing that she might be capable of drugging me so she could steal our money, when she's devious enough to swap her engagement ring behind your back and set up those horrible pictures of me. *The morning after* the money vanished, she spent a huge amount of cash on that ring. You don't think that's odd? And how much do you really know for sure about Kelly – and her past? You've been together for eleven months. That's nothing!'

'So now you're suggesting she's made this stuff up about her mother?' Will looks at me in alarm.

'No,' I admit. 'I'm not. I know that's true and I'm very sorry for her. But I think it also might have been what made her do things that perhaps you don't know about. She's very far from being a totally innocent victim in all of this.'

'I completely refute that my being with Kelly for eleven months is in any way relevant. Someone you've known for eleven years is just as capable of turning out to be completely untrust-worthy, and whether you think it's crap or not, Kelly needed to lose some more of her dad's money, and she thought that spending it on the ring was a really nice way to do it. It meant something to her, and—'

'Oh Will, please!' I interrupt. 'It's the most ludicrous story I ever heard! I love you, but really – how stupid are you?'

He stares at me. 'That's enough, Sal. Whatever your reason, it's not acceptable to speak to me like that.'

'Oh, shut up!' I finally lose my temper. 'Stop speaking to *me* like you're a bloody counsellor. I wound up in a fucking taxi at the other end of the country and yet not a single member of my own family is listening to me when I tell you all that something is badly wrong, and I can't remember what happened. Then when it becomes apparent to me who *is* to blame, no one believes me because your lunatic fiancée has done such a great job of making me look like *I'm* the crazy one, and now, to cap it all, you think I've gone to the press, when actually, *I've done nothing wrong.*'

'Well, Sally, you certainly did something. You had a suicide note on you. Your phone messages were all cleared, you had a large amount of cash to pay the taxi, and you've tried to do it before. Maybe you don't want to remember it, but it *did* happen. And what was the first thing you did when everyone let you go off on your own? Go to the flat to confront Kelly! You cannot refute that you have become completely obsessed by your dislike of her... Irrationally so, to the point of deliberately making public something I trusted you with.'

'What was the first thing I did when "everyone let me go off on my own"?' I repeat in astonishment. 'I wasn't aware anyone had *let* me do anything.'

'You know everyone is very concerned for you right now, Sally, and paying close attention to what you do. That can come as no surprise, so don't pretend otherwise.'

'The Friday night I was abducted—'

'Oh Sally! Come on! Abducted?'

'Yes, abducted!' I insist fiercely. 'I had shopping lists on my phone that I intended to use, I had a sleep log, I was timing Theo.

The so-called note was something I'd written to Matthew earlier in the week. I was *not* planning on killing myself. Why would I even do that? What logical reason could I possibly have?'

'What logical reason does anyone ever have?'

Through the monitor, Theo grizzles briefly. Great – we've woken him up.

'I would never do that to my kids,' I continue, lowering my voice. 'And I'm amazed that you all seem to have disregarded everything you know about me, and the fact that I'm *telling* you I didn't do it! I know you think that I've become obsessed with Kelly, but she isn't the person you think she is.'

'Fine,' he says angrily. 'Come on then – let's entertain this bullshit theory of yours for a minute. So, according to you, Kelly comes over, sees a bag of cash under the stairs, then what – drugs you while we're having our champagne together, presumably?'

I meet his gaze squarely. 'She was on her own with the drinks for long enough to put something in them. That's what I was looking for in your flat – I think she's on really strong prescription-only sleeping pills. If she'd have put one of them in my drink, I'd have been out of it within about half an hour to an hour.'

'Then what?'

'She came back to get her "forgotten" phone, stole the bag while I was upstairs, waited outside for me to pass out, then put me in the taxi and made off with the money.'

'And you think her dad leaving some cash in his loft is implausible?' He shakes his head in disbelief. 'This is farcical. What about the fact your mother-in-law was in the house?'

'I'm sorry – you're suggesting *Caroline* did this?' I gaze at him incredulously.

'I actually meant you don't think Kelly would have been concerned about Caroline hearing you being dragged down the stairs? But yeah – Caroline was there too; why can't we point the finger at her?'

'Er, why in the hell would my mother-in-law – a well-respected psychiatrist, who I've had a close relationship with for years – drug me to steal her *own* money?' I stare at him.

'I don't know – you tell me, Sally! You seem to have developed a pretty fertile imagination over the last few days.'

I take a deep breath and try to calm down. 'In answer to your point about Kelly worrying Caroline might hear something, I told Kelly that Caroline had gone home. As far as she knew, I was there on my own with the kids. You'd already both seen Matthew leave. And Caroline wouldn't actually have heard a thing – she had earplugs in, to block out Theo's crying.'

Will laughs harshly. 'Of course she did! Silly me! Anyway, let's carry on. How did Kelly get into the house once you were allegedly upstairs sparko?'

'When she came back to get her mobile, she deliberately woke Theo up. I remember because I was really pissed off with her. I left her downstairs on her own while I ran up to close Theo's door so he didn't wake Chloe. Kelly would have had plenty of time to pick my keys up from the side. I wouldn't have noticed they were gone when I came back down. I just wanted to get rid of her. She could have just let herself in once she saw my bedroom light go off.'

'What about the note you had on you, then? How do you explain that?'

'It was an apology I'd written to Matthew about a row we had. It was on my bedside table. Kelly got lucky with that. She must have been delighted to find it.'

'She got lucky...' he repeats slowly. 'Wow. I just don't know what to say to you, Sal.'

'I'm telling you, I *know* she's dangerous. You have to trust me.'

I refuse to implicate Caroline now, as it seems Kelly is about to end it with Will anyway.

'I have to trust you, and yet you can't tell me what it is that you apparently know?'

'No, I can't. I'm sorry.'

'How convenient.' He closes his eyes briefly, and looks as if he's trying to plan what he's about to say next very carefully. 'I really don't think you understand the implications of what's happened, Sally. Given everything that appeared in the papers this morning, Kelly's told me that if she stays with me, it's on the understanding she never has to see you, or have you in our house. Try and understand the position that puts me in when I love you both.'

'No, she's talking about ending it with you because she's got her cash – so now she's off.'

Will just stares at me. 'What even started this? Is it to do with her being famous or something? It's completely taken you over.'

I stand my ground. 'You know what, Will? I can live with you thinking this is all my fault, and that I've gone completely insane. I'd still rather you thought that – and Kelly is out of our lives – than do nothing, and she stays in them. The only thing I care about is protecting all of you.'

There is a moment of silence, and then Theo starts to cry properly upstairs.

'I have nothing more to say to you.' Will gets to his feet, picks up his bag, and quietly leaves the room.

'Sally, I've asked Matthew to come and get you, and take you home after tea. I'm so sorry, love, but I honestly think it's for the best.' Mum looks at me with concern as we're both sitting on the bed in my old bedroom. 'I feel completely torn, but the truth of the matter is Will's got nowhere else to go.'

'He's got his own flat! He should be there. If Kelly wants to leave him, she should do exactly that, and just go.'

'She is. She's moving her stuff out tomorrow. She told him an hour ago.'

'What?' I'm flabbergasted. 'But he told me earlier she was thinking things over, and he was giving her the space she needed.'

Mum sighs. 'Well, she seems to have made her mind up already. She doesn't want to see him before she leaves, she said.'

'She came to this decision remarkably quickly – and all because of what appeared in the papers today?' I exclaim.

'I think what happened between you and her at their flat frightened her very badly,' Mum says carefully.

'Oh, come on! She made the whole thing up – you weren't there, I was. It was all an act. I get that she's beyond hurt that everything is in the papers about her mum, but would you actually end a relationship over something like that? So much for her threats that she wouldn't let anything separate her and Will.'

Mum doesn't say anything.

'Does Will want me to go home?'

'He's very hurt right now. He doesn't want you to feel pushed out, and he's said if you need to stay, you can, but I think he'd find it easier if we could just let everything settle down a bit first. You probably should know Kelly asked him to cut you out of their lives completely, and he said no. That's when she said it was over. I don't want you and the children to go, Sal, of course I don't. I want to look after you,' she says, 'but under the circumstances, I think it's the only solution. Caroline is going to stay at yours for the next couple of days while we work out a better plan.'

'Yes, Will mentioned you all think I need some "help". Someone to supervise me?'

'No! To give you a hand, love, that's all,' Mum says wearily. 'I promise.'

'Right, well, what do you want me to tell Chloe?' I say, more quietly.

'Just that it's time to go home, only a little bit earlier than we thought it was going to be. She'll be fine. Caroline will make a fuss of her. Get her to take Chloe on a few "Granny and Chloe" trips out. Come on.' She pats my leg. 'Let's get you all packed. I don't know how long Theo's going to hang on with Dad downstairs, and Matthew will be here before we know it. Oh Lord! Is that the door now?'

'It wasn't me, Sal,' Mel says desperately as the wind whips a wet strand of hair across her face and plasters it against her red cheek. She yanks it away as she stands on Mum and Dad's doorstep in front of me. 'I would never do that to you. I mean, I told Ed about it, I admit that, and he joked – we both did – about ringing the papers and selling our story, but we'd never actually do it. Not in a million years.'

'But you're the only person I told.' I hold onto the front-door latch. 'So if it wasn't you...'

She stands a little taller. 'It wasn't Ed,' she insists. 'Christ, Sal, I've been with the man for twenty-five years. I know what he's thinking before he does.'

I can't help but remember Will's comment about time spent together not equating to trustworthiness, and look down at the floor uneasily, not wanting to contradict her.

'He wouldn't, Sal, I promise you. You're one of my oldest friends!'

'Did *you* do it because I said I wished there was some way of getting rid of Kelly?' I ask quietly.

'No,' she insists. 'I didn't. What, you think because you didn't actually ask me not to say anything and it was just implied, *technically* I'd think I wouldn't be doing anything wrong?'

'I didn't even think about that,' I confess. But now you mention it...

'I know you'd do anything for me, Mel,' I say. 'And I was very upset yesterday, but...'

'It wasn't me.'

We look at each other in silence.

'OK.' I give up. 'Look, Mel, I've got to go back in. I'm sorry, but we're going home in a bit. Matthew's on his way, and I need to get sorted.'

'You're leaving early because of this?' She looks distraught.

'Mummy!' calls Chloe from inside the house. '*Bing* has finished and Granny Sue's upstairs changing Theo!'

'I've got to go in, Mel.'

'Please – ring Will and tell him I'm really sorry, and it absolutely wasn't me.' She reaches out and grabs my arm. 'You will tell him, won't you? And your mum and dad, I don't want them thinking badly of me either. Could I at least come in and talk to you while you finish packing?'

'Will's here, so I don't think it's the best idea,' I say uncomfortably.

'What, now?' Her eyes widen. 'Why? Is everything OK? They haven't—'

I shake my head. 'I can't say anything more, Mel. I've said enough. I've really got to go. I'm sorry. I *will* call you when I get back though, I promise.' I gently remove her hand, give her a quick, kiss, and close the door. From the sitting-room window, I watch her walk back down to her car, wiping her eyes, before getting in and driving off.

I sink down heavily onto the sofa, putting my head in my hands – and I'm very glad when Chloe wriggles over, pulls my hands away, and gives me a warm kiss on my cheek. 'I love you, Mummy.'

I smile, trying very hard not to cry in front of her. 'I love you too, Clo.'

'You never, ever stop loving me, even when you're cross.'

She's evidently picked up on all of the tension. 'Never, ever,' I assure her. 'There's nothing you could ever do to make me stop loving you.' I hug her to me. 'I'll always be here, and I'll never let anything happen to you, Chloe. I promise.'

'We're on our way back now, actually,' I say quietly into the phone, the hum of the motorway beneath us dampening down my voice, as Chloe and Theo sleep peacefully in the back of the car. 'I thought maybe we could call in and see you tomorrow? At least then Kate and Chloe can have a play together. It'll be something for Chloe to look forward to when she wakes up, and hopefully take the sting out of coming home early. Or you can come to us, if you'd rather?'

'Whatever's good for you,' Liv says, slightly stiffly. 'Matthew probably doesn't want a house full of kids, though – I assume he's working from home tomorrow?'

'Oh, that'll be fine, leave him to me.'

There's a pause, and for a moment I think I've lost her. 'Liv? Are you still there?'

'Yes. I am. Listen, Sal, I just wanted to say sorry – for everything. I'd like to explain myself properly tomorrow, if that's OK? It's probably better you come to us. We're in until at least two anyway because I've got a new mattress being delivered.'

'Fine. I'll call you in the morning then, shall I? I'll look forward to it.'

'Me too.'

'You're genuinely seeing Liv tomorrow then?' Matthew asks as I hang up. 'Are you going to tell her what's happened?'

I try to ignore the 'genuinely' bit and reply, 'Probably just the edited highlights: Will's now unexpectedly at my mum's, so we had to come back early.' I pause. 'I'm sorry this didn't turn out to be the breathing space that you all hoped it would be.'

Matthew hesitates. 'We wanted you to have a bit of distance from everything, that's all. No one is trying to stage-manage you, Sal.'

'Well, thank you for coming to get us again.'

'It's fine. I said I would.'

'You must be shattered, though.' We drive for a moment more, and I think about poor Mel, insisting her innocence. 'Do you think Kelly leaked the story herself?'

'And why would she do that?' Matthew says slowly.

'So she has an excuse to say to Will how vindictive I am; "It's the final straw, I'm so frightened of your sister", *blah blah blah*; then she gets to walk away with the cash.'

Matthew pauses. 'I was actually going to ask if you told Mel on purpose, knowing there was a risk she might not be able to keep everything to herself?'

I shake my head. 'Will asked me the exact same thing. I did tell her I wished there was something I could do to get rid of Kelly, but I didn't in a million years expect her to do anything.'

'Well, whoever it was – Kelly is out of your life, for good.' He glances at me.

I feel suddenly weak with relief as I realize he's right. 'Everything appearing in the papers today must have been dreadful for her, but I can't even tell you how terrified it makes me to think Will might have actually married her,' I say quietly. 'I just wish I could fast-forward him through this bit to the moment where he meets the person who *is* right for him. He's still convinced Kelly is completely innocent.' I look out of the window. 'I suppose, of course, now I'll never know for sure what she did to me on Friday night, but at least I'm OK. We all are.'

'You still believe it was Kelly then?'

'Well, she certainly seems to have pretty ruthlessly cut her ties, doesn't she? But you know what? I really do just want to close the door on the whole affair now. I suspect your mum feels the same way too?'

'Er, yes. I think she'd be happy to never have to see Kelly again.'

I fall silent for a moment. God knows what the story really was between Kelly and Caroline. I guess I'll never know about that now, either.

'We haven't had a chance to talk about them properly yet. I imagine your mum is pretty angry with me for telling you about her being Kelly's therapist?'

'She wasn't thrilled, no, but she understood why you wanted me to know. As do I.'

'I don't really get why she didn't tell you anyway,' I reflect.

'She did, on the Friday night you went missing. She explained to me that in the heat of the moment on seeing Kelly, she'd reacted impulsively and just blurted out their connection to you. We discussed it all, though, and I was happy that there wasn't anything else we needed to do about it, in terms of any risk Kelly might have posed – and especially now they've split up. The really important thing is that you haven't told anyone else what Mum divulged. As she said to you, she could face really serious repercussions, Sal. Breaching patient confidentiality is no joke, even when it's done with the best of intentions.'

'I've not told anyone else, I swear, and Will hasn't brought it up with me, so Kelly can't have mentioned her relationship with Caroline either.'

He looks relieved. 'Good. Well, let's just keep it that way, and hopefully now Kelly's no longer on the scene, everything will just settle back down.'

'Are *you* OK with walking away from all of that money, though?' I ask. 'If it was my mum who'd lost such a huge amount, I think I'd be very angry.'

'She didn't lose it, we did. She just offered to cover it, and I'm very grateful to her,' he says simply.

How on earth can it be so straightforward and uncomplicated to him? It must be a bloke thing.

'The money isn't my priority anyway, to be honest,' he continues firmly. 'You are.'

I fall silent for a moment. 'We're all right, aren't we?'

He looks at me quickly. 'What, you and me? Of course.' He reaches out, picks up my hand and kisses it briefly.

'It's been nice; things starting to feel... better... between us, I mean,' I say hesitantly. 'But you do definitely think it was Kelly now, don't you?' I add quickly. 'You don't still think I went to Cornwall to kill myself, or that this was a crazy plot on my part to get your attention? You believe me?'

'Yes, I do.' He looks straight ahead at the road in front of us. 'You know what, Sal? If this week has taught me one thing, it's anything's possible. Anything at all.'

CHAPTER TWENTY

As we pull up at the house, the curtains are drawn and the lights are on. It's rather odd to see my own home as an outsider would.

'Before you say anything,' Matthew whispers, 'I know the kids are going to wake up unless it's dark inside, so Mum and I have already prearranged everything. Hang on.' He pulls out his phone and quickly sends a text. Sure enough, seconds later, the sitting-room light goes off, followed by the hall one – then the front door opens to reveal Caroline. She waves, then puts her finger to her lips and tiptoes off, back into the gloom.

'I'm impressed,' I admit. 'That's incredibly organized.'

'You just stay in the car with them while I dash in and do the blackout on Theo's window, plug the monitor in, and put his wind machine on.'

'Could you do his thermometer too, please? It's just he's used to it as a nightlight.'

'I know,' Matthew says patiently, placing his hand on the door.

'And leave the car engine running, won't you?' I say instantly.

'Of course. Oh, hang on.' He reaches up and switches the car lights off.

'Good call,' I breathe. 'So, when you come back, you take her, and I'll do him. Shit!' We both freeze as Theo begins to stir, sensing the movement has stopped. 'Go! Go! He's waking up! We haven't got much time!'

Hastily, Matthew climbs out, rushes around and barely audibly unclicks the boot, grabs the overnight bag, then runs up to the house and dives in through the front door, as if he's on some sort of special ops mission. I glance anxiously in the mirror at Theo – who is moving his head from side to side, and rubbing his nose, although his eyes are still closed – and send a silent prayer to the patron saint of sleeping babies. It's so ridiculous that we have to go through all of this, just to get in the house. I glance at Chloe, who is thankfully out for the count, her head lolling forward. Not even a megaphone would rouse her right now. One day Theo will be the same. One day...

Caroline must have helped Matthew, because he reappears remarkably quickly, giving me the thumbs-up before going around to Chloe's side. I climb out, and simultaneously we open both back doors, and in a practised manoeuvre, start to unclip belts as our children stir at the cold air hitting their skin. I begin gathering Theo up, glancing over at Matthew, who already has a completely floppy Chloe in his arms. He grins at me, and I smile back, before – in one swift movement – lifting Theo and beginning to walk smartly back to the house. Theo huddles closely into my body and I'm suddenly struck by the realization that Matthew and I won't be doing this for ever, carrying our babies back to the safety of their cots and beds, and I hug Theo a little tighter.

We're actually making a pretty good team – everyone appears to be staying asleep for once. I step into the welcoming warmth of the house. God bless Caroline, she's had the heating on. She's standing silently in the dark, waiting in the sitting-room doorway as I mouth 'Hello!' and pass with her sleeping grandson.

I pad up the stairs softly, Matthew a couple of steps behind me, then we peel off into the respective kids' bedrooms. Just as I realize I've made a fatal error in forgetting to tell Matthew to lay Theo's Grobag out – unzipped so I can pop him straight in it – I spy it on the change mat bathed in the orange glow of the night-light, neatly waiting for me. Wow. This is seamless. If I had a spare hand, I'd pinch myself.

I'm feeling just as stunned, less than three minutes later, to be silently creeping out of Theo's room, gently drawing the door to behind me. He actually went down. This is a miracle. I tiptoe over to Chloe's room and peer in. She's already in bed, snoring gently – no sign of Matthew. I hastily beat a retreat while the going is good, only stopping off in our bedroom to pick up the monitor. I have another quick listen, but all I can hear is the sound of Theo's wind machine gently whirring. I make my way back downstairs in a state of disbelief.

The sitting-room door is closed, but the light is on again. I push it open and blink slightly as my eyes adjust, to find Caroline now sitting on the far sofa, cup of tea in hand, doing the crossword in her folded-over paper. Mum left everything here tidy, but Caroline has taken it to the next level. The whole room smells wonderful: a combination of the new Jo Malone Pomegranate Noir candle burning on the table, and beautiful fresh flowers on the hearth of the otherwise disgustingly monstrous white-tiled fireplace I've almost become used to living with. Far more alluring, though, are two trays carefully balanced on the coffee table, each carrying a glass of red wine and a plate of crackers, olives, cheese and pâté, alongside a neatly folded napkin.

'I thought you'd both be hungry after such a long journey.' Caroline puts down her paper. 'Although Matthew says you've made excellent time. He's just getting the bags in from the car – via the garage, though, so the children aren't disturbed. I can't believe they've both stayed asleep. Well done you!' She gets up. 'Sit down and I'll pass your tray over.'

'Thank you so much for this,' I say, amazed, as I obediently flop down. 'I am starving.'

'Isn't it strange the way long journeys do that to you?' agrees Caroline, taking a seat again, having handed my supper to me. 'Don't drink the wine if you don't fancy it. I can make you a cup of tea instead, if you'd rather?' She half rises again.

'No, no – this is lovely.' I take a mouthful to prove my point, and it really is delicious. I can feel the alcohol creeping through my veins, and start to relax. I smile gratefully at her. 'Really, thank you so much.'

'You're very welcome. And welcome home, too.'

'Thank you,' I say, a little more soberly. 'It is actually nice to be back. Things took – as I'm sure Matthew has told you – a rather uncomfortable turn at my parents'. My brother arrived this morning and he needs some space. Away from me.'

'Oh dear!' Caroline says, making a sympathetic face, and yet her tone is totally bland, just as she might have sounded if I'd said I had a slight headache coming on, or something equally as insignificant. Thrown by this uncharacteristic indifference, I pause momentarily. Matthew *has* told her what's happened, surely?

'You know that he's split up with Kelly?' I say slowly. 'Or rather, that Kelly's left him.'

'Yes, I do. Now, tomorrow, I thought that while Theo naps, I could take Chloe out so you could have a rest, although I think you also have plans to see a friend, possibly? I'm more than happy to stay this weekend too, but I think I'd quite like to go back to mine on Sunday night, if that's all right – I'm chairing a big meeting at Abbey Oaks first thing on Monday – although I will of course drive over after that so I can look after both of the children while Matthew takes you for your scan in the afternoon.'

'Thank you, that's very kind.' I look at her carefully. 'Caroline – is there something wrong?'

272

She holds my gaze, regarding me steadily for a moment. 'Should there be? Now, I had a text message from your mother earlier. We've been thinking about the possibility of a nanny or an au pair, on a short-term basis. What do you think? We could—'

'Caroline, are you sure nothing's wrong?'

'Well, I was very sorry to hear that Kelly and Will have separated – it's always extremely painful when significant relationships end. I can appreciate that, as an outcome, it's not an unhappy one for you, however, and I understand completely the reasons for your relief. That said, I think the way in which this conclusion has been reached is, at best, utterly irresponsible and, at worst, devastatingly cruel.'

My mouth falls open. There is a pregnant silence as Caroline continues to look at me unfalteringly.

'You're angry with me?' I manage, eventually. 'You think the stuff about her mother in the paper is my doing?' Caroline and I have never exchanged words like this, ever.

'When a parent commits suicide – especially, research shows, a mother – they leave a very complicated legacy of pain that the child can spend years trying to work through. It's the job of a dedicated professional to ensure that trauma doesn't become long-lasting, or something that consumes the child completely. One can only imagine what it must then feel like to have that scar freshly sliced through, in the name of public consumption.'

I wince at her graphic choice of words. 'While I've made no secret of my feelings towards Kelly, I would never, ever do something like this.'

'You, in particular, understand better than most what Kelly is going through today, surely?'

Wow. I tense up completely. Does she mean because of what she thinks I was going to do in Cornwall last week? We're not really going there *now*, are we?

'I actually agree with everything you've said.' I keep my tone conciliatory. 'I think it must have been horrendous for Kelly today, and in spite of everything, I feel very sorry for her.'

'I'm not advocating that if you see a child in the playground, who beats all the other kids up because they're having a horrible time of it at home, you let them carry on hurting everyone around them. Of course you don't,' Caroline says. 'You remove the bully to protect everyone else – but it's never necessary to annihilate them in the process.'

'I agree!' I repeat. 'It wasn't me who did this. I understand why you would think that I might, and why that would make you so angry, because of your professional relationship with Kelly, and how hard you must have worked with her to overcome the damage her mother's suicide caused. But I swear, I did nothing except unwisely tell a close friend of mine at home about Kelly's past – in the context of everything else that's happened, I hasten to add – and she told her husband. One of them has now let me down very badly.'

Caroline pauses, eyeing me carefully.

'It's the truth, Caroline. But am I glad she's out of our lives? Yes, I am. I can't lie about that.'

'Yes, well, as I said, I appreciate why you feel that way. I think we're all rather relieved, for one reason or another.'

I look down at the floor. 'Yes, about my revealing your professional relationship with Kelly to Matthew... You must be upset with me about that too, and I do owe you an apology on that score.'

'No, Sally. I'm not upset. I'm disappointed, perhaps, that you didn't trust *my* judgement when I told you I didn't think we needed to do anything further about Kelly – and instead you sought a second opinion, as it were, from Matthew, but I know he's not going to say anything to anyone, as he understands the full implications for me.'

'I do too,' I say, 'and it's not information I will disclose to anyone else, I give you my word.'

Mercifully, Matthew walks in at this point, his eyes lighting up at the sight of his tray of food. 'Oh thanks, Mum, that looks great.' He picks it up, comes and sits down next to me, and lowers it onto his lap. 'I'm starving. You all right?'

'Yes. I'm fine,' Caroline says, and then meets my gaze once again as she adds, 'I was just saying to Sal, it's very nice to have her back.'

I'm forgiven? I start to relax again.

'Yes, it is.' Matthew puts his hand briefly on my leg before removing it to pick up his wine glass. 'I missed you all loads. I'll try and hold onto that thought tomorrow morning when Theo gets up at crack of dawn.'

'I hope you took advantage and had a lie-in?' I ask. 'I would have.'

Matthew looks sheepish. 'Well, I was still working both days, but I might have slept in a bit later than usual, yes. It really is good to have you all back, though. The house was too quiet without you. I didn't like it.' He takes another sip of wine.

'Well, no one's going anywhere now,' I reassure him quickly.

'That's good to know. By the way, tomorrow, when you go to Liv's, Mum will drive you.'

There's an awkward pause.

'Um, why?' I ask, and laugh uncertainly.

'We all just think it would be a good idea to help you out a bit more, while you get back on your feet properly.' Matthew takes another mouthful of wine. 'It's no big deal. Mum doesn't mind, and she won't come in with you, obviously. Just drop you off and go and have a coffee somewhere.'

'But,' I begin, 'I'm completely safe to drive. Is this your way of telling me you think I'm going to black out at the wheel because of the enormous brain tumour I might have after all?'

'Sally! Of course not!' he exclaims. 'Although, that's true, from an insurance point of view, until you get the results back, I wonder if you're even covered to drive at the moment? I ought to check it out... Really, though, I'm just asking you to be kind to yourself, that's all.'

'You want to pay me close attention,' I repeat Will's phrase slowly, looking between the two of them. 'As opposed to monitoring me, while I'm with the children, of course? Matthew, you said in the car that you believed me, that—'

'Sally, we really do just want to help you.' Caroline leans forward in her seat. 'That's all this is. No one is monitoring you. If any of us had felt you were a danger to yourself or the children at any point since Friday, we *would* have acted, all of us together: Matthew, your parents and me. We have all discussed the options at length, as and when it's been appropriate, and we haven't felt it's been necessary for us to step in and make any decisions that you might not be capable of. '

'I'm sorry, you're talking about me being sectioned again?' I'm astonished, but try to keep my voice calm.

'If we'd felt we had to go down that route, we would have done, yes,' Caroline says truthfully. 'You and I talked about this very possibility the other night, before you broke into Will's flat, but it hasn't needed to be the case. You are, however, very tired, you're stressed, you've been up and down the country. You've got medical tests coming up – and did I mention two small children? I'm offering to drive you because it saves you doing it. That's all. I promise.'

As I climb quietly into bed, and lie very still, listening to Theo beginning to stir through the monitor – I honestly don't know how he does it, does he sense the vibrations of us coming upstairs or something? – the momentous events of the day replay through my mind. I can't believe Kelly is actually out of our lives.

She's gone.

I know Will is incredibly hurt and angry right now, and that he will never truly appreciate the extent of the situation he was in, but maybe eventually he'll make his peace with it regardless – and with me. Kelly'll probably do something similar to another bloke soon, and perhaps he'll see it then. At the very least, I'm sure he won't be single for long. He'll meet someone else. Men always do. And this time, it'll hopefully be a nice, kind, *normal* girl, who loves him for the amazing person he is, and would never dream of doing something so unkind as to take back the ring he bought for her, never mind all the deeply psychotic shit Kelly pulled.

I think about standing on top of that lonely clifftop, disorientated and terrified. It was almost exactly a week ago today that I climbed into this bed and closed my eyes, suspecting nothing. I remember Kelly's furious expression back at the flat when she thought I'd planted something to incriminate her, shortly before she twisted it into one of fake fear for my mother's benefit, then finally imagine her merely inches away from my unconscious face, as I lay in this bed, prodding me to make sure I wasn't going to wake up – maybe lifting my lifeless, heavy arm and letting it drop.

I shudder and pull the duvet more tightly around me. If the last of her legacy is that Matthew and our parents are going to continue watching me like a hawk, I can probably live with that. Although – I consider with deep disquiet Caroline saying they'd all talked about 'options' for me – now Kelly's gone, there won't be any further confusion about my behaviour in any case. Everything will return back to normal.

We can *all* finally move on with our lives.

So long, Kelly. It was not nice knowing you.

CHAPTER TWENTY-ONE

I wake up to the sound of Theo chattering happily to himself in his cot. Stretching, I reach for my phone to check the time. Ten to seven? Wow! He's actually done – I count it through on my fingers – five hours back to back! That's amazing! I blink a couple of times and yawn. I think I actually dreamt last night; the first time in six months. I go to sit up, but Matthew reaches out and pulls me towards him.

'Just five seconds with my wife before another day starts,' he murmurs, and I collapse back into his arms. It feels good.

It literally is five seconds, though, because Theo shouts suddenly, having decided he's bored of being on his own after all.

Matthew groans, but as I start to get up again, he says, 'It's OK, I'll go,' and throws back the covers.

As he leaves the room, I gratefully reach for my phone and go straight to the news. There's nothing more about Kelly, but then I guess there won't be until she moves her stuff out of the flat later today. I sigh. The papers are going to love that – poor Will. I'll ring Mum in a bit – see how he's doing.

I put the phone back down and wriggle under the duvet again. Theo's nappy change will buy me another minute or two, but I jump as a small muffled voice alongside me says, 'Mummy. My tummy feels achy.'

I open my eyes. Chloe is standing right over me, looking rather pale. 'Hello, darling. Achy in what way?' I peer up at her blearily.

But she doesn't answer, just opens her mouth and with a graphic '*Bleuarhhhh!*' she pukes on my head.

'Urgh! Oh my God!' I shout, sitting up in shock. A glob of sick plops from my fringe into my lap, and poor Chloe bursts into tears.

'Oh, darling, don't cry! It's OK! Mummy isn't cross!' I reach a hand out to her, while looking around urgently for a cloth of some sort. 'It's all right – poor girl. Hey, do I look funny?' I try to smile, but then gag; the smell is horrendous. I can feel it dripping down my neck.

'MATTHEW!' I yell, scrabbling to my feet and grabbing a clean towel from the pile waiting to be put away, next to the bed. Quickly, I wrap a turban around my head to contain the vomit. 'See?' I say, eager to reassure Clo. 'We're all fine!' I put my head up, just in time to see her give me a frightened stare.

'Mummy! I'm going to be sick again!'

I look around me desperately, but there's nothing bowl-esque, just my open make-up bag on the floor. No way. I lunge for another towel, just as the poor little thing gags again and her tiny body heaves. A torrent of puke cascades onto the carpet, then onto the towel that I finally manage to shove under her mouth.

'What's up? I'm trying to change Theo's... Oh Christ!' says Matthew, appalled, appearing in the doorway with a half-naked baby balanced on his hip. 'What's happened?'

'Clo's been sick,' I answer, equally as unnecessarily.

'Oh God,' he groans. 'It's all over the carpet...'

Chloe looks up at him worriedly, her eyes streaming.

'That's OK, Daddy,' I say warningly. 'Clo couldn't help it, and she's been very brave.'

'Yeah, sorry – of course,' he says. 'Well done, Clo.'

'Do you feel like you want to be sick again, sweetheart?' I ask.

She shakes her head silently and looks down at the vomit.

'OK, well, go with Daddy and brush your teeth while I just sort this out,' I say brightly.

'What's wrong with her?' Matthew asks, taking Chloe's hand. 'Is it something she's eaten?'

'Let's just get sorted, shall we?' I say firmly. 'And think about that in a second?'

'Why have you got a towel around your head?' Matthew says suspiciously.

'Chloe was also sick on me.'

Matthew's eyes widen. 'Oh.'

'Yeah, never mind. It was just an accident.' I smile at poor Chloe again.

But Matthew has already stopped listening. 'Theo! No!' He looks down in dismay to see a large, spreading wet patch on his pyjama leg, as our nappy-free son looks around him disinterestedly, then yawns.

Matthew looks up at me incredulously, and for a second I can see he has no idea what to do. 'MUM!' he yells instead, over his shoulder, in the direction of the spare room. 'Can you get up and help? We've got a situation here!'

'How are you feeling now, darling?' Caroline looks sympathetically at Chloe, tucked up under her blanket on the sofa. 'Better?'

Chloe nods, without taking her attention from the *Tinker Bell* movie I've put on for her.

'It went *everywhere*.' Matthew peers at Chloe anxiously. 'What do you think it is, Mum?'

'Matthew, Chloe's really fine.' I smile.

Matthew frowns. 'Well, she's not, is she? She was just violently sick. Are you not at least *concerned*?'

I nod furiously towards the door, and they both follow me out into the hall.

'Of course I am! I'm deliberately downplaying everything in front of Chloe as I don't want her to worry she's ill, or that it's going to happen again,' I explain. 'And I was all bright and breezy upstairs because the first thing you said was about it going all over the carpet, and I didn't want her to think she'd done anything wrong, either.'

'Oh, I see,' Matthew says. 'Sorry.'

'I wonder if it's related to Theo having that strange crying fit earlier in the week?' Caroline says. 'Have they eaten something odd, do you think?'

I look at Caroline, puzzled. 'But Theo wasn't sick, as far as I know. Chloe's probably just picked something up.'

'She hasn't been anywhere where she might have caught something, though, has she?' Caroline persists.

'Well, she was in the shop with my parents,' I say slowly, not sure where this is going. 'I honestly think it's nothing serious – but I'll keep an eye on her this morning.'

'OK,' Matthew says.

'Would you mind if I sort my hair quickly?' I ask, gesturing to the towel twist on my head. 'It's just it'll dry funny if I leave it much longer.'

'Well, I can't have Theo, I've got to get on with some work,' Matthew says.

'I'll take him.' Caroline reaches out. 'We'll pop out for a breath of fresh air for twenty minutes before his nap. Take as much time as you need – I suppose Matthew is in his office right there if Chloe wants anything – and it'll give you a moment to recover yourself.'

'Thank you. I can set the pram up for you now?' I offer.

'Yes, please. I'll make sure we're back for a quarter to ten. Come on, Theo!'

I decide to do my hair in the playroom, once I've made sure Chloe is still all right, so I'm within easy reach if she starts to feel sick again. Head upside down, as the hairdryer hums, I watch Caroline out of the window, happily pushing Theo down the drive before disappearing off around the corner.

Of *course* I'm concerned about Chloe, but she doesn't have a temperature, she's drinking plenty. It's not irresponsible of me to suggest we just keep an eye on her; it's sensible. I might try and call Mum in a moment too, before Caroline gets back. I want to ask her about this nanny and au pair plan that apparently they all have, and while Will won't want to speak to me, it's also important he knows I'm staying in contact, thinking of him, and I don't take what happened yesterday lightly.

Another movement catches my eye, and I look up to see Ron walking stiffly up the drive towards the front door. Sighing, I turn the dryer off, put my hairbrush down, and make my way out into the hall. He's only my elderly next-door neighbour, I know, but earlier this week he saw me on the doorstep in my nightie, now he's catching me with mad, half-dry hair. It would be nice for people to find me looking normal for a change.

He actually does a double take when I open the door, as well he might to find Tina Turner standing in front of him.

'Hello.' I smile. 'Please excuse my hair, I was halfway through drying it. My daughter was sick in it this morning, the poor thing.' There's a stunned silence as he stares at me. 'Anyway,' I continue brightly, making a mental note to also try to attempt more social interaction with adults before I lose my already limited social skills completely, 'what can I do for you, Ron?'

'I just wanted to say first of all, I wasn't spying on you,' he says gruffly. 'So don't think I was.'

It's my turn to look wary. 'OK,' I say slowly. 'I'm sure you weren't, but what are we talking about, exactly?'

'This.' He holds up a small plastic box, in camouflage colours.

'Sorry, what is that?' I stare at it, still none the wiser.

'It's an Invisible IR Hunting Camera with PIR sensor and SD card recording.'

'Right.' I pause. 'Sorry, Ron, did you say it's a *hunting* camera?'

'Yes, but I got it to film the bats that I think are roosting in *your* loft, not mine. I'm about to have a bat survey done, you see, because we want to put another bedroom in the attic, and maybe extend out the back, only you can't do anything if there are bloody bats. It's lunacy, the planning regulations. Never mind a house is built for *people*. Anyway, these surveys aren't cheap, so I thought I'd see what was what first. And I bought this,' he holds the box up again, 'because it films infra-red and you can see exactly what's going on at night. I set it up to film last week. That's when I saw it.'

'Saw what?'

He looks a little shamefaced. 'All the coming and going here. I was going to wipe it then, honestly I was, but then I showed Shirley.'

'Shirley, your wife?' I say, still confused.

'Yes,' he says. 'I shouldn't have, I know, but she's such a fan of hers, I couldn't not.'

I go very still. 'A fan of who – Kelly Harrington? You filmed Kelly here?'

'Yes.' He looks embarrassed. 'I didn't intend to, but I watched it back, and there was Kelly, three sheets to the wind... I said to Shirl, the state of her... She couldn't even stand when you put her in that taxi. But then when everything was in the paper yesterday it made more sense, the poor old girl. We think she was smashing in *EastEnders*. Anyway, you should have it. Our son wants us to sell it to the papers.' He holds the box aloft again. 'He reckons we'd make a bob or two. But that's not right. You can't go doing things like that – and that's why I've brought it around to you now, so you can destroy it. I'm very sorry I even got it in the first place. We only caught it by a whisker – it started filming about a minute before the taxi turned up. I really *was* only after the bats, though.'

'Just to be completely clear, Ron,' I try to keep my tone neutral, 'you're saying on that camera is a film of me putting Kelly in a taxi, and she's drunk? When did you record this?'

'Last Friday night.'

My heart gives a thump. 'Can I watch it right now?'

'Of course – if you've got a computer?'

I hold the door wider. 'Come in.'

Grabbing my laptop from the hall sideboard, I take him into the kitchen, placing the computer on the table and starting it up. 'This film is *definitely* from last Friday night? You're absolutely sure?'

'Yes. I am.'

'And you can see our house in it?'

He rubs his neck awkwardly. 'Yes, but like I say, I was only trying to see the bats. Which you have got, by the way. I counted three. Well, you can see them for yourself, now.' He removes a small card from the camouflage box and inserts it into the side of my computer. We both wait, and my stomach lurches with apprehension as an icon appears on the screen.

'May I?' says Ron, and I stand aside.

He clicks on it and quickly opens a file. He's surprisingly computer literate for an older man, and just as I'm beginning to worry he might actually not be telling me the truth about why he was filming our house, I forget everything as a black-and-white image of our empty drive appears on the screen.

'I'll just start it... *Now...* There, you see?' Ron says, points out a flickering movement. 'That's the bats. Oh, and here's the taxi arriving.'

I watch, stunned, as an unmarked car pulls onto our drive, but Ron's right – it's a taxi. I *know* it is, because I recognize it. It's the car that I woke up in last Saturday morning on the clifftop. My heart starts to speed up, and my skin prickles, as next, I watch the front door to our house open.

'Oh my God...' I breathe, as I see myself emerge and appear on screen.

Ron looks at the floor uncomfortably. 'I'm very sorry,' he says again, but I don't answer. I can't say anything. I just start to shake as, transfixed, I watch myself struggling to stand, arm slumped across her shoulder, because Ron is wrong, of course, it's not Kelly who is unconscious – it's me. It's not possible to make out the faces clearly, but there's no doubt in my mind who is who. I'm so lifeless that one of the cab doors opens, and the driver gets out hurriedly to go and help.

'This cannot be happening...' I whisper, staring at the two female figures he rushes over to assist.

'I know.' Ron misunderstands me. 'You have to actually lie her on the back seat there. See? Dear oh dear...'

'There isn't any sound, then?' I manage to ask, as evenly as possible.

'No, this sort of film is about getting a visual rather than audio. It's quite clear, though, considering it's pitch black, isn't it? Although, to be honest, I'm not entirely convinced a newspaper would have been able to identify Kelly from this—'

Which is probably why you haven't sold it, I can't help but think silently to myself.

'—but Shirl and me knew it was her, because of course we'd seen her arrive earlier.'

We continue to watch – me in horror – as they shut me into the car, the driver firmly closing the back door, before getting into the front seat and driving off, stealing me away. *She* stands there for a moment longer on the doorstep, before turning calmly, and letting herself back into *my* house, where my children lie upstairs asleep, vulnerable and unprotected.

'Can I keep this, Ron?' I straighten up suddenly.

'Of course. And just so you know, I haven't done any more filming since then. We got what we needed on the first go.'

And thank God he did. The second I've managed to get rid of him, I rush back to the computer and watch the film again. I have to sink down onto a chair because my legs won't hold me up.

'Mummy?' calls Chloe from the other room. 'I need a drink!'

'Coming,' I whisper, barely audibly – once more reaching the part where the cab drives off with me in it, and she stands there watching it leave with her arms composedly folded. I hit pause and stare at the slightly grainy figure so hard, it starts to blur, before suddenly covering my mouth with my hand, as I think *I'm* about to be sick. I close my eyes, and once the nausea has dissipated, I open them again and look right at my perpetrator on the screen, completely unaware she has just been caught red-handed.

I hit play again and watch once more, as Caroline turns, walks back into my house, and calmly closes the door.

CHAPTER TWENTY-TWO

I make my way over to the sink on autopilot, to do Chloe's drink. I can see why Ron made his mistake. He saw Kelly arrive at our house, but presumably missed her leave. The height difference between Caroline and me *is* very similar to the one between Kelly and me – but ultimately, he saw on the film what he wanted to see: Kelly the celebrity, pissed. Only it wasn't her.

It wasn't her!

I start to fill the small plastic cup on the draining board. I accused Kelly. She and Will have separated – and all along it was *Caroline*? She did all of this?

But *why*?

For a moment I can't move. I'm completely unable to process what I've just seen, and the cold water begins to splash all over my hand. I look down at it and suddenly a hideous thought slams into my mind: Chloe. Is that why she's been sick this morning? Has Caroline done something to hurt my little girl? I shut off the tap and dash into the living room, spilling water everywhere in my haste.

Chloe is still sitting quietly on the sofa.

'I've got your drink, darling.' I close the door to Matthew's office quickly and hurry over to Chloe, putting my hand on her forehead. It's still cool, and her cheeks are a normal colour. I kneel down and peer at her closely, placing my fingers on her wrist to feel for her pulse, which doesn't seem to be faster than usual. I listen carefully to her breathing, which is normal too. Her pupils aren't dilated, and she's sitting upright, not floppy-limbed or unresponsive.

'Clo, did Granny give you anything to eat or drink this morning?' I try to mask the panic in my voice, and force myself to smile at her.

Chloe shakes her head.

'And you don't feel really, really sleepy, or like you want to be sick some more, nothing like that?'

She shakes her head again.

'Granny didn't tell you it was a secret, what she was giving you, and that you shouldn't tell anyone?'

'No.' Chloe looks thrown, and I can see I'm now confusing her. 'Can I have my drink now?'

I pass it to her and watch her sip carefully. Should I just take her straight to the doctor? She seems OK, but… Caroline wouldn't hurt Chloe, though, surely? She adores her. Doesn't she?

'It doesn't hurt when you swallow?'

'No, Mummy. I can't hear the TV.'

'Sorry,' I say anxiously. 'Just stay right here, I'll be back in two seconds.'

I dash back into the kitchen and pick up my phone. I dial my mother and simultaneously pull the computer towards me, pressing play and intently watching the film as it re-runs and I wait for Mum to pick up. I cannot believe how calm she is. Caroline appears completely unperturbed – as if putting her comatose daughter-in-law in the back of a taxi with some stranger is a perfectly normal occurrence. Anything could have happened to me in that car.

Mum picks up. 'Hello, love! How are you? I was just about to call, but you beat me to it!'

'I can't really talk, Mum. Chloe's just been sick. You and Dad haven't got anything, have you?'

'Oh *no!*' Mum exclaims. 'Dad doesn't feel quite right this morning, actually, he's got a dicky tummy. I didn't think to let you know, love, I *am* sorry!'

'No, that's really great, actually.' I feel wobbly with relief. 'Thanks. I've got to go.'

I hang up just as it gets to the part where Caroline serenely turns to make her way back into the house, and I shiver, as if someone standing behind me has just breathed on the back of my neck. While I'm now reassured that Chloe is probably all right, Caroline remains unquestionably dangerous. This woman I have known for nearly a decade, who I've trusted, has not only betrayed me completely, she tried to hurt me. How the hell can this be?

I watch her close the door to my house and, as if I've been struck, I ball up my fists, still holding my phone, and press my knuckles into my temples, drawing my elbows tightly into my body, in total disbelief as I think about staggering around on that clifftop, confused and completely spaced out as I nearly fell… What did she give me to make me feel like that, to be so out of control and not be able to remember a damn thing? My breathing begins to speed up as the enormity of my discovery starts to sink in. If I'd fallen, I'd have died.

Everyone would have believed I'd killed myself.

I gasp as it hits me – is *that* what was really supposed to happen?

I lift my head wildly, just in time to see, out of the window, Caroline appear around the corner, pushing my son up the drive, apparently happily singing to him.

I slam the lid of the laptop shut and, fingers shaking, yank out the small card, shoving it in my pocket, before rushing to the front door and flinging it open, just as she arrives in front of me.

She smiles, slightly flushed from the effort of the walk, and turns the pram so I can see Theo lying there happily. 'Hello, Mummy!' she says. 'We had a lovely time, didn't we, darling?'

I fight every single instinct in my body to dart forward and rip my son out of the pram before slamming back into the house, so I can lock her out. She drugged me. This is real, and there must be a reason why she's acting as if there's nothing wrong now. Does she have something else planned? That has to be why she's had no problem in staying here so much – unfettered access to us all. I stare at Caroline, terrified. Swallowing, I try desperately to gain control over myself so that she doesn't realize that anything is wrong.

She looks at me, puzzled, putting her head on one side. 'Sal, are you all right? You look like you've seen a ghost.'

For a moment my mind goes blank, but then my mouth just opens, and from nowhere I find myself blurting, 'It's Chloe.' I move forward carefully and start to undo Theo's straps with fumbling fingers, before lifting him out and clasping him to me tightly. 'Her temperature's shooting up and I've just discovered I've got no Calpol.'

She frowns with concern. 'Poor little scrap. It sounds like she's got gastroenteritis. Do you want me to pop out and get some?'

'Would you mind?' I gabble desperately. 'I don't want to leave her, and obviously Matthew's working.'

'I'll go right now. Let me just get my purse.'

'No! I've got cash here.' I grab for my handbag – thankfully lying open on the floor of the hall, its contents already spewing out onto the carpet – and reach for a ten-pound note. She mustn't come in and see that Chloe isn't feverish; she'll know instantly that something is up. 'Here.' I shove it at her. 'Take this.'

'I need my car keys, Sal,' she says slowly, looking at me.

I turn away instantly so she can't see the fear in my eyes, and, thank God, there are her keys sitting on the sideboard. I snatch them up and thrust them at her too.

'I'm sorry, Caroline, I don't mean to rush you, I'm just really worried about her.'

'She hasn't got a rash or anything, has she? Her feet and hands are a normal temperature?'

'Yes, they are, and there's no rash. It's just the fever.'

'OK, well try and remember that's a good thing, her body is fighting off whatever it is. Just keep her hydrated. Where's the nearest chemist? Actually, anywhere will have Calpol, won't they? I'll nip to the garage, that's probably easiest, I'll be able to park faster. I'll be right back, don't worry.'

I nod mutely and watch as she walks smartly to her Mercedes, blipping it open before climbing in and reversing out of the drive carefully. I listen until I can't hear the car any more, and slam back into the house before breathlessly leaning on the closed door as I try to think what to do. I've probably got about ten minutes at the most before she comes back. Do I go and tell Matthew now? Show him the film? But he's going to be appalled – he'll confront her instantly, and the children are here. It will escalate, maybe even furiously, and now I know what she's capable of, I can't risk that. None of us are safe, potentially not even Matthew. It's incredible that this can be true, but I have to get the children away from here – as soon as possible.

Theo bounces around on my hip as I hurry into the sitting room and crane to see if I can hear Matthew on a call. I can. Thank God. He won't notice a thing.

'Chloe, darling,' I hasten over to the sofa, 'we've got to pop out for a little bit. Can you come and get your shoes on?'

She looks up in dismay. 'But I've only just started watching this.'

'I know, but I need you to come out with me.'

'But I don't want to. My tummy's still achy.'

'That's why we need to go out, to get some sweets to *help* your tummy.' I try to smile. 'Come on, the sooner we go, the sooner we're back again. You can choose the sweets,' I cajole.

She considers this. 'Can I get one of the chocolate eggs that has a toy inside it?'

'You can get two if you come right now.'

Her eyes widen in amazement and she rather shakily gets to her feet. She really is under the weather, the poor little thing, but we have to leave. Immediately.

Buckling them both into their car seats, I shove the change bag and the food bag containing Theo's bottle, a drink for Chloe and a couple of baby pouches into the passenger footwell, carefully strap my laptop on the seat itself, and set off.

'That's fast, Mummy,' remarks Chloe after a moment or two.

'It is a bit, isn't it? Sorry,' I agree, trying to smile as if nothing is wrong. 'Tell me if you feel sick again, won't you?' I glance at her anxiously in the rear-view mirror.

'Where are we going to get the chocolate eggs from?'

'Well, we're going to get them in a little bit. We'll have a drive first,' I say, trying to think straight. What am I going to do? I can't take them to Mum's. Any sudden dramatic disappearance will make everyone think I'm having another breakdown or 'crisis moment', only this time they'll tell the police I've got the children with me. I feel nauseous at the thought of being pulled over en route by a wailing squad car, blue lights flashing – then a terrified and ill Chloe and Theo being dragged out of the car by a police officer, for their own 'safety'.

'Hang on a minute, Clo,' I say, and I take a sudden right-hand turn off the main road into a housing estate, then turn left into a small cul-de-sac. There's no chance Caroline will happen upon us here on her way back from the garage. I pull over and reach for my phone to text Matthew.

Just taken Clo to doctor. Sure she's fine, but so hot I think they should check her out. Didn't want to disturb while you were on phone. Could you tell your mum I'll be back soon, so she doesn't worry?

He's going to say do I want Caroline to come down to the surgery, I know he will. Sure enough, he texts exactly that, seconds later. Will it look suspicious if I don't say yes? I chew my lip worriedly.

No, it's OK thanks. Chloe will want to go back in her car if she arrives and don't want to risk Clo being sick in it. Tell your mum I'll be back in an hour at most.

There, that's plausible, isn't it? Caroline probably won't think anything more than I'm just being neurotic about Chloe. So now I have about an hour before either of them will begin to suspect something. I lift my head, stare out of the windscreen for a moment, then make my decision and return to my phone.

Hi Liv. Sorry I didn't call earlier, and hope it's OK, but I'm on my way over now. You still in? x

I hit send. Please be there, Liv. Please don't have already had your delivery and gone out...

Thank God, the three scrolling dots of her typing a reply appear instantly.

Definitely still here. See you in a bit xx

I throw the phone down on the passenger seat in relief and, checking over my shoulder, pull out onto the road and start to turn around.

'Are we going to get my eggs now?' says Chloe.

'Yes. We're going to get them on the way to Liv and Kate's.' I give her a wide smile in the rear-view mirror, and she looks doubtfully back at me.

'Am I well enough to go to Kate's house?'

'Oh, I think so, yes, darling!' I lie airily. 'You're fine. You don't still feel sick now, do you?'

'No.'

'Well, there you go then!' I smile at her again, and she looks marginally less worried, before, unusually for her, lapsing into silence and staring out of the window. I glance over at Theo, who has already fallen asleep, and exhale heavily. This *is* the right thing to do. I can't go to Mum's and I can't go to the police either. All the film shows, as far as they'd be concerned, is Caroline putting me in a taxi. That's hardly illegal. I have no proof that she drugged me – and Caroline knows that. She'd explain it all away to them, and who would they believe anyway – the nutter they picked up on the clifftop in her pyjamas, or the respected psychologist with an unblemished record?

Matthew is the person who really needs to see this film – and Liv knows enough about the situation to understand the significance of it too. I can trust her with this, I'm sure I can. I'm still angry with her for telling Matthew what I did all those years ago – but I can at least see she had good intentions, which were rooted in her caring about me. She will understand exactly why I want to get the kids away from Caroline, once I tell her the whole story.

Except, what is the whole story? We reach the main road and I pull out into the anonymous flow of traffic. I have absolutely no idea why Caroline has done this to me. I've known her for years. I've liked and respected her; I thought she felt the same way about me too.

How, then, can she have let me believe this was all Kelly's doing? I even thought at one point that I might be seriously ill. She watched me flounder around in confusion, and all along she knew – *she knew* – exactly what had happened, and she was totally prepared to let Kelly, an ex-patient, take the blame for everything.

Maybe *that's* it. Perhaps this is about Kelly, and not me. Has this been about her using me to get back at Kelly somehow? What really is the deal between those two?

But even if it *has* been Caroline's intention all along to ruin Kelly, why would she put me at such serious risk?

I shift in the driver's seat uneasily. There is no escaping the fact that she did me actual bodily harm. She drugged me. Was it when she and I had the second glass of champagne, after Will and Kelly had gone home? She had plenty of time to slip something in my drink then. Jesus – this is horrific – she talked me through all of the various drugs that can cause memory loss, utterly calmly, when she knew what she had done? That's psychotic.

And I *begged* her to back me up by telling Mum, Dad and Will about Kelly's toxic past. No wonder she didn't want to! In fact, what's to say it's even true? I don't know what to believe any more.

I grip the steering wheel more tightly and think about her telling me that sixty-five thousand pounds was a small price to pay for Kelly disappearing off into the sunset and leaving us all unscathed. I trusted what she said implicitly, while all along, she was the one who had hurt me.

I still don't understand.

Why has she done this?

CHAPTER TWENTY-THREE

'Oh my God,' breathes Liv, watching the film intently. My laptop is balanced on her knees, as the girls sit on the opposite sofa, completely absorbed by *Frozen* on the TV, and I jiggle Theo. 'You're right. It's definitely you being put in the taxi, and it's definitely –' she peers closely at the screen – '*not* Kelly who's doing it.'

'Would you say it's this woman?' I hold out my phone, showing a family shot of me standing next to Caroline in our kitchen, who is holding a four-week-old Theo, while Chloe stands delightedly in front of both of us.

Liv gasps. 'Isn't that Matthew's mother?'

I nod.

Liv's eyes widen in shock. Her voice drops to a horrified whisper. 'His *mother* did this to you?'

'Yes.'

'You'd gone to bed, totally as normal?' Liv asks eventually, apparently, like me, trying to make sense of this.

'Yes. I remember I could barely keep my eyes open, but I'm like that all of the time. I felt a bit sick too, but I assumed that was just me not being used to drinking any more.'

'Then you woke up the next morning in Cornwall, in the back of that taxi?' Liv points at the screen, and I nod.

'And all along, you really did have no idea what had happened to you, until you saw this film?'

'Yes.'

'What are you going to do?'

'I need to show it to Matthew, so he can see it with his own eyes, because I don't ever want her near my children, or me, ever again.'

'You don't think you should just go straight to the police?'

I shake my head. 'This doesn't prove she drugged me, and they won't be able to charge her with anything. When Matthew watches this, though,' I lower my voice, so the girls can't hear, 'he'll realize that his mother has been lying all along, and that she's dangerous.'

'I don't think you should risk going back to the house to show Matthew if she's there too,' Liv says, concerned. 'What if she becomes really nasty and turns on both of you? Who knows what else she's capable of?'

'I'm not going to take the kids. I know this is a huge ask, but can they stay here with you?'

'Of course,' she says instantly.

'Thank you so much,' I say gratefully. 'I've brought all of Theo's stuff, and Chloe probably won't want much to eat, if anything. I'll be back by two.'

'And if you're not?' Liv says. 'Who do you want me to call in the event of an emergency?'

'My parents,' I say instantly. 'I'm going to leave you their numbers, and one for my brother too. Don't let the kids go to anyone else.'

Liv starts to look frightened. 'Even Matthew?'

'No, sorry, I meant anyone other than him or me. But don't worry, I'll be back, Liv.' I reach out and put what I hope is a steady hand on her arm. 'I promise I will.'

'I *really* don't think you should go back to the house. Make Matthew meet you in a public place somewhere so that if she insists on coming too, she can't make a scene.'

I consider that. 'OK,' I agree. 'You're probably right. It might help contain Matthew's reaction too. This is going to devastate him.'

'Here.' Liv folds up the laptop and puts it on the floor next to her, before holding out her hands to take Theo. 'You have to show Matthew. He absolutely must see it. Theo will be totally happy to nap in his pram upstairs then, you think?'

I pass Theo over to her. 'To be honest, probably not. And I'm really sorry if he kicks off.'

'Well, we'll give it a go anyway.' Liv smiles at Theo. 'Won't we, little chap?' She looks up at me again. 'You've already put the pram in our bedroom, though, with his food bag?'

'Yes. There are pouches, his spoons, his milk stuff – everything is in there.'

'Great. Now don't worry about anything here, Sal, we'll be fine.'

'Thank you,' I say sincerely, as I bend to pick up the laptop before turning to my utterly focused daughter. 'Clo? Hello, Chloe?'

She looks up with a jump as I raise my voice to get her attention. 'Yes, Mummy?'

'I've just got to pop back home to get something, so you and Theo are going to stay here with Liv and Kate.'

She looks between us warily. 'When are you coming back?'

'After lunch.'

'Which is pasta,' Liv says. 'But you don't have to have any if you don't feel like it. You might just like some plain with no sauce.'

'Yes please.' Chloe nods, then turns back to the TV.

'OK, go,' instructs Liv.

'I'll text you the numbers for my family en route. And thank you again.'

'No problem. Email a copy of that video to yourself, just to be sure. And, Sal?'

I stop as I reach the door, and look back at her.

'I really am so sorry for my part in all of this.'

'It's forgotten.' I smile briefly. 'I have no memory of anything, remember?'

'Take care.'

'Will do.' I wave to my children and blow them a kiss. Chloe doesn't even look up. I should be grateful that they are so unperturbed by my leaving, but as I get into the car and strap myself in after placing the laptop in the footwell and starting the engine, I have to fight a ridiculous urge to run back into the house to hug them again, and tell them how much I love them, and promise I'll be back before they know it.

I've been driving for just over half an hour when my mobile starts to ring. It's Matthew. I pull over quickly and call him straight back.

'Where are you?' He doesn't even bother with hello. 'You've been gone ages. What has the doctor said?'

'Chloe is absolutely fine,' I say truthfully. 'Listen, I've actually had a bit of a problem.'

'Oh?' he says instantly. 'What sort of problem?'

'With the car. I was just about to ring you. I've called in to Tesco on my way back to get some rehydration salts from the chemist for Chloe –' God is going to strike me down for these lies – 'but I've just come back out to the car and discovered we've got a flat tyre.'

'OK,' he says slowly. 'Completely flat?'

'Er, yes.'

'How did that happen? Didn't you notice it when you were driving? Can you see around the car? Is there any glass on the floor or anything? You definitely didn't drive it while it was flat, did you, or you'll have warped the wheel itself?'

Oh God, Matthew... 'Look, it's fine,' I say, realizing I should have said it was a slow puncture. 'I'll call the AA when we get home, but could you borrow your mum's car and pop around to get me and the kids? Chloe obviously isn't very well, and Theo's tired – we need to get back. I think *you* should come rather than Caroline, though, so you can take a look at the wheel and make sure it's not been damaged.'

'I'll leave now.'

'And just remember, if your mum drives, there won't be enough room for all of us in her car once we've got the kids' seats in the back, so you'll have to come on your own, OK?'

'I'll be with you in five.'

I take a deep breath. 'See you then.'

He hangs up, and I glance at the clock. If he's leaving now, I'll be there just before him.

I start the car up again and ease back into the traffic, selecting the inside lane. I sit at the red lights in front of the turn-off to the supermarket and drum my fingers on the steering wheel. Come on! I still need to forward Mum's number to Liv. And Will's.

The lights change to green and I drive into the busy car park full of mums with pre-school children, and older couples parking or returning trolleys. I choose a space a little further away from the shop front, but still plenty busy enough, just in case. Although surely she won't come; I've made it practically impossible for her to.

I turn the engine off and forward Liv the phone numbers. She replies instantly.

Thanks. All OK here. Theo fast asleep and Chloe watching Tangled now. No rush. Please be careful.

At least everything is fine there.

I scan the car park – no sign of Caroline's silver sports Mercedes yet, but he'll be here any minute. I reach down into the footwell for the laptop and set it up on the passenger seat. I'm not going to say anything, I'm just going to let him watch the film for himself. I also take Liv's advice and email the film to myself, just in case.

Still I wait, but he doesn't arrive. Frowning, I look up and down the lines of cars – which is when I notice a blacked-out Audi slowly cruising past the mother and child spots. I watch it absently for a moment, before realizing it isn't someone trying to park, as they drive past an empty space. The driver is looking for someone.

It indicates and quietly pulls into a disabled space. A tall, heavily-set man climbs out, before slowly starting to walk past the parked cars, casually peering in here and there, before coming back and saying something through the Audi window.

The back passenger doors open, and another man climbs out of one side, then Caroline out of the other. I freeze instantly – then, horrified, watch her start to turn, very slowly on the spot, hand shading the bright sun from her eyes as she begins to scan the car park for me. She stops still as she catches sight of our car – and then I see her point, and the two men look over, right at me. My heart leaps with fear. Who the hell are they?

All three of them begin to walk in my direction, and, as they get closer, I see that the men are actually wearing uniform: black trousers and dark tunic tops, with a distinctive gold oak emblem on the left breast pocket. They're from Abbey Oaks? The private hospital Caroline works at? Oh my God. I know then exactly why they are accompanying her. Panicking, I pull on the door handle and scramble out rather than starting the car. This isn't leading to some reckless and dangerous car chase – I hear the echo of my promise to Chloe that I'll come back, as I look around desperately for an escape route. They are still some six car lengths away from me. Do I scream for help? Run? Won't that make me appear even more insane? Is anyone going to help me if I start to struggle with these two men? They're going to force me into that car!

'No!' I gasp audibly as Caroline walks calmly towards me... But then the silver Mercedes suddenly appears at the other end of the car park, roaring up towards us.

Matthew.

Matthew is here. Oh thank God!

The car swerves slightly as he swings erratically into a space, and then jumps out. 'NO! Mum! Stop!' I hear him shout, and he sprints towards her. He reaches out and grabs her arm, pulling her around to face him. I can't hear what he says, they're not close enough, but she takes a sudden step back from him. I can see Matthew's chest rising and falling as he tries to catch his breath, and says something else, gesturing angrily at the two men. A moment more passes, and then, apparently at Caroline's instruction, the men fall back and return to the Audi. They climb in and close the doors, but they don't leave. The car just sits there, as Caroline turns and resumes her walk across the car park, Matthew hastening after her.

Caroline arrives right in front of me. 'I gather you have something I need to see.' She isn't smiling. Considering, however, that I'm about to accuse her of a crime that has the power to ruin her and rip her from the life of her beloved only son for ever, neither does she appear particularly concerned. 'Show me.'

I ignore that – and her – before taking a deep breath. Everything falls still, a moment of hush before the bomb explodes. Then I look at my husband and say earnestly, 'Matthew, I'm so sorry – but there's something you need to know.'

CHAPTER TWENTY-FOUR

'You stay back, though,' I instruct Caroline. 'If you take so much as a step towards me, I'll scream, and then I will tell anyone who will listen *everything*, including your two employees over there.' I hold my phone up. 'And just so you know, I'm also now recording this conversation.' I hit the voice memo and start it running.

'Sal?' Matthew looks at me, frightened. 'Tell me what's going on. Why are you talking like this?'

'It's OK, Matthew,' Caroline says coolly. 'Let's just listen to what Sally wants to tell us.'

'My laptop is on the front passenger seat, Matthew. I want you to go around and hit play on the film that's on pause at the moment.'

He hurries away and I hear the click of the car door opening as Caroline and I stand in silence, not taking our eyes from each other. 'You actually brought two Abbey Oaks staff with you,' I manage. 'You were going to try to force me there?'

She doesn't answer me, and we're interrupted anyway by Matthew exclaiming, 'Oh my God!'

Caroline frowns slightly, but then draws herself up a little taller than before, and stares me down as Matthew reappears.

I glance across at him. He is ashen. 'It's a video of you, Mum, and you're putting Sal in the back of a taxi. She's completely out cold! It's an actual film!'

'Our next-door neighbour brought it over earlier,' I explain. 'He was filming the bat activity around our house. He thought it was me putting Kelly in a cab. But it isn't, is it, Caroline?'

'Show me,' she repeats.

Matthew carries around the laptop and rests it carefully on the bonnet, then presses play. I watch Caroline – her face barely flickers. All she does at the end is sigh, reach to the drive, extract Ron's card, and very precisely, she snaps it in half. Then, with a tiny, almost imperceptible push, she slides the laptop off the car, and it shatters as it hits the concrete car park floor.

I gasp and look across at Matthew, expecting him to say something, but he's stunned, and simply stares at his mother wide-eyed.

'How very annoying of your neighbour,' Caroline says.

'Smashing my laptop won't make any difference,' I stammer. 'I've already emailed it to myself, and the only person I needed to see it has now.' I nod at Matthew.

She shrugs. 'Well, it made me feel a bit better, anyway.'

'How can you be so calm?' I stare at her in disbelief. 'All this time,' my voice starts to shake, 'you've known exactly what happened. You've watched as I've struggled to work it all out, when you knew, *you knew* I hadn't tried to kill myself! I talked to you, I *trusted* you!'

She says nothing, just looks at me, and then, to my astonishment, simply smiles.

'This isn't a joke!' I shout suddenly, and a couple of people a few cars away look up. 'You tried to hurt me! I know you put something in my drink that made me black out to the point that I was unable to remember anything!'

'Mum!' Matthew exclaims suddenly, seemingly shocked into action by what I've just said. He puts both hands on his head. 'This is actually happening. This is *actually fucking happening*!'

'Calm down, Matthew,' she says instantly.

'Calm down?' he exclaims. 'Did you not hear what Sal just said?'

'You honestly think I put something in your *drink*?' Caroline cuts right across him, directing her comment straight at me. 'You're so pedestrian, Sally. Credit me with a little more imagination. Do you know there was a man who injected his wife with HIV while she slept? Perhaps you read about it? I'm very skilled at sedation, actually. It's years of practice.'

My heart is beating so fast I think I'm going to be sick. 'You're actually admitting you drugged me?'

'Mum!' cries Matthew, brokenly.

'Yes, I am,' she says quickly.

'But why?' I ask incredulously.

She shrugs again. 'I just don't like you.'

'You just... don't *like* me?' I repeat foolishly. 'I'm the mother of your grandchildren! You engineered everything to look like I'd attempted to kill myself – and when I refused to accept that, you let me believe Kelly was to blame. Do you not understand the damage you've done to so many people? I thought I was seriously ill at one point. You even just brought two men with you, presumably to help forcibly section me – and you say you did all of this because you don't *like* me?'

She doesn't respond.

'Did you steal Kelly's phone, so she had to come back to the house and I'd think it was her?' I ask slowly. Then my eyes widen. 'Oh God, did you break her shoe as well, so I'd know she'd been in the cupboard under the stairs, where the money was?'

Caroline snorts. 'Oh please! There never was any money in the holdall! Just my clothes and belongings. Only a complete idiot would actually leave that amount of cash lying around.'

I persist, doggedly, 'What did you do after you told me you went to bed? Drug me, then call me a taxi? Clear down my phone?

My God, you must have been delighted to find that note to tuck in my pocket. Talk about a God-given gift.'

She shrugs. 'There might have been one or two small moments of luck, but everything would have worked just as well without them; I had thought it all through. To be perfectly honest, Sally, it was your antipathy towards Kelly – and vice versa – that pretty much took care of everything. It's so tragically easy to manipulate women of your generation because you're all primed and ready to destroy each other at the earliest opportunity, underneath those fake smiles. All I did was exploit your natural jealousies and insecurities – don't let's forget, no one *forced* you to break into your brother's flat. You did that all on your own. I will tell you I took the holdall out of the house inside my empty and capacious suitcase when I left on Saturday night, though. I hadn't actually been to Barcelona, you see.'

'You told me that Kelly was dangerously unstable.'

'No,' she corrects me, 'I didn't, actually. I said someone close to the children had the potential to be dangerously unstable. If we're being pedantic, one could argue that everyone has that potential – it's a totally meaningless phrase. But I told you that someone close to the children might be about to behave in a toxic manner that could do long-term damage to them, and I felt duty-bound to intervene and prevent it. You filled in the blanks incorrectly yourself. I was actually talking about *you*.'

'Me?' I am horrified, and look across at Matthew, who appears to have frozen once more.

'I had reason to believe that you might be about to do something that would harm Chloe and Theo unnecessarily, so, as I promised, I intervened and stopped you. That's all that this has been about.'

'That's complete *bullshit*!' I cry angrily. 'I would never hurt my own children. Don't you dare try to justify what you've done! Everything you said was deliberately designed to mislead me!'

'You heard what you wanted to hear,' she insists. 'You wanted to believe Kelly was a liar and a thief.'

'No, I didn't! What's the real deal between you two?' I say. 'Why are you trying to hurt her as well as me?' I gasp suddenly. 'Oh dear God – *you* told the papers about Kelly's mum, didn't you? How could you do that? I accused my oldest friend of betraying me, when it was you! You wilfully broke Kelly's patient confidentiality, and after that pious lecture you gave me?'

'I had no idea about her mother's suicide until you told me, so there is no conflict of interest in my contacting the press whatsoever.'

'Of course there is! You were her counsellor!'

'No I wasn't. The first time I met her was at your house the night they came to tell you of their engagement.'

The ground feels as if it's falling away from under my feet. 'W-w-what?' I stammer. 'You *weren't* her psychiatrist?'

'No,' says Caroline simply.

'You made out as if you'd recognized her!'

'I did – she *is* famous, after all.'

'No, I mean recognized her from the past. You *know* that's what you did! You told me you'd treated her, that you knew secrets about her,' I cry. 'Dangerous secrets. You even told me she couldn't have children.'

'No, I told you some anorexics have issues with fertility. That's just a statement of fact, like the sky is blue. I said nothing explicit about Kelly in the slightest. How could I, when she was a perfect stranger to me?'

'I can't believe this. You don't know her *at all*?' I clutch my hands to my head in complete shock. 'But if you'd never met her, you can't have been doing this to get back at her...'

'That's right,' she says patiently, as if speaking to an exceptionally stupid child.

'That almost makes it worse! You simply used her? But what about the sixty-five thousand pounds you said was a small price to pay for not enraging Kelly?'

'Well, it *was* a small price to pay, because she never took the money, did she?' Caroline shrugs. 'Kelly never had any involvement with any money at all. Did you not hear what I said a moment ago? *There was no bag of money.* Matthew lent sixty-five thousand to me, and then I repaid it straight back into his account. End of story. Here's the thing, Sally – if you create enough of a sense of chaos, your adversary won't know who the enemy is, and they certainly won't be able to aim the gun... And I think it's a little disingenuous of you to start raising concern for Kelly, in any case. You've got exactly what you wanted: Kelly is gone. You can thank me whenever you feel ready. And if you *really* want to know the truth, I actually *don't* like you. I never thought you were the one, right from the first time Matthew brought you home.'

'Mum!' Matthew steps in finally.

'You criticize my son constantly,' she continues, ignoring him. 'Nothing is ever good enough for you. You live in a house he works his fingers to the bone to keep you all in, and all *you* can go on about is how dated it is, how everything has to go. Well, why don't *you* go and make the money to pay for it all then?'

'*Mum!*' Matthew says again.

'No, Matthew!' she cuts him off, suddenly very angry indeed. 'She needs to be told! You have no idea how bloody lucky you are!' She swings around to face me again, furiously. 'Two healthy children, a husband that loves you, a roof over your head. You don't deserve any of it. That's what I really loathe about women like you, Sally: your sense of entitlement. You have the world, but you want more, more, more. And everything is someone else's fault. I dragged myself up by my bootstraps, and I built a life for me and my child. What have you ever done? Except complain bitterly about your lot? It would have done us all a favour if you *had* fallen. That was certainly my preferred outcome, and God knows you had enough meds in your system to make it happen.'

I take a step back, unable to believe what she's just said. 'You are never to come near us, or our children again,' I tell her, my voice shaking wildly. 'We want nothing to do with you.'

'We? *We?* So you're going to make him choose all over again? This is *exactly* what I'm talking about! *You* want to go to America, so Matthew has to leave his whole life behind – just like that.'

'Jesus Christ, Caroline! That was years ago! You've been holding onto this all that time?' I'm appalled. 'I mean it – if you come near us again, I will ruin you. I will play everyone and anyone this recording,' I hold up my phone, 'so they all know exactly what kind of woman *you* really are.'

'You do whatever the hell you like, my darling,' she says.

'Mum, no!' Matthew says, his voice breaking. 'This has gone too far. Stop it. Now.'

'Shut up, Matthew!' she warns him.

'You can't do this!'

'It's already done, Matthew!'

'But it's not fair, or right,' he cries out suddenly. 'I can't let you take all of the blame for everything when it wasn't just you, Mum.'

I gasp as if someone has suddenly grabbed my head from behind and shoved it under water. Unable to breathe, I jerk my head around to look at him.

He has tears in his eyes. He is not angry; his face is full of shame.

He looks like a man who has just confessed.

'*You* were part of this?' I can hardly get the words out. My whole body starts to shake.

He swallows.

'Don't say anything more, Matthew!' Caroline says, now genuinely frightened. 'I've already admitted it was all my doing. There is no need for any of this to happen. *Think* about what this will mean. *Please,*' she begs.

'Yes, I knew,' he admits to me. 'I knew what Mum was going to do. We planned it together.'

'Oh God!' Caroline whimpers. 'Oh shit, Matthew! You stupid, stupid child!'

I hear myself make some sort of weird, guttural moan of pain. 'You planned it *together*?' I repeat, looking at my husband in horror. 'But seconds ago you looked horrified when you saw the video.'

'Because she said no one would ever know. We both talked about it – how you wouldn't get hurt. I promise you, Sally, it wasn't supposed to go this far. You were only meant to wake up in Cornwall and be a bit confused and frightened, that's all. I thought you'd believe that perhaps… you weren't well. Especially given the note I put in your pocket. You were right, I did read it.' He takes a step towards me. 'But I swear I didn't know that you'd had genuine troubles in the past, Sal, and tried to take your own life before, I promise you, or I'd never, *ever* have agreed to it. You must know that?' He reaches out and grabs my arms desperately. 'And I want you to know you *were* safe. All the time, you were safe. You had money on you, and we knew exactly where you'd gone.'

'I wasn't safe at all!' I cry, pulling away from him. 'Why have you done this to me?'

He looks at me wildly. 'I let something really stupid happen.'

'Matthew, SHUT UP!' Caroline cries. 'You will lose *everything*! Is that what you want?'

'What have you done?' I whisper, my heart starting to pound.

'It was a mistake,' he says. 'A dreadful mistake. What she

wanted would cause so much pain to so many people, all of the children, and… it's not worth it. It could never be worth it. I don't want the kids to suffer, and I don't want to start all over again. I love you, and I changed my mind. I even started to worry you'd found out and you were going to leave *me.* Then she said she was going to tell you everything, that she could see I was too afraid to leave you, and she'd make the decision for me. I panicked. I took all of our money out, so at the very least you couldn't leave me with nothing. I knew you'd divorce me if she told you what we'd done.'

'The money from the flat sale? You said you lent it to her for the refuge?' I gesture at Caroline, thinking that's whom he is talking about.

He swallows and shakes his head. 'None of that was true. I withdrew it, but then Mum had her Cornwall idea, and I needed to put the money *back* again, but I also needed an excuse for why I'd removed it in the first place, in case you saw it on the bank statement or something. I really believed the money had gone missing on Friday night, by the way. Mum told me it had, so that I looked genuinely worried. She thought I wasn't going to be able to pull everything off convincingly enough otherwise… But you *have* to know that when I discovered what had happened to you all those years ago, I was terrified, and I wasn't acting then either. Every word I said to you about all of that was true.'

'Wait – what do you mean you'd cause pain to "all" of the children?' I say slowly. 'What other children? Who is this "she" you're talking about?'

'Perhaps I could be happy with someone else.'

There is a pause.

I stare at him. 'Matthew, have you been having an affair?'

He closes his eyes in shame, as if somehow that means he won't have to answer my question with what I now see is the truth.

'Who is she?'

'She's irrelevant,' he whispers. 'It's over, and it's you I want to be with, you—'

'It's relevant to me! Oh my God, Matthew!' My eyes fill with frightened tears. 'Everything you told me? You actually asked me if I'd orchestrated this to get your attention... When all the time it happened because of what *you'd* done? How can you not have been going to say a single thing about any of this – either of you! If I hadn't been given that video, purely by chance...'

'It wasn't meant to turn out this way! When Will told me he was getting engaged, I knew it was going to upset you, and when Mum thought we could use their announcement so that it would look like *that* was what had triggered you having a breakdown, it seemed perfect. You were supposed to come home focused on getting better; I was going to help you. You were going to realize that you needed me. And everyone else would see how fragile you were, how vital it was that I stayed with you. It was the perfect excuse for me not to leave you. No one could carry on pressurizing me to walk out on you under those circumstances.'

I back away from both of them. 'But if you hate me so much, Caroline, why not just encourage Matthew to leave me? Wouldn't that have been easier?'

'And have you take Chloe and Theo off to the other end of the country where we'd never see them again once you divorced my son? I don't think so.' Caroline looks at me scornfully. 'And while I may not like you, I like this other one even less. I told you, I was simply trying to protect you from hurting the children with an unnecessary divorce. I knew there was no way you'd be prepared to live with Matthew's mistake – you're too immature for that – but children shouldn't be brought up by single parents when it's avoidable. It's not fair on them when it isn't *their* fault. I won't have it happen all over again. I *won't* keep my counsel and say nothing this time. I want more for Chloe and Theo than that! Much, much more – and you should too!'

'Please, Sally.' Matthew steps forward again. 'I know what I did was wrong, very wrong. I've made some dreadful mistakes. To be honest, I think it's me who hasn't been myself recently – I've struggled a lot. Maybe *I* have some sort of post-natal depression!' He laughs desperately. 'I know it's no excuse, but since Theo was born, I—'

'No! Don't you dare!' I yell. 'Don't you *dare* blame him! You've been seeing someone else behind my back? We've just had a baby?' I can't believe the words I'm saying out loud. 'And as for you,' I swing around to face Caroline wildly, 'if I had fallen for real, confused and drugged out of my mind, everyone would have believed I'd killed myself: the children, my parents. You'd have kept that secret for ever? You were really prepared to risk my *life*?'

'Sally, please! Of course no one intended you to actually fall.' Matthew reaches out and grabs my arm. 'Mum was just trying to pull the attention from me when she said that. I told you – it wasn't supposed to go to these extremes. I would never have done it if I'd known about your previous struggles. I have been genuinely frightened for you this week, after you broke into Will's flat and—'

'Did you know she was bringing those men from Abbey Oaks with her, just now?' I nod across at the stationary Audi. 'Oh my God, you *did*, didn't you?'

'But we stood them down again – you saw us do it!' he says eagerly.

'That's hardly the point, and they're still *right there*. Just let me go!' My only thought is to get away, back to Chloe and Theo. The man I love *allowed* this to happen to me? 'You're never coming near me or the children again!'

He pales. 'Don't say that. It's you and the kids I want, not her. I made a mistake.'

313

I break free and stumble backwards, turning away from them, terrified.

'No!' I hear him shout. 'I won't let you do this, Sally!'

I start to run, blindly.

I don't see the car driven by the eighty-six-year-old man, who will fail to react properly to the person suddenly appearing in front of his bonnet, as if from nowhere. In fact, in his panic, he will accidentally slam on his accelerator by mistake, rather than his brakes, dramatically increasing the force of impact.

All I hear is Caroline scream, 'NO!' at the top of her voice.

And then the whole world falls silent.

FIVE MONTHS LATER

CHAPTER TWENTY-FIVE

We sit in silence on the clifftop, staring out at the tide coming in on the beach beneath us. The evening sun is still warm on my face and it's a balmy evening for the first weekend in September, but I shiver suddenly.

He looks across at me. 'Want my coat?'

I shake my head, and we lapse back into silence again until he breaks it. 'Penny for them?'

I exhale. 'I was just thinking about Chloe. I'm struggling more than I thought I would with her starting school on Monday. It's come around so fast, and she seems so small. I just worry about… how she's going to cope.' I turn away because I know he can hear the sudden tremble in my voice.

He reaches out and takes my hand for a moment, squeezing it briefly before letting go. 'Of course you do. Has she talked any more about it all?'

I shake my head. 'No. But today Theo bowled over into a tower she'd been making from the blocks in his little push-along trolley, and she was just furious. She screamed, and then burst into floods and floods of tears. She didn't know where to put herself, and all I could do was hold her. I could *feel* her missing him, and it was so desperately sad, Joe.' My voice breaks. 'I can't explain what it's like to watch her hurt so much, and to not be able to make it OK for her. Sorry,' I whisper, and wipe my eyes.

'It's OK,' he says, and passes me a tissue from his jeans pocket. 'It's been a horrendous week for you.' He pauses. 'Do you want to talk about what happened at the inquest?'

I look down at my hands as I start to twist the tissue into a point. 'Not really, but thank you.'

He nods, understandingly.

'The coroner recorded a verdict of accidental death,' I say, however, moments later, discovering that actually I do want to talk about it.

Joe looks confused. 'That was a given, though, surely?'

'Well, not exactly.' I squint out to sea. 'The police had done quite a lot of investigating, and all of that information is passed to a coroner once they're happy there isn't a criminal case to answer.' I take a deep breath. 'Matthew wasn't hitting his targets at work, just before he died, and things like that were mentioned. He also withdrew a very large sum of money from our savings two weeks before it all happened.'

'Shit!' Joe is appalled. 'They thought he might have stepped in front of the car *deliberately*?'

'It was a possibility that had to be ruled out, yes. But I was able to confirm I knew about the cash,' I say carefully. 'He was making some investments on behalf of his mother. A loan, really, which she repaid. It wasn't suspicious in any way. Ultimately the coroner concluded, from the supermarket's CCTV and some witness statements, that Matthew didn't appear to see the car coming because he was concentrating on trying to catch up with me; although we were right at the back of the car park, and the film isn't particularly clear because the camera was almost side on to Matthew. You see him step out, but you can't really see his face.'

'But no one suggested it was your fault in any way?' Joe says quickly.

'No, no. I explained that I had felt very violently sick, very suddenly – and I was running to the loos in the shop. My father and Chloe had the same bug. Matthew was worried and was following after me. His mother confirmed that was what had happened too.'

'Was it hard to see her again?'

'Very. We've not had any contact since the funeral, as you know. His dad wasn't there. He said it was too far to travel from Sydney.'

'Incredible.' Joe shakes his head in disbelief. 'And I find it just as weird that his mother doesn't want to see Chloe and Theo now, when they're her only link to her son.'

'I think that's probably why; she finds it very hard to be reminded of Matthew,' I say slowly.

'Maybe, given time, they will become a comfort instead?' Joe suggests.

'I don't think so. It's incredibly sad, but I know it's a situation that won't change. She's never going to see them again.'

There's a silence, and then Joe says, 'I'm sorry, Sally. That must be really hard for you. Especially when you could have supported each other through this. And you must miss her.'

I pause. 'I miss what she used to be to me.'

Before I discovered that she'd never liked me. I don't think Caroline was making that up, just to cover for Matthew. I've thought quite a lot about the advice she gave me when I was upset about Will marrying Kelly – keep quiet and smile, because he'll do it anyway. Is that how she felt about me marrying her son? She certainly risked my safety – I'm sure it was all her idea – because she wanted to. I don't doubt for one moment that she privately hoped I would end my life that night.

And I still don't know what to do with that horrifying knowledge. Despite what Matthew said, just before he died, *did* he mean me to fall too, or was he telling me the truth: he'd changed his mind, and didn't want to leave us after all?

'I'm so sorry,' I can hear him saying to *her*, 'but Sally tried to kill herself. My kids need me. I *have* to stay.' Who could have argued with that? Liv certainly wouldn't have – being a mother herself...

Because the identity of the woman Matthew was sleeping with turned out to be very relevant indeed, of course.

It never occurred to me in the heat of the moment in the car park, to wonder how Matthew had appeared to know about the film before I'd had a chance to tell him. Almost as if someone *else* had warned him.

The only other person I'd shown the film to, in fact.

Ironically, had Liv not warned Matthew, perhaps I'd now be sitting in Abbey Oaks, having been involuntarily sectioned in that very same car park. Nonetheless, I find it a challenge to feel grateful for her intervention.

I considered playing Liv the recording of Caroline and Matthew's confession, after the event, deciding that it was important she knew what actually happened, so Matthew's death didn't hold a resonance for her that it didn't deserve; but really it was because I wanted her to hear my husband say that she was irrelevant, and a mistake. Instead I sent her a text message that she was not to come to his funeral, and that she wasn't to contact me again. I finished with:

You were my friend. How could you?

I think that was pretty unequivocal, and I haven't heard from her since. I have no idea what made Matthew choose one of my closest friends, of all people, to have an affair with – perhaps she made the first move. I don't want just her side of the story when Matthew won't ever be able to give me his, and I have kept the extraordinary and horrific truths I do know to myself.

I've also, however, been forced to consider Caroline's stinging accusation – that women these days are far too quick to turn on each other – at great length. For my part, I'm ashamed to admit she was probably right, although I genuinely believe I was driven by a desire to protect Chloe and Theo from the threat I thought Kelly posed, rather than simply wanting to be rid of her.

Even now I can't imagine how on earth that first conversation between Caroline and Matthew began. 'Darling, I've been thinking, Will and Kelly are getting engaged, let's use it to make Sally think she's having a nervous breakdown, shall we?' It has to have been Caroline's idea. The alternative is unbearable. I look down at my hands, and, more specifically, at my wedding ring.

'I'm so angry with him, Joe,' I whisper suddenly.

'I think that's a very normal part of loss and grief,' Joe says.

'Yet I feel so guilty, too,' I continue, not really listening. 'If I hadn't been running...'

'Sorry, but *that's* crap,' Joe says bluntly. 'It was an accident.'

'But if I hadn't called him and told him to come and get me—'

'You'd had a hideous morning! Your first morning to yourself in months and you got a flat tyre, you needed to get back to the kids – of course you had to call Matthew to come and get you! That's what husbands do. The good ones, at least.'

We need to change the subject. I can't cope with this. 'Anyway,' I say purposefully, 'are *you* all right? How was it seeing the boys?'

'Lovely, although it broke my heart to leave them again. Kim had some news. She's met someone, and he's moving in with them. So that's nice.'

'Oh, Joe,' I exclaim in dismay. 'I'm so sorry. That's rather... fast.'

'Yes, I think it's fair to say she's moved on. Anyway, I told her I was happy for her, and actually that's not a lie. I *do* want her to be happy. He seems nice, her new bloke – and the boys like him, at least, which is good... The bastard...' he adds after a moment more, then smiles at me. 'On the upside, I signed the lease on the house yesterday.'

'That's great,' I say sincerely. 'Congratulations.'

'Thanks. It's only a six-month let, but it means the kids can see me in my own home when they come up to visit, and my mum's thrilled, obviously. We'll see how it all goes. Have you made any decisions about buying yet?'

'No. I think Chloe needs the stability of being at Mum and Dad's for a bit longer now she's starting school. It's too much change, otherwise; she needs to anchor herself to something, and being at my parents' will do that. I don't want to be off the property ladder for long, though, so I reckon I'll buy something after Christmas, I think. Somewhere close to the school.' I take a deep breath at the thought of everything that's to come... How different to the path I thought I'd taken. 'Anyway, talking of being at Mum and Dad's, I need to get back.' I look at my watch. 'Will and his wife are coming up later this evening and staying over. Chloe is hyper excited to see them in the morning. I'm kipping in with Theo tonight, though, so I'm less thrilled.'

'I saw your new sister-in-law on TV yesterday,' Joe muses. 'She was playing some rookie vigilante cop with, what I suspect we will discover in episode two, a raging alcohol issue, that I *think* is going to put her career on the line.'

I grin and get to my feet. 'She's good, though, isn't she? Thanks for the walk and the chat. You're right, I do feel better for getting out for half an hour.'

'You're very welcome. Want me to escort you back?'

I shake my head gently. 'No thanks.'

'I think your mum would be cool with it.' He looks up at me. 'I promise not to try and kiss you on the doorstep or anything.'

'Shut up, Joe.' I smile at him.

'At least not today, anyway.'

There's a pause and suddenly Matthew is everywhere – I can hear him saying sceptically, 'He just bought you flowers? He didn't want anything else?' I hear Matthew a lot, just as I see him in

Theo's smile and feel him with his arms around us when Chloe holds me tightly, tells me she loves me, and then makes me promise that I won't die too. We miss him.

I miss him.

And yet I hate him too.

'Night, Joe,' I say lightly, and I turn and start the walk back down the coastal path from the top of the cliff towards the village and my parents' house, where my children lie sleeping safely in their beds.

But halfway down, I pause and look out over the bay. The red sun is low in the sky – soon it will slip out of sight completely – but for now it is a beautiful sunset, over a calm sea. I hesitate, then slip my wedding ring from my finger. Suddenly, and with all my might, I hurl it towards the water, giving a gasp of surprise as I see it arc through the air and disappear over the edge. I hadn't planned to do that. I had actually wondered if Chloe might want it one day. But given everything, it wouldn't be right, surely? Not that she will ever know what really happened, of course.

I reach into my pocket and pull out my phone. I have listened to the recording hundreds of times since Matthew died, more specifically the moment where he calls after me, 'I won't let you do this.' Even now, I couldn't be sure if he meant, 'I won't let you do this, and now I'm going to step out in front of this car deliberately to make you come back', or 'I won't let you do this, and I'm so focused on stopping you, I haven't seen this car I'm about to step out in front of'.

But what I *do* know is that I was not prepared to let Chloe and Theo grow up with any burden of doubt about their father's death. And neither was Caroline. We have at least successfully protected Matthew's memory. It was the final decision she and I made; the last time we spoke. The remainder of my deal was simple: no further contact = no recrimination. No public recrimination, more accurately. At the inquest it was evident that she was a heartbroken woman, devastated by the death of her only child. She no longer practises, I believe. She is alone – the one thing she was most afraid of. And it is her own fault. I don't want to feel anything towards her at all, but in darker moments, I can't help but hope she has to live with that knowledge for a very, very long time. I also sometimes like to imagine her a patient at Abbey Oaks, driven quite mad by grief, although I have no idea if that's true or not.

So now, I do not want to keep this recording any more. Caroline, of course, doesn't know that I'm going to erase it, but I don't want to risk Chloe or Theo ever stumbling across the last moments before their father's death.

I hit delete, and the recording vanishes for ever. Then I start to walk home. Only one other person heard it. Someone who really did deserve to know the truth about what Caroline *and* Matthew did – for so many reasons – but I know it's a secret they can keep.

She's a very good actress indeed.

The End

ACKNOWLEDGEMENTS

My grateful thanks to Sarah Ballard, Sara O'Keeffe, the teams at UA and Corvus, Emily Eracleous, Nathan Johnson, and all of the bloggers and authors who have provided me with such invaluable support.